LUKE IRONTREE & THE LAST VAMPIRE WAR

Book 0 - The Centurion Immortal
Book 1 - Dark Fangs Rising - March 22, 2022
Book 2 - Dark Fangs Raging - April 19, 2022
Book 3 - Dark Fangs Descending - May 17, 2022
Book 4 - Blood Empire Reborn - August 23, 2022
Book 5 - Blood Empire Avenged - September 20, 2022
Book 6 - Blood Empire Infiltrated - October 18, 2022
Book 7 - Blood Empire Burning - November 15, 2022
Book 8 - Ancient Sword Falling - March 21, 2023
Book 9 - Ancient Sword Unyielding - August 22, 2023
Book 10 - Ancient Sword Shattering*

The Luke Irontree Historical Adventures
Rise of the Centurio Immortalis - April 5, 2022
Fall of the Centurio Immortalis - May 31, 2022
The Moonlight Centurion*
The Highway Centurion*

*Forthcoming
Titles and release dates may be subject to change.

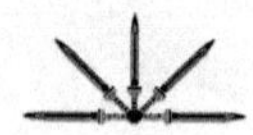

BLOOD EMPIRE BURNING

LUKE IRONTREE & THE LAST VAMPIRE WAR
BOOK 7

C. THOMAS LAFOLLETTE

EDITED BY
SUZANNE LAHNA

BLOOD EMPIRE BURNING
C. Thomas Lafollette

A Broken World Publication
13820 NE Airport Way
Suite #K395495
Portland, OR 97251-1158
Blood Empire Burning
Copyright © 2022 by C. Thomas Lafollette
ISBN 978-1-949410-79-2 (ebook);
ISBN 978-1-949410-82-2 (paperback)

Cover Design: Ravven
Developmental Editing by: Suzanne Lahna
Copy/Line Editing: C.D. Tavenor
Proofreading: Amy Cissell

CONTENTS

CONTENT WARNING

This book contains some gore and body horror. There is also gun and sword violence.

PRONUNCIATION GUIDE & AUTHOR'S NOTES

Pronunciation: Latin names and words are mentioned throughout the book and are intended to be read with the classical Latin pronunciation. For instance, "c" is always pronounced hard, like a "k." "U" is always a short "oo" sound. "V" typically sounds like a "w." There are plenty of resources on the internet if you wish to learn more about Classical Latin pronunciation.

- Lucius – Loo-kih-oos
- Silvanius – Sihl-wahn-ih-oos
- Ferrata – Fehr-rah-tah
- Jung-sook — Yoong-sook
- Jan - Yeahn
- Roxiustanta - Roks-see-oo-stahn-nah
- Surena - Ser-rehn-nah
- Selene - Sehl-lee-nee
- dōšagīh - doe-shah-GHEE

Latin Words: Latin words are used for effect and to add to the "flavor" of the story, not to reflect Latin grammar/declensions/conjugations.

CHAPTER
ONE

LUKE STARED at the sheet music on the piano's desk, the notes blurring into blotches on the page. He'd hoped disappearing into music would allow him some respite from the torment of watching the woman he loved die.

Roxi had come back to him, but if something didn't change, she'd be leaving again, and this time there'd be no rescue for either of them. Taking in a deep breath, he let the weight of his forefinger depress the key, releasing the soft sound of a slightly out-of-tune note into the dim music room. He hadn't pulled the heavy curtains back after wandering in, looking for a quiet place to avoid the activity of the rest of the cottage. His friends avoided venturing outside into the stinging mix of snow and sleet, preferring to cluster inside in noisy groups to enjoy the warmth and Luke's booze.

The room needed a good cleaning if he were to use the piano more. He'd have to find his tuning tools; it had been a long time since he'd tuned the poor instrument.

"Luke?" Maggie's soft voice sounded from behind him. She slid her hands over his shoulders, squeezing them. "Are you OK?"

He didn't answer, keeping his eyes on the sheet music. When she gave another affectionate squeeze, he slumped slightly, letting his head droop. "No."

"Still feeling weak from your encounter with the entity?" she asked.

"I don't know. Maybe? But that's not it." He swung his legs around so he faced the pretty blonde doctor. "I've watched everyone I've ever loved before die. I'm not sure I'm strong enough to go through it again, not like this."

Maggie stepped between his legs and pulled him into her, cradling his head against her chest as she stroked his hair. "You are one of the strongest persons I've ever met. You've gone through so much and come out on the other side. Wounded, definitely, but your humanity survived." She pushed back and aimed his face toward hers before laying a kiss on his forehead. "I know this isn't an easy thing to hear, but you're strong enough. You're going to have to be, for her…and for yourself. She has no one else in this world who cares about her as deeply as you do. No one she cares about as fully as she does you."

He sighed and nodded. "I know." He stood up and folded Maggie into his arms. "I'm going to go check on her."

Maggie smiled sadly at him, caressing his cheek. He gave her hand a squeeze and departed the dusty music room to make his way up to his suite where Roxi rested. Careful to turn the doorknob quietly, he pushed the door open.

A tall Black woman with a high-top fade turned her head toward the opening door. She closed the book she was reading and stood, joining Luke outside his suite.

"How is she doing, Patrice?" he asked.

"Doing alright, all things considered. I put a new bag on her IV. We talked for a while before she dozed off," Patrice replied.

"Thank you. I'll keep her company for a while. Why don't you take some time off?" He reached out and patted her shoulder.

"Thanks, Luke. I think there's a beer downstairs calling my name." She lifted her book. "I just got to the juicy part, and I'm feeling a bit thirsty."

Luke chuckled and stepped quietly into the room. The chair creaked under him as he let it take his weight.

"Hello, Luke," Roxi said groggily, her eyes fluttering open.

"Sorry for waking you up."

"That's OK. I'd rather spend my time with you awake instead of haunting my own dreams. Besides, I need to visit the bathroom. If you'd help me get up…"

Luke stood, pulled the blankets back, and helped her swing her legs off the bed and onto the floor. Then, he gently pulled her to standing. He kept a firm hold on her as she wobbled. When she felt steady enough, she patted Luke on the cheek and shuffled toward the bathroom, using the rolling IV stand as a third leg to help her move across the room.

He watched her, glad to see her mobile but ready to move if she looked like she was about to lose her balance. He wanted to carry her everywhere to help save her strength, but he knew she needed to move on her own—both to keep her strength up and so she didn't feel like a burden to others. Still, his heart ached for her.

Once the door to the bathroom closed, he used the opportunity to freshen up the linens, grabbing a spare set of sheets and stripping the bed quickly. He dropped the last pillow into its case when the door opened. Roxi stood in the door frame, using it to hold herself up.

"You're a handy fellow to have around." Roxi gave him a wan smile and shuffled to the bed.

Luke moved out of her way so she could slide between the wall, chair, and the side of the bed she'd been using. Once she got her stand situated, she stuck her arms out toward Luke and pouted, a twinkle in her eye. He chuckled and shook his head. Kissing her pouty lower lip, he helped her back into the bed then spread the duvet over her.

Patting the empty side of the bed next to her, she smiled wearily, her eyelids already drooping. He couldn't imagine how exhausted she must be, yet she kept going. He'd give anything to take some of the burden from her, but with no solutions available, frustration and anger vied for dominance in his gut. But Roxi's needs were paramount, so he kept them tightly contained. He pulled his T-shirt off, kicked off his slippers, and crawled under the duvet, lying flat on his back with his arm out so Roxi could roll over and snuggle into his side.

"You smell nice," Roxi said, rubbing her hand over his chest. "How are you doing?"

"I'm alive. I'm glad to be here with you." He kissed the top of her head, her messy black hair tickling his nose. "Maggie says you're ready for some more solid food. They're preparing a nice soup for dinner."

"I'd rather have something solid like a steak or maybe a piece of pie. Or maybe both? A cottage pie? Or a really spicy curry." Roxi sighed. "Though I doubt your pretty doctor will let me have one of those. I guess soup will have to do for an upgrade over broth."

"I'll run your request by her, though displaying an appetite is probably a good sign. Do you feel up for joining everyone in the solarium? It looks quite festive. Those who celebrate Christmas have decorated. It looks properly pagan with the tree and pine boughs."

Roxi chuckled. "I'm not a Northern European pagan, but it'll have to do in the absence of anything else. Besides, as long as they have twinkle lights, it'll make me happy. I do like twinkle lights."

"That they do."

"Good. I'm dying to get out of this room. I think an adventure downstairs will do nicely." She snuggled in tightly, giving him a squeeze.

He lay there quietly, stroking her wild hair. "Roxi. Can I ask you a question?"

"You may." Her voice had a dreamy quality to it.

"Wh…where did you go when you left Portland?" He'd nearly asked, "where did you go when you left me?" but substituted Portland instead. He'd thought about nothing else since she'd left him that note after they'd let their burning attraction spill into reality.

She didn't answer, her breathing steady. He thought she might have fallen asleep until she took a deep breath.

"Armenia." She exhaled noisily. "I tried to go back to the mountain, back to where it all began."

A warm, wet drop fell on his chest. Lifting his head, he kissed the top of head and pulled her in tighter.

"I hoped…"

"That if you returned to the wanderer's temple, he could help you? Heal you and fix your rudis?"

She nodded. "I couldn't find it. I found the right mountain. It's indelibly seared into my memory. I'd visited a few times throughout the years. But I couldn't find an entrance. I thought I'd found a path that wound up the side of the mountain, but at some point, a rockslide had sheared off most of it at its highest points. The entire side of the mountain was covered in rubble. Either the entrance was destroyed, or I was being denied entry."

"Is that why you headed to Halberg? To see if you could reach him via the shrine there?" An ember of anger rekindled in his chest as the feeling of Mithras turning his back on him flashed through his mind.

"I tried to find a few of the old spots along the way but had no luck."

"Then you were hunted and ambushed by vampires." He shook his head, pursing his lips as his jaw clenched.

"I don't remember much clearly. Just vague flashes of terror and brutal fighting. When I finally recognized you in that castle ruin, that was my brain's first clear moment in a while." She sighed forlornly. "At least I get to be myself and with you at the end."

Her words cut him deeply. He wanted to counter her and say she wouldn't die, but that wasn't a promise he could make. He couldn't rob her of the comfort of accepting the logical conclusion of her current path. Forcing his jaw to unclench, he took a slow, deep breath and held it, letting it quietly slip from his lips, carrying his anger and frustration away.

He needed to be present for her. Without a functioning rudis, there was no way for her to turn back the compulsion. And no amount of vitriol on his part could make the burnt and warped remnants of her old rudis functional. If he couldn't stop her decline, he couldn't deny her or himself the precious little time they had together. He cared for her, loved her too deeply to steal her peace and offer only anger in return. As her breathing steadied into the peaceful rhythm of slumber, he stroked her hair, soaking up her presence by his side. When she rolled over and off his arm, he slid out of bed and pulled the covers over her shoulders. Kissing his fingertips, he gently touched them against her cheek before dressing and slipping silently out of the room.

He nodded at but didn't speak to anyone he passed as he made his way to the bar by the entrance to his cottage. Flipping one switch on, he left the rest off so he could stew in the dim quiet of the empty, windowless room.

Once he was behind the bar, he poured himself a glass of pils and grabbed a chair at one of the small tables in the back corner, brooding and sipping his beer. He wasn't sure how long he sat there, but when he put glass to lips and came up empty, he stood to get another.

As he refilled his glass, Pablo poked his head in the door. "Mind if I join you, buddy?"

Luke thought about it for a moment, unsure if he wanted even his best friend to intrude upon his solitude. When he realized he did want Pablo's company, he grabbed a second glass and filled it, sliding it over the bar toward Pablo. With a twitch of his head toward the table he'd just vacated, he retook his seat and waited for Pablo to get comfortable across from him.

They sat in silence, drinking their beers until Pablo cleared his throat lightly. "So, the crew said you looked pretty pissed when you came downstairs. Anything you want to talk about?"

Luke huffed, looking inward. The muscles of his face, neck, and shoulders were bunched up tight. He took a moment to run a breathing exercise and untense his body. He took another sip, then looked across the table, locking his gaze with the kind eyes of his friend.

"I didn't come across nearly two thousand years of pain and loneliness to give up on Roxi now that we've found each other."

Pablo reached across the table and gave Luke's hand a squeeze. "I know. You're not the type to give up. Whatever you need, I'm here for you."

"I know. You're a true friend, Pablo. I just wish I knew what I needed to do." He shook his head and frowned.

"I mean, I don't know much about your whole deal, but is begging your Mithras an option?"

"We tried that before Roxi left Portland. We were ignored." He narrowed his eyebrows. "I don't even know if he heard us to ignore us." He paused for a drink. "That's why she left—to find the original temple where we were both given this mission, in the mountains of Armenia."

"I take it she didn't have any luck?"

Luke snorted. "No. She couldn't find an entrance to the temple. Then she tried locating any of the old holy spots that had once been shrines and temples. That's why she went to Saarbrücken. Either Mithras wasn't interested in listening, or the vampires pursuing her didn't allow her enough time to properly seek him out."

"Well, there are no vampires here and you have a temple across the yard…" Pablo gestured in the vague direction of the cliff that backed the property and held most Luke's hidden infrastructure, including the temple.

Luke pursed his lips, shook his head, then sighed. "Yeah. I think it's time I pay my respects to the Wanderer."

Pablo leaned across the table, staring intensely into Luke's eyes. "I don't know what is between you and your god, but Roxi is worth it. You adore her, and she is smitten with you. You need to do whatever it takes to earn her life back."

Luke nodded, first tentatively, then more firmly. "Yeah. You're right." It had been a week since he'd rescued her. He didn't know how much time she had left if he continued doing nothing. He drained the rest of the small glass of pils, then set it down firmly on the table, the clack of glass on wood sounding loud in the empty room.

"What can I do to help?" Pablo asked.

"Refill our beers while I find a pad and a pen. I need to make a list for Émile." Luke stood up and wandered the first floor of the house, looking for anything to write on. Finally, he took a small whiteboard and marker off the wall in the kitchen and brought it back into the bar with him. Once he sat across from Pablo, he took a drink from the refilled beer and began writing a list of the supplies he'd need his caretaker to assemble. Only a few short days remained before the winter solstice, before the feast celebrating the birth of Mithras and the rebirth of the sun.

CHAPTER
TWO

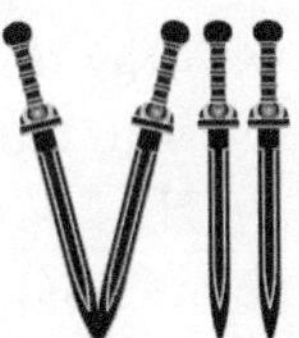

MAGGIE POKED her head into Luke's suite. "Luke, dear, Émile is here with Anne-Marie."

He poked the bookmark into his book and set it on the night-stand. After laying a gentle kiss on Roxi's head, he slipped out of the room and into the waiting hug of Maggie.

"How's she doing?" she asked.

"About the same. Exhausted. Resigned." He shook his head and ran a hand through his untidy brown hair. "At least she's here and safe. Mithras may have abandoned her, but at least he's keeping the property protected."

"I'm sorry, Luke. Do you think your plan will work?" She slipped her hand into his as they descended the wide staircase.

"I don't know, Maggie. I just don't know. It's all untested long shots at this point. I hope going back to the basics will work. Old gods sometimes demand old rituals." He chuckled bitterly. "Not like we can run a double-blind clinical trial. Not with a sample size of two." He stopped on one of the landings and rested against the wall, taking both of Maggie's hand in his. "I just feel so powerless. She deserves better than this, and I can't do anything to help her. Rushing out to slay vampires would salve my anger, but it would get me no closer to helping heal Roxi."

Maggie's brow furrowed as she drew her face into a pensive expression. "Luke, I'm going to ask you a tough question, but I think it needs to be asked."

He nodded, squeezing her hands.

"Does she want to get better at this point? She seems at peace with the direction things are going. Is she tired of the fight? Is she ready to move on?"

He stared into the calm pools of Maggie's blue eyes, thinking about what he'd just been asked. "I don't know anymore. This life is so hard, and it's been rough for her for a while now. The compulsion is…wearying. I've gone through it enough times. Even with having the solution immediately at hand, it's exhausting. I can't imagine what it's like to know the one thing that you can use to make it all go away is corrupted and beyond your reach. But I…I don't want to lose her now that I've found her."

Maggie stepped forward and slid her arms around his waist, laying her head against his chest. "I know. I can see the struggle in your eyes. But make sure you check in with her, so she has a choice and say in the matter, OK?"

He nodded and kissed her forehead. "I will."

"Luke," Pablo called from the first floor. "Your caretaker is waiting."

"Go. I'll go keep Roxi company in case she wakes up."

"I'll be there in a moment," he called down to Pablo. He smiled at Maggie. "Thank you. I'll talk to her when she wakes up."

She turned and ascended the stairs. He watched her for a moment, then hurried down the last flight of stairs into the entry hallway. Émile, Anne-Marie, and Pablo stood in the entryway with their arms full of boxes.

"Let's put those in the bar. Is that everything?" Luke asked.

"No, there are a few more boxes in the back of the car," Émile replied.

Luke helped them with the last boxes, stashing everything in the corner of the bar so they'd be out of the way until needed. When they finished, he thanked them before they departed. He went back inside with Pablo.

"I appreciate the gesture. It is the gift-giving season and all, but you really shouldn't have," Pablo said.

Luke chuckled. "Unfortunately, these aren't presents for you, Pablo."

"Always breaking my heart, dude, always so cruel to your old pal Pablo." He shook his head sadly and walked away, doing his best sad shuffle off on his way to get himself a beer.

Luke wished he could join his friend but needed to check on Roxi and see if she was awake yet. "Don't worry, you can have all the beer you want. As a gift from me."

"I guess it'll have to do."

Luke waved and vaulted up the stairs.

Maggie closed the door behind her as she left the suite. "Ah, I was just coming to get you. Roxi is awake."

Luke nodded, anxiety and dread warring for dominance in his stomach. He wanted Roxi to live, wanted her to choose to keep fighting, but he'd respect her wishes no matter how much they hurt. But that didn't mean he wanted to rush into finding the definitive answer, not when he could live with the dream that his plan would work. She'd be free from the pain of the compulsion, even it was tied to a repaired rudis.

"Thanks, Maggie."

She smiled kindly. He could see the concern and understanding in her eyes—he appreciated her generous soul. Taking a deep breath, he gripped the doorknob and twisted, releasing the breath as he stepped into his suite.

"Hey, stranger. I woke up to a pretty blonde." Roxi stretched and yawned.

"Sorry. You'll have to deal with this beat up old mug now," Luke replied, taking his spot in the chair next to the bed.

"It's a good face, though. Lots of character." Roxi reached out and patted his knee, her hand thin and bony after the ravages of her compulsion. She furrowed her brow, a wrinkle between her eyes running up her forehead. "You look worried."

He smiled softly and scooted the chair forward, taking her nearest hand in both of his. "Roxi, I need to ask you something important. Take your time if you need to think about it, if you need to."

She nodded, raising an eyebrow. "Alright."

"Tonight's the winter solstice, and I have a plan. But I don't want to enact it if you… If you don't want me to."

"What's got you so out of sorts, Luke?"

"Do you want me to keep fighting? For you? To stay alive?"

Roxi looked away for a minute, then returned her dark brown eyes to him. "I'm resigned to my lot, though I'm not sure I'm at peace with my impending death. But Luke, I don't want to die." She squeezed his hand weakly. "Not now that I've met you. I want to see this through to the end. Maybe before this all I would have succumbed to this destiny, but these months with you and your friends… It's shown me what life can be again. It's the closest I've felt to a family and a community in centuries. Luke, I see a light at the end of the tunnel, and you're there. If you have a plan, I trust you."

He swallowed and blinked hard, trying to get his emotions in check. "I can't make any guarantees. I don't want to get your hopes up."

Chuckling weakly, she gave him a lopsided grin. "My hopes are always up when you're by my side, and they're always well-contained after nearly two thousand years of this existence. Do what you can. You have my support and my blessing." She sighed. "I think I'm going to take another nap now."

"OK. I'll be back in a bit with some soup, and I think I smelled bread baking when I was downstairs."

"Mmm, butter too?"

"I didn't smell any of that baking, but I'm sure I can find some to go with the bread."

She shook her head. "You're a silly man." Her eyes drifted shut.

Standing, Luke pushed the chair against the wall and bent over to kiss Roxi's forehead.

She opened her eyes. "Luke, I want you to know that I love you."

Caressing her cheek, he smiled. "I love you, too, Roxi."

He slipped out of the room and made his way to the Solarium to grab a snack. The cooks were preparing a special meal for the winter solstice later, but they'd laid out meats, cheese, pickles, and breads for snacking, as well as other options to meet the various dietary needs of those assembled. On the way, he stopped in the bar and grabbed a glass of dubbel before heading into the solarium.

The leadership team—Ahmed, Delilah, Jung-Sook, Maggie, Pablo, Sam, and Simone—were assembled around a table having a lively conversation that involved lots of broad gestures and laughter. Standing back for a few moments to watch them, Luke smiled at Pablo's antics as he worked the table with one of his stories.

Maggie caught Luke's gaze and stood, walking over to slide an arm through his. "Did you have the talk with her?"

"Aye. We keep fighting."

"Good. I'm glad you're both on the same page. It makes it easier for you."

He nodded. "It does, but if she wanted to stop fighting, I couldn't subject her to it and keep going on my own. I couldn't do that to her."

"That's because you're a good man, Lucius Silvanius Ferrata. And that's one of the main reasons I love you."

"I love you, too."

"Why that silly grin on your face?"

His cheeks flushed with heat, and he looked at the ground before making eye contact with Maggie. "Roxi just told me she loved me."

"I'm glad that you two have finally admitted the obvious. So how does it feel?"

"To be loved by Roxi?"

"Yes, but also by me." She gestured toward the table. "And everyone else. How does it feel to be loved by so many people who care about you and want you to be happy?"

He quietly watched as Sam started a loud story, apparently trying to top Pablo. It had been a very long time since he'd had so many people in his life he truly cared about, and there were even more back in Portland he could add to the tally.

"Scary."

"Even now?" Maggie asked, raising an eyebrow.

"Especially now." He set his beer down and pulled Maggie into a tight hug. "But I've committed to many things in my life that frightened me."

"Why is love so frightening?" She sounded more like she was probing as opposed to curious.

"Opening myself to people has always taken the most courage, and it's the thing I've failed at the most." He sighed heavily. "I'm tired of failing."

Maggie pushed back enough so she could tip her head up and kiss him.

"Get a room, you two!" Pablo called from the table.

Pulling back, Maggie turned her head toward the table. "Hush, Pablo."

"I supposed we should go sit down," Luke said.

"Go get a snack. I'll grab a chair for you." Maggie returned to the table, adding another chair to it as everyone scooted around to make room.

Once Luke fixed a plate, he grabbed his beer and took the empty chair. "Don't mind me. Continue the conversation you were having. It looked entertaining."

"We were just telling stories about old friends, and Pablo and Sam had to get competitive about whose friend did the most outrageous stuff," Jung-sook said by way of filling Luke in.

"Was there a winner?" Luke asked.

Delilah laughed. "When Sam and Pablo try to one up each other, we're all the winners."

"That's true." Luke stuffed a bite into his mouth and leaned back in his chair as they went around the table talking about old friends.

By the time they made it around to Luke, he'd finished his snack and was feeling decidedly content as he sipped his beer.

Simone leaned on the table, looking at him. "Are you going to tell us a story, Luke?"

He sat up and gazed around the table, his friends all staring back. "Let's see… Have I ever told you about my friend Pisakar?"

With the exception of Maggie who'd heard the full tale of meeting his first wife Marpesia, they shook their heads no.

Luke exhaled and took a sip of his beer. "Pisakar was probably the best officer who ever served under me in the two hundred and thirty years I was in Rome's legions." Luke laid out the tale of how he met and recruited the man with highlights from his career up until he placed their legion in the way of the emperor's son's legions in an effort to rescue Luke from the boy's grasp. "Whenever I think of the message he sent to Constantius, it always makes me smile. 'Legatus Pisakar says that when he is finished with you, he'll send condolences to your father and congratulations to your brothers. Your bones will lie where they fall.'"

Delilah chuckled. "Damn, that's cold."

Luke nodded. "Pisakar was a brilliant leader and a brutal fighter. I miss him."

Maggie squeezed his thigh under the table, smiling at him reassuringly. He appreciated her tenderness, knowing digging up the old story about his friend and the time he'd met his first wife would bring up old sorrows.

Ahmed folded his arms across his chest. "See, you really need to write that series of memoirs."

"What's this?" Sam asked.

"When we were in Monaco, Ahmed and I suggested to Luke that he needed to write an autobiography," Jung-sook said.

"You totally need to do that, buddy. I've only heard a fraction of your stories, and I know I want to hear more," Pablo added.

Luke looked around at his friends, seeing eager faces and nods affirming their desire to learn more about Luke's life. "Maybe. We'll see how this all ends. Maybe Le Mousquetaire and the entity will relieve me of the burden of typing my fingers to nubs." Staring at Pablo, he narrowed his eyes. "Not sure I'd be able to get an agent selling a story about an immortal man who hunts vampires as an autobiography."

That elicited several laughs from around the table.

Pablo leaned forward, his eyes growing wide with excitement. "Even better! You sell it as urban fantasy. You know the genre. It would be the greatest joke played in all of literary history."

Delilah smirked at Pablo. "He's right. That shit would probably sell like hotcakes, and no one would be any the wiser that they're actually reading an autobiography with a true look at history."

Luke shook his head, a faint smile on his face. "While that would indeed be humorous, I'm not sure I'll have time to commit my life to paper and ink."

"Why not?" Sam asked. "If we end this and you don't have to hunt vampires all the time, what else do you have on your schedule?"

"We'll see." Luke pulled out his phone to check the time. "I need to go prepare for tonight." Luke nodded at his friends then stood and walked away.

He didn't really need to get set up quite yet, but the turn the conversation had taken made him uncomfortable. Locked in a seemingly eternal struggle against the vampires, he'd never really thought about a time after. Not anymore. It didn't seem like a thing he'd ever achieve. A time after… Only in his earliest days of fighting what he then thought of as di inferi—before the word "vampire" came into the lexicon—had he entertained the idea of a life after hunting.

Leaning over, he opened a large box and pulled out a wide, circular plate with tall walls around the edge and pedestal on the bottom.

"It's quite beautiful," Maggie said softly.

Luke jolted, surprised to hear someone behind him. "Sorry. Didn't hear you."

"I'm sneaky." She stepped in front of him. "What is it?"

"It's a special plate for the presentation of the food for the ceremony."

"Would you like some help unpacking everything and getting ready?"

He smiled warmly. "Thank you."

"You know they were just teasing you, right?" she asked, opening another box.

Luke pursed his lips and nodded. "I do, but I also think there's enough of a thread of seriousness that it makes me uncomfortable."

Maggie reached out and squeezed his forearm. "It wouldn't be the worst thing in the world to have a few things on your schedule. It doesn't have to be concrete, but some goals might help you see a future beyond the life you've known for so long."

He looked down, focusing on unpacking boxes while he thought about what she'd said. "It's been a protection mechanism. To think of a future was to think of a something unattainable. Something I couldn't have. It was too painful, so I gave up on thinking about all my tomorrows." He sighed. "Hope is a dangerous thing."

"It can be, but it's also one of the most beautiful things." She pulled a chair from under a table and sat down. "When I was in the camps, it was the only thing that kept me going. When someone gave up hope…" She paused to collect herself. "It kept me going. A tomorrow. And eventually it did come. I have a loving partner. A boyfriend I love. And a wonderful community that sustains me and gives me purpose. All of those things were born out of the ember of hope I kept kindled in my heart against impossible odds. Without that ember, I wouldn't be here today."

Maggie pulled out another chair and placed it next to hers, patting it to encourage him to sit. He took her invitation, giving her a kiss on the cheek as he sat. Once he was settled, she took his hands.

"That's why you're doing all this. Why you drove hours in the middle of the night to find her. Why you're prepared to do something tonight you haven't done in ages. Because deep down, you have hope. Hope you can save Roxi. Hope you can have a future together. I know right now you might not be comfortable thinking beyond making a better life while you hunt vampires. It's a simple hope that doesn't force you to stretch too far. It keeps you from opening yourself up to more hurt."

"It'll have to do for now, but I'll give it some thought." He smiled and leaned forward for a kiss. "You always give me the best advice. Thank you for being patient with me. I'm sometimes a bit dense about such matters."

"You're not dense. Let's just say you have a pretty thick callus on your heart. You have armor to protect your body. The callus grew to protect your mental health."

He chuckled. "It didn't do a very good job."

Maggie laid a hand on his cheek. "You came through all this, and you still care and love deeply. You still feel. It did pretty well, all things considered."

He nodded, letting her words sink in. After a few moments sitting in silence, he looked up. "Will you help me prepare for this evening?"

"Of course." Maggie looked at the watch on her wrist. "You should go check on Roxi."

Luke gave her hands a last squeeze then stood up, leaving her in the bar next to their pile of cardboard and the accoutrement for tonight's attempt to save Roxi. She was the reason he was willing to go through with this. As Maggie had pointed out, he loved Roxi deeply, and he'd do anything for the ones he loved. Tonight was about her. Tonight, he faced the one who'd set this whole journey in motion.

Tonight, he reminded Mithras of his duty to his hunters.

CHAPTER
THREE

LUKE STOOD STIFFLY while Maggie straightened the long black wool cloak the caretaker had commissioned. On the back in white embroidery, a Roman-style sun took up most of the space. Over his heart, he'd placed Selene's moon. Though the sun of Mithras and Sol Invictus was prominent, the moon's placement spoke to his true loyalties. Over the right breast, two crossed stakes balanced the moon.

He'd deliberately kept the design simple for ease of construction on a short timeline. That, and he didn't want it to look like the NASCAR robe of religious symbols. He was the Centurio Immortalis, Mithras's Dux Belorum. He didn't need a showy robe to demonstrate his position. He was *power*.

Clad from top to bottom in high-quality replica Roman armor augmented by the few original pieces that hadn't been stolen from him, he felt almost himself, though he wouldn't feel entirely right until he took his armor back from Mathis. He skipped the helmet. Reaching down, he rested his left hand on the pommel of Roxi's Parthian sword—the weapon she'd carried for nineteen hundred years. She'd asked him to wear it in her honor for tonight's mission.

Maggie, fishing carefully around his neck, pulled out the medallion Selene had given him to carry her magic and aid in his disguises.

She set it visibly between the sides of his cloak, sitting over his armor-covered heart. "You don't need to disguise yourself. You may as well display Selene's gift."

He nodded, running his hand over his short hair. He'd been keeping his hair and beard shorter than his preferred length to aid his disguise as the Comte, per Selene's instructions. "Am I all set?"

"Yes. Everything is prepared in your Mithraeum. You're all dressed." She stepped back, taking in the full image of Luke as she looked him up and down. "You look magnificent."

"It seems like I've come full circle." He looked down at his legs, bare from his knees down to his feet. "I should have had some trousers made. It's cold outside."

Maggie chuckled. "You have lovely legs though. The tunic shows them off nicely."

"I'm glad you approve." He reached out and took her hand. "Would you walk with me?"

"Of course."

They stopped in the entry way so Luke could put on a pair of new caligae—he didn't want the hobnails to damage the floor of his house. With his Roman military boots strapped on, he stepped outside and stopped, his jaw dropping. All of his friends had assembled in the yard, forming into two lines with a central walkway for Luke and Maggie to walk through. Everyone carried a lit candle. At the end of the line, blocking the walkway, stood the dark-haired and pale-skinned moon goddess Selene, a soft silvery glow surrounding her as she stood a foot taller than everyone else.

Maggie squeezed his hand. "Why'd you stop?"

"Why is everyone here?" he asked.

"They're here to support you. Your friends wanted to wish you luck. They like Roxi and know how much she means to you." She tugged lightly on his arm.

Out of the darkness, Brutus shuffled toward the goddess. He made a low friendly bark and wagged his tail before sticking his head under her hand. The goddess smiled down at the huge dog and scratched behind his ear and down his neck until she found a spot that set his leg to thumping. The dog was still a mystery, but one that didn't trip his or Selene's danger senses.

Luke walked down the column, nodding at his friends as he passed. When they reached Selene, she smiled fondly at him before letting her face fall into an expression he was seeing more frequently —a mix of sadness and thinly veiled anger.

"Thank you for coming tonight, My Mistress." Luke bowed before the goddess.

"We've been in this together for a long time, Lucius."

"That we have. Do you think he'll relent and heal Roxi?"

"For her sake and our mission's sake, I hope so." She clenched her jaw briefly as a wave of frustration passed over her face. "I've grown quite fond of her in the short time I've come to know her. And I feel she's a key piece to ending this. Are you sure you don't want me to join you this evening?"

Luke shook his head. "No. This is between him and me. I don't want to drag you into this."

"Very well." She nodded gracefully. "May I at least accompany you to the border of the cave?"

"Of course."

Selene took his hand. With Maggie on one side, Selene on the other, and Brutus following along, Luke strode across the yard toward the shed hiding the secret entrance to the cave he'd turned into a Mithraeum centuries ago. When they reached the door to the shed, he let go of Selene's hand and turned to Maggie, giving her a kiss.

"Thank you, Maggie," he whispered.

Maggie ran her hand over his cheek and left him with the goddess. Unlocking the door, he led Selene into the shed and punched the code in for the secret retracting wall. They walked through the rough tunnel, stopping at the entrance of the Mithraeum. Selene raised her hand, igniting the silver lamps inside the cave.

Bending over, she laid a kiss on her forehead. "Go with my blessings, Lucius."

"Thank you, My Mistress." Lucius placed his fist over his heart and bowed deeply.

Turning, he strode confidently into the Mithraeum. The faint scent of paint lingered from the touch ups Anne-Marie had done in preparation for tonight. A small table stood before the bull scene. On it was the large wooden plate he'd unboxed earlier. A wooden dome covered it.

Once he stood in front of the bull scene of the altar, he pulled Roxi's sword from its scabbard and dropped to one knee, resting the tip of the sword on the stone floor. Wrapping both fists around the handle, he bowed his neck and rested his forehead on the pommel of the sword.

"I greet you, Lord Mithras, on this the eve before your birth into the new year."

With no one else and nothing but stone surrounding him, his words echoed faintly. It had been a long time since he'd held the feast celebrating the rebirth of the sun and the birth of Mithras—at least a century, but probably over two centuries ago. And even then, it had been more a formality than serious devotion. It had felt too hollow then—or he had felt too hollow—and he'd decided not to bother the next year or the following until it became years of spiritual neglect.

He tried to keep his annoyance and anger buried deeply, wanting to find pieces of the wonder he'd once felt in the presence of the god that had so radically changed the course of his life. His devotion had been strong when he first accepted his mission and formed his legion of vampire hunters. The intensity of his fervor had energized his recruits.

Now, he felt little for the god who'd set him on this mission save for anger and loathing. All of that, he packed away in a deep dark walled-off spot inside himself. Burying his feelings in the dark recesses of his psyche was something he was exceptionally good at.

"May your strength blossom in the new year and guide my hand to fulfill your mission." He stood up and sheathed Roxi's sword.

He walked to the back corner of the Mithraeum where a small brazier contained a tiny flame—not enough to provide warmth or fill the room with smoke, just enough to provide fire. Reaching next to it, he picked up a plain metal incense burner with a chain attached to it. He opened the lid to make sure the incense was inside. Satisfied, he picked up a set of tongs, plucked a small ember, and set it carefully inside the burner. After a moment, the incense caught and smoldered.

They'd found some cherry wood to burn, and it added its fragrance to the pungent blend of scents from the incense. Remembering the ceremony his wife Marpesia shared with him in their little hideaway, he wished he could drop a few nuggets of cannabis into the burner.

A faint trail of smoke and scent followed him to the table with the large wooden plate. He removed the dome and set it aside carefully. A large piece of grilled beef sat in the center, its juices creating a small pool around it. Along the edge, on a small stand to elevate it, stood a mini loaf of bread. A crock of butter and another of honey stood sentinel by the loaf's side.

Reaching under the table, he pulled out two crystal wine glasses and set them on the table, one on the north side facing the bull scene and the other on the southern side. He retrieved a decanter of dark red wine. He'd had Émile find something special from his cellar for tonight, not wanting to appear cheap to the god Luke needed to heal Roxi. After he poured two glasses, he set the decanter to the side.

With the incense burner back in his hand, he spun the plate on its rotating base, sending it slowly revolving clockwise. The action was smooth and hardly lost any speed as it spun. He'd need to relay his compliments through Émile to the craftsman who'd produced such a fine piece on short notice.

He walked around the table counterclockwise, giving a gentle swing to shake more smoke from the burner at each of the cardinal points of the compass. The first pass around the table was dedicated to Mithras, whose birth the feast celebrated. The second honored Sol Invictus, whose rebirth signaled the renewal of the sun's covenant to return to prominence. The last time around the table, he held Selene in his heart, thanking her for her guidance and the centuries of devotion she'd shown him.

While the plate still rotated slowly, shedding speed as it neared the point it would return to stillness unless Luke gave it another spin, he hung the incense burner from an iron hook affixed to the wall near the bull scene. He paused, closing his eyes, and reached out, hoping to feel the approach of Mithras. Nothing.

He tucked away his frustrations and returned to the table. He picked up the glass and ran it under his nose. The wine smelled positively decadent. He took a sip and set the glass down. Next, he took the loaf and tore it in half—setting the larger half toward the north side of the plate—then ripped off a small chunk, dragging it through the butter before dipping it into the honey. He popped it into his mouth and savored the mix of relished butter and sweet honey. Last, he pulled his dagger from his belt and carved a piece from the beef, revealing the red and pink inner portion. The meat was cooked perfectly. He chewed and swallowed the bite of meat.

At the sound of a small whine from just outside the entrance to the Mithraeum, Luke smiled and cut off another piece of meat, carrying it to the giant dog laying on his side. He looked up, his tail thumping on the ground as Luke approached.

"Here you go, Brutus." Luke made sure the dog saw the piece of beef before he dropped it. With a speed that belied his size, Brutus snatched the morsel out of the air and chewed it noisily, his tail beating harder. Luke bent over and gave him a quick scratch behind the ears.

Now, he waited. He grabbed his glass of wine, took a seat on the nearest bench, and sipped it, trying to keep his mind in the right frame. Working to keep his anger with Mithras contained and out of sight was proving to be one of the more challenging tasks he'd undertaken in a while, but for Roxi, he'd do it.

He'd do anything to bring her back from the edge of death; he just hoped he didn't have to go as far as he was willing to go. Some bridges shouldn't be crossed and burned behind him. But if he had to, he'd kindle an inferno without a second thought.

When he finished his glass, he refilled it and set it on the table. He spun the plate counterclockwise this time. Taking down the burner, he repeated the sequence he'd performed earlier, save for this time he walked clockwise.

He pushed out his awareness, hoping to feel the powerful presence of the god, but he felt nothing. Taking a moment, he breathed to calm himself before he let slip his emotions. Once he felt under control, he pulled the lid off the burner to check on the incense. He grabbed a few more nuggets and dropped them in to keep it burning.

This time, he dropped to the ground and sat cross-legged, keeping the table between himself and the altar. He could never quite get the hang of the full lotus position, rather settling for the easier option. He tried to slip into a deep mediation but couldn't get beyond a calming breathing rhythm. After a while, the cold stone become too much for his ass and legs.

Standing, he nearly fell, his legs going numb as pins and needles washed over his lower half. Once he revived the sensation in his legs, he repeated the circuit around the table, reversing the directions again.

He repeated the ceremony several times throughout the night, sometimes drinking and eating some of the food, other times sitting on a bench to calm his mind and return it to a place of respectful welcome.

The only nod to modern technology in the cave was his phone, which he left just outside the entrance to the Mithraeum. When the alarm sounded, he turned it off and made another circuit around the table at the moment of the solstice. After he returned the incense burner to the hook, he stood on the south side of the table and watched the altar, waiting and wondering.

The sun chariot of Sol Invictus and Selene's moon chariot briefly flared to life with gold and silver flashes of light, respectively, before returning to their previous states of paint on stone with only the faintest of glows remaining. Yet the figure in the center remained motionless and devoid of life.

As Luke stared at the stone carving of Mithras, his anger and frustration grew. When the vibrations of his teeth grinding resounded through his head, he forced his jaw open to unclench the muscles.

"Joyous tidings on the occasions of the anniversary of your birth, Father of Fathers." He had trouble keeping sarcasm out of his voice.

Still, nothing.

Turning his back to the altar, he stretched his arms out to his sides gesturing toward the empty benches. "Behold! The bounty of your followers, all gathered in one place to pay homage to you."

He strode to the back of the cave and turned around, once again raising his arms. "Down through thousands of years, all your true followers have gathered to pay their respects. This is it. Empty benches. And me."

Stalking forward, he stopped in front of the altar and pointed violently, nearly touching the image of the god. "Your other follower, one who is more devoted than I, sought you out in her time of need, and you ignored her. Now she lays not far from here, dying. Abandoned by the god she served loyally for so long. I may not have been as devoted, but together we've kept your mission alive. And now, with an end in sight, you have abandoned us and failed in your duty to protect your remaining adherents."

He hung his head for a moment before looking up again. "She traveled halfway around the world to pay her respects and to renew her covenant with you. When you failed to give her entrance to the cave, she sought every old place she could, but yet you ignored her."

He shook his head, pursing his lips. He wanted to say more, but he was about to tip fully into the realm of blasphemy—a place he might not be able to come back from. Thinking of Roxi, he couldn't indulge his anger and vent his spleen. Instead, he turned crisply and exited the cave with long, powerful strides.

Brutus stood and followed Luke out into the morning light. Instead of heading into the cottage, he walked around it, passing to the north side to avoid the solarium in case people were up early. Following the concrete path, he stopped at its terminus overlooking the Meuse River. He stared out over the river, running wide and high from the winter rains and snows, until his eyes blurred.

When a hot drop hit his hand, he moved toward a nearby chair, stumbling. Brutus inserted himself under Luke's hand, bolstering him until he could sink into the chair, resting his elbows on his knees. The giant gampr licked his hand then laid down behind him. The gentle passage of the river disappeared behind the trickle of tears from his eyes. When he looked down, his hands trembled.

Behind him, Brutus growled low and ominously.

"Oh, hush, you," said a feminine voice tinged with a Polish accent.

The growling stopped. Instead, he gave a low huff of greeting, his tail thumping on the ground.

"Luke. Is it OK if I join you?" Maggie asked.

He nodded. Pulling a chair over to him, she sat next to him, resting her hand on his forearm. She didn't say anything, only sitting there providing comfort.

With a deep sigh, he brought up his other arm and wiped the tears from his cheeks and sat back. "I've failed her, Maggie."

She tsked. "You haven't failed her. You've done everything you can think of; it just hasn't been successful yet."

He looked over at her, his eyes pleading. "How do I tell her?"

"You're an honest man. Tell her the truth. She probably knows it was a long shot. The effort and the attempt will mean something, even if you didn't achieve success." She gave half a shrug. "It's at least something."

Luke nodded, looking at the ground and thinking over her words. "I feel like this is my fault. If I'd been more devout…or kept up my religious duties all these years…"

"You can't blame yourself. Self-recriminations will get you nowhere, and they'll distract you. She's going to need you whole and present." Maggie set her hand on Luke's cheek, rubbing away a tear with her thumb. "She's lucky to have you by her side."

"Thank you, Maggie. I'm lucky to have you by my side."

She smiled mischievously. "I know." She leaned forward and kissed him. "You smell of wood smoke and incense."

"I had the incense burner going all night. It's good to get some fresh, clean air. I should get cleaned up and tell her."

"You should show off your outfit first. You look very dashing."

He chuckled. "Did I tell you about the first time we met?"

"The arena in Wyoming, right?"

"No. It was in Armenia in 117 CE. She'd led a group of Parthians pursuing the remnants of my cohort. By the end, it was just me, another legionnaire, and an Armenian boy. They'd chased us across the snowy mountains until we managed to get across a narrow bridge over a ravine. We formed a two-man shield wall. It was quite pathetic. She probably had about a hundred Parthians with her. After they shot some arrows at us, she tried to talk us into giving ourselves up."

"Why didn't you?" Maggie asked.

"I didn't fancy the options—interrogation and being sold into slavery after if I survived, or they might just decide to execute me. Besides, I'd just been given a mission." He shook his head. "That went well."

"How'd you escape?"

"The Armenian boy's sister showed up with a small army. Have I never told you about Ariazate and her brother Tigran?"

Maggie shook her head.

"She was something else. Strong, fierce, smart. She claimed to be a direct descendant of Tigranes the Great."

"Was she?"

He shrugged. "The Armenians in the mountains believed them enough to follow her into a potential battle with their occupiers and then to hide her after. The Parthians believed it enough to make her and her brother a threat worth hunting. After we wintered in the mountains in some village, I talked her into fleeing Armenia. When we reached Belgica, I had my parents adopt her and Tigran. They became my brother and sister and took over my father's business since I was going to be otherwise occupied."

"What happened to them?" Maggie leaned closer, a faint smile gracing her face.

"Eventually, I lost track of Tigran's line as they ventured away from Belgium."

"What about the girl…Ariazate?"

"You've met them. Émile, Anne-Marie, Alexandre. They're the direct descendants of Ariazate."

"And they've served you all this time?"

He nodded. "Ariazate raised her offspring to be truly loyal as did they with theirs. I've taken very good care of them throughout the centuries. With all the turmoil this country has gone through, it still amazes me that I didn't lose more of them, especially since I've often been gone for decades at a time." Reaching out, he patted Maggie's knee. "I should go check in on Roxi."

She smiled and stood up, taking his hand as they walked into the house. After he slipped off the caligae and stood, Maggie pulled him into a hug, cupping the nape of his neck as she leaned in, standing on her tip toes. "Be strong for her."

Luke nodded and headed upstairs. At the top, he yawned, holding his hand over the doorknob that would lead him into the suite where Roxi waited. He took a steadying breath and turned the knob gently, slipping in. Roxi, her hair disheveled, was sitting up in bed, propped on a pile of pillows and drinking tea.

"Good morning, Luke." She smiled weakly at him.

He did his best to feel strong while filling his eyes with love.

"Oh..." Her hand trembling, she set the teacup on the nightstand.

Sliding the chair close to the side of the bed, he sank into it, taking her hand in his. "I'm so sorry. I held the vigil all night and welcomed in the new year and congratulated him on his birth at the moment of the solstice. He didn't show up or even speak to me. I've ignored him too long..."

"Don't blame yourself. You and I have served loyally for centuries." She sighed. "I'm so tired of fighting, Luke. I'm exhausted. I think I want to lie down. Lay with me for a while?"

Luke nodded. "Of course."

He walked over to the closet, stripped off his armor and Roman garb, and slipped on a comfortable pair of pajama pants. After he slid into the bed, he pulled Roxi into him and she rested her head on his chest. If this was all he could have of her, then he'd savor every moment. Together, they dozed in each other's arms.

CHAPTER
FOUR

A GENTLE RAPPING on the door woke Luke from the deep sleep he'd fallen into. At some point, Roxi had rolled over, though she still had her back pressed into him. Careful to not disturb her, he extricated his arm from under her head and slipped out of bed, pulling on a T-shirt and sliding his feet into some slippers.

He opened the door and snuck out, finding Pablo waiting. "Yes?"

"Sorry to disturb you, buddy, but you left your phone in the cave. I wouldn't have woken you for that, but you've got messages from Mathis. I know you need to speak with him to make sure he was still on the hook after we left Antwerp, then the whole Roxi rescue thing."

Luke nodded. "Yeah. Lead the way."

When they reached the ground floor, Pablo squeezed his shoulder. "I'll go make you a coffee and bring it out to you in the Solarium. Sam has your phone there."

"Thanks, Pablo." Luke stepped into the restroom to use it, then splashed some water on his face after washing his hands. The water perked him up some but did little to revive his spirits. Leaning over the sink, he stared into the mirror.

Dark bags underscored the bone-weary exhaustion he felt. He

splashed more cold water over his eyes, dabbed them dry with a towel, and gave up against the losing fight. Coffee awaited.

When he entered the Solarium, those closest to him—Delilah, Maggie, Pablo, Sam, and Simone—were seated around their usual table. He hesitated before closing the distance, afraid to meet their eyes and see the sympathetic looks they no doubt wore. Sighing, he made his way to the open chair next to Maggie and sank into it.

Pablo slid a coffee toward him. "Quad shot. Figured you could use a little extra boost after everything."

Maggie grabbed a cherry pastry off a platter and put it on a plate in front of Luke. "I know they're your favorite."

The kind gestures brought a small smile to his face. They really were the best people.

"Thank you. For everything." He took a bite of the pastry and closed his eyes, savoring the balance of sweet and tart. With a sip of his coffee, he added bitterly. "I hope y'all had a more profitable evening than I did."

"No one felt like celebrating much," Pablo said.

"Oh?" Luke asked.

"Yeah. I think everyone's mind was with you." Sam reached over and squeezed his hand. "How's Roxi doing?"

"Exhausted. She didn't say anything, but I could see the disappointment in her eyes." He shrugged. "I feel so powerless to help her. Everything we've tried has failed."

"I'm sorry, buddy," Pablo said.

"If there's anything we can do, you know Simone and I are here for you." Delilah patted Simone's forearm.

Simone nodded. "You've done so much for me and my brother. If there's anything…"

"Thank you, I appreciate it. If any of you know where I can track down a wayward god and are willing to hold him down while I remind him vigorously of the duty he owes Roxi, that might be handy."

Pablo scooted away. "Um, he's not one of those lightning throwing gods, is he? Because I'm not interested in being smited."

Delilah snorted.

Pablo turned to Delilah, his eyes narrowing. "What?"

"I think the past tense of smite is smote." Sam reached for pastry, a faint smile on her face.

"Smoted smited. Either way, not interested."

Luke chuckled. "I'll be sure to keep my blasphemy to occasions where you're not within in smiting distance. Sound good?"

"I guess it'll have to do." Pablo stood. "I think I could use another coffee. Anyone else?" Once he collected the orders, he disappeared into the house.

After Pablo delivered the requested coffee drinks, he returned to his spot, though he did cast a periodic furtive glance toward the sky as if expecting retributive lightning bolts. He took some of the seriousness from the gesture by accompanying it with a wink.

"So now that we have more caffeine, what's the plan?" Sam asked.

"On the hunting side, that's entirely up to Delilah and the teams." Luke gestured toward her and used the movement to grab another pastry.

She leaned forward, resting on her elbows. "I think we'll keep things up as is, though for the holidays, we're taking volunteers. I figure the fangers will take advantage of the chaos to feed. I'd like to have some protection out there to keep the vamps from ruining too many holidays."

Nodding along, he swallowed his bite. "That works. I doubt we'll need a bunch of people for any big assaults now that we've got Roxi, but let's not spread our people too far."

"That's probably not a bad idea," Sam said. "If what you say is true, and the entity recognized you, then that makes things more precarious if he spreads the word."

Pablo cleared his throat and set his coffee cup down. "I've been thinking about that. Would he reveal Luke's existence?"

Luke narrowed his eyes and tipped his head to the side. "What do you mean?"

"Since your capture and then your faux death, the toothy bastards have been on a steady path of expansion. I'm sure there's probably more going on around the world than just here in Belgium."

Sam looked a Pablo for a moment, an eyebrow raised. "He could be right. Last time I talked to Holly, she said they've been seeing more vampires sniffing around Portland again, though not enough to create problems. Plus, they've been getting calls from other packs in other cities asking for aid."

Pablo smiled smugly and put his hands behind his head as he slouched into his chair. "Don't look so surprised, Sam. I'm more than just a pretty face."

Luke chuckled. Pablo always could lighten his mood. "Don't let it go to your head, buddy. You know how Sam and Delilah like to deflate you when you get a bit too full of yourself."

"What about your part, Luke?" Sam asked.

"No changes. I keep pressing Mathis and Jan."

"Are you sure it's safe after the incident with the entity?" Maggie asked.

Luke shrugged. "I'm not trying to sound blasé, but it's been dangerous from the moment we set foot in Europe. This is the closest I've been to achieving some serious hits against the vampires' hierarchy." He paused and looked around the table, exhaling noisily through his nostrils. "And I know y'all aren't going to like hearing this, but the entity is part of our end goal. Whoever or whatever it is, it's controlling and driving the vampires. The more I learn about it, the better chance I have to eliminate it and maybe end this."

Eyes flicked from face to face as the team checked in with each other, the only sound the rain falling on the glass roof of the solarium.

Simone, her brow furrowed and her lips pinched tight, sat up straighter, sliding an arm through Delilah's. "Do...do you think the entity is the god of the vampires?"

"I don't know, but I'm having strong suspicions," Luke replied.

Everyone sat still, silent. When a loud buzz vibrated Luke's phone against the tabletop, they all jolted. Simone even squeaked.

Chuckling sheepishly, Luke picked up the phone. "It's another message from Mathis. I'm going to give him a call, so let's keep things quiet… After a bathroom break, those two coffees Pablo poured into me are doing their thing."

After Luke returned, he sat down and picked up his phone. "Hello, Mathis. It's Pierre."

"Ah, Your Excellency. So good to hear from you. You've been hard to get a hold of lately." Mathis sounded extra smarmy.

"My apologies. It's been a very hectic few days, especially with the impending holidays. To say it's been chaotic would be an understatement. I hope you conveyed my respect and apologies to Mr. van den Bergh about missing our meeting."

"I did. Don't worry about Jan. I was able to smooth things over with him. He can be a bit prickly if he doesn't feel respected, but I persuaded him it wasn't a personal insult and merely the fortunes of dealing with an important and busy man." Mathis was laying on the charm.

With their enhanced hearing, his friends could hear the conversation, especially since he'd turned up the volume on the phone to aid their eavesdropping. Sam rolled her eyes.

Pablo chuckled silently and rubbed the tip of his nose. He mouthed "brown nose" at Luke.

"I appreciate your efforts, my friend," Luke said. "Please convey my regards to Mr. van den Bergh and if you feel the timing is right, inquire about another meeting. I liked what I was hearing in our first meeting and would love to continue the conversation."

"That's good. It's always hard to gauge Jan's reactions. I'm sure he'll be eager to continue the conversation. It sounds like the venture you're proposing will be profitable for all."

"Yourself included?" Luke asked, raising an eyebrow.

Mathis chuckled. "A little something for everyone is the best kind of deal, especially for friendly brokers."

Pablo sucked his lips in between his teeth to keep them clamped closed.

Luke did his best to give what he hoped sounded like a friendly laugh. After his failure with Mithras last night and only a few hours of sleep, he didn't have the patience to deal with the conniving money and power grubber, but he'd have to fake it as best as he could.

"Those are indeed the best deals. I always like to see my friends get ahead. If things go the way I think they will, the commission I offered will turn out to be quite the tidy sum." He drummed a finger on the table.

"Music to my ears. What is your schedule like in the coming days?" Mathis asked.

"Oh, for you and this port deal, I can be available."

"I doubt Jan will want to meet before Christmas, but I might be able to persuade him to meet before New Year's." Mathis tried to sound casual, but Luke could hear the thinly veiled eagerness in his voice.

"I'm willing to work around Jan's schedule. Please give my regards to your wife."

"I shall. Merry Christmas, Your Excellency."

"And to you." Luke hung up the phone and tossed it lightly onto the table. "Gods, I hate that greedy bastard."

Maggie slid her hand onto his thigh, squeezing it. "He's truly despicable."

He turned and kissed Maggie on the cheek. The gesture softened the disgusted expression she wore. Normally serene and even-tempered, she couldn't hide her distaste for the man who'd orchestrated Luke's kidnapping.

"Hey, waffleboy!" Pablo called.

Pieter walked into the solarium, looking rumpled and tired, a slump in his shoulders.

"Hello, Pablo. It's good to see you. Luke, Maggie. Sam. Delilah and Simone. A pleasure." He sagged into a chair across from Luke.

"Need a coffee?" Pablo asked.

"That would be splendid. Make it a double if you don't mind. It was a long trip," Pieter replied.

Luke looked his friend over. Pieter's clothes were wrinkled, and he hadn't shaved in several days.

Lifting his arms, he stretched his back left to right, cringing. "I stink. You know what, I'm going to run upstairs and take a shower.

I'll be back in fifteen minutes. When I get back, we need to make some plans."

Pieter stood and strode out of the solarium. It was rare to see Pieter this disheveled. Luke wondered what had brought his friend from his assignment in the south of France all the way back to Belgium in such a hurry. Whatever it was, he hoped it would be good news, though that rarely was the case. He'd just have to wait and see.

CHAPTER
FIVE

INSTEAD OF CLEARING THE SOLARIUM, Luke moved to the sitting room. Pablo brought Pieter's coffee in and set it on an end table while they waited. A few minutes later, Pieter walked into the room with wet hair, wearing a clean pair of jeans and a tight black T-shirt that showed off a lean, muscular body.

"That's much better." Pieter sank into a wingback armchair and picked up his cup of espresso. "I've been on the road for nearly twenty hours."

"What's so urgent? Is everything OK with Owen?" Luke asked, scooting forward in his chair as he rested his elbows on his knees and held Pieter's gaze.

"Sorry, I should have been more specific. Everything is going fine on that end of things. He's finalizing a deal. We were meeting with our contact in a little place deep in the Pyrenees. That's why it took me so long to get here." He tipped the espresso back and sighed happily. "I could use a few more of those."

Pablo stood up and patted Pieter's shoulder, then disappeared with the empty cup.

"That's good at least," Luke said. "But could you let me know what's going on? I'm not exactly in the mood for the long play right now. It's been a rough few days, and my patience isn't what it should be."

"Apologies, my friend. I've been on the phone constantly and my brain's a bit scrambled from everything." He rubbed a hand across his eyes and sat up straighter. "Let's see. It started a couple days ago. Amiata called me with a request to speak from one of her contacts here in Belgium. Apparently, my brother's leadership isn't exactly winning over some portions of the pack. That, combined with those who've fled his purge, has led to an underground movement to seek new leadership."

Luke leaned forward, his eyebrows raising. "That's very interesting. Have you spoken with the contact directly?"

"Aye. He was one of the people I spoke to, along with some of my other contacts." He paused and pursed his lips, making a light popping noise. "They haven't been relaying much information to me as of late. I guess I seemed too disinterested in the problem for their tastes. Either way, they confirmed the rumors Amiata relayed."

"What do you want to do, Pieter?" Luke asked.

"It plays right into our hands. Jan has to be getting desperate trying to juggle everything with Jamaal draining the funds. If we could integrate a rebellion into our plans, it would work well."

"But what do *you* want? Do you want to remove your brother and take over the pack to restore your father's legacy?"

Pieter slumped into the chair with a heavy sigh. "I don't know, Luke. Two years of being free of those obligations felt good. Like years of weariness had been lifted from my shoulders though the how and why haunts me." His brow furrowed as sadness filled his eyes. "I miss my father still. Being this close to my ancestral home has been a lot."

"I can understand that probably better than most, my friend. We both have too much history here, both distant and recent."

"That's partially why I wanted to go with Owen—to put some distance between me and here. Also, I didn't want to be seen by anyone who might relay my location to my brother." Pieter rubbed his temples with his middle and forefingers.

"You know you have my support for whatever course you take.

We don't need to foment a rebellion to take down your brother. If you want to go back to Portland and live there, then I'd be delighted to have my friend in the same city. However, if you want to replace your brother, you'll have my full support and all the resources I can bring to bear." Luke pushed off the chair and leaned close enough to pat Pieter's knee reassuringly.

Pieter, resting his elbows on the arms of his chair, steepled his hands in front of his face. He sat quietly, staring somewhere in the middle distance as he thought. "I don't know what I really want, but it would be a shame to pass up this opportunity to strike against Jan. Plus if we take him down, we need to have people ready to take over the pack functions whether I'm at the top or someone else."

"So… We assist the opposition?" Luke asked.

Pieter nodded first, lightly, then more firmly. "Yes. I think it's the right course for us. Now comes the fun part, arranging a meeting."

Luke chuckled, leaning back in his chair. "Yeah, we still need to keep our identities under wraps."

"You're going?" Pieter raised an eyebrow. "Isn't that a little…unwise?"

Luke reached into the neck of his T-shirt and pressed his fingers against the moon amulet Selene had given him as he formed an image in his head. Pieter's eyes opened wide as he sat back rigidly. Luke had practiced the image in front of the mirror enough to know what Pieter saw—a handsome man with black hair and vaguely Middle Eastern features.

"That always makes my blood run cold when you change images." Pieter gave an exaggerated shiver.

"Where did you come up with that image, buddy?" Pablo asked.

"When I went to make up another, an old memory jumped front and center. It's especially linked to his place." He looked around the room at his friends, a faint smile on his face. "Remember when I told you about the caretaker's family origins? This is the face of Tigran, at least as he appeared as a man of about thirty." He chuckled and shook his head. "The first time I tried to execute the image, I ended up with the face I'd first seen when I met him in 117 CE. He was a boy of twelve then."

Sam barked a laugh. "I bet you looked ridiculous with a twelve-year-old's head on your body."

"I would pay good money to see that," Delilah said, a broad grin on her face.

"If the price is right, I'd consider it. But no cameras or cell phones," Luke said.

"Spoil sport," Pablo said.

Pieter looked Luke over. "I guess that solves the problem of not revealing you're still alive or ruining the Comte's public image. I'll get the ball rolling." He paused. "Where do you think we should hold the meeting? I'm loath to hold it near Antwerp or Brussels."

"Yeah, they're definitely out," Luke replied.

"What about Paris?" Pablo asked.

"Sorry, buddy. I know you didn't get any fun time on the last trip. Normally, I'd say yes, but I'd prefer not to cause mischief in Jean-Paul's city. I'm still unsure of our potential relationship and I'd like to keep it on the positive side. I don't know if Jean-Paul's annoyance has worn off yet. Also, I want to avoid Le Mousquetaire. He appears to be gaining traction there. I don't want to move against him without gaining the Paris Pack as a firm ally first. Give me a little bit, and I'll come up with something. Then we can compare notes and find a few likely places to propose."

"That works for me," Pieter said.

"Just check with me on dates and times so we can make sure I'm not double booked. I've got a lot of balls in the air right now."

Pablo snorted and snickered, mumbling, "balls."

Sam rolled her eyes.

"I guess on that note, I'm going to go check in on Roxi." Luke departed the room, casting a wave behind him.

"ARE you sure this is the squad you want to take?" Sam asked. "They've never done any covert operations with you before."

"That's kind of why I need them. You all might be recognized as my associates. And I can't compromise the Comte's bodyguard personnel. If they're seen and linked to any of the people involved in this rebellion, that would be bad for everyone involved."

Sam pursed her lips and folded her arms over her chest. "I know. It's the logical choice. I just don't like sending you into the unknown without your core teams."

"They're all well trained. All they have to do is be on hand if I need a little muscle. Besides, I'm just there to function as Pieter's escort. No one needs to know I was ever there."

"I guess so." Sam pulled out her phone and pulled up a list. "I've got Agatha, Connor, and Joe on deck for you. They've been briefed. The caretaker dropped off a rental vehicle for you earlier."

"We're just waiting on Pieter then?" Luke shoved his hands into his pocket and jingled his keys nervously.

"I'm here." Pieter stopped in front of Luke. "Damn. Every time I see you in one of your fake faces, it sends chills down my spine."

Luke nodded. "Imagine me looking in the mirror. I've had my face a lot longer than you've had yours."

Pieter chuckled. "I guess so, though mine is a far more interesting one."

"Interesting is a good word choice." Luke grinned at his friend.

Sam checked a message on her phone. "Your team's loaded up."

"Let's roll, Pieter." Luke turned and exited the cottage. He climbed behind the wheel and buckled in.

Once Pieter was settled in the passenger seat, Luke reversed and drove up the ramp and out of the property. Luke waited until they were off the windier roads and headed east before breaking the silence.

"OK. We're not anticipating any trouble, but be on the alert. Watch me for your signals and err on the side of caution. We're here to make allies and further our plan. As long as we're smart and pay attention, everything should work out fine," Luke said. "And remember, don't call me Luke. For this mission, Alex is my name. Got it?"

"Right you are, Alex," Connor replied. Joe and Agatha nodded along.

"Good." Luke nodded toward Pieter. "Any last-minute updates?"

Pieter rotated in his seat so he could more easily look toward the back seat. "I don't have an official count, but there shouldn't be too many people there. They're as worried about leaks as we are. We're being allowed weapons, but they should be visible. Nothing concealed."

"Do you all have your silver alloy daggers?" Luke asked. "I don't know if they'll be able to feel the silver on them, but we'll be prepared if things go badly with the werewolves. Let me lead so I can sense any vampires. If I pick up any, we just fade away and get out of there. I am not interested in confrontation."

"I can sense the silver on my belt," Joe said. "Though we haven't tried a range test."

Luke nodded. "That's a good idea. When we get back, we'll test them out to see if there's any difference in ranges depending on size."

"You're always thinking of plans and solutions, aren't you?" Pieter asked.

"I haven't survived this long by being lazy and unorganized. At least mostly."

He snorted quietly, remembering the admonishment Sam had given him after she'd joined the team for his weak plans. It wasn't that he wasn't making plans, he just didn't care that much since it was only his body and life on the line, two things he was increasingly tired of as his loneliness grew. Now, he had friends, loved ones, and a pack to protect. They deserved his best efforts, and he was going to give it to them.

Once they pulled off the larger road, they wound their way through the Belgian countryside until they arrived at the first set of coordinates. As they parked, the sun dipped down and disappeared. Pieter pulled out his phone and sent a message to their contact.

"OK. We have our next set of coordinates," Pieter said, stuffing his phone into his pocket and stepping out of the car.

They joined him at the back of the SUV and helped each other gear up with Kevlar vests. Each of them carried a belt with magazines for their pistols, machine guns, and their dagger. Pieter had chosen to only go in with two 9mm pistols. Agatha, Connor, and Joe had a pistol and the APC9K compact machine guns the team was growing fond of. Luke carried the AK-47 he'd taken from the freighter nearly three years ago. It wasn't the most efficient weapon, but it looked intimidating and had a long reputation of violence. He wanted to look dangerous. Sometimes the best way to ward off violence was to look scary.

"If everyone is ready, let's proceed. I'll take the lead. Pieter, you're behind me. Keep your ears and eyes open." Luke loaded a magazine into the magwell of the AK.

"Can you see well enough?" Joe asked. "What I mean is…"

"I have excellent night vision. It's part of my whole deal." He pushed the button on the fob to lock the car, then slid the key into his pocket. "Let's move out. We have about a mile to go."

Using all his woodcraft skills, Luke picked a trail through the trees, keeping on a westerly course, adjusting as needed when Pieter whispered a correction or a change in direction. After they reached their destination, a small meadow, Pieter received another set of coordinates.

"They're not the trusting sort, are they?" Connor asked.

"Do you blame them? They're planning a rebellion against a patricide who's allied with vampires." Luke pulled a canteen off his belt and took a small drink. "Ready?"

When no one objected, he waved them after him as he slipped into the trees heading south. After another mile, they stopped to take a breather and wait for the next set of instructions.

"I hope we're not wandering around out here in the woods all night. I'm getting cold," Agatha said.

Luke snorted, giving her a friendly smirk. "A little jog will help with that. You got the new coordinates?"

"Yes." Pieter pointed to the southeast. "That way."

"Is this our last round?" Luke asked.

"I don't know. They didn't say," Pieter replied.

Luke kept his thoughts to himself. He knew his friend was already worried about meeting with people from his old pack. He didn't want his brother finding out he was in country and working against him. Nor did he want to expose anyone to danger, especially if some of the people he was meeting with were already on Jan's enemies list.

Luke felt for his friend, but he was concerned this was a wild goose chase or a way to expose Pieter. Though they had backup teams ready, with all the tromping through the woods, it would be a hard fight to hold off any ambushes while they waited for extraction.

The longer they traipsed through the woods, the more alert he grew. Every noise drew his attention. When an owl flew overhead across the field of the moon, adrenaline dumped into his veins. He had to restrain his hand from pulling back the charging lever of his AK. Once his heart rate calmed a bit, he started the team moving again.

"Do you smell that?" Pieter whispered.

Luke held up his hand, halting the group. Poking his nose into the air, he searched for an out-of-place scent on the wind. There it was. A hint of wood smoke. As the breeze shifted slightly, the smell intensified.

"It's in the direction we're headed. We must be close," Luke whispered. "Extra vigilance."

Luke slowed their pace so he could more carefully pick his steps and keep their advance as silent as possible. With each minute, the smell of smoke grew stronger. Five minutes after they first smelled it, Pieter slipped up behind Luke and placed a hand on his shoulder.

When Luke turned to Pieter, he had a finger over his lips and then pointed into the woods. It took Luke a moment to see what Pieter was pointing toward—two wolf eyes reflected in the moonlight. Then he pointed to the other side. Another set of eyes.

"They know we're here. I guess we can just move forward without the extra stealth," Luke said quietly. "Don't point your weapons toward them. Just keep them ready but relaxed."

Luke took the lead, moving quickly toward the smell of the smoke. When they rounded a hill, he saw the faint glow of a fire in the near distance. The flickering light illuminated ruined stone walls. At one point, they might have belonged to a castle or fortification. There were certainly enough ruins littering southern Belgium. This one looked far more run down than most.

He pointed toward the fire. "Is that our destination, Pieter?"

"I believe so." Pieter checked his phone, then nodded.

They closed the last distance. Luke's eyes swept around them, tracking the two wolves as they escorted them from a distance. He didn't see anyone else in the woods, but his body had slipped into hyper vigilance, picking up every sound or movement around him.

"Any fangers?" Pieter asked.

"I don't sense any, but let's slow it down just in case."

Luke stopped them about thirty meters from a gap in the ruined stone wall leaking fire light. "Give them a shout. I don't want to walk in blind."

Pieter stepped in front of Luke and placed his hands around his mouth to shout. "You, in the camp. Show yourselves."

A shadow poked its head out from behind the wall. "Who comes to call?"

"A wayward son from across the ocean," Pieter replied with the code phrase.

"Oceans are wide and deep; rest and be welcome," the shadow replied.

Luke looked over at Pieter, who nodded, confirming the correct code had been given in return. Stepping in front of Pieter, he kept his hands on his AK-47, though he kept the weapon pointing down. When they reached the gap in the wall, they stopped. A Black man stepped from behind the wall holding up his empty hands.

"Pieter, it has been too long," the Black man said in Flemish Dutch with a Congolese accent.

"Augustin Lusamba, it has. You're looking well," Pieter replied, stepping from behind Luke. He pulled Augustin into a hug, patting his back. "Until Amiata called saying you wanted to meet, I wasn't sure you'd survived my brother's purge."

"Too few have escaped his murderous rampage. Who are your friends?"

"These are my escorts Alex, Agatha, Connor, and Joe. They don't speak much Flemish or French, so you'll have to pardon me if I have to translate anything, but they're good people. Sorry if we're a bit heavily armed."

"Troubled times." Augustin turned back into the gap in the wall. "It's all clear."

Luke relaxed but didn't take his hand off the AK. Augustin led the way back into the ruins. Four people relaxed in various poses around the fire—each of them held a gun as well. The two wolves flanking them into the camp blurred into naked people and quickly pulled their clothes on, steam rising from their bodies.

"I hope the trail in wasn't too unpleasant. I tried to pick a route that wasn't too arduous."

"Better cautious than dead. If it were summer, it would have been a pleasant hike." Pieter slipped his hand into his pocket.

"Please, tell your people to warm themselves by the fire. I have hot water in a kettle if they'd like some tea," Augustin said.

Pieter gestured toward the fire, then spoke in English. "You can get warm by the fire. Anyone want any tea?"

Luke raised his hand, as did Agatha, Connor, and Joe.

"Make it five teas, please," Pieter replied to Augustin.

The two men talked idly while one of Augustin's people prepared five cups of tea in enameled tin camping cups, handing them out when he finished. Luke cradled the cup in his hands, letting its heat sink into his frigid fingers.

"So what are you doing back in Belgium, Pieter?" Augustin asked, folding his arms across his chest.

"I can't get into too many details, but suffice to say, I'm working toward the same ends you are."

"How have you remained undetected? I know your brother has a standing order for all his people to keep an eye out for you, no matter where they go." Augustin squatted near the fire and poked a log into a better position with a stick.

"I haven't been in Belgium. I've been working on another project."

Augustin gestured toward Luke with his head. "Are you going to topple Jan with an army of mercenaries?"

"I'm not comfortable discussing those details with you at this point, Augustin. What are your goals?"

"Sit with me, and we can discuss it." Augustin waved someone over.

They set up two simple folding stools with cloth seats.

Augustin stared at Pieter for a moment, then sat up straighter. "What started this all?"

"I'm not sure what you've heard from Jan and his allies, but this is what I've pieced together from various sources." Pieter's eyes flicked briefly to Luke, who gave the barest of nods. "I'm not sure who initiated it, but at the behest of a vampire lord through the alpha of the Luxembourg pack, Jan assassinated my father."

"What?" Augustin nearly tipped over on his stool. "He said the kidnappers did it."

"Lies. He orchestrated the whole thing. The kidnapping and the assassination. I don't know how long he's been under the thumb of the vampire lord, but he's been feeding them information for a long while. That's how we lost the south to the vampires after we worked so hard to take it from them."

"Do you swear this is the truth?" Augustin asked, leaning forward.

Pieter nodded solemnly. "I saw the assassination with my own eyes. The rest is information I've assembled from various pieces I and my allies have picked up in the intervening time."

"Why didn't you stop him?"

"How could I? I didn't know. He had a couple of his goons knock me in the head, then hold me down. I barely escaped. I should have seen it, though, seen Jan's betrayal." He shook his head and sighed heavily.

Augustin leaned forward and squeezed Pieter's shoulder. "I'm sorry, Pieter. Your father was a good man and a dear friend. We've all been mourning his loss. How could one of his sons have fallen so far from the tree?"

Pieter didn't answer the rhetorical question, instead staring into the fire as he wiped a tear from his cheek. Taking a drink from his tea, he exhaled steam after swallowing. "I don't know, Augustin. I've been thinking about that question non-stop since he murdered our father. How? How didn't I see it?"

Luke wanted to reach out to his friend, but he couldn't in his current role as bodyguard. Augustin gave Pieter a moment to collect himself.

"Now, back to our earlier conversation. What are you goals? Why have you asked to meet me?" Pieter asked.

"Amiata says I can trust you," Augustin replied.

Pieter nodded. "I'd die to keep Amiata and Olivia safe. They're my family, and that still means something to me."

"Because she trusts you, I'll extend that trust to you. I want to put a stop to Jan's predations. To stop the disappearances of families that don't hit his ideal of who belongs in the pack. I want the pack to return to the welcoming place your father fostered. I want peace and prosperity."

"That's not a small list, though it's a worthy one." Pieter took a drink of his tea. "I want the same thing."

"Now, the important part. What are you doing to achieve it?" Augustin asked.

"Right now? I'm working with a consortium of people interested in bringing down Jan. I can't reveal much beyond that until I discuss this meeting with them. But they've authorized me to explore any alliances that seem legitimate."

Augustin sat up straighter, his eyebrows rising. "As subservient partners?"

"As equal partners."

With Pieter's assurances, Augustin warmed up to his old friend as they discussed some potential plans, but only in the vague terms both of them were currently authorized to make. Luke focused on Augustin, trying to get a feel for the man. Taking down Jan was the plan, but a power vacuum in an important pack would be a disaster for the region and Luke's plans. Augustin just might be a good ally.

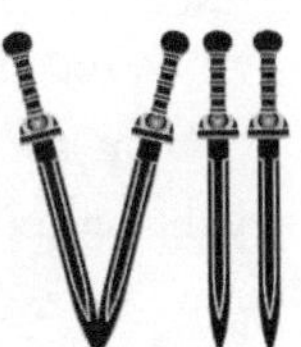

CHAPTER
SIX

LUKE'S SLEEP had been troubled, lying next to Roxi as she weakly tossed and turned all night, unable to find comfort even in sleep. The compulsion Mithras placed upon her ate away at her body and mind. He'd tried to sleep on the twin bed at the foot of his bed so she'd have her own space and comfort, but he could be near if he was needed. Without him lying next to her, she thrashed and moaned in pain. During her few brief moments of lucidity, she'd ask for him to lie next to her and hold her. It was the only thing that allowed her even the barest respite from the agony her life had become. He'd never deny that comfort to her, no matter how much it affected his sleep. He'd have given anything for her to feel better.

Over the days after they'd successfully rescued her, Luke rarely left her side, sitting in a chair reading a book and holding her hand if she wanted it. Reading aloud to her if she needed to hear his voice. The doctor had stabilized her, putting several bags of fluid into her.

Luke looked up from the book at the sound of a knock on the door. "Yes?"

Sam poked her head in. "I brought some food up for you two."

"Thanks, Sam. Bring it in." Luke placed the bookmark in the book and set it on the nightstand.

"How's she doing?" Sam asked, wheeling in a service cart.

"I'm feeling absolutely capital, Sam," Roxi rasped out quietly.

Sam chuckled and caught Luke's eye when he stepped forward, blocking the line of sight between Sam and Roxi. In her eyes, he saw the worry he felt reflected along with the profound sympathy and love of a dear friend.

"What do we have for lunch today?" Luke asked.

Sam took off the silver dome covering the food. "We have some fresh baked bread and butter, along with a nice chicken noodle soup."

Inhaling deeply, a smile crept over Luke's face. "That smells wonderful."

"I can't claim the bread, but the soup recipe is one of mine." Sam wheeled the cart out of the way alongside the wall.

"Thanks, Sam. Anything I need to know about?" Luke poked his nose out, pulling in the aromas wafting up from the steaming serving bowl.

"Not much we can't handle. If there is, we'll come get you. Everyone knows their duties." Sam smiled warmly. "I'll leave you two to your lunch."

Luke followed her out of his room. "Thanks, Sam. Are you sure there's not somewhere I'm needed?"

"There is, Luke." She reached up and laid her hand on his cheek. "Right here. Roxi needs you more than anyone or anything right now. Let us handle things until you're truly needed for something."

Luke nodded, giving her a lopsided smile. "Thanks, Sam."

"Go to her," Sam instructed.

Luke nodded and slipped back into his room, closing the door behind him. Roxi smiled weakly, her eyes barely open.

"I like soup," she whispered.

Luke grabbed a bowl and dipped the ladle in, filling the bowl half full. Setting it on the nightstand, he handed Roxi a cloth to drape across her chest, then helped her sit up, propping her up with pillows. Last, he grabbed the tray and laid it across her lap, setting a piece of bread on it before smearing butter over the warm bread. Once everything was settled, he placed the soup on the tray and laid a spoon next to it.

Roxi looked at the tray, then up at Luke, a tiny note of mischief in her eyes. "I want you to feed me."

"What?" He grinned. "Not feeling strong enough for a spoon?"

She shrugged. "I just want you to baby me."

Some days, she barely could lift the spoon without a tremor shaking the soup out. He didn't know if today was one of those days, but he didn't care. If she wanted special attention from him, he wouldn't deny her. He nodded gently. "OK."

He scooted the chair closer to the bed and sat down, lifting the bowl and scooping some soup into the spoon. With the steam rising from the bowl, he blew on it before lifting it to her lips. She slurped it in, humming in appreciation at the soup. Spoon after spoon he fed to her until it scraped against an empty bowl. Taking the bread, he tore off a piece and wiped it around the bowl before popping it into Roxi's mouth.

"Are you full or would you like more soup?" Luke asked.

She yawned, her eyes drifting low. "I think I'm good. I have a belly full of soup and now it's time for a nap."

Luke lifted the tray and set it aside before helping her lay back down. Behind him, his phone vibrated on the nightstand. He picked it up, saw Mathis's name flash across the screen, and silenced it, letting it go to voicemail. Bending over, he kissed Roxi on the forehead and tucked her in.

"Mmm, thank you, Luke."

"Sleep well, Roxi. I need to make a call, but I'll be nearby." Luke wasn't sure if she heard him, though, as her breathing slipped into the steady rhythm of sleep.

He reached for the phone, but the aroma of soup distracted him as his stomach grumbled. Mathis could wait until after he had a full belly. He fixed himself a bowl and grabbed a hunk of buttered bread. The soup was indeed excellent; he'd have to get the recipe from Sam.

Looking over Roxi, he moved a strand of hair out of her face, smoothing it into the halo of black hair wildly flared over her pillow. With a sad smile, he grabbed his phone and stepped out of his room.

Luke hit the call back button. "Hello, Mathis. What can I do for you?"

LUKE SHOOK JAN'S HAND. "I'm surprised to hear from you so close to the holidays. I'm not a religious man myself, but we do live in a society that likes to avoid work during the winter holidays."

Jan chuckled obsequiously. "Thank you for coming to Antwerp on such short notice."

"It's a beautiful city, especially decorated for the season."

The sudden change in attitude threw Luke for a moment. Previously Jan had been aloof, almost haughty. Now…he was overly polite and friendly. This was a side he hadn't seen of the Flanders packleader. He tried to keep a pleased smile from spreading across his face.

"Well, after you rushed off, we missed the opportunity to really dig into the business you wanted to conduct. Your proposal was so interesting, I couldn't let it sit unattended. Time is money after all, Your Excellency." Jan gestured toward a chair.

"Indeed." Luke sat, crossing a leg over his knee.

"Can I get you something to drink? A snifter of Cognac? I even bought some Bourbon in case you were feeling homesick." Jan pasted a fake smile on his face. Even with its wattage, it couldn't overpower the cold calculation behind his eyes.

"Cognac will suffice," Luke replied.

A few moments later, Jan handed Luke a generously filled snifter of amber brown liquor.

"I'd like some cognac as well, Jan," Mathis said.

"You know where the glasses are, Mathis." Jan negligently waved his hand toward the sideboard cabinet where he'd just poured Luke's glass as if lazily swatting a fly.

As soon as Mathis stepped out of Jan's field of view, he scowled at the Belgian. Luke covered a snort of humor with a cleared throat.

"Once Mathis wets his whistle, we can proceed," Luke said, his lip quirking up at the corner.

"We don't need Mathis to discuss this deal, it's merely a courtesy to your friendship that I've allowed him in the room." Jan's eyes narrowed as a small, vicious grin tugged at his lips. He seemed to enjoy the wince and uncontrolled scowl he drew from Mathis.

"That is true. I have promised Mathis a finder's fee for introducing us, but I've come to recognize him as a fine judge of where to find financial gain and tenacious in getting it." Luke swirled his snifter and peered over the edge, his gaze boring into Jan's, and took a sip. "Now, since we're being forthright here. Let us proceed to the meat of the matter. What can you do to make your ports an attractive option to base my European businesses from? Consistent and reliable transportation is key to the success of this venture."

"You can't find better hubs with access to roads, rails, and canals than Antwerp and Rotterdam. They're the second and first largest ports in Europe, respectively." He tipped his head to the side and raised his glass.

"Indeed. Though I may be an American, that doesn't mean supersized is actually the better option. Bigger ports can mean bigger delays." Luke shifted in his chair, slouching slightly, and sat as if he owned the room. "Amsterdam and Hamburg are both well situated to meet my demands."

"Ah, but I hear you're trying to reinstate your Belgian titles with His Royal Highness. Bringing more commerce to the lands of your titles certainly wouldn't go unnoticed." Jan leaned forward, an ingratiating smile smeared across his face.

"You're well informed." Luke raised his glass toward Jan. "I do believe your own king's line comes through Germany, Saxe-Coburg and Gotha, if I'm not mistaken…"

Jan chuckled. "You know your history, but after nearly two hundred years, they're fully Belgian. Something you can't claim to be, Your Excellency."

Mathis leaned forward, sitting straighter. "Now, now, Jan. We're all citizens of the world. Denizens of commerce, if you will. There's no need to be picky about what dirt we were born on when the real reason we're all here is for the same purpose."

Jan lifted his glass and tipped it along with his head toward Mathis. "You are correct, Mathis. My apologizes, Your Excellency."

Luke chuckled and smiled, not letting it reach his eyes. "No apologies necessary. I appreciate a plain spoken person. Better a person who speaks unpleasant things to your face than one who smiles prettily before stabbing you in the back."

"Indeed. There are far too many deceitful men selling sweet lies. The trick is knowing which is which, is it not?" Jan replied.

"You're a wise man, Mr. van den Bergh. Now, back to business. We were speaking about what you can offer me that your Dutch friends in their capital or our German neighbors can't." Luke raised an open hand and nodded with a smug smirk affixed to his face. "Since you prefer plain-speaking men."

Jan snorted, then chuckled, until it broke into a full laugh. "You continue to be an interesting man, Your Excellency. Most entertaining, if nothing else."

Luke let the smile fall off his face. "I'm glad I amuse you. Yet you still haven't answered my question."

"You Americans are direct, aren't you? So be it. I can offer preferential handling of your containers so they spend only the bare minimum time on the ground before they're moving again. If you have... Let's just say *special* containers that need discreet handling, we can make those arrangements as well, for a modest per unit gratuity."

Luke raised an eyebrow. "'Special containers'? That makes for an interesting offer. Do you often handle special shipping requests?"

Giving a half shrug, Jan took a drink of his cognac. "For a few important customers."

Luke stared at Jan for a moment. He'd suspected the vampires shipping into Portland via Rotterdam had been assisted by Jan. Luke wondered how long before Jan had murdered his father had he been the plaything of the vampires. He kept his eyes firmly planted on Jan, not wanting to give in to his urge to check out Mathis, the man who'd likely brokered the whole betrayal. "Ah, to be a special customer is a fine thing. But what does it take to become a preferred shipper via the ports you control?"

"Well..." Jan gestured with the hand holding the glass, sloshing brown liquor around in it. "Based on the numbers you presented to Mathis... I'd say a startup fee of fifteen million euro to cover all the paperwork would facilitate things and then a modest one point five per annum. To renew the contract and services."

Luke's eyebrows shot up. "Five."

"Oh, what is the saying? Something for something, nothing for nothing? Five is nothing." He pushed out his lips and thought for a moment. "I'm feeling generous. Twelve point five."

"For twelve point five million, you can afford to feel generous. Seven million and one per annum." Luke took a casual drink, admiring the swirl of the cognac in the glass.

"I see you're a man who expects to get what he wants. Fine. Let's say ten—"

Luke leaned forward and opened his mouth.

Jan held up his hand to stall the response. "And I'll throw in season tickets to Royal Antwerp F.C. It's probably best if you get used to the preferred sport in, well, the entire world except for your small corner."

"Make it Anderlect or Brugge, and we have a deal. They're easier to get to from my estate in Maubeuge."

"If proximity is a factor, I can get you tickets to Charleroi?"

Luke snorted. "Make the deal four million euros, and I'll take the tickets for the Zebras."

Jan's eyes narrowed as he stared at Luke for a minute, then he slapped his knee and barked out a laugh. "Ten, one per annum, and the Anderlect tickets. Plus, I'll host you at the next home game Belgium plays before the World Cup."

"I do enjoy watching the Red Devils. You have a deal." Luke stood up and offered his hand to Jan.

Jan stood and shook Luke's hand. "Would you care for another glass to toast our deal?"

"Of course." Luke offered his glass to Jan, then sat.

Jan turned his back and walked to the bar with both their glasses. Mathis stood to get his own refill, not trusting the hospitality of their host to offer, even after a successful deal had been struck.

Luke slipped his hand into his pocket and pulled out the tiny bug, then slipped it into the crack between the back cushion and the bottom cushion. He stood again and took his glass and raised it. "To a successful partnership."

"To commerce." Jan raised his glass.

Mathis shoved his way in and tapped his glass against both glasses before they could pull them away. Smirking, Luke took a sip and savored the fine flavor of the expensive cognac Jan was plying him with.

After a satisfactory sigh, he gave a relaxed smile. "You have excellent taste in drinks."

"Thank you, Your Excellency."

Luke tipped his head toward Mathis. "And many thanks to you for arranging this meeting, my friend. Don't worry, I won't forget your finder's fee. I'm sure you'll be most pleased with my thank you. I'm very generous with those who make my life easier."

Mathis relaxed slightly and nodded his head in a mini bow. "It's been a pleasure making your acquaintance and helping you feel welcome in our little corner of western Europe. Your thanks is merely a happy extra, Your Excellency.

Jamaal cleared his throat and set his hand on Luke's shoulder. "Excuse me, Your Excellency. You wanted me to remind you when we neared your appointment."

"Ah, yes. Thank you." Luke nodded at Jamal. "I'm afraid I'll have to cut this little celebration short. I have a call with my associates in the states, and I need time to return to my room. Jamaal, my coat please."

Jamaal stepped forward and held open Luke's overcoat. Once it was settled on his shoulders, he reached into his pocket and pulled out two envelopes made from thick paper with gold embossed seals holding them closed. A ribbon dangled from the seal. Jan's and Mathis's names were written in beautiful calligraphy on the front. Luke handed Jan's to him first, then gave Mathis his.

"Gentlemen, I'm hosting a little soirée at my place to celebrate its renovation and to—well, not to sound too conceited, but—announce my arrival officially. It should be a splendid party. Dress attire and the other details are contained within. I look forward to your RSVPs."

"I'm honored, Your Excellency. I'll do my best to clear my schedule if there's any overlap," Jan replied with a slight bend of his back to offer the most minimal of bows.

Mathis's bowed lower, placing his right hand on his chest. "I look forward to it, Your Excellency."

Luke nodded. "Let me know when the paperwork is ready so I can have my lawyers peruse it, Mr. van den Bergh. Adieu, gentlemen."

Luke cast a wave over his shoulder as he walked through the door Ahmed held open for him, Jamaal following him out the door. When they walked into the brisk evening air, Luke popped his coat's collar to keep the wind from biting deep. He'd forgotten his scarf. Checking his watch, he turned off their route and strode toward a shop carrying locally made products he'd seen on an earlier trip. While Ahmed paid the clerk, Luke wrapped the superfine merino scarf around his neck and stepped back into the night.

CHAPTER
SEVEN

AFTER THEY RETURNED to their suite, Luke sent Ahmed and Jung-sook to bring back food. Jamaal disappeared into the room shared with the other two—though one person was always awake and on guard duty, leaving one of the beds empty. He appreciated their sacrifices for the cause.

He opened a bottle of sparkling water before texting Roxi. *I just got back from my meeting. How are you doing?*

Terrible. I'm having trouble sleeping without you here. A moment later, a picture of Roxi's pale and emaciated face appeared. Her eyelids drooped as if she was struggling to keep them up even that far. The attempted smile confirmed the bone-deep weariness and highlighted her hollow cheeks.

Even though she'd tried for a bit of a smile, it only twisted the knife in his heart as he watched her losing her battle.

I miss you too. I wish I could be with you, Luke replied.

I know. Maggie and everyone else is taking good care of me. There's only so much they can do.

He felt terrible about leaving her alone, though the house was a hub of activity with his friends and packmates moving through constantly. He also worried the compulsion might take over and force her out of the bed to hunt, but so far she'd stayed safely in bed, letting Luke's friends care for her.

Can I hear your voice? Roxi asked.

He called her. "Hey, I'm sorry you're not sleeping well."

She sighed heavily. "I haven't slept well since I fled Oregon. When you're here, I do a little better, but the compulsion haunts me day and night." She paused, catching her breath. "I'm so tired today, Luke." She sighed. "At least yesterday was decent. I had dinner with everyone in the solarium."

Luke clenched his jaw, squeezing his eyes shut. He hated what the compulsion had done to her, how it had robbed her of her vitality and her joy. The selfish part of him hated that it had robbed him of her, just when he'd found her and their friends freed them. The compulsion had settled in hard for her after going too long without renewing her connection with the rudis and through it, Mithra. Every day he watched her deteriorate—even on the good days, she spent more time asleep than awake. On the bad days, she no longer could make it to the bathroom unassisted. Each day he hated the vampires who'd destroyed her rudis more, but behind it all was the towering resentment for the god who'd set them on this course all those years ago and hid this curse within the covenant they'd shaken hands on.

For nearly two thousand years, he and Roxi had hunted and slain vampires. Luke had raised an entire legion and maintained it for two centuries, moved it back and forth the length of the empire, and even beyond, doing Mithras's bidding to make the world safer from the fanged monsters who preyed on humanity. The god owed him and Roxi for the services they'd rendered.

When the door opened, the scent of food drifted across the room. Jamaal stepped out of his room to join the rest of the freshly returned team to eat.

"Luke, would you sing me that song, please?" Roxi asked, sounding tentative.

"Hmm? Yes. Of course." He sat up and cleared his throat, then sang the lullaby his mother had sung to him as a boy, the same song he'd revived in the deep, dark cell of the vampires' arena a year ago.

In the background, he heard the soft voices of conversation until they realized Luke was singing and stopped. When Luke finished his song, he listened to her breathe.

"Thank you. I'm going to try to sleep again," she said, struggling to speak through her exhaustion.

"Good night, Roxi. I hope you sleep well."

"Good night." She hung up.

He set the phone down on the table and stared at the wall for a few minutes while they set up the food.

"You have a nice voice, Luke." Jung-sook poured some more water into her glass.

Luke stared ahead. "Thank you."

Ahmed looked up from helping Jamaal. "What was that song? I didn't recognize the language."

"You wouldn't. The language has been dead for over a thousand years. It was a lullaby my mother used to sing to me when I was young." He picked up his glass and took a drink, letting the burn of bubbles in the back of his throat coax some feeling back into his mind.

"It sounds sad," Jamaal said.

"It is. It's filled with a lot of poetic symbolism about the wolf and the eagle killing all the boars and stealing their boarlets to feast upon in faraway lands." He covered his eyes with his left hand and rubbed his temples, one side with his thumb, the other with his middle finger.

"What does it mean, though?" Jung-sook asked, getting a beer from the fridge for herself.

"It's about the genocide of my people at the hands of Julius Caesar."

He removed the hand from his eyes and blinked a few times, then looked at his friends as they stared blankly at him.

"Before Caesar came, historians estimate about three million Gauls lived in France, Switzerland, and the Lowlands of Belgium and the Netherlands. If Caesar is to be believed, he killed a million and sent an equal number to Rome as slaves, though historians estimate half those numbers are more accurate," Luke said quietly.

It had happened over a century before his birth, but it haunted the world he'd grown up in, even if he was too young to see it at the time. Then, as a fresh-faced legionnaire, he participated in removing Dacia and its people from the map, killing thousands as huge swaths of survivors were sent to the slave auctions of Rome. He'd spent the rest of his life fighting against the vampires, a force that sought to subjugate humanity, turning them into cattle.

"Even at half…" Jung-sook shook her head.

"You know, I don't think I'm hungry right now. I'm going to go lay down." Luke stood and headed to his room.

"We'll leave you some leftovers," Ahmed said.

Luke sagged onto the edge of his bed, resting his elbows on his knees, and stared at the floor. He loathed Mathis and Jan for dragging him away from Roxi when, in reality, he had no idea how much longer he had with her. They were convenient targets for his vitriol.

But they were already in his crosshairs and it was almost time to pull the trigger. They'd get theirs. And even though they were nominally the reason for his absence from Roxi's side, neither of them were the reason she was sick. Neither of them were the reason she was dying.

There was only one being who deserved his ire — Mithras.

LUKE SIPPED his cup of coffee idly while Jamaal, Jung-sook, and Ahmed talked quietly as they finished the last of their breakfast. When he reached the bottom of the cup, he refilled it.

"Are you ready to listen to the recordings, Luke?" Jamaal asked, rubbing a napkin between his hands.

Luke nodded and returned to his chair. "Assuming they didn't find our bugs."

Jamaal chuckled, shaking his head. "Doesn't look like they did. At least from the sample I listened to."

He set a blue tooth speaker on the table and pointed it toward Luke, then set his laptop down in front of himself. After his fingers finished clacking over the keys, the speaker crackled to life, filling the quiet with static and what sounded like rustling in the background.

"Ten mill—" Mathis started.

"Shh." Luke guessed it was Jan. "Ludo, is he gone?"

A door opened, then closed. "Yes, sir."

"Good, you can wait outside," Jan replied.

The door opened and closed again.

"You've gotten paranoid, Jan," Mathis said.

"One man's paranoia is another man's cautious. And when we're under my roof, you'll do well to remember which man you're talking to." Jan sounded annoyed, as he often did when speaking to or about Mathis.

"Of course, of course. So you did quite well there. A nice little payment plus a yearly fee and whatever you can squeeze out of him for the actual freight handling."

"He'll get his money's worth and then some out of my ports, if he's the businessman you say he is."

Mathis chuckled. "By all rights, he's supposed to be something of a prodigy. Though he comes from a long line of wealthy men."

"Have you managed to slip your hand into his pocket yet, Mathis?" Jan asked, sounding mildly curious.

Mathis grunted. "Not yet. He's been fairly stingy on that end so far."

"He did rescue you from these mysterious kidnappers. Isn't that enough for your ungrateful heart?"

"What has he done for me lately? Besides, I can't *afford* to be sentimental right now."

Jan chuckled. "Have you figured out who's trying to fuck you over?"

"No." Mathis bit out. "Everyone seems to be astonishingly closed mouthed now that they don't owe me money."

"Even those who you owed money to?" Jan sounded amused.

"No one will say anything other than they sold the mark and to contact the new owner. Every now and then, someone shows up at my house with one of the marks and demands payment. Fortunately, it's just been the smaller marks I owe, but I'm running out of liquid assets. Especially since some people—"

"I suggest you alter this line of thought right now, or you'll find yourself swimming in the Scheldt," Jan interrupted, his earlier trace of humor gone. "If you need money so badly, ask for your finder's fee. I know you didn't bring him here out of the goodness of your heart." Jan snorted. "You'd have to have either goodness or a heart for that to be true."

Mathis mumbled something.

"What now?" Jan asked, deadly quiet. "I don't think I quite heard what you said there."

"Jamaal, can you pause?" Luke asked.

Jamaal clicked a button. "Sure thing."

"Can you clarify what Mathis said? I'm curious." Luke set his empty cup down, turning his chair toward the speaker.

Jamaal ran the segment back and worked it over, trying to enhance it. After a few minutes, he sat up and tied the computer back into the speaker. "I think this is as good as I can get it. I'm not an audio tech and this software is only so good. Ready?"

Luke nodded.

Loud static proceeded the mumbles, but Luke thought he heard the words "own father" and maybe "murdered" or "removed;" he wasn't sure.

"Did any of you hear what he said?" Luke asked. "My hearing isn't as good as a werewolf's."

"Um, Luke, they're not speaking English," Jung-sook said.

"Really? Shit. I didn't think of that." He'd been so distracted by thoughts of Roxi and Mithras that he'd just listened without thinking about it being in Flemish and translating it for his team. He took a moment and recounted the conversation back to the team.

"That Mathis is a real petulant little shit, isn't he?" Ahmed asked.

"Yeah. He's the kind of person who's a poor winner and a poor loser. I'm thoroughly enjoying bringing his house of cards down around his ears." Luke stood and stretched, working some of the tension from his shoulders. "Go ahead and play the rest. I'll try to translate or summarize as we go."

"On it," Jamaal said, focusing on his computer.

Jan's voice announced the resumption of the playback. "What now? I don't think I quite heard what you said there."

"Nothing, just had a little something in my throat. I think it's clear now," Mathis said obsequiously.

"If you don't watch your mouth, you'll find it hard to clear with your teeth shoved down it. Understand me?" Jan replied.

"Yeah."

"No. Do you understand me?" Jan raised the intensity of his voice.

"I understand you."

"Be sure that you do. You're quickly outliving your usefulness, especially if you keep running around with your hand out. Now get out of my sight. I'm tired of looking at your smug face. I'll let you know when the deal is done so you can extract your fee from your up-jumped *Comte*."

Feet stomped across the floor followed by a slamming door as Mathis exited. A minute later, the door opened and closed again, this time quietly.

"You know he has no loyalty," a new voice said.

"Mathis?" Jan snorted. "Only to himself and his entertainments."

"He'll betray you if the price is right."

Jan barked a harsh laugh. "Who is left to trust him? Someone is stripping him of his wealth. I'm about the only one of his associates that'll see him. If he wants his money back from me, he'll remain loyal. He may shoot his mouth off, but he knows we are tied with ropes thicker than money." He sighed and let silence hang for a minute. "I sometimes wish I'd never listened to him."

"A silver blade in the back and you'll never have to hear him again. A forest. A cave. A canal or a river. There are plenty of places to dump his body in this country where he's unlikely to be found. A concrete block tied around his ankles and a short trip out onto the North Sea and he's fish food. What use is he anymore? You have his money and his contacts. You don't need him anymore."

Jan chuckled. "Don't underestimate the need to keep around someone you can feel superior to."

Luke thought he heard a bit of loathing in Jan's voice. He could have misheard it, but it was a feeling he knew all too well, though he'd never done anything as loathsome as murdering his own father.

After a couple minutes of silence, Jamaal perked his head up. "You think that's it?"

"Let it go for a little more." Luke reached for the coffee carafe. "Damn. Empty."

"I'll go grab another," Ahmed said. "I could use some more myself."

"Thanks."

When Jan started speaking again, Luke was glad he'd decided to wait.

"Have you found out anything about our little *Comte?*" Jan asked.

"Not much beyond what we already know. He's private and keep his presence in the world to a minimum. Every lane I travel down seems to lead to legitimate places." The unknown voice sounded unsure.

"You don't seem too confident."

"I don't know. I have an itch on the back of my neck like I'm being watched. Everything seems too clear. Too well curated."

"Could he be a fraud? Or, he could be a very wealthy businessman with a lot of family money. The ultra-wealthy are often very good at keeping their profiles low. They have no need for flashiness."

"That could be it. He sure seems to throw around a lot of money at antiquities auctions and on refurbishing his estate in Maubeuge. The place is crawling with contractors."

Jan laughed. "He must be burning through money to get the French to work that hard around the holidays."

"I've even seen a few vans and trucks from Germany."

"What do you make of this?"

Floor boards creaked as someone walked. A moment later, heavy paper rustled.

"An invitation to a party at his estate? Will you go?" the unknown voice asked.

"It might be interesting to see what an American thinks makes for tasteful decor for a European aristocrat. I'm also curious to see if anyone worth knowing shows up."

"It could be a good opportunity to see who this Comte really is and make some more connections of your own."

Jan snorted. "I'm not sure I'm ready to kiss an American's ass, especially one that's putting on airs as an aristocrat. We already have too many blue bloods running around as is. We don't need to import more and pretend their titles are worth bowing to."

The voice chuckled. "Your background is showing."

"If you have no more information for me on the American, you're dismissed," Jan said.

"Of course."

A moment later, the door opened and closed. The clink of glass signaled a drink being poured.

"I don't think there's anything after this. All I see on here is pretty much a flat line. Want me to shut it off? I can check over this morning's recordings to see if there's anything. You can tell me if they're worth listening to."

"Sounds like a plan." Luke chuckled, shaking his head. "I should have brought another Dutch speaker with us so I wouldn't be the only one who can translate."

"Yeah. That probably would have been a good idea. I can read code, but I don't know Dutch from the Swedish Chef."

"That was poor planning on my part, but I don't think we have a lot of Dutch speakers who aren't known by people here."

"Yeah. That'd blow our cover," Jung-sook said. "At least it was an interesting conversation once you remembered to translate."

"It was…very informative. I think Jan is regretting some life choices, though it's far too late to put those horses back in the barn, not after he also burned it down." Luke took a drink from the refilled coffee cup and stared off at nothing, narrowing his eyes.

"It's good to know the plans are working. Everyone seems to be feeling the squeeze," Ahmed added.

"Yeah. I'm glad all this effort isn't for naught," Luke replied.

The phone rang, interrupting them. Ahmed picked it up. "Yes?" He paused. "Very good. I'll be down in a moment." After he hung up, he shoved the phone into his pocket. "Someone left a letter for you at the front desk."

While Ahmed went to retrieve the letter, they waited quietly. Once he returned and handed over the letter to Luke, along with a thick manila envelope, he disappeared into the bathroom.

Luke opened the envelope. It was an invitation to a meeting in the morning to finalize the contract. The thick manila envelope contained a printed version of the contract along with a thumb drive. He held it up. "Jamaal, I believe this is your department. He says it's just a digital copy, but I'm loath to just plug it into the old laptop."

"Come to papa," Jamaal said, taking the drive. He pulled out a second laptop and plugged the drive in after firing it up. "Give me some time to work on this, and I'll have your verdict for you."

Luke nodded and went to the bedroom to take a shower in his private bathroom. Letting the hot water cascade over his head, he ruminated on the tangled web Jan and Mathis had woven and how he'd been captured in it. A smile tugged at his lips as he wiped water off his face. Now it was his turn to be the spider. Once he felt water-logged, he dried off and dressed in jeans and a button down. If they had the day, he might as well head out and enjoy the city.

"Thought you were gonna try to swim away in there," Jamaal said, looking up when Luke emerged from his room.

"Nah. Just enjoying some quiet time to think." Luke grabbed a chair across from Jamaal.

"For a solitary cat like you, I bet all this time surrounded by people has to be a bit of a break from your normal routine."

"Something like that. Most of the last couple centuries have been spent moving about on my own with brief intermittent injections of people. It's been a change for sure. It didn't take long to get used to Delilah and Pablo, then Sam. Now I'm getting used to your presence. It's different, but not bad."

"I know what you mean. I'm usually on a solo mission at the keyboard. I like it that way, but all this covert work with you is definitely shaking up my day to day. You ready to talk thumb drive?" Jamaal asked.

"Lay it on me."

"It's a good thing you had me look this over first. The contract is on the drive, but there's also a sneaky little Trojan horse along with it."

"What kind of Greeks does it have inside?" Luke asked, smirking.

"The hairy kind with swords. Though I can't tell yet if they just want to look around your castle or if they want to burn it down. I've extracted it from the file, though. I don't see anything else attached to it, so you should be safe."

"Good. Send it to that lawyer Johann put us in contact with. I wouldn't want to accept it and find something slipped into it that might blow our cover. And when you're done with that, I think I'd like to take a spin around the city, if you're up for it."

"I think I'm due for some solitude. I'll stay here and dig into this file and the Trojan horse," Jamaal replied.

"Suit yourself. Ahmed? Jung-sook?" Luke asked.

"Sounds good. Besides, we can't let the Comte de Maubeuge wander around without his scary bodyguards, right, Jung-sook?" Ahmed stood and walked toward the room they shared. "Just let me change."

⚔

LUKE relaxed into a decadently upholstered antique couch as Mathis paced around the waiting room in Jan's mansion office. The building was another one of those old Antwerp brick numbers with crow-stepped gables and at least four-hundred-years-old. His decor could best be described as tasteful and luxurious. The man, before he'd become a patricide, had been a talented artist with excellent taste.

Luke kept a nonchalant expression, relaxing as much as he could —partially to keep up his facade as the wealthy Comte, but also to fuck with Mathis, who seemed to take the long wait as a personal insult to his own importance.

A man in a suit Luke assumed was a werewolf stepped into the room. "Your Excellency, Mr. Heinen. Mr. van den Bergh will see you now."

Luke nodded politely, though he thought he heard Mathis mumble, "About time."

After standing, Luke followed the man through a hallway and into a plushly appointed study and office. Ahmed and Jung-sook tucked in behind Luke, taking up their posts in the back of the room.

The man stopped in the middle of the room and gestured toward a pair of chairs sitting opposite a large, dark wood desk. The leather executive chair behind it currently sat empty. Luke sat, looking relaxed, his elbows on the arm rest and his hands steepled in front of him. Mathis wiggled in his chair, trying to get comfortable or unable to sit still due to his irritation.

A few moments later, Jan appeared from a door in the back corner. He wore a three-piece suit minus the jacket, which hung in the other corner. He had his sleeves rolled up to his elbows, though that was the only nod to relaxed or casual in his impeccably tailored suit. He had a pocket watch chain dangling from a pocket of his waistcoat.

"Pardon me for keeping you waiting. I had an important call with Rotterdam that ran long, then I needed a brief restroom break." Jan stepped around his desk and sat, staring across the room at Mathis. "Mathis, I don't recall inviting you to this meeting."

"That would be my fault," Luke said. "I invited him along to witness the auspicious occasion since he brought us together."

"Ah. It's not a problem. You are the man of the hour, Your Excellency." Jan stared daggers at Mathis.

Luke sat so he could watch Mathis out of the corner of his eye. The packleader from Luxembourg looked quite smug with himself.

"I hope my delay didn't bother you," Jan said.

Luke dismissed Jan's almost-apology. "It's not a problem. While I'm in Antwerp, I'm at your disposal. You're my only purpose for being here."

"My people tell me you got to play the tourist yesterday. How did you enjoy our fair city?" Jan asked, raising an eyebrow.

"Keeping an eye on me?" Luke kept his tone neutral—the kind of neutral that contained a well-hidden edge for those paying attention.

"I like to ensure the safety of my business associates while they're in my city. Two or three bodyguards don't seem like much of a security detail for one of such eminence."

Luke laughed. "You've already sold me your port deal. You don't need to sell past the close by trying to flatter me. It was a good day, despite the weather. Enjoyed a few drinks. Visited the Mayer van den Bergh museum." Luke furrowed his brow. "Say… Any relation of yours? An ancestor perhaps?"

Jan paled visibly before his cheeks flushed as he clenched his jaw. As quickly as his uncontrolled reaction appeared, it disappeared to be replaced by his usual slightly aloof expression. "Not that I'm aware of it. Van den Bergh is a reasonably common surname, Your Excellency."

"Fair enough. Anyway, on to business. I forwarded the digital copy to my lawyer. He says it's all fairly boiler plate for such deals. I'm more interested in our private deal." Luke leaned forward, sitting on the edge of his chair, and looked intensely at Jan. "I'd like to see we have clear verbiage on our private deal."

"Of course, though this isn't strictly something you should run by your lawyer." He picked up a piece of paper and held it up. The man standing behind him took it and delivered it to Luke.

Looking it over, he nodded as he read over the simple language used to convey the agreement they'd made. "This looks exactly like what we discussed. Excellent."

Jan nodded. "Who would you like to use as a third party to maintain a third copy of the contract in case we need to discuss any miscommunication that might arise?"

"In a deal like this? I think Mathis here will suffice to hold the contract if ever the occasion should arise that we need a third party."

The flame of hatred returned to Jan's eyes briefly before he quashed it. "That is acceptable to me."

"Then I think we are in agreement, and we can sign the paperwork."

Jan's man handed Luke a pen. Once everything was signed and sealed, Jan broke out a bottle of Champagne to celebrate the deal.

"Here's to new partnerships!" Jan raised his glass.

"And to a successful trip to Antwerp," Luke added.

They clinked classes and drank.

After a round of refills, Ahmed approached Luke. "Your Excellency, we need to get going soon for your next appointment."

Luke nodded to acknowledge his bodyguard.

"I thought you said I was your only purpose in Antwerp," Jan said, an eyebrow raised.

"That is true, but this meeting isn't in Antwerp."

Jan chuckled. "Ah, you've got me there."

Luke drained the last swallow of Champagne. "Have your accountant send me your bank information, and I'll forward your fee. The email on the card I gave you should suffice."

Jan stuck out his hand. "Thank you for such a pleasant opportunity to serve your growing business empire, Your Excellency."

"Jan, it's been a delight." He took his coat from Ahmed. "Let us depart."

"Your Excellency, can I speak with you for a moment?" Mathis asked, a note of desperation coloring his voice.

Luke caught Ahmed's eye. His bodyguard gave a subtle, but not too subtle, shake of his head.

"I'm sorry, Mathis. I'm afraid we're tight on time. Give me a call and we can discuss whatever you need." He patted Mathis on the shoulder, then spun around and followed his bodyguards out the door.

By prearranged agreement, no one said anything until they were on the road back to their hotel to pick up Jamaal.

Jung-sook laughed from the front passenger seat. "You shut Mathis down quickly. I wish I had a picture of the look on his face."

Ahmed smiled and shook his head. "I'm sure Jamaal can play the recording of sound after we left. I'm sure he's whining to Jan, and Jan is eating it up. He was not happy about Mathis intruding on his meeting."

Luke pulled his phone out and queued up The Pierces' "Secret."

"Why do you think I made a special point of inviting him? If I can't antagonize my enemies before I bring about their ruin, what even is the point?"

After Ahmed and Jung-sook helped Jamaal load up the last of their gear—Luke offered to help but was told it was unbecoming of a count to help with the luggage—they headed south to inspect the work on his manor in Maubeuge.

"Jamaal, do you have the money ready to go?" Luke asked.

"I sure do."

"Here's the information. Is this one of the accounts you know about?" Luke handed Jamaal his cell phone with the emailed information.

"Let me check…" Jamaal's fingers flew over the keyboard on his open laptop. "Indeed I do."

"So you know what to do?" Luke asked.

"Yup. As soon as they give confirmation of receipt, I give confirmation of pilfering it back." Jamaal looked up from his keyboard with a broad grin on his face.

Luke laughed. "Music to my ears. Also, I think I'll need to send my factor to visit Mathis and collect some more debt."

"You're a cruel, cruel man, Luke," Jung-sook said. "I like your style."

"Thanks. I'm deeply loyal to my friends and allies, but I can be vindictive when someone betrays me." Luke slouched in the seat. "Now, if you'll excuse me, I need a little quiet time. And keep an eye out for anyone suspicious following us."

He opened his texts and sent one to Roxi. *On our way back. See you shortly.*

After taking the time to answer other texts his team had sent him, he checked if Roxi had returned his text. Nothing. He sighed. She was probably asleep like usual, with the compulsion nearing its brutal finale.

Right now, he had too many enemies. The earthly ones he had a good bead on, but the divine ones were proving harder to pin down. He just never thought Mithras would be one of them.

CHAPTER
EIGHT

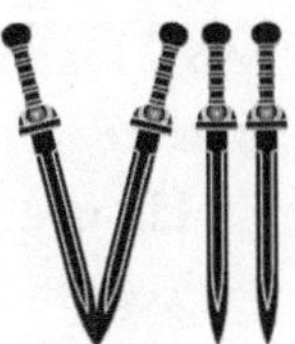

LUKE OPENED the door to his suite quietly, not wanting to disturb Roxi if she was asleep. She lay motionless, her chest rising and falling shallowly.

"I'm awake. I'm happy you're back," Roxi said.

"Sorry to disturb you."

Roxi smiled softly. "Your presence is never a disturbance."

Luke stepped into the suite and closed the door behind him before sitting in the chair next to her side of the bed.

He took her hand in his. "Roxi, I want to make one last attempt to persuade Mithras."

"He doesn't seem interested in listening," Roxi replied weakly. Her eyes fluttered open, then she squinted, taking in his face. "You look so angry."

"I am." He tried to unclench his jaw, wanting to soften his expression while he was with Roxi. "I'm sorry. I don't mean to be mad around you, but I'm so angry for the way you've been treated. I mean to address it. If you'll let me."

"You have my trust, as always, dōšagīh."

"For this, I'll need you as well. Are you willing to go to my Mithraeum with me and stand before Mithras?"

Roxi nodded slightly. "I will stand together with you. Though I'm not sure I can stand for long." She pulled the blankets back slightly on the empty side of the bed. "Now come snuggle me back to sleep so I can rest before it's time."

Luke took his jeans off and removed his T-shirt before crawling into bed next to Roxi. As weak as she was, it didn't take long for her to fall into a restless sleep. Even though he could have slid out of bed at any time, he need to reconnect with Roxi and feel her presence next to him.

He needed her by his side. He needed her whole. He loved her.

Together they could be a true force to be reckoned with—one capable of overthrowing the tyranny of the vampires and stopping them before they grew all powerful. He wanted to see a world after vampires. He didn't know what would happen if they could take out the dark entity that drove them, but he sure as hell wanted to find out. And he wanted Roxi to find out as well.

After he redressed, he sat in the chair watching Roxi sleep. He used the quiet time to clear his mind and prepare for his next act, for the potential folly he was about to commit. When the alarm he'd set for an hour after moonrise went off, he woke Roxi and helped her to the restroom before bundling her in warm, comfortable clothes—borrowed, of course.

Instead of forcing her to walk down the stairs with him, he scooped her up in his arms, carried her to the sitting room, and placed her in the love seat by the fireplace, draping a blanket over her legs. It had been almost no effort, she'd wasted away to skin and bones under the cruelty of the compulsion.

With a kiss to her forehead, he slipped out quietly and made his way to the cave and his Mithraeum. The moon shone above as he strode across the yard to the small outbuilding blocking the entrance from view. The coded doors passed, he stopped just inside the entrance of the Mithraeum and stared at the altar, ignoring Mithras and the bull. He focused on Selene's moon chariot.

"I need you, My Mistress." He cast the thought into the ether.

A moment later, a gentle glow brightened the room, solidifying into the beautiful form of the moon goddess. She stood in the center of the Mithraeum, her hands held primly in front of her stomach.

"How may I aid you, my brave soldier?" she asked.

Luke strode forward then sank to one knee, bowing his head. "I need to consult with you about something potentially very dangerous."

Selene sat on one of the benches and patted the spot by her side. "Please rise, Lucius. You don't have to stand on such ceremony with me."

Luke moved next to the goddess, staring at the wall. She'd always been kind to him—for that he appreciated her more—but she'd also provided him with her strength many times. For that, he'd rely on her once again.

When Luke didn't fill the silence, Selene chose to. "How fares your Roxi?"

Luke frowned, fighting back tears, and hung his head. "Not well, My Mistress. She's weak and is getting weaker. She can barely stay awake. I can barely get her to eat. I know she tries for me, but her body is failing her."

Selene took his hand in hers, stroking the back of it. "I'm sorry. She deserves so much better."

"She does." Straightening up, he looked into Selene's silvery blue eyes. "I need to ask an important question."

"If it's in my power to answer, you know I shall," she replied.

"Are Roxi and I the last of Mithras's hunters?"

Selene closed her eyes, slumping a bit. "I think so. Not all his chosen paid worship to me as part of their binding—the children of Ahura Mazada and those further east even. But I've watched over the world for countless nights after Mithras set about this project. I've come to know the feel of his chosen hunters. To my knowledge, you are the last of my children and Roxi is the last of his others that still follow the path."

Luke nodded, a smile threatening to pull the corners of his lips up. "And he has raised no others in the last few centuries?"

"No. We are not what we once were. I'm not sure he could bring the power to bear. And to be open with you, I'm not sure I'd help him after how roughly you and Roxi have been used." The only physical cue that betrayed her feelings was a bit of tightening around her eyes.

However, her voice surprised Luke with the amount of anger and sadness infused into the last sentence of her statement. He bowed his head to her, acknowledging her admission.

"What do you have in mind, my brave soldier?" She eyed him with friendly suspicion.

"This is between me and The Wanderer." Squeezing Selene's soft hand, he looked into her eyes, conveying his deep regard for her, the goddess who'd always been so kind. "But no matter what happens, know that you shall always have my loyalty and affection."

"Of that I've never had a doubt, Lucius." She leaned forward and kissed his cheek. "What can I do to aid you?"

"Can you invite The Wanderer here?" He gestured to the surrounding Mithraeum.

"And if he won't come?" Selene asked, an eyebrow rising up her forehead.

"Then he'll no long have his last two hunters. He will have failed and be shunned for it."

The other eyebrow joined the first. Apparently, whatever she'd thought Luke was going to do, that wasn't near the top of the list. Once she schooled her expression back into her normal, serene visage, she nodded. "I'll call to him."

"OK. I'll be back shortly." Luke left the Mithraeum and strode across the yard between the cliff wall and his house.

Maggie, Pablo, Sam, Delilah, and Simone waited under the shadow of the entry awning, keeping out of the wind.

"Well?" Sam said. "Are you on?"

Luke nodded and strode through the entry hall to the sitting room. His friends followed in his wake. He'd brought Roxi down and laid her on one of the couches in the sitting room. Before he picked her up, he strapped her sword around his waist and fixed his rudis to it. Grabbing a nearby backpack containing Roxi's rudis, he threw that over his back.

He ran the back of his fingers over her cheek, bending over to kiss her forehead. "Roxi, are you ready?"

She wobbled her head in the affirmative. "You look angry."

Luke pushed the anger to the back and softened his expression, smiling at the woman he loved. "I am angry—angry that after all you've done in service to Mithras, he's abandoned you to wither and die in agony. He's a cruel master, and I aim to present his failings to him…and offer him an alternative."

"Um, dude. Are you about to piss off a god?" Pablo asked, sidling away from Luke.

"If it comes to it…"

"Are you sure that's wise?" Sam asked.

"Probably not, but that's never stopped me before," Luke replied.

Roxi chuckled weakly. "You're so fierce." She inhaled weakly, trying to fill her lungs.

Luke knelt by her and ran his hand over her forehead, trying to push back her messy hair. "This will be over soon."

"I know." She closed her eyes, seeming to doze off.

He carefully slid his arms under and lifted her, cradling her to his chest. Her weight was hardly a burden after her body had degenerated from the compulsion. He stalked through the entryway and out onto the grounds, heading straight for the entrance to his Mithraeum. Maggie ran ahead and keyed in the code to the outer door, then the secret inner door.

"Thanks, Maggie." Luke smiled nervously.

"Good luck, Luke." She reached out and rubbed Luke's shoulder, then squeezed Roxi's hand, dangling below her, before picking up and laying it across her body.

He nodded, then stepped into the cave mouth leading to the Mithraeum. Selene waited for them inside the entrance and fell in beside Luke as he carried Roxi toward the altar.

"Poor, child. She has been used poorly."

Luke nodded, too angry to speak. He wanted to save the emotion for the proper time to use it. To a cunning soldier, it too was a weapon to be deployed at the right time. Before Mithras's altar, Selene had spun a high bed for Roxi. Though it was made of her moonlight, it looked solid as stone, though soft and inviting on top. Luke laid her on the bed, arranging her body so she'd be comfortable. Looking toward the foot of the bed, he wished there was a blanket to cover Roxi; a moment later, one appeared. He pulled it over her, tucking it under her chin.

Luke leaned down next to Roxi's head, stroking her hair gently. "Roxi, Selene is here. She wishes to speak with you."

"Alright," Roxi whispered, not opening her eyes.

Stepping back, Luke moved out of the way so the goddess could take his place. "Roxiustana Surena, I've held back the compulsion as best as I can so you'd have some peace, but it grows more difficult since you are unable to accept my full blessing. I can't hold it off forever, but I can hold it for a while longer. Will you accept me into your heart and receive my blessing in full?"

Roxi wobbled her head. "I will, My Mistress." She tried to wet her dry lips. "I will hold you in my heart and honor your light."

"Done." Selene's voice sounded in Luke's head.

Selene placed one hand over Roxi's forehead and the other over her heart, then bowed down and placed a kiss on Roxi's lips. Roxi seemed to relax as a gentle silvery light suffused her body, slowly soaking in. She inhaled, taking the strongest breath he'd heard since finding her on the wall of a castle ruin.

"Luke?" Roxi's eyes opened.

He stepped up to the bed. "Yes?"

Roxi's hand moved under the blanket toward the edge. Scooping her hand into his, he brought it over her chest and squeezed it, refusing to let go. The tightness around Luke's heart eased seeing Roxi relax. Selene had helped once they were able to get Roxi back to the cottage, but even then, Roxi's suffering was like a dagger in Luke's heart. For the first time, she looked relatively peaceful.

Selene laid her hand on theirs. "My blessing upon you both." She looked up at Luke. "He comes. Do you wish me to stand by your side?"

Luke shook his head. "This is between me and The Wanderer."

Selene nodded and faded out, the warmth of her hand lingering on his skin.

"Luke?" Roxi whispered.

"Yes?" he smiled gently.

Through eyes lidded with exhaustion, she struggled to make eye contact. "I love you."

"I love you, too, Roxi." He leaned over and kissed her softly.

"In case…" She trailed off.

Luke quickly understood what had caused her to stop—presence. Not yet visible, Mithras could be felt. Patting Roxi's hand, he carefully withdrew his fingers and took half a step back so he'd have room. Opening the door to his anger, he let some leak out, stiffening his spine and erasing the soft tenderness displayed for Roxi. He replaced it with a hard expression of determination with just a hint of underlying hostility. Luke meant business, and he needed Mithras to know it.

As soon as the god materialized, he expanded to tower over the two humans, his head nearly reaching to the tall vaulted ceiling. **"You dare summon me like a servant?"**

"I dare." Luke said, quiet but steely, not quailing before the god's divinely infused anger. "It's time you take responsibility for your actions. We've called to you to no avail."

"I do not need to answer to those who have not paid me the respects deserved." Mithras folded his arms across his chest.

"What of the respect you owe us? What of your failed duties?"

"What duties do I owe two failed hunters? You have yet to fulfill your contract."

Luke scoffed, letting more anger out. "A contract with hidden clauses." Luke gestured toward Roxi. "Look what your failed duties and obfuscation have done to her, and she was far more diligent about maintaining her faith in you. Look where it got her. You have failed to hold inviolate your part of the covenant. Without telling us all the details, you gave us this power, then cast us out into the world to do your bidding. Yet in secret, you placed this compulsion on us. This hateful sickness. Then, through no fault of your servant's, the one means to protect herself was destroyed by your enemies. And you won't correct the error?"

Luke turned his back on Mithras and walked several steps back before whirling and jabbing his finger angrily through the air at the god. "I hold you in violation of what is owed us. For nigh on two thousand years, we have fought your fights and carried out your will on this earth to only be cast aside when we need you most."

The god tried to contain his anger, attempting to look airy and above this distasteful interaction. **"What I do with my tools is none of your business. When I use them up, it is my decision if I wish to toss them in the refuse heap."**

"Roxi is not refuse to be thrown away. Choose your next words carefully, godling." He rested his hand on the pommel of Roxi's sword. "This room contains your last two true worshipers in all the world. Without us, you are nothing. You are a trivial inquiry for academics. A name mentioned, but no longer worshiped or cared about. Make an enemy of me, and I will tear you down. I have soaked continents in the blood of my enemies. Don't think I won't hesitate to soak your altar in your blood."

"You would slay a god over a woman?" Mithras spat the question.

"I would slay a god to bring justice to this woman." Luke's voice, deadly quiet, rang with the truth of his intention and belief in his ability to do it. "I am Lucius Silvanius Ferrata. I earned the Ferrata. My will is iron. Where I walk, vampires tremble in fear. When I draw my sword, my allies fight ferociously. I have saved countless humans who spoke my name to the heavens in thanks. Make me your enemy, and I will chase you through every plane of existence until I have spent your life onto the ground."

"Do you think I fear you? Who has failed to defeat your enemy after all this time? I can raise up an army of men superior to you."

Luke thought he heard the barest hint of doubt in the god's voice. The silver glow of the braziers intensified, but Luke kept his wrathful gaze firmly fixed on Mithras.

"You do fear him." Selene's voice broke the silence. "You know he is powerful if he seeks the full strength within him—and combined, these two could bring your ruin." The goddess appeared next to Luke, towering to match the height of Mithras, and laughed. "There will be no more of your issue, Mithras. You do not have the power to do it unaided, not anymore, and my brother and I will not lend you ours."

Mithras's eyes narrowed. **"You would betray me for this pathetic mortal?"**

"You betray yourself and our mission. They are closer than anyone has ever been to finding the wellspring of the vampires' power and bringing it down. Lucius has confronted it twice and survived. You'd throw away all our work because you were called out for your negligence as a master?" Selene shook her head. "Not only will I betray you for this brave soldier, but I will lend my strength to his arm if you choose to stand against him. For nearly two millennia, these two fine souls have stayed true to the mission you laid upon them all those years ago, in spite of your petty compulsion and your lack of support."

The goddess flexed her presence, filling the Mithraeum. "There is no where you can hide from me and my brother. You may be The Wanderer, but we…see…all."

Luke's finger bounced on the pommel of the Roxi's sword, his hand itching to draw it.

"Don't draw the sword," Selene's voice sounded in his head. *"I know you desire it, and I'd like to see it, but that might be a move beyond walking back for him."*

Luke stopped tapping his finger, lifting his hand—

"Don't remove your hand from the pommel. And let your finger bounce. It's making him nervous." There was a hint of laughter in her tone.

He let his finger tap out its steady rhythm of anger and annoyance.

Selene shrunk to more human proportions, but still stood a bit taller than Luke—the gesture meant to act as a peace offering to deescalate the situation. She held her hands in front of her, palms open and empty, facing upward. "Keep your compulsion, but repair the child's rudis so she may join forces with Lucius to bring ruin to our enemies."

The warped and twisted rudis, which had been in Luke's backpack, appeared in her hands, lying flat over her palms. Breathing shallowly, his body wound tight, Luke kept his gaze forward and ready in case Mithras stepped into violence. The god's eyes broke contact with Luke and moved to the warped and burnt piece of wood. When Mithras shrunk to less intimidating proportions, although he chose to appear taller than both Luke and Selene, Luke wanted to sigh in relief. But he held his composure.

The god stepped around Roxi's bed and bent over, looking at the blade in Selene's hands. He looked up at the goddess. **"May I?"**

She nodded firmly.

Reaching out, he made to wrap his hand around the hilt but pulled back as if it had burned the skin where it made contact. Steeling himself, he grabbed it and lifted it from Selene's hands. He turned it around and looked every inch of it over.

He shook his head, still examining the rudis. **"This cannot be remade. If it were to be used, it would do…evil work upon the user."** He raised his eyes and looked at Selene. **"How did this happen?"**

"I found it this way in the vampires' stash after I'd broken free of their captivity," Luke said. "It feels like the dark entity that confronted us outside their arena, then again not far from here at Château de Franchimont. It claims to be Zalmoxis, but that name doesn't feel right."

Mithras nodded, not looking over at Luke. **"I'll keep this and investigate further."**

The warped rudis disappeared into thin air and was replaced with a new one identical to the one currently on Luke's hip. Turning around, the god picked up Roxi's hand and wrapped her fingers around the hilt, closing his hands over hers. The silver of the blade and filigree glowed gold for a brief flash, then returned to normal. With gentleness, he laid her hand down on her chest, the rudis clenched in her grip, the blade laying down her stomach. He placed a hand on her forehead, then looked at Selene, scowling at her for a moment, then returning his attention to Roxi.

Roxi and Mithras glowed gold, growing brighter until Luke could no longer keep his eyes open. When his vision returned to normal and he raised his eyelids, Mithras was gone, but Roxi looked restored, or at least returned to a more robust state. Luke rushed to her side, caressing her cheek.

"Roxi? How do you feel?" He held his breath, waiting.

"Almost human," she replied.

Luke exhaled explosively, the tension and fear draining from his body. Closing his eyes, he lowered his head, rested his forehead on the back of Roxi's hand, and cast a prayer of thanks to Mithras. Although begrudgingly, the god had healed Roxi and given her a new rudis. Luke owed him the thanks.

Smiling down at Roxi, his smile broadened into a grin as her eyes fluttered open.

"Why are you crying?" Roxi asked, looking puzzled.

"Not all tears are sadness." He kissed her. "You're healed, and you have a new rudis. It was a good day."

"It was a good day." She lifted her head and looked around. "Can you help me up?"

Luke nodded, taking the rudis and setting it on a nearby bench. Sliding a hand under her back, he helped her sit up and swing her legs over the edge of the bed as it lowered itself, bringing her feet into contact with the ground, then stopping. With one hand on her back and the other taking her hand, he helped her to standing. Her legs wobbled, then gave out, but before she could fall, Luke scooped her up and squeezed her tightly against him.

Roxi laughed, the sound pure ecstatic music to his ears. He spun her around, kissing her cheek and face.

"Put me down, you ridiculous man," Roxi said between bouts of laughter.

"Never," Luke whispered, stopping.

He lowered her feet but kept an arm around her back, both to keep her steady and to prevent her from falling if called on. "How are you doing?"

She stared down at her feet before looking up at Luke and smiling. "Wobbly, but good. I think I can stand for a bit."

Luke forgot they weren't alone, but when he looked to Selene, she had a wide, closed-mouth smile across her face as she looked at them. She glided forward and kissed them both on the forehead.

Stepping back, she left her hands, one for each, on their cheeks. "I am most glad your health and life are restored, Roxiustana. You two can be far more powerful together than as individuals, and for the coming fights, you'll need that strength to lift each other up. Go with my blessings, my children."

The flash of her silver light was more gentle than the golden flare of Mithras, but she left Luke with the warmth of her hand on his cheek, her blessing in his heart, and Roxi in his arms.

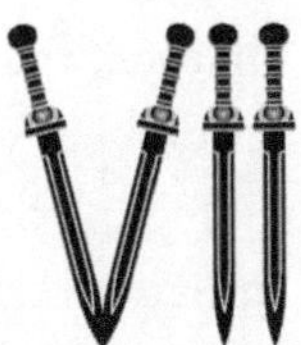

CHAPTER
NINE

WHEN ROXI and Luke emerged from the Mithraeum out into the grounds, everyone waited for them, his inner circle—Maggie, Delilah, Pablo, Sam, & Simone—standing front and center.

"So, what's the good word, dude?" Pablo asked.

"She's walking out, even if Luke's helping here. That's got to be a good sign," Delilah said.

Once they reached the front of the group, Luke stopped. "I don't know what it'll cost me later, but I got Mithras to relent."

Roxi snorted. "Relent? You threatened to cast him down and kill him. And when he threatened to wipe us out and raise new hunters, Selene stepped in and called him out on his lack of power and refused to lend her or her brother's to it. It was one of the most reckless things I have ever seen." She kissed him on the cheek.

Simone's eyes were wide with shock. "You...you threatened a god?"

Luke nodded.

Pablo laughed and slapped Luke's back. "That's my buddy."

"How are you feeling, Roxi?" Maggie asked.

"Tired. Exhausted might be more accurate, but I feel better than I have since before... You know." Roxi trailed off, still uncomfortable talking about her captivity. "And famished, now that I think about it."

"We have food prepared," Sam said. "We didn't know how long we'd have to wait, plus we wanted to have a little celebration for you and Luke if it was successful. It's mostly cold snacks—meats, cheeses, fruits, and veggies and the like. We can warm up something special for you if you'd like?"

"No, Sam. Whatever you have ready sounds superb." Roxi smiled at Luke's friend.

"I can deal with that. I'm going to head into the bar and start pouring drinks. You want something, Luke?" Delilah asked.

"Sure, pour me the strong dark."

"Roxi?"

"I think I'd like a little something. I'll have a small glass of whatever Luke is having," Roxi replied.

Delilah nodded and headed back into the house with Simone following along. Maggie fell in beside Luke, laying her hand on his forearm and giving it an affectionate squeeze. Pablo and Sam stepped in front of Luke and Roxi and cleared the way through the crowd who wanted to pay their respects to their leader and the one they'd worked so hard to save. They knew what she was—that she was like Luke—and what that could mean for their efforts.

"We've set up everything in the bar," Sam said, guiding them toward it after they'd entered. "Figured it would be more intimate and people would be in the mood to drink one way or the other. Our usual table is set up in the back." She turned to Pablo. "We should add another small table or grab a bigger table now that we have Roxi to add in."

Luke smiled as some of the tension leached from his body, though he couldn't get rid of all it. They still had a lot of work to do to take down Mathis, Jan, and Le Mousquetaire, and a lot of planning along the way. They still had his masquerade ball to prepare for while Delilah kept up her constant assault on the vampires of France and Belgium. And he had to really dive into his piano practice. But that could wait for tomorrow. Today, they would celebrate Roxi's reprieve.

A MEAN SMILE spread over Luke's lips when he saw the caller ID. He hit record on the call recording app as he answered. "Mathis, my good man. How are you doing?"

"Excellent, Your…Excellency." The unusual cheerfulness seemed to have thrown Mathis for a loop. "You sound like you're in a good mood."

"Tis the season, as they say. What can I do for you?"

"Well… I hate to bring up such matters, but we had discussed a small token of appreciation for helping you strike a deal with Jan van den Bergh." Mathis sounded almost desperate and small.

"Right you are. Tell you what, are you planning on coming to my little get together?" Luke asked.

Mathis chuckled falsely. "I'd hardly call a costumed ball a 'little get together,' Your Excellency, but I wouldn't miss it for the world."

"I'll have a suitable gift prepared for you for all you've done for me. I'm sure you'll find it more than fair." Luke chuckled. "Don't worry, it will be suitably liquid."

"Ah, of course, Your Excellency. Um, I was just hoping I would see it a bit sooner. This is embarrassing…"

"More embarrassing than finding you tied to a chair in the French mountains after you'd been abducted from your mistress's flat? Out with it, Mathis." Luke thought he heard a carefully squashed growl from Mathis.

"I've had a touch of bad luck recently and don't have the liquid assets available to address some of my obligations."

Luke had trouble containing the cruel grin on his face so he could speak. "And you were hoping my gift would cover it? I still haven't received confirmation from van den Bergh that he's received his fee. I can't very well pay out a tip for a service that isn't yet complete."

Mathis mumbled something Luke didn't hear.

"Sorry, my reception must not be great. What did you say?" Luke asked.

"Nothing really." Mathis inhaled then sighed loudly. "I hate to do this, Your Excellency, but I'm in a bit of a pinch after a bit of bad luck. Is there any way I could borrow some money from you? I offer excellent rates, and I'm renowned for paying my debts."

"Hmm." Luke paused, letting Mathis hang. "We have become reasonably friendly in the time we've known each other... But I don't loan money to friends. It's how I keep my friends my friends. I am willing to do business with you though."

"What do you mean?" Mathis asked warily.

"We both share a love of antiquities. I'd be more than happy to buy that set of lorica and the gladius from you for a very nice sum," Luke replied. "They'd be splendid additions to my collections."

"Well... Let me think about it for a moment."

"What good are possessions if you can't part with them when you need to?" Luke wished he could see the look on Mathis's face right now. The sword and armor were the prizes he kept in his home office, their pride of place in his personal items, not the more publicly displayed pieces that burnished his public image.

"No. I can't part with them. They're too precious. I'd be willing to sell you nearly anything else." Mathis paused for a moment. "You seem to have taken a liking to my wife. I could arrange... Well. Use your imagination."

Luke's jaw dropped. He didn't think Mathis would stoop that low, but apparently there was no floor for his depravity.

"Your Excellency? I assure you it would be worth your time," Mathis added, his voice growing even more smarmy.

"Mathis. I'm going to pretend I didn't hear that. If you need money and none of your other sources are available, you know my price. Good day." Luke hung up the phone.

As Luke stood and stared at nothing, his mouth hanging open, Maggie walked in. Seeing his expression, she stopped.

"What's the matter, Luke?"

"What?" He shook his head to clear it. "Oh. I just got off the phone with Mathis. I don't know how he managed it, but he lowered my already dismal opinion of him."

"What did he do?"

"He tried to pimp his wife out to me so I would loan him money."

Maggie, already pale, blanched. "What? I'm not Gabriela's biggest fan after our dinner, but that's warped. How could he?"

"He'd sell his own mother to further his own interests. He's a thoroughly depraved man." He lifted his phone and sent a text message. "I think it's time to call in more of his debts. I want to make that twisted piece of shit sweat."

"Do you think your messenger will be in danger? If he's getting that desperate?" Maggie asked.

"I don't think so. His reputation is based on his financials. If he harms someone coming to collect, he'll anger his business contacts. If he loses his reputation, he loses his ability to influence and control, not that he has much left at this point since I own almost all of it. We'll see if he has any more money to pay or if we've completely tapped him out."

When Luke's phone rang, he held his hand up to forestall any comments, then picked up. "Mr. van den Bergh, to what do I owe the pleasure?"

"Good day, Your Excellency. I just wished to take a moment to let you know that we are now officially in contract with each other. Your generous token of thanks has been received," Jan replied.

"Excellent! It's a load off my mind to have a home for my shipments. Once I begin the next round moving, I'll be in touch."

"I look forward to it. Now, if you'll excuse me, I do have to get going." Jan sounded stiff and a cool.

"Of course. Thank you for the news. I look forward to our next meeting," Luke replied.

"As do I. Goodbye." Jan hung up without waiting for an answer.

Luke smiled.

"That's a wicked looking grin."

"Have you seen Jamaal? I need to let him know he's free to recover our money."

Maggie chuckled, shaking her head. "You're having too much fun destroying your enemies financially."

"I aim to bring them low and ruin them before I fully destroy them. I'm not interested in being generous, Maggie." He pulled her in for a hug.

"They're bad men and deserve justice. I'm just glad you're alive and able to deliver it to them."

"Me too. When I'm done with Jamaal, would you like to take a walk with me?"

Maggie laughed. "It's starting to snow."

"We'll bundle up."

"I'll go get my coat and gloves." Maggie turned and headed up to her room, a little extra sway in her hips.

He watched until she disappeared, then pulled out his phone and put in a call to Gabriela. "Hello, Gabriela. It's Pierre."

"Your Excellency! It's good to hear from you," Gabriela replied.

Luke cleared his throat and took a deep breath. "I hope you can make some time for me. We need to talk…"

CHAPTER
TEN

LUKE SAT QUIETLY at the piano, his fingers playing over the keys without depressing them. His nerves wrestled with weasels in his stomach. It'd had been about a century since he'd really performed in anything resembling a public setting. He flipped through the pages and made one last check to make sure his sheet music was in the right order. Staring at the flurry of black splotches and lines scattered over the page like overzealous shotguns blasts, he wished, not for the first time, that he'd picked something simpler.

It was too late now. He'd committed to the piece before him and dedicated hours to practicing at the piano in the cottage. Like battles, his nerves would calm before the plunge into action. He'd be fine. If he said it enough, he'd believe it.

Out of the corner of his eye, movement drew his attention to Charlie, who stood behind him and to the side. He was there to flip pages on the sheet music while also providing added security.

He reached down and pulled on the ends of his white frilly sleeves, making sure they lay properly and weren't bunched up inside his beautiful burgundy silk coat covered in a gold embroidered stylized floral pattern with black velvet collar, cuffs, and lapels. Gold buttons ran up the edges of the lapel and cuffs, giving the coat a military flair. He'd forgone a waistcoat in favor of the elaborately engraved steel breastplate he'd worn as a Hussar fighting against Napoleon. The centerpiece on the front of the plate was Selene's moon engraved in a field of stars. On the back, he'd commissioned an engraving of a large Roman-style sun, though it wasn't visible under the coat. An elaborate silver masquerade mask finished the outfit.

"Hey, buddy. Are you ready to go?" Pablo asked.

Luke started at his sudden appearance. "Sorry. Didn't see you coming. I'm as ready as I'll ever be."

Pablo wore tight pants and knee-high boots. Under a plain breastplate, he had on a simple white shirt. His face, save for his lips and chin, was covered in an elaborate black masquerade mask featuring simulated dragon scales.

"You always are. Somehow, you always are," Pablo replied.

"Thanks for your vote of confidence. How are things looking out there?"

"Good. You've attracted a bevy of guests—the wealthy, the elite, the important, and the famous—all here to see the mysterious Comte de Maubeuge. They're happily drinking your fine wines and snacking on your exquisitely prepared petit fours. If I knew it was going to be this kind of high-powered party, I'd have smuggled in some beer and tried to wrangle an international deal for Howling Moon."

Luke snorted then chuckled. Pablo always could lighten his mood. "I'm not sure if the European elite set is really into craft beer, especially those trying to hobnob with an aristocrat."

"You can drink from a pint glass with your pinky up." Pablo pretended to drink from an imaginary glass, his pinky held high and proud. "Indubitably, my good sir. This is a positively smashing glass of beer."

"I'm sure that's exactly how it would go." Luke held up a crystal snifter filled with expensive Scotch whisky and nodded toward Pablo before taking a drink of the peaty liquor. "Are our marks here?"

"Mathis is, though suspiciously without his wife. I don't know if I've ever seen him so agitated." Pablo grinned broadly. "It's a look I like seeing on him."

"Did he bring anything with him?"

Pablo nodded and grinned. "He had a large crate brought in. Ahmed and Jung-sook stashed it out of the way."

"Good. What about Jan?"

Pablo shook his head. "He is conspicuously absent."

"And Jean-Paul?" Luke asked hopefully.

"Sorry. Haven't seen him either, though he didn't RSVP."

Luke nodded tightly. He'd hoped the invitation might intrigue the wolf master of Paris, but it looked as if Luke had some work to do on that flank. "Damn. I guess we make do with what we have."

"Your Excellency," Jung-sook said then bowed quickly. "It's time for the servers to take their stations."

Luke held a deep breath for a few seconds before releasing it. "OK. Let's get this party started. Pablo, once the servers are in position, alert the team to let in the guests." He took another drink. "You all know your roles. Tonight is just like any other mission night."

Jung-sook stifled a laugh. "Yeah, not sure a fancy schmancy ball where we'll be surrounded by civilians is what you'd call a normal mission night, but you can rely on everyone here. We won't let you down, Your Excellency."

After Pablo and Jung-sook walked away, Luke checked over his sheet music one last time. Feet moving across the floor of the wide hall and the murmur of voices alerted Luke to the presence of the servers. Pablo rang a small bell, signaling that everyone was in position, and went to fetch the guests from the various rooms they were waiting in. With a couple deep cleansing breaths, he set his fingers. Once he depressed the first keys, his nerves receded to the background, replaced by Beethoven's Piano Sonata 18, known as "The Hunt."

A minute later, Jung-sook and Ahmed opened the large double doors and people dressed in historical finery and masks streamed in chatting animatedly. Since the people waiting had been diverted to various sitting rooms, the groups intermingled as they saw people they knew. Luke tried to focus on his sheet music.

He knew his people were moving through the crowd, keeping an eye out for any unwelcome guests and ensuring the invited guests were well taken care of. When he reached the end of the current page, Charlie reached over and pulled the sheet music, opening it to the next section.

A few people, music lovers apparently, stood near the piano watching him play. He did his best to ignore them and focus on the sonata. Even though he wished he was done performing, finishing meant he had to go mingle, which seemed a far worse option. So, he withdrew into the music. When he reached the last note of the sonata, he folded the sheet music and unfolded the next piece he planned to perform. There was a smattering of polite applause.

Laying his hands in his lap, he waited. A man with a trumpet stepped onto the balcony from a room on the second floor. Lifting the horn to his lips, he played a regal fanfare that silenced the crowd and drew their attention.

While everyone's attention was focused on the trumpeter, Luke quietly slid off his piano bench and stood next to piano, leaning against it. He'd picked a pose straight out of a portrait of a 17th or 18th century nobleman.

Holding the trumpet to his side, the trumpeter stepped up to the banister, his empty hand holding his lapel. "Ladies, Gentlemen, Gentlefolk, welcome to His Excellency's home. He hopes you all feel welcome and enjoy the offerings. Now it is my great pleasure to introduce you to His Excellency, Pierre Luc-Thibaut Archambeau, Comte de Maubeuge." With a flourish, the trumpeter bowed toward Luke, giving a gesture that directed everyone's attention.

Luke bowed his head and deployed a wave any aristocrat would be proud to have given. Looking over the crowd with a half-smile quirking one corner of his lip, he returned to the piano bench and sat down. He lifted his hands; silence fell over the room, and he launched into Beethoven's eighth piano sonata, often known as Pathetique.

It wasn't the easiest of Beethoven's sonatas, but it was one the master had taught him all those years ago in his apartment in Vienna. Memories of the wild haired composer and virtuoso brought a soft smile to his face as he let the practice combine with the muscle memory of Ludwig's tutelage.

Once he made it through the first few quicker runs without making any serious mistakes, he settled in, moving through the rest of the first movement without incident. By the end of the second movement, he felt the fatigue of too much piano and not enough conditioning. As he started the third movement, he focused, using his reserves of mental and physical stamina to drive toward the end. When he made a couple mistakes, Ludwig's words snapped into his brain.

"Never mind the mistakes, just keep going as if they hadn't happened."

He heaved a sigh of relief as the last note rang out through the room packed with elaborately dressed guests. As soon as he stood up, a raucous round of clapping broke out. Bowing elegantly, he stepped off the dais and grabbed a glass of champagne as Jung-sook and Ahmed stepped into position on either side of him and half step behind.

With smiles and nods toward his guests as they lobbed compliments on his playing, he made his way across the floor to the staircase winding up to the balcony.

He stopped at the midway point of the balcony and looked over the crowd, raising his hand and drawing the crowd to silence. "Welcome all to my little soirée. I am so pleased to see the wonderful effort you've put into your costumes tonight." He raised the Champagne flute and waited for the people below to raise their glasses. "To new friends and opportunities. Be at home. Eat, drink, and be merry!"

He raised the glass further and then brought it down to take a drink. Once he finished the toast in English, he repeated it in French and Flemish Dutch. "Now, my friends, please enjoy some more music. I'll be down shortly to meet you all, if time permits."

While he'd distracted the crowd with his toast, musicians had set up on the dais. With a last wave, he exited the balcony into the room set up as his office.

"Can you help me off with this coat? It looks splendid, but damn it's too hot, especially over this armor," Luke said. "I think the cape will do."

Ahmed helped Luke remove the coat. Jung-sook draped a short midnight blue cape with a moon and stars stitched into the velvety cloth over his back and shoulders. Luke caught the chain and fixed it into place.

"For a guy who wears a hoodie most the time, you are a dapper dresser," Jung-sook said.

Luke chuckled. "A gentleman must know the proper attire to wear to each occasion." He took a couple calming breaths and checked his appearance in the mirror to make sure everything was in place. Reaching up, he straightened his sleeves so they flowed properly.

"Are you ready, Your Excellency?" Ahmed asked.

"One moment," Luke replied. He grabbed a bottle of water from a small fridge hidden in a cabinet and chugged it. "Gotta stay hydrated. Now, let's go."

He swept out of the room with this bodyguards behind him as he strode across the balcony and down the stairs. As the crowd noticed him, he received bows and introductions from people longing to meet the mysterious Comte de Maubeuge. With the flick of a couple fingers, he summoned one of the servers and took a glass of Champagne from her tray, nodding his thanks before she wondered off to resume her station.

"Such a lovely house, Your Excellency! I don't think I've ever seen this place looking so good," said a woman wearing a purple mask.

He didn't remember her name, forgetting it in the flurry of introductions. "Thank you. I shall be sure to convey your regards to my designers and work crew. Without them, this place would still be falling apart at the seams."

A few grumbling people parting reluctantly alerted Luke to a minor disturbance as Mathis shoved his way through the crowd.

"Your Excellency, it's excellent to see you again," Mathis said, giving a perfunctory bow. He'd skipped the party's requested dress code and simply wore a suit while also eschewing a masquerade mask.

"Mathis, my good man, it is indeed a pleasure to have you here this evening," Luke replied.

"I didn't know you could play the piano."

"I'm a man of many parts."

"Indeed. You play very well. You must have trained for a long time." Mathis hitched a winning but insincere smile onto his face.

"I learned from the best."

"Your Excellency, if I could beg a few moments of your time, I would be most grateful," Mathis said, giving a half bow.

"But you already have." Luke smirked. When he saw the flash of disappointment on Mathis's face, he raised a placating hand. "I'll tell you what, if I get a free moment, I will make myself available to you, out of courtesy to the bond we have."

"That is much appreciated, Your Excellency."

"Now, I must attend to my guests." Luke nodded at Mathis and turned away. Ahmed inserted himself between Mathis and Luke as he moved through the crowd and exchanged more empty greetings.

He took a moment to speak to a woman who wore an elegant gown that would have been at home in the French court and laid out on a guillotine.

"I must compliment you on your choice of dress, madam. And your hair matches it perfectly." Luke bowed to her.

Blushing, she held a fan over her lips and lower cheeks. "You are most gracious, Your Excellency. What a lovely breastplate that is, if you don't mind me saying so."

"I don't mind at all. It was worn by the first Comte de Maubeuge, well, at least of my line, when he fought against Napoleon."

"It fits so splendidly, Your Excellency."

When the musicians struck up a waltz, Luke smiled toward the woman. "Would you care to join me for a waltz? If you're familiar with the dance, of course."

"I'd be delighted." She curtsied.

Luke bowed as Ahmed and Jung-sook cleared a space. Finding the beat, Luke took her hand in his and rested the other on her waist, guiding her in a simplified waltz. He wished it was Maggie or Roxi in his arms, though he didn't know if Roxi knew how to waltz. After tonight, he'd have to avoid strangers for a month to recuperate from the random interactions. When the song finished, he thanked the woman for the dance and worked his way through the crowd until he neared the hall leading to the kitchen.

Movement drew his gaze toward Mathis, trying to shoulder his way through the crowd. Catching Pablo's eye, Luke ducked into the hallway.

"No one is to follow us," Pablo instructed the pair of packmates serving as security as he followed Luke into the hallway.

Luke worked his way through the hall and around a couple corners until they were in an empty room. Taking the opportunity, he bent over and stretched his legs, then tried to loosen the muscles in his shoulders and neck. Unfortunately, the breastplate and the stress of the evening made that a fruitless enterprise.

Pablo crossed his arms and leaned against the wall. "So... Do you need some help stretching, or did you have a reason for drawing me away from the tasty nibbles?"

"I think it's time to deal with Mathis, otherwise he's going to create a disturbance."

"Are you ready?" Pablo asked, raising an eyebrow.

"I have all the material ready. He's desperate."

"I can't say that I'm disappointed to see him knocked down a few pegs."

Luke nodded then stared off, his jaw clenching.

"But that's not what I'm really asking, dude. Are you ready to *deal* with him? This is the man who orchestrated the death of your friend, then your kidnapping. You were sold into slavery and forced to perform for your enemies."

Luke mulled over the Pablo's words, pacing slowly through the middle of the small room. "I'm not sure this falls into the normal range of major life moments a therapist can prepare you for." He stopped and looked at Pablo. "But whether I'm *ready* or not, it doesn't matter. The time is right and the pieces are in play. It's Mathis's time to fall." Luke fixed a sinister grin onto his face. "Then… Then the rest of the dominoes come tumbling after."

CHAPTER ELEVEN

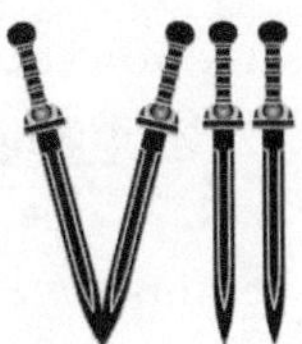

LUKE SET his mask on the desk, running a hand through his sandy blond hair, and drew back a hand damp with sweat. "What's got you in such a tizzy, Mathis? You should be enjoying the ball."

Mathis clenched his jaw, the muscles working in his cheek. "This is below my dignity, but I've run into another streak of bad luck, Pierre. I don't know who else I can turn to…"

"Ah, is it to be money again?" Luke asked.

Mathis hung his head and nodded.

"In that case, I'd prefer it if you refer to me as 'Your Excellency' if we're going to talk business." Luke kept his tone in the neighborhood of warm, but injected a note of steel into it.

"Of course, Your Excellency," Mathis replied obsequiously, curling his shoulders in to reduce his size.

Luke wanted to smile, knowing how much pretending to be subservient to a man he thought only a human must be galling Mathis, but kept his face relaxed and slightly haughty. "What's the problem, my friend?"

Mathis paced back and forth in front of Luke's desk, his hands behind his back. "It's a conspiracy to destroy me. It has to be, otherwise why all at once? Someone is trying to bring me down, and I don't know who I can trust anymore."

As Mathis spoke faster, he moved his hands in front and gripped them tightly, wringing them. "I owe money to some powerful people, and they've all called it in. All of them. They're trying to bring me down, bring my whole business crashing around my ears."

Luke feigned shock. "Surely there must be plenty of people who owe you money or favors you can call on?"

Stopping, Mathis turned and pressed his palms onto the edge of Luke's desk, looming over it staring at Luke, fury on his face. "Someone bought my marks from them and they're refusing to pay. It's a fucking conspiracy!" He pushed off of Luke's desk and resumed pacing.

"Calm down, man. You'll wear a hole in my rug." Luke knew he was pressing, but he held all the cards, literally.

Mathis flexed his entire body, then exhaled before flopping into a chair.

Luke sat back in the tall leather office chair, resting his elbows on the arm rests and steepling his hand in front of his chest. "I'm not opposed to helping you out, as a friend. But as they say, nothing for nothing…"

Mathis gave one curt nod. "I thought you might say that. I've brought a token of my friendship as a gift and down payment. I had my man bring it to your people. It should be outside with your bodyguards. May I?"

Luke thought about it for a moment before nodding. "Very well." He stood up and opened the door. "Please bring in the item Mr. Heinen brought."

"Of course, Your Excellency," Ahmed replied, nodding toward Pablo in his masquerade mask.

Pablo stepped out of sight then reemerged carrying a large, heavy looking secure crate.

"Set it next to Mr. Heinen." Luke gestured lazily with an open hand. He had to check that his hand wasn't shaking as he pulled his eyes away from the crate he hoped carried his precious armor and sword.

Pablo set the crate down with the latches facing toward Luke and his desk, then left the room, pulling the doors shut behind him.

Turning the crate slightly so he could reach both latches, Mathis rotated the dials to unlock the latches then opened the lid. A piece of black egg crate foam covered the contents until Mathis pulled it out, setting it behind the crate. Luke couldn't see the contents sitting back in his chair, so he leaned forward, resting his elbows on the desk. The glint of light on steel brought a small smile to his face.

Mathis reached in and grabbed something, lifting it out. When the edge of Luke's gladius cleared the top lip, he had to restrain himself from leaping across the desk and yanking it from the filthy hands of the man who'd betrayed him, stealing two years of his life and his property in the process. Careful not to touch the silver-alloy blade, Mathis held it so it wasn't pointed toward Luke, but flat in front of his body.

Luke stared at his old friend covetously. "Set it on the desk, please." Luke cleared his throat to cover the slight quaver in his voice.

He could see the steel of his lorica—and the way it poorly reflected light because of the engravings covering every band. Leaning forward, he gripped the handle of the gladius, feeling the power of his old friend caress his senses. Frankly, he was surprised Mathis hadn't tried to foist carefully recreated forgeries on him. Mathis truly was desperate.

Still playing the game of keeping his origins a mystery, Luke was careful not to touch the blade as he brought it closer to inspect. "It's beautiful." Pulling his eyes away after a few seconds, he nodded toward the crate. "Is that the lorica?"

Mathis nodded, looking disgusted at the proceedings. Luke set the gladius down on the desk then stepped around, peering into the crate. He reached out a hand and ran it over the Selene's symbol engraved on the steel that ran over his heart. His babies were home. Closing his eyes, he lowered the lid, then moved it against the wall. He gave the crate one last glance before cracking the doors and poking his head out.

"Ahmed, would you send in the accountants please?" Luke said, leaving a gap in the open doors and striding across the office. "As it turns out, I can help you with your plan. We'll solve this little money problem of yours and handle both sides of your debt."

Luke returned to his office chair. As he gazed across the room, he ran his fingertips over the bone hilt of the gladius from hilt guard to pommel and then back. Mathis's gaze narrowed but Luke thought he caught a bit of confused hope in the Luxembourgian alpha's eyes. Holding Mathis's gaze, Luke stared, pouring steel and power form gaze and into the werewolf's eyes. All the times Luke had caught Mathis's expression when he didn't think Luke could see, he saw nothing but contempt for the American human playing with his wealth and titles.

For the first time, there were hints of loss of control and fear. His expression made it clear he didn't want to talk, his jaw hard and his eyes cold. He returned his finger to the hilt of the sword, sliding it over the ridges until he dragged it over the hilt and let it hover over the blade, slowly carving a circle above it before pressing it down on the silver-steel alloy. The feel of Selene's crescent moon simultaneously soothed and stoked his need to exact a reckoning from the fucker sitting in front of him.

Mathis did everything in his power not to squirm under Luke's baleful glare but couldn't contain his discomfort. Below, the band started playing again. The first notes of a strumming guitar drifted through the cracked doors, chased by the dramatic tones of a trumpet laying an ominous melody.

When Delilah, Sam, and Pablo, dressed and masked for the ball like everyone else, appeared in the doorway, they pushed aside the doors, turning up the volume. Each of them carried a lacquered box approximately the size of a shoe box. One by one, they set them down on the table by Mathis, then stepped back—Delilah and Pablo taking up station on each side of the door while Sam stood near the wall by the crate containing Luke's lorica.

Luke held up his hand to keep Mathis from opening the boxes then stood up, grabbing the gladius, and stepped away from the desk so nothing stood between himself and his betrayer. Letting the sword dangle between fore and middle fingers, he clasped his hands behind his back and turned toward the window with its curtains drawn back where he could watch Mathis in the glass's reflection. The gentle glow of Selene's silvery light caressed his face as the sound of the trumpet soared.

"Do you know what El Degüello is, Mathis?" Luke asked, voice just loud enough to carry to Heinen's sensitive werewolf ears.

"No…"

"General Antonio Lopez de Santa Anna had the bugle core of his Mexican army play it as they laid siege to the slaver army of Texans at the battle of the Alamo. It means 'the throat-cutting.' No quarter given."

The clack of Mathis's marks rattled against the inside of the box as the wolf opened the lids and looked into the first box containing the debt markers he owed, then the second with the markers owed to him. "What is this? What are you playing at?" The chair scooted across the wood of the floor as Heinen stood. "Did you orchestrate this all—"

Luke didn't turn around. "Sit. Down." Not bothering to raise his voice, the words still cracked like a whip between them.

"You own my debt and what's owed to me… Are we even?" Mathis ventured, a mix of timidity and boldness.

Luke shook his head slowly. "Oh, no, Mathis. We're not done here."

In the reflection in the mirror, Luke watched Mathis open the third, slightly larger box and pull out a folder. When he opened it, the blood drained from his face as the papers fell from his shaking hands.

"H…how?"

Leaving the hand with his sword dangling from it behind his back, Luke brought the other one around and touched the medallion that triggered his disguise. Watching his own reflection, he smiled as his disguise melted away, revealing his dark, curly hair, then his face and ears. Mathis's eyes went wide as his whole body trembled.

"You…" Mathis hissed. He scrambled back, knocking over the chair, his legs tangling in it as he went down.

In a heartbeat, Luke whirled around, his gladius in his hand, and laid the flat of the tip against Mathis's cheek. The faint sizzle of flesh accompanied the stench lifted into the air by the trickle of smoke rising from the edge of the blade. Tangled as Mathis was, he couldn't move, not that he could escape the gravity of the loathing pouring from Luke's eyes.

"Mathis Heinen, we will never be even, you and I. I've taken everything you have—your money, your pack's money, and your pack." Luke leaned closer, sneering at Mathis. "Now, I'm going to take your freedom."

Delilah stepped forward and snapped a collar around his neck before he could react. Working together, Sam and Pablo clamped manacles around his wrists and ankles. With Mathis rendered inert, Luke let the corner of one side of his mouth quirk up. Slowly, Luke dragged the blade along Mathis's cheek and jaw, giving the sword a flick just before it left the werewolf's skin. Blood welled up from the slice along his cheek.

"Don't try to break through these. You'll just hurt yourself against the anti-werewolf enchantment," Delilah said, patting his uncut cheek condescendingly.

Standing up, he set the gladius on the desk and reached over, opening a drawer. Reaching inside, he pulled out a tranquilizer gun.

"I believe you're familiar with one of these, Mathis?" Luke opened it to make sure there was a dart inside.

Mathis's eyes went wide as he tried to push away, but the sole of Delilah's boot propped against the top of his head stopped him. He made to speak, but as soon as his mouth opened, Delilah shoved a ball gag into his mouth and locked it tight around his head.

"I suggest you hold still or I might miss and put the dart somewhere sensitive, like your face or your balls." He waved the gun casually, so the barrel swung over and around Mathis's body.

Mathis froze, closing his eyes. Pulling the trigger, he put a dart in Mathis's stomach, causing the man to grunt through the gag as his whole body twitched from the impact. A few moments later, the Selene-enchanted dart did its work and knocked Mathis out, his body relaxing.

Luke tossed the gun back into the draw and grabbed a cloth from the desk so he could wipe the blade clean. Sheathed in a clip-on scabbard, Pablo helped him attach it to the back of the steel breast-plate so it was mostly hidden under the cap with its high cowl. Leaving his friends to handle the pile of offal, he glided toward the door, grabbing the rapier with its scabbard and baldric he'd set aside earlier.

"Uh, buddy. Are you forgetting something?" Pablo asked.

"Ah, yes." Luke turned around and swiped the mask from the desk.

"You're forgetting your other mask, Luke," Sam said, laughing.

He chuckled and ran his finger over the medallion, then tied on the mask. Stepping through the door, he squinted. The light of the ball washed over him as he leaned on the railing overlooking the dance floor below. With a shake of his head at the couples dancing to Degüello, he pushed off the rail and strode down the stairs curving down and onto the dance floor. Ahmed and Jung-sook followed at a discreet distance.

As he stepped off the last stair, a feminine form caught his eye and he abruptly changed course with a swish of his cape behind him. Stopping in front of the woman wearing tight dark brown riding pants tucked into polished black thigh-high riding boots folded just below the knee, he bowed elegantly. She wore a silver shirt with ruffles at the collar and sleeves and a velvety midnight blue waistcoat with embroidered silver stars and moons. It was equal parts corset and vest and came up just below her breasts. Her thick, black wavy hair was plaited down her back. She'd paired a simple silver mask with a black tricorne hat with silver stitching around the brim. At her hip, she wore a long rapier with an elegant but simple basket.

"You look lovely, my dear," Luke whispered in the middle Persian they used to secretly communicate. He sketched a florid bow. "Would you like to dance?"

Roxi curtsied elegantly. "How could I turn down an offer from such a handsome gentleman?"

Luke had made several turns around the dance floor with various guests throughout the night, but none had been preceded by such intensity from the Comte's gaze or such an elegant bow. Holding out the sheathed rapier on its baldric, Ahmed took it, then took Roxi's as she pulled it from her belt.

After Luke's first waltz, the crowd had left space for dancing. Many people availed themselves of the dance floor and the music. So when Luke led Roxi to the space, his bodyguards didn't have to clear the floor.

After his hand clasped hers and he felt the warmth of her body through her waistcoat, he smiled his first genuine smile of the evening.

"You have such a warm smile," Roxi said.

The band let the last note of the current song drift to silence before starting the next one. The piano led the band into the first notes of "Mi Ankla" by Mindy Gledhill as a singer stepped forward to pick up the Spanish lyrics.

Seamlessly, Luke and Roxi slipped into the 3/4 waltz rhythm of the dance, starting simply until they got used to each other. Like in the arena, they soon melded naturally into each other, seeking to complement and enhance each other's movements and forms until they gracefully moved across the dance floor, their elegant magnetism drawing eyes.

For the first time that evening, Luke lost himself in the moment, staring into Roxi's eyes as he guided her body, though in truth, their movements were harmonious with no need for the pressure of a hand on a waist to direct their path. He could have lived in that moment forever.

As the music faded, Luke and Roxi parted. A loud, slow clap interrupted the harmony of the moment. Looking over Roxi's shoulder, he saw a man strutting through a parting crowd. Dressed as a French musketeer, he wore an elaborate masquerade mask under his jaunty wide-brimmed hat with its long red feather. With him, he brought backup and the overpowering sense of vampire.

Le Mousquetaire had arrived. Luke had been too wrapped up in his dance with Roxi to notice the approach.

"Bravo, Your Excellency. Bravo." He slowed his clap. "I searched the world for you, yet you were right under my nose the entire time, you and your doxy." He stopped about fifteen feet from Luke. "A masquerade, how appropriate. And all this time I thought you were a paper nobleman playing with a bought title, but low and behold, I find the noblest of all living humans with more titles than the kings of Europe playing dress up on their thrones, and here you are hiding under a nothing title. Comte de Maubeuge. Ha!"

Luke's pack sidled their way through the crowd, working their way near the front without looking too obvious in case they needed to interject themselves between the intruders and Luke's guests.

"Welcome." Luke bowed his head. "If you aim to dance, let the band strike up a number to your liking, though I don't believe I planned refreshments to your tastes."

Le Mousquetaire laughed, looking around at the richly dressed guests. "The snacks here are quite posh, no need to worry about that. But I do aim to dance. You and I started a number we never got to finish, and I've come to collect what's owed to me."

"Your Excellency," Ahmed whispered behind Luke.

Reaching up, Luke unclasped his cape and draped it over his right hand. He stuck his left arm up, allowing Ahmed to drape the baldric over his head so The Mistress's rapier lay against his left hip.

"My Lady," Ahmed whispered, handing Roxi her rapier.

Roxi took it and returned it to her belt.

Le Mousquetaire stared down at Luke's hip. "Ah, I see that's where my pupil's blade went. I'll be most happy to repatriate it back into my collection where it belongs."

"I defeated two of your pupils and took it by right of conquest from the second. If you want to reclaim it, you'll have to earn it." Luke flicked his eyes around as his security forces moved through the crowd, trying to cull any humans and take them to a safe place to evacuate them. While he'd not anticipated Le Mousquetaire showing up, he'd never do anything this grand without at least some contingency plans in place. He'd have to rely on his friends to handle those pieces. Le Mousquetaire was an enemy too deadly to give anything but his full attention.

Le Mousquetaire smirked, walking around the edge of the forming circle of bodies. "And I see you've reacquired your short sword. Archambeau? You are indeed bold. Always hiding in plain sight, even with your word play names. You do it nearly as well as our kind. But I digress. Seeing as you've been playing that fool Heinen, I've come to collect him. My master has use for him still."

"I'm sorry, but he's a bit tied up elsewhere at the moment. I'll be sure to convey your regards when next I see him." Luke stalked around the edge of the circle, keeping the vampire on the other side.

Le Mousquetaire clicked his tongue. "My master will be most disappointed."

"Based on his henchmen, it's probably a feeling he's used to by now." The snickers of his pack friends tugged the corners of his lips up slightly.

The vamp shook his head at Luke's insult. "I appreciated the Degüello earlier. No quarter asked." Le Mousquetaire nodded left and right, signaling to his goons to spread out and press back.

"No quarter given." Luke flipped the cape to his left hand and pulled the silver-infused and Selene-enchanted rapier from his scabbard. Although he was sad his party had been interrupted, the thought of extracting an extra dose of vengeance for the evening excited him. There was a debt between him and Le Mousquetaire, and he was in a mood to collect.

CHAPTER
TWELVE

AT THE SIGHT of their naked blades, the last few civilians took the advice of the security forces and allowed themselves to be ushered away as Luke and Le Mousquetaire stared across the dance floor at each other.

Roxi laid her hand on Luke's arm over the cape and leaned in and kissed his cheek. "Destroy him, Roman."

"With pleasure, Parthian," he replied in middle Persian.

She backed away, ensuring plenty of space.

"Are you ready to resume our dance?" Le Mousquetaire asked. "I aim to finish what I started in that arena."

"I'm not weakened and injured this time. I'm surprised you even showed up knowing I'm at full strength. Doesn't seem your style to face someone who can fight back properly. I've defeated two of your protégés. Defeated your little army in the arena. Nearly took you down while I was severely injured."

Le Mousquetaire chuckled, circling forward. "Do you think to intimidate me? I'm the finest swordsman in all vampiredom."

Luke took a couple steps forward. "Then get to carving or get out of my house."

With a yell, Le Mousquetaire lunged forward, thrusting low. Curving his sword around, Luke knocked it aside and flicked out his blade in a tight slash. The vamp leapt back in time to only take a cut to his tabard. Not letting Le Mousquetaire reset, Luke attacked.

With mix of thrusts and slashes, Luke drove the vampire to the edge of the room. After an intense exchange of blows, Le Mousquetaire reversed Luke's attack and spun them around before disengaging to open space.

Luke shook his cape down to his hand and gripped it, covering his palm and draping it over his forearm. On Le Mousquetaire's next pass, Luke stepped to the side and shoved out with his cape-covered hand, knocking the blade aside, and tried to foul the vamp's blade in the cloth. As the fanger yanked back, Luke flicked out with the cape, snapping it toward Le Mousquetaire's face, and followed it with another fast slash. Missing flesh, Luke cut another slice of fabric, this time from the sleeve of the vampire's white shirt. The spectators gasped at the near miss.

Not letting Le Mousquetaire recover, Luke swung his left hand around, letting the cape flare out, up, and around clockwise and following it with a high, downward thrust that penetrated into the vampire's left shoulder. He let out a short scream as the silver burned and yanked back, grabbing Luke's blade with his glove-covered left hand and shoving it away.

Savoring the scream of pain from his enemy and onetime tormentor, Luke yanked his blade back and thrust out with his left arm. Although he missed his target of grabbing Le Mousquetaire's sword, Luke snapped the cape down and knocked the blade off target. With a deft parry, he slid his rapier along the inside of the vamp's blade, raising a line of dark blood along his forearm and another yelp.

Luke let his hatred pour out of his eyes as he pressed the attack, exchanging blows with the vampire—who was redoubling his efforts after Luke erased his initial arrogance. Raising his hand in time to catch the vamp's blade, Luke thrust toward Le Mousquetaire's stomach. He snatched the tip, gripping it tightly, and tried to yank it from Luke's grip. With each sword captured, they tugged back and forth. The corner of Luke's lip curled into a sneer as he yanked back hard. When the vamp yanked at his own sword in return, Luke let go, sending the vampire stumbling backward until he tripped onto his ass.

The ballroom filled with laughter as Luke's friends added insult to the injury of a smarting ass. Had this been a gentlemanly fight, Luke would have let his opponent regain his feet. Instead, he lunged forward aiming for Le Mousquetaire's heart. The aim was true, but someone leaped from out of the crowd and turned the blow aside so that it only penetrated Le Mousquetaire's thigh.

He scrambled backwards, yanking the blade from his leg. As he tried to get back to his crowd, he moved too close to Luke's friends. A foot lashed out, kicking the vamp in the back. Rolling to the side, Le Mousquetaire slipped away from Luke's partisans and crawled back toward his vampiric escort. Luke recovered from his deflected thrust, exchanging blows with the interloper. Recognition stirred as the blond hair whirled out of her face. It was Antoinette from the casino—he'd played cards with her before she'd introduced herself as Robert Beaufort's wife.

From out of Luke's peripherals, a blue and silver blur darted in and skewered the interloper through the chest with the moon-enchanted rapier. Roxi let out a low, satisfied yell as she yanked the blade out. Antoinette's body collapsed in on itself as she fell into a pile of dust and empty clothes.

"No!" Le Mousquetaire screamed.

The pieces clicked together in Luke's head as suspicions and rumors became fact. The man who'd orchestrated the fall of the Flanders Pack and the murder of its packleader as well as the abduction of Luke was none other than Robert Beaufort—and Antoinette's widower.

Luke didn't hesitate or give him time to move into an en garde position. He attacked. The vampire's sword met Luke's and pushed into a counter thrust. Flicking it aside with his cape, he knocked Robert's blade down and across his body, getting in deep, and punched out, striking the fanger in the face with the basket hilt of the rapier. As Le Mousquetaire staggered back from the blow, Luke captured Robert's blade and pulled him off balance. Leaping back to open space, Luke slashed at the vampire's back, the tip of the blade whipping through cloth and into flesh. As steel cut and silver burned, Le Mousquetaire screamed in pain for the fourth time that evening.

Luke wouldn't be satisfied until the vampire who'd caused him so much pain perished. Unlike Le Mousquetaire, Luke didn't plan on playing with his food. If he got a kill shot, he wasn't giving up the opportunity. Catching his balance, the vampire twisted hard, knocking Luke's next thrust aside, and followed it with a quick flick. The blade cut into Luke's sleeve and bit flesh underneath it, raising a thin line of red along his right bicep.

Stepping back on his right foot, he twisted and knocked Robert's blade away with the cape. With Le Mousquetaire out of position again, Luke stepped in with his left side and kept the blade pushed away as he raised his rapier above his head. Only a quick dive and roll saved Le Mousquetaire from the vicious thrust made toward his face.

"Don't just stand there, fucking kill them!" Le Mousquetaire shouted as he popped up away from Luke.

"It's only me," Roxi said. "I have your back, dōšagīh."

"And I yours," Luke replied, parrying an incoming thrust.

The groups had intermingled as they'd watched the duel between Luke and Le Mousquetaire. Now everyone punched and clawed to separate toward their own people. Those armed worked to pull their weapons. Due to the nature of the party, a lot of werewolves pulled swords they weren't truly comfortable with, even with the instruction Luke, Delilah, and Sam had been giving them. As the ballroom sorted itself out, Luke didn't like the odds as more vampires filtered into the ballroom—Le Mousquetaire had left most of his contingent outside the room when he made his appearance.

"Should we get out the heavy artillery?" Ahmed called.

"Do it, or we're going to be in for some hurt." Luke lunged out, thrusting low into a vampire's thigh.

Roxi had gone after the same one, but thrust high, piercing the heart. When they both withdrew their swords, the vampire sluiced to fluid, ruining the clean dancing floor. Luke unwound the cape and laid it out over the puddle.

"It was such a nice cape," Roxi said.

"A gentleman always covers a puddle for a lady. Unfortunately, between sword fighting and vampire goo, I don't think the cape will look so jaunty anymore." He blocked and counter-slashed, enjoying the feel of blade slicing through vampire flesh.

Growls joined the increasing sounds of fighting as werewolves stripped their clothes and shifted to their bipedal werewolf forms before launching themselves into the fray. So far, Luke had only seen vampires, but lately he'd never seen vampires without their furry bullies. Without his cape in his offhand, he pulled the gladius from his back.

"Where's your sword and armor?" Luke asked, blocking a sword slash to his head.

"Nearby." She slashed out.

Stepping around the cape and puddle, Luke lashed out with gladius and rapier. "Go! This is going to get worse."

"I've got her stuff," Jung-sook called.

Luke stepped to the side, blocking the way to Roxi. "Jung-sook, help her."

"Aye, *Your Excellency*," Jung-sook replied tartly.

Luke barked a quick laugh as he waded into the front line the vampires had established. He wasn't sure, but it looked like the crowd was thinning out toward the back. As his wolves surged around him, he stepped back and scanned for Le Mousquetaire, looking for the jaunty hat with its bright red feather.

Growling when he didn't see him, he stepped back into the mess, slashing and stabbing. As the edges of his anger surfaced, his speed increased and his precision bit deep, removing limbs, striking hearts, and driving back the vampires who were learning what it meant to stand against the Centurion Immortal. His wolves fought harder, inspired by their leader.

"I am with you, dōšagīh," Roxi said, stepping into the space next to him.

He risked a quick look. She'd pulled on her scale armor over her costume, the elaborate silver sleeves of her shirt poking out. The tails of the armor dropped to mid-thigh. Underneath, she'd pulled up the boots over her knees to add extra protection. Like Luke, she had her

Parthian sword in her left hand and a rapier in her right. She'd put her tricorne hat back on and looked bold as brass in the mixed outfit.

He contemplated getting his lorica and shucking the steel breast-plate. Longing to feel its familiar weight on his shoulders, he'd missed it like a long-lost friend. It would also provide better protection with its magically enhanced steel. The breastplate would not deflect a bullet.

The wolves had the line held, so he stepped back to confer with his heads of security. "Jung-sook, can you get your Steyr and scout the balconies?" He wiped the sweat from his forehead. "Let us know what's going on outside. Shoot if you have the shot."

"How you doing? Holding up?" Jung-sook asked.

"Yeah, all the training has helped." He looked around. "Roxi, can you hold the line? I'm going to make a wardrobe change."

"Of course, I'll see about ejecting these uninvited guests from your hall." She put her blade against her lips and used it to blow him a kiss.

Chuckling, he followed Jung-sook upstairs, leaving her at the keypad-locked door of the room set up as an armory. As he turned into his study, electronic beeps trailed off. Pulling off his baldric, he unbuckled the leather straps and buckles enclosing him in the steel breastplate. At the sound of a footfall, Luke reached for his sword but relaxed once he saw it was Rhonda.

"You're a bit jumpy, though I can't blame you. Thought I'd come up and grab some shotguns from the armory in case we needed them. Also figured you could use a hand." She stepped in and opened the crate, lifting out his armor, and held it open for him. "Pick up your collar so it doesn't bunch around neck."

Luke lifted the frilly collar so he could lay it over the neckline. He'd have to find a new scarf to use as a focale, though he should have had one ready. Not wanting to count his chickens, he'd avoided it out of some sense of superstition that planning too much would jinx it, no matter how foolish a thought it really was. The frilly collar would have to do to protect his neck for now, but he wouldn't even mind a little chafing from his beloved armor. As Luke tied the front shut, Rhonda grabbed the baldric with his rapier and placed it over his arm and head when he was ready.

"That's better. You looked sharp in the fancy breastplate, but you look right in your proper armor." She smiled and squeezed his forearm.

Luke followed her into the armory, passing Jung-sook as she headed into Luke's office to look through the windows. A couple other werewolves had gotten the same idea and were currently grabbing shotguns and ammo belts. Taking one for himself, he strapped it around his body and grabbed one of his Winchester M12s. As he looked around, he found one of the tactical bandoliers he used for his gladius and snagged it, snapping on a generic scabbard that would do the job for now.

With a troop of shotgun-armed werewolves, Luke led the way down the wide staircase, pumping a shell into the firing chamber and flicking the safety off. Seeing the armed squad coming down the stairs, the remaining vampires made a break for it.

"Hold up," Luke called, seeing a few people trying to pursue the fleeing vampires.

Once he had everyone's attention, he sent those who wanted guns upstairs to the armory. Those who preferred their wolf form, he sent off in pairs to take station at every door as well as a few groups to sweep through the basement and first floor to ensure no pockets of vampires were left.

"Don't hold a door if the group coming in is too big. Run back and we'll reinforce you. For now, we're gathering information on what's waiting for us outside. Find out what happened to our people watching the doors into this place. Until we know better, stay out of view of the windows and keep all your senses active. This ballroom is the central point, so I'll post up here. And remember, save your shots. We're not exactly flush with ammo right now." He looked around the group. "Shit. Has anyone seen Delilah, Pablo, or Sam?"

He got nothing back but nos and shaken heads. They must not have returned yet from depositing Mathis back at the cottage.

"Fuck. Everyone to your posts. You know your tasks." He pulled out his phone and dialed his friends.

When they didn't pick up, he left voice mails with each, then sent a group text. Checking the time, he calculated where they might be if they'd gotten away clean. If all had gone well and they'd left before the vampires showed up, they'd be arriving at the cottage or just on their way back. The warmth of a hand in his drew him back into the room.

Turning to face Roxi, he smiled. "How are you doing? Holding up OK?"

"I'm a little tired, but I'll be alright. If we can get a couple vampires for me, I'll be able to recharge up for real."

Luke pulled her in close. "Another armored hug. Sometime we'll have to try this out when we're both healthy and not bedecked in steel."

Shifting from foot to foot, Roxi lowered her eyes. "Luke... I'm sorry—"

"Please, Roxi, you don't have to apologize. I was mad when you left, but I understood, even if I didn't agree. All I care about is that you're alive and here." He chuckled. "I'd add 'safe,' but the present circumstances might beg to differ."

Roxi laughed, squeezing Luke's waist. "Yeah, I don't think safety is something either of us really knows, but if I'm going to be in danger, at least I'm with you."

Luke ran his hand along her cheek and jaw. Hooking her chin with his forefinger, he lifted it up so he could look into the deep pools of her dark brown eyes. The longing mixed with sadness nearly bowled him over. The tip of his tongue parted his lips, wetting them as he lowered them to Roxi. As soon as his lips touched hers, his knees nearly gave out as heat and electricity surged through his body. When Roxi pushed back into his lips, their kiss intensified as he coaxed her mouth open with his tongue. He lost himself in the depth of his feelings for Roxi, losing track of how long they kissed.

"Ahem."

Reluctantly, Luke pulled back after giving Roxi one last squeeze. "Sorry. We got a little carried away."

Rhonda chuckled. "No worries. You two have had a bit of a time lately. No harm seeking a little solace in the middle of a battle."

Luke blushed. "So what's the word?"

"Everyone's to their spots. Jung-sook says she sees them milling about out near the tree line surrounding the property. They're blockading the road in with their vehicles. She can't see anything beyond that." Rhonda winked at Roxi.

"Thanks, Ronda. Ge—" The muffled sound of automatic gunfire interrupted Luke. "Sounds like the southeast side. Go check there."

Louder fire, likely returned fire from inside the house, punctuated Luke's order. Rhonda gave a curt nod and jogged off in the direction of the gunfire.

"I'm glad you took the minute to go change into your armor, if it's their guns." She caressed his cheek now that they were alone. "Since the vampires know who you are and where, can you put away this face? I'd rather look at yours."

He grinned mischievously. "Are you sure? This one is much handsomer. Noble even."

Chuckling, she shook her head. "Be that as it may, I prefer the face I got to know staring through a hole in a stone wall. It's my face."

Luke bumped the medallion, then stepped back and made a square over his face like he was framing a shot with his hands as the disguise disappeared from his face. "Does this look more familiar?"

Roxi smiled, a twinkle of mirth in her eyes. "That's much better. The other face is made of too precious of stuff, it's not a work a day face like this one. It's not my face." She pushed up on the balls of her feet and gave him a quick kiss. "Let's watch each other's back and get out of this alive."

"Agreed."

They both turned their heads when they heard running feet. A moment later, Rhonda tore around the corner from the other end of the ballroom. "They're aiming for the kitchen door. I sent one of the search parties to reinforce the two there."

"Good. Go find the rest of the search parties. And bring them here. I want them centralized so we can send out reinforcement parties anywhere we need." When the crack of the Steyr sniper rifle went off, he turned his head upstairs. "Roxi, can you check in with

Jung-sook and Connor?" Remembering the stairs and Roxi's fatigue, he added, "Rhonda, send me someone to act as a runner so I have Roxi to lead parties after this first check."

"Got it. Good luck." Rhonda gave a half salute and jogged off back into the depths of the manor.

Roxi gave Luke's hand one last squeeze, then headed upstairs to check on the snipers. He watched her work her way up the stairs, glad she was here, but wishing she'd stayed at the cottage. With much recovery still needed, he hoped she wasn't risking her health further. He needed her and now that he had her back, he didn't want to see her hurt before she could fully recover.

When gunfire sounded to the northwest, Luke sighed and shook his head. The second round of violence had begun.

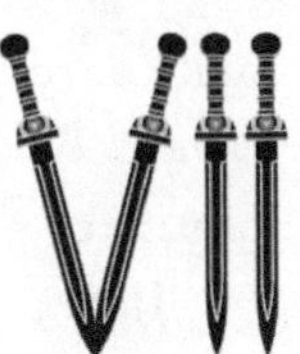

CHAPTER
THIRTEEN

LUKE WIPED the sweat from his brow, his breath finally returning to more steady levels. Around him, his packmates caught what rest they could, some newly arrived from their last round of fighting, others with a bit more time between bouts. Roxi, getting slower with each journey to whatever part of the manor the vampires were attempting to break through, sat on a cushioned dark wood bench against the wall.

So far, they'd repelled several minor incursions as the vampires outside probed Luke's defenses. If it had only been the vampires that had crashed his ball, they'd have no problem matching their numbers if they'd had all their people on hand. But they'd hoped to distract the local fangers from their event by hunting them on the streets, leaving Luke shorthanded against an all-out assault the vamps appeared to be bringing. Luke's manor was far enough out in the country without much in the way of other properties nearby, so the chances of anyone calling for aid would be low, assuming the vampires wouldn't just blockade the authorities out and glamour them. They were on their own.

He pulled his phone, making a disgusted noise when he saw the cracked screen he'd forgotten about. The last message he'd received from Sam was "message received, standby." At least they were still alive—or most likely alive—with a message like that. Then, he'd dove out of the way and landed funny, breaking the screen. He couldn't tell if the phone even worked anymore. Tossing it out of the way, he asked Rhonda to see if she could get in contact with Sam.

"And Rhonda, have someone do a quick ammo check. I want to make sure we're not getting too low." Catching Roxi's eye, he started toward her when another muffled burst of gunfire stopped him. A minute or so later, one runner sprinted into the ballroom.

"Incoming, we need help. Side entrance on the north side. We have one wounded." They skidded to a stop in front of Luke.

"Understood. You rest here." Turning to the crowd milling about, he raised his hand to stifle the various questions and conversations. "I'm going to need seven people—the people who've been resting the longest. Two will bring back the wounded to here so they can be bandaged up. Four of you, go bring down more ammo and the remaining guns. Roxi, you hold the post down here."

When the group split into three, the two with orders plus the unassigned folks resting, Luke waved the reinforcement group after him as they jogged toward the designated entrance. The closer they were, the louder it got. Luke slowed them down and called a halt before they could dash into the hallway.

"Damn it, Luke," Rhonda panted. "Next time, get a mansion with fewer doors. This running around stuff is bullshit."

Several people chuckled, shaking their heads and smiling at Rhonda. A few nodded their heads in agreement.

"I'll ask the real estate agent for a more defensible house next time."

Luke peered around the corner to survey what waited. He could make out a pair of people firing out the door and side windows, the occasional muzzle flair highlighting the shadowy figure stretched out on the ground.

"Reinforcements behind you!" Luke called.

Someone looked back their way. "Terwilliger."

"Flanders." Luke gave the return call.

Since the majority of the werewolves here were from the various northwest Oregon packs, he'd used Portland street names to add a bit more security to their operation. He'd hate to have friendly fire take someone out.

Luke stepped around the corner, waving everyone to follow, and crouch-walked, staying low and in the shadows. Carefully stepping around the wounded wolf on the ground, he racked a bullet into the chamber and stepped into an empty spot. With a quick look over the ledge of the window, he found an easy target. He raised his gun and aimed, pulling the trigger immediately. The vampire exploded into a pile of viscous goo, splatting to the ground on the stone walkway.

"You two pull back to the ballroom, reload, and grab a breather." Luke drew another aim and fired, missing a kill shot but sending the vamp to the ground screaming as the silver burned its flesh.

With a quick wave, the two pulled back, opening spots for comrades to relieve them. Soon, Luke had four shotguns poking out the shattered windows. When he checked over his shoulder, the wounded wolf was gone, leaving two people crouching in the shadows. Luke squinted into the dark, his eyes adjusting to the brighter interior of the manor. Off in the distance, he saw another wave sneaking through the shadowy landscaping around the manor. He'd paid for a decent chunk of work to be done in the yard, but fortunately the work was only partially done and the plants were still young and well-trimmed, having had no time to get established and bushy.

"Hold fire until they're in range. Three of you duck down. Everyone to the front and ready to fire." Luke tried to stay out of sight as best as he could while still keeping an eye on the vampires scampering toward them.

One of the vamps poked their head out, scanning the entrance to see what the resistance looked like. He probably saw the corner of Luke's head, but to see no one would have been equally suspicious. With a bit of a gap between the landscaping and the entrance, the vampires made a break for it. Eight shot out from the shadows, sprinting for all they were worth, and with their vampiric speed, they were worth a lot.

"Now," Luke said quietly enough for his team to hear.

They all popped up and opened fire, six shotguns barking to life as they spit flame, silver, and death toward the vampires who had committed to their attack. Too deep to turn around, Luke's crew left seven of them dusted or splattered about the stone walkway. Only one still moved.

Rhonda held up a stake. "Want me to get it?"

"No, I think I'll take it back to Roxi as a present."

With a snort, Rhonda shook her head. "You're a real romantic, Luke."

Peeking out the window, Luke pulled his gladius and set the shotgun down. With the way clear, he darted out, keeping low, and decapitated the vamp, then dragged it in by its ankles.

"I need two volunteers and a runner to cover this door." Luke nodded at the hands thrust up. "Great, the rest of you are with me back to the ballroom. And if someone could help me with this body, that'd be great."

One of the men grabbed the arms, leaving Luke the legs, and together they hauled it back through the house, setting it in the far corner of the ballroom out of the way of paths in and out. After dropping it, Luke strode across the big room to Roxi.

Smiling at her, he squatted in front of her, taking her hands in his. "I brought you a little present. Hopefully it'll give you a bit of energy."

"If it's cocaine, I'm going to be disappointed. I've heard about you playboy aristocrats and your habits." She winked at him slyly.

"Alas, I'm fresh out of rootie tootie booger sugar." He shrugged, tipping his head to the side and looking sorry.

"What? Ha!" Shaking her head, she reached out and caressed his smooth cheek. "You're a ridiculous man, do you know that?"

"Anything to make you smile." He took her palm and kissed it. "I did bring you a vampire, though. If you want to give your new rudis a proper blood blessing."

Roxi nodded nervously, reaching out for him to help her stand. Once he was fully upright, he pulled her up, directing her across to the body.

"It's not every man who brings his lady friend a headless body," someone said as they walked by.

"Did you know? Headless vamp is this season's diamond bracelet. All the fashionable people will want one," someone else replied.

Several people laughed. He liked that his people were joking and keeping their spirits up. Today's event had been designed to snare Mathis—and Jan, if he'd showed up—not draw in all the vampires for a pitched battle. Their armory wasn't up to full snuff yet and everyone knew it. Sam had something cooking; they just needed to hold out until she could relieve them.

Standing over the body, Roxi clasped her hands and looked adoringly at Luke, batting her eyelashes. "Ah, Luke! It's just what I wanted. You sure do know the way to a woman's heart."

Luke smiled smugly. "I do. Through the ribcage."

"Well, here goes…" Roxi pulled her rudis, letting Luke help her down onto her knees.

She held the wooden sword with its silver filigree and steel-silver alloy blade in a reverse grip with both hands and plunged it into the vampire's chest. Standing behind her, he tried to block her off from the rest of the room, though he could feel the eyes burning into his back. He knew Roxi was nervous, afraid the rudis wouldn't work—that Mithras might have betrayed them—but they had no choice but to try it. Roxi inhaled deeply, then let the air out slowly before bending over the corpse and placing her forehead on her rudis. He knew the words like they'd been etched on his bones. His lips moved to speak the incantation as Roxi voiced it.

When he saw the white light start at the top of the pommel and slither down the blade to disappear into the fanger's body, he held his breath while it made the return trip up the rudis and into Roxi.

"It worked," she whispered.

Luke exhaled explosively. She stood up, looking stronger and haler than she had a minute ago. He couldn't help but smile, his lips splitting into a wide grin. Grabbing her shoulders, he pulled her into a tight hug. Tears burned in his eyes as relief washed over him. If he thought he could get away with it, he would have sung and danced.

"Are you alright, Luke? You're practically shaking," Roxi whispered into his ear, stroking his hair soothingly.

He took a moment to get his emotions in check before responding. "I was terrified it wouldn't work. That you'd have to go through everything again. That...that I'd have to live in a world without you."

"Oh, Luke." She squeezed him tightly. "You'll have to throw me out to get rid of me now."

She pushed back and tipped her head up, closing her eyes as she went in for a kiss. Behind them, the werewolves broke into applause, the sound of hands clapping mixing with the padded sound of wolf paws coming together. Luke tried to ignore them, but the heat of his flushed cheeks told him he was failing at it, though he truly didn't care. The pack was more than just his army. They were his big extended family, and they wanted to see him happy. And if Roxi was truly staying with him, the pack would become her family too.

The sound of renewed gunfire put a quick halt to their shared joy as reality reimposed itself rudely. Tilting his ear toward the conflagration, his brow furrowed as the amount of gunfire robbed his face of the smile, pushing the corners of lips down.

"Roxi, you stay here and keep an eye on everyone." He gave her a quick kiss on the tip of her nose before stepping away from her. "I need six guns with me. Everyone else, make sure you're fully loaded and ready to go."

Rhonda held up an ammo belt full of shotgun shells. "Luke, give me yours and I'll refill it."

Luke unbuckled the ammo belt and handed to Rhonda, replacing his with the one in her hand. "Thanks."

Giving Roxi a quick nod, he jogged toward the door that led to the kitchen, his six volunteers forming up behind him. There were two ingress points in this section they'd have to check. As they busted into the kitchen, carnage greeted them. One of the wolves, in their human form—it looked like Rebecca—dragged a packmate by their hairy arms, both of them cover in blood. With two wounded, they'd be dangerously light on responding fire.

"Situation?" Luke called out.

"Too many. They overwhelmed us. We just barely got out, but took more shots on the retreat. Agatha is doing the best she can. It sounds like the other entrance was hit too," Rebecca replied, panting from the fight and the excursion of moving her wounded packmate while also having injuries.

"Get back to the ballroom. We'll see if we can plug the gap." Luke didn't wait for an answer, running through the kitchen toward the hallway, the trail of blood their wounded had left guiding them to the fight. At the junction to the entrances, Luke stopped. "You two, down there to reinforce the other door. The rest, with me."

Luke ran left, following the trail of blood. When they reached the halfway point, Luke opened fire. Agatha took the moment to reload her shotgun. Luke could see the blood staining her wooden bayonet. Dark wet spots gleamed in the dim light, highlighting blood. Whether it was hers or the vamps, he couldn't tell at this point.

"Fall back, catch your breath," Luke ordered.

They let Agatha through while Luke and his squad emptied their shotguns down the hallway, dodging out of the way at returned shots. While they killed more than they missed, the numbers pressing into the hallway were greater than any assault faced so far.

"Fuck! Pull back slowly. Rhonda, go get the other group moving so they're not cut off from us." Luke stepped back to let someone else take his spot so he could shove shells into the magazine of his gun. The trench guns were proving themselves yet again in the tight confines of Luke's manor house.

Once reloaded, he let his front line step behind him. He opened fire, not so much picking targets as filling the hall with wood and silver shrapnel, hoping it found flesh to bite. With each shot, he took a step backward. As he fired his last shot, he stepped behind the next line to let them take up their turn. He looked over his shoulder. The muzzle flash of shotguns lit up the other side of the hall. They were getting close to the exit into the kitchen.

"We need to hold our ground until the others get to us," Luke barked out, shoving shells into his gun. "Two by two."

When the two firing emptied their guns, Luke and Agatha stepped forward, trading fire to extend their time.

"Shit!" Joe screamed, dropping his shotgun.

With a quick glance down, Luke saw blood covering his shoulder as he cradled his arm. "Get him out of here. Get back to the ball-room. Damn, out."

He picked up the dropped shotgun and fired off the last few shots. Charlie stepped forward while James helped Joe up. With all his enhanced speed and dexterity, Luke shoved shells into first one, then the other shotgun. As soon as Agatha fired empty, Luke stepped up, James joining after getting Joe moving toward the ballroom.

Without speaking about it, they set up a three person rotation, sweating to reload between each round or dodging returned fire.

"Luke! We got to get out of here," Rhonda shouted.

"All clear your way?" Luke yelled, shoving shells into the shotgun.

Each time his hand moved over empty loops and he had to go looking for a shell, his anxiety intensified. The rest of the team had to be running near empty as well.

"Yeah."

"Get back to the ballroom and get us some reinforcements." Luke stepped up to take another around.

"You two stay and help Luke," Rhonda ordered.

Luke backed up, checking to make sure everyone else had made it through the door before jumping through it. He sprinted behind the nearest stainless steel counter and slid to the floor, breathing heavily as he scrambled to find more shells. He tried to ignore the ringing of his ears in the momentary quiet of the storm before the vampires realized the halls were empty of defenders. The occasional shot rang out, receiving an answering from the other side. After a rat-tat-tat of an automatic, several shots popped from the other side. So far, no vampire had dared pop their head through the door into the kitchen.

He looked around for anything to barricade the entrance but found nothing with sufficient size and weight to be worth the effort. Everything else was attached to the floor or walls.

With his gun loaded, he popped up and took aim toward the door —still no vampires, yet they kept shooting. He started chuckling until it turned into laughter. When it finally trickled to a stop, everyone stared at him.

"They don't know we abandoned the hallway. They're shooting at each other." He gave a last chuckle and shook his head.

When the door leading from the ballroom blasted open, Luke heaved a sigh of relief as a half dozen werewolves poured into the room. He pointed half to one side of the kitchen and half to the other side so they could keep multiple angles on the door. Then he waved everyone else over, had them strip the remaining shells from the belts, and sent them off to fetch more ammo.

With a reload on shells, Luke refilled his ammo belt and waited. With the vamps still firing at each other, the tension ramped up in the kitchen.

"Luke?" Rhonda called a bit above a whisper.

He beckoned her over. "What's up?"

Rhonda took a moment to catch her breath. "We're getting hit at two other entrances. Roxi's been leading sorties, but she's struggling again. I think she used up that one vampire."

"Fuck." Luke shook his head, handing Rhonda the loaded shotgun. "You're in charge here."

He pulled off the ammo belt and laid it on the counter for her, picking up the spare shotgun, then jogged out of the kitchen. Roxi was catching a breather on the stairs—a half dozen wolves were scattered about, grabbing some water or reloading on ammo. Sliding onto the stair next to Roxi, he leaned over kissed her cheek.

"How you doing, Rox?"

"I'm getting tired again. They just keep coming, Luke. We're running out of ammunition and taking more injuries than we can replace. I've got them moved upstairs where they'll be safe for now." The weariness staining her voice tugged at his heart.

"Anything serious?"

"Enough to make them a liability in a fight. Maybe a couple might wolf heal enough we can pull them back into the fight if we're getting truly desperate." She wound her fingers through his, leaning her head against his shoulder.

Luke laid his head on hers. "We're fast approaching desperate. Anyone heard from Sam yet?"

"Just a quick text about thirty minutes ago saying 'hold on.' I hope that means she's on her way. I finally have my life back and a future to look forward to. I'm not interested in dying for the cause tonight."

"Me either." He perked his head up when he heard several shotguns bark to life from the direction of the kitchen and sighed. "I'd better go check on that."

He stood up, body creaking with fatigue, and grabbed his shotgun and a filled ammo belt, strapping it around his chest.

"I'll go check in on the other two fronts." She forced herself to standing. "Luke, do be careful."

He turned and gave her a tired smile. "You too, Roxi."

Flicking off the safety, he ran toward the hall that lead to the kitchen. Even at the jog, his muscles burned. When he turned the last corner for the kitchen, a percussive explosion blasted the door open, spewing fire and shrapnel, and knocked Luke to the ground. His ears, already whining from a steady diet of gunshots, screamed in agony through a wash of static. Tiny points of pain blossomed on his face, arms, and legs.

The door to the kitchen teetered off its hinges, crashing to the ground revealing chaos and flames in the kitchen. He thought he heard shotguns blast back to life in front of him but couldn't be sure as he tried to blink the smoke out of his eyes and regain his sense of balance and hearing. Through a pillow, he thought he heard someone calling his name. When werewolves poured in from the ballroom, he shook his head, wincing at the motion, and waved them off, trying to get them to move into the kitchen.

"Get our wounded and fall back," Luke yelled, choking on smoke as he inhaled sharply. Those flames were too high for a fire extinguisher and the battle too hot to risk a fire team.

He clawed at the wall, trying to pull himself up and balance himself, only to slide back to the ground. Having no other choice, he sat back and tried to stay out of the way as people in human and wolf form jumped over him to reinforce the kitchen and see to the wounded. As his eyes drifted down, motion next to him caused him to startle. Someone had tossed down a body Luke didn't recognize.

"Luke," they shouted. "Vampire. Drain it."

It took a moment or two for the words to filter through to his brain and make sense. The person, seeing Luke's slowness, grabbed Luke's rudis and stabbed it into the vampire. Luke let gravity do the work and fell toward the vampire, using his hands to stop his descent. Wrapping his hands around the hilt, he set his forehead onto the pommel and whispered the incantation. The relief, once the light disappeared into his forehead, was immediate. He still felt like he'd been in an explosion, but the fog smothering his mind receded, as well as the whooshing hell of his broken ear drums. He hated broken ear drums and concussions. Between them and broken ribs, he always seemed to be recovering from one or the other the last few years.

Someone tossed down a second body for him. Without prompting, he pulled the rudis, groaning as the first fanger dissolved into goo and soaked his pants, and drained the next one. After the second vamp, he began to function. With help so he didn't slip in the sludge of the two vampires, he stood up. The bark of the shotguns cracked more clearly now. He worked his way along the wall, trying to stay in the shadows so he could assess the situation in the kitchen.

When two bodies emerged from the smoke and shadows, he pressed against the wall, allowing them space to get their wounded packmate out of the way. Something metal bumped into his hand. Someone held his shotgun. He took it and pumped it. Seeing no shadows in his way, he crouched and broke through the door and out of the way behind the back row of steel counters. He stood up and made sure the way was clear, firing off a couple rounds toward the door.

A couple more wolves opened fire at the door, blindly shooting to keep the vampires from advancing. One of the pack had gone full wolf and was crawling around between the rows of counters, checking for any other wounded.

"Luke, let's clear out! We got everyone," someone shouted.

Luke waved everyone out and stood up, firing off his gun steadily as he backed into the door. Once he made it through, someone else stepped up and kept up the fire as they backed toward the turn in the hall. As soon as they cleared it, they dashed backwards toward the ballroom. Luke, having trouble getting air into his lungs, staggered several times, a hand always reaching out to prop him up and help him along. After they burst into the ballroom, Luke ducked out of the way and slid down the wall. He stared blankly across the room until something clicked into place.

"The hall…" he gasped out.

Rhonda, blood covering her clothes, nodded and grabbed several people, disappearing back into the hall to find a place to make a stand. Rolling onto his hands and knees, he forced himself up as people boiled into the ballroom from the other entrance, a few taking up post to shoot down the hall leading into the ballroom. A limping Roxi made her way to him after her eyes landed on him.

He thought she called his name, but he could barely hear. He tapped his ear with his empty hand. "I can't hear well."

Roxi nodded. "We lost the other hall. We've got to fall back."

He squinched his eyes tightly, taking a deep breath and coughing. "OK. Rhonda's holding the back hall. Get someone to run down and tell them we're pulling back." He tried to force his mind into action but was struggling. They didn't plan on a pitched battle in the porous manor. No one was supposed to notice Mathis's disappearance until well after the party. "Third floor. Get the wounded and all the weapons and ammo. If there's anything in the armory, clear it out. I'll organize the last stand here, then pull out once we've got everyone moving."

"Are you sure?" Roxi's eyebrows furrowed in concern.

"We don't have a choice." He wiped the sweat from his brow with the back of his hand. It came back pink from a mix of blood and sweat.

"Alright, I'll get everyone moving." She turned to carry out her part of the plan.

"Roxi." He waited until she turned back around. "I love you."

"I love you, too, Roman. Now don't die on me. We have things to do."

"I won't, Parthian. Good luck."

"You too," she replied.

He closed his eyes briefly. *"My Mistress, I know I call on you too often, but we're getting desperate. Any aid you can provide would be welcome."*

Selene's warmth filled him, easing his pain and lightening the symptoms of his various wounds. He felt slightly refreshed, though still exhausted.

"I can loan you a little of my strength. What else can I do?" Selene's voice asked in his mind.

"Can you bar entrance to this ballroom when we need to withdraw?" Luke asked.

"I can for a brief time. Something strengthens our enemies and my strength fades, but I'll do the best I can for you, my brave soldier."

"Thank you, Selene." Luke opened his eyes and dashed to usher Rhonda and her team into the ballroom.

Once everyone was contained within, he saw a brief flicker of silver light casting a sheen over the doorways. Luke poked his shotgun through the barrier and fired. When a vampire poked their head around the corner and shot back, the barrier flared briefly and the bullet slowed and fell through, robbed of all its velocity.

"Pick your shots," Luke called. "We're running short on ammo. Selene can provide some protection, so let's not waste what we have."

Stepping away from the door, he turned to check on Roxi. A couple of the pack were moving a wounded person upstairs, but the rest had already been cleared out. Roxi ushered the last of the pack up the stairs, then gave him a wave and a sad smile before limping up the stairs to finish overseeing the evacuation of the armory and the snipers stationed at the windows.

"Oh, shit!" someone shouted.

Luke whipped his head around as everyone dove out of the way. Luke quickly saw the reason. The vampires had tossed another fragmentation grenade. Not even thinking of the barrier, he dove toward the wall just as the grenade exploded.

Luke's ears popped and whined, but he hadn't felt any shrapnel or the explosion, save for a softened shock wave. Trying to catch his breath, he rolled onto his butt and rested his back against the wall as he tried to will the adrenaline coursing through his veins to calm down.

"Luke! Are you OK?"

Luke looked up. Roxi's head poked over the banister along the second-floor balcony that overlooked the ballroom.

"Yeah. Just a little rattled." His body shook, still coming down.

"We're clear up here. We'll cover your retreat."

"Understood," he replied.

Roxi's head disappeared. Luke forced himself to stand, propping himself against the wall with a hand.

He cleared his throat to make sure his voice was still working. "Everyone, fall back to the stairs. We're heading up to the third floor. Keep it organized."

No one had to be told twice. As a group, they stood up and dashed toward the stairs. Luke jogged behind.

Selene's voice broke into Luke's awareness, her voice urgent and stressed. *"Lucius, I can't hold it much longer. Something dark comes…"*

Luke skidded to a halt. *"Is it him? Has he come?"*

"No, it's something else, something less powerful. Now run!"

Luke took off after everyone, gasping for air as he flew up the stairs, taking two at a time. Ahead of him, three people stood at the banister and opened fire as vampires poured into the ballroom. As soon as Luke passed them, they fell in line, making for the rickety stairs leading up to the third floor.

CHAPTER
FOURTEEN

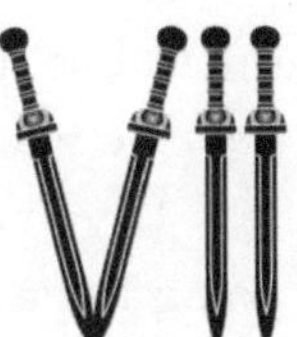

THEY'D RAN out of time to finish the third floor repair before Luke's planned party, so it remained untouched. As his feet pounded up the stairs, he thought he heard a board or two crack, but he couldn't be sure as everyone thundered up, sending up a din of squeaking boards. Stopping at the top, he waited until the last person ran past. With a quick glance, he watched as vampires took the first tentative steps up the stone steps leading to the second floor.

"Luke, get in here," Roxi ordered.

"Right." He turned and entered the hallway.

Werewolves, their hands full of old broken and moldy furniture, waited until he passed, then started chucking everything down the stairs to foul the approach. The next round took longer, heavier pieces and blocked the top of the stairs, forming barriers they could shoot from behind.

"What's with all the other detritus?" Luke asked.

Roxi shrugged and gave him a wicked smile. "It's hard to climb stairs if you're dodging crockery. As busted up as this stuff is, it'll do yeoman's work."

"Good thinking. That'll help us extend our ammo." He looked around. "Where are the snipers?"

"They're searching for a window they can look through, see if they can spy Sam's approach." Roxi unbuckled the partial ammo belt strapped around his torso and handed it to a Rhonda and another wolf. "We can only put so many people up front, so we're going to pass empties back to reload and keep up a constant fire."

Luke slid his hand behind Roxi's neck and pulled her in for a quick but intense kiss. "I'm glad we've got you here. This is the best defense we could organize, considering the circumstances."

"If you're going to kiss me every time I do something smart, I'm going to have to keep up the good work," she teased.

He chuckled. "You're irresistible."

"Sure. I'm sweaty, covered in blood and vampire goop. Very sexy."

"To me, you'll always be beautiful." He gave her a lopsided grin.

"You're flirting while we're busy prepping for another fight?" Rhonda shook her head. "Y'all are weird."

Luke squatted down by Roxi as she organized the weapons and ammo pile. "Sometimes you have to say what needs saying when you can, Rhonda. Anything I can help you with?"

"Nah, got it all wrapped up while you two were smooching. I guess I've got to cut you some slack since she's been sick for so long." Rhonda sighed. "I hope Patrice is safe."

Luke squeezed Rhonda's shoulder. "I'm sure she's doing everything in her power to help Sam break us out of this mess."

"I'd rather she stays back at casa de Luke, but I guess you're right. I'm sure she wishes I were safe somewhere else, but alas..." She placed her hand on his, squeezing it. "Thanks for being a friend."

"Luke, I think you need to come up here," one of the wolves watching from the barrier called back.

Luke grabbed a shotgun and joined the pack members using the small landing at the top of the stairs as their first line of defense for the third floor.

"I think they've been checking out the other rooms first. A couple have been milling about down there to make sure we stay up here," Charlie said.

"What did you need me for?" Luke asked.

Charlie moved out of the way. "Here, take my spot and see if you can look down toward the stairs down to the ballroom. The lights are doing something funny. Something that seems like it's more your department than mine."

Luke chuckled and squeezed into the slot where Charlie had been. The trans man was quite a bit smaller than Luke's bulk, especially in his armor. Once he crunched down into the nook, he moved his neck around until he found the top of the stairs and followed them down.

The light pulsed. It didn't look like a power issue; the dim bulb hanging from the hallway ceiling back behind them burned steady, shedding its light over the dusty, dingy hallway. It reminded him of the arena back in Wyoming, outside when Zalmoxis made his presence known, although not as intense or dark. Where his power had been a raging inferno, this felt like a candle in comparison, a pale copy, at least Luke hoped. It could be the soft probing before bursting to full power. He'd have to be careful.

Luke unfolded himself and let Charlie have his previous spot. "If anything changes, send someone to me. I'm going to check in with the snipers.

"I can handle that," Charlie replied.

Luke patted him on the shoulder and headed into the hallway, finding Jung-sook laying on the dusty floor, her sniper rifle pointing out a window. She'd pulled a couple boards off the window frame and busted out the window so she could point the barrel out.

"No need to look up, Jung-Sook. It's just me. How's it looking out there?" Luke asked.

"Not much going on. I can see some occasional movement deep in the woods, but nothing worth shooting at."

"If you want to shoot, you can see down into the stairwell up to the second floor from our little barrier on the landing."

Jung-sook looked up, a wicked smile on her face. "That sounds more useful than staring off into the woods."

"Who has our other rifle?" Luke asked.

"Connor had it the last time I saw him." Jung-sook got up and grabbed her sniper rifle. "Am I free to shoot?"

"Yeah, take anything out that you can put your scope on. Make them wary of coming any further." Luke stepped out of the way.

"With pleasure."

Luke followed Jung-sook out into the hall and explored around, seeing how his people had set up while he held the first floor. The first room he peeked into contained the wounded. Most looked in OK shape, their werewolf healing going a long way to heal their wounds. Some of them might be available if they were truly needed. The small room next to the wounded contained a sadder sight—three bodies covered in blood with flesh desecrated by the grenade that had gone off in the kitchen. He knew there were other bodies that should be in the room that they'd not recovered yet, including those who'd been on door duty before Le Mousquetaire crashed his party.

In the largest room, he found most of the pack, resting and getting ready to fight when next called upon. Someone had grabbed blankets from downstairs for the wolves who'd gone bipedal, leaving their clothes elsewhere. Now that they were taking a break in their human forms, the breezy third floor wasn't the most comfortable option.

"Who removed the boards and broke out that window?" Luke asked.

"Connor. He climbed out onto the roof so he could see all around," Joe said.

Nodding, Luke looked over his brave crew, giving them a smile, and hoped he looked like a calm and confident leader who'd get them out of this mess and out of here alive. He thought about finding a mirror to see if he could even convince himself. "That's not actually a bad idea, but can someone slide out and make sure he's careful? Sam is supposed to be coming anytime now, and I don't think she'd appreciate it if we shot at her and the people she's bringing to spring us. And if he sees our people out there, let me know," Luke said.

A few people chuckled. A slim woman with a pixie cut got up and headed to the window, ducking out quickly.

Someone Luke didn't immediately recognize said, "That'd be a rude welcome."

The sound of the Steyr SSG 69 cracked to life, drawing Luke's attention back toward the landing. He assumed some vamp or one of their pet wolves had been dumb enough to poke their head out so Jung-sook could remind them to be cautious, but when a second, third, and fourth shot rang out in quick succession, Luke turned around and jogged back to their font line, halting just before stepping onto the landing. Jung-sook opened fire, emptying the ten-round magazine in quick order, and grabbed another.

"They're making a break up the stairs." James handed Luke a shotgun.

Rhonda stood up from her well organized arsenal and handed Luke a couple of leather holsters. "I found something for you."

"My 311s!" Luke set down the Winchester M12 and strapped his two Stephens 311 sawed-off shotguns on, one to each hip.

Roxi stepped up and looked him over. "You're looking very martial."

Rhonda chuckled. "He kind of looks like some Roman cowboy. He shoots pretty well from horseback too, if you can consider a dirt bike a modern horse."

Luke laughed. "I guess so. I'm a decent shot from horseback with a gun. Never could get the knack of horseback archery, no matter how much my first wife tried." He shrugged. "I was a better shock troop than archer, anyway."

"Luke!" Charlie called.

Sighing, Luke slid up to the entrance of the hallway, staying off the landing and out of Jung-sook's way. "What's happening?"

"They're coming up the stairs hard, running fast. I think I saw a couple grappling hooks fly over the banister, too."

"Fuck. I'll get everyone on standby up here." Luke stuck his head out, twitching each time the Steyr went off. There were no shortage of targets for Jung-sook. "Anyone got those compact machine guns?"

Charlie held up one, grinning evilly. Agatha held up another.

"Feel free to open up. It'll be like fish in a barrel now that they're rushing up. Has anyone attempted our barriers?" The angle wasn't right for Luke to see the bottom of the staircase up to the third floor.

"Not yet," Charlie replied.

Agatha opened fire, spraying bullets down onto the second floor in controlled bursts. Charlie turned and joined her. When he turned around, several people who'd been resting were arming themselves.

"I went back and got them moving when you mentioned it," Roxi said.

He smiled at her warmly, though he could feel the weariness as his lips and cheeks struggled with the gesture. "Thanks, Roxi."

Waning tinnitus kicked back up with the constant crack of the sniper rifle and the rat-tat-tat of the APC9K compact machine guns. He worked his jaw, trying to get his ears to pop.

"Ears?" Roxi asked, raising her voice to carry over the noise of the guns and the whining in Luke's ears.

"Yeah. I fucking hate guns."

The APC9Ks went quiet.

"Luke, we're out." Charlie slid the APC9K down the hall, picking up his shotgun.

Agatha followed suit. Ammo wasn't as easy to come by in Europe, especially for things like machine guns. Owen hadn't secured a reliable source yet, though he said he was close to making a deal with some shady arms dealer. If he ever got to the other side of this, he'd be perfectly happy to never touch another gun ever again.

Rhonda grabbed the APC9Ks off the floor and stashed them out of the way in a bag so they'd be easy to tote out later. Backing away, Luke made room for a couple people whose job it was to hand reload shotguns to Charlie and Agatha. They had enough shotguns that they could keep a loaded one ready for the shooters while someone else did the reloading.

Jung-sook poked her head into the hallway. "Luke, I'm down to my last magazine. Want me to save it?"

"Five or ten?" Luke asked, not that it really mattered.

"It's a tenner," she replied.

"Let's save it."

"Want to hand me a shotgun?" Jung-sook asked.

"No, stay with the gun. We can have someone else pull a shotgun trigger." Luke hit the floor as shots thudded into the wall near his head.

"Um, they're shooting back now," Charlie said.

"No shit," Luke mumbled, sitting up. "They hitting your barrier?"

"Not yet. Gun," Charlie handed back an empty M12, its barrel smoking.

He didn't like how thin the pieces of wood they'd used were. "I need some wolf muscle."

Luke stepped into the infirmary. He'd remembered seeing them using a slab of a table to fix up wounds. Now, it was empty as everyone currently wounded was treated and out of the way.

"I hate to do this, but we need the table," Luke said.

"What if we have more wounded?" Brielle, one of Maggie's newer trained medics, asked.

"If I don't take the table, we'll definitely have more wounded. It's solid oak and thick. It'll protect our shooters from shots."

Brielle nodded, clearing off her medical supplies. With the help of James, Luke flipped the table onto its side. Spreading his arms wide, he figured there was enough room on the landing. Together, he and James jimmied it out of the room and down the hall.

"Alright, on my mark, I need you all to move and get out of the way so we can get this table down," Luke commanded, his voice straining under the weight of the thick table.

"Understood," they replied.

"Ready," Luke warned them. "Mark."

Charlie, Agatha, and Rebecca scrambled out and flatted themselves against the wall of the hall. As soon as they were out of the way, Luke and James slid onto the landing and slammed the table down, shoving it forward against their existing barrier. Then, crouching low so as not to attract unwanted bullets, they crawled out of the way, allowing their shooters to set up in their new and improved shooters' nest.

"Rhonda, how we looking on shotgun shells?" Luke asked.

She held up her hand and wobbled it side-to-side. "Not great, not if we're going to be here for a while."

Luke turned and crouched near the landing, keeping his head down. "Let's go light on our shots. We're getting low."

"Understood," Charlie replied.

Slinking back out of the way, Luke looked from person to person, seeing tension and worry on every face. All they needed was time and ammunition; they had very little of either. And now they were running out of space to defend. Up to the roof or over the sides would soon be their only options, but the house was surrounded. The vampires had committed considerable resources to this assault, and if they didn't find relief soon, it might just pay off for the vampires. He felt his breath growing shallow as his muscles tightened up.

Roxi stepped up next to him and took his hand in hers. "Luke, we'll get out of this."

He wished he was as confident as she sounded. "How do you know?"

"Because I have to believe." She looked up into his eyes, caressing his cheek. "I have to believe there's a light at the end of the tunnel. I can see it, and it's you. If I have to, I'll kill every last one of them and pull this house down in the process to save you."

Her voice sounded soft and gentle, but the words rang true. Roxi really would destroy everything to protect Luke, to save the potential future of being with each other. He drew in a deep breath, her words stiffening his spine. For Roxi, he could give no less. To get back to Maggie, he would ignite the kindling Roxi had made of the house. To see Gwen grow up safely, he'd gut every vampire—and the gods who'd made them.

"Luke," Charlie called. "They're using those grappling hooks to pull the junk off the stairs."

"Rhonda, do we have some of those bayonet stakes?" Luke asked.

"Yeah. Why? Luke, what are you thinking?" Rhonda asked, her voice strained.

Luke lifted his head and looked down the hall at everyone staring back at him. "We can either wait until we run out of ammo so they can corner us up here like rats and tear us apart, or we can remind them of who we are and what we can do to them. We can remind them why they fear us. Together, our deeds can spread terror across the world's vampires, forever making them tremble at the mere whisper of our names."

The fire of Luke's words spread down the hall, igniting the resolve of his friends and packmates as they looked at each other, nodding at their friends and loved ones, the collective strength of will and character psyching everyone up.

"It's time to bring the pain," Luke said. "Rhonda, load up every gun we can, but leave an ammo belt for three shooters. Charlie, you three are going to hold that barrier if they get past us and protect the wounded. Understood?"

"Yes, sir!" Charlie responded.

"I will not order you to accompany me, but I am taking volunteers."

As one, hands rose down the hallway.

"OK. Shooters, grab a gun and make your plan for when ammo runs out. Everyone else, pick your wolf form of choice and get ready to rumble."

Everybody started stripping their clothes, shooters and non-shooters, to save themselves the effort later. Some started their transformation, most of them going with the hulking bipedal form, though a few chose to go with the full wolf form. As soon as Rhonda divvied out the ammo to the three staying and the rest of the guns to those going, she stripped her clothes and changed into a bipedal wolf that practically dwarfed most of the others.

"So that's why they call you 'Big Rhonda.'" Luke chuckled.

She chuffed and winked at him, her tongue lolling out.

Roxi picked up a shotgun and stepped up next to Luke. "Once again, we fight together, dōšagīh."

Luke nodded and kissed her quickly, then turned to everyone. "We don't have any reload. We need to leave it here to protect the wounded. Empty your gun, then step back so the next shooters can take the lead. Once we've spent our ammunition, drop your gun and make our enemies pay. Try not to get separated from each other."

"Luke… They're getting close," Charlie called.

"Ready, Roxi?" Luke asked.

She nodded and pumped a shell into the firing chamber. Luke joined her.

"Let's go. Charlie, take three shots each to clear the stair, then move aside. We're coming through."

Nine shots fired out in quick succession, then stopped. Luke leapt over the barrier and landed on the top of the stairs, the wood groaning under foot as Roxi's weight joined his. Taking aim, he fired. Roxi squeezed the trigger, blasting a vampire running away. With each step, they fired, hitting something with every shot, killing most, but wounding many. As soon as they fired their last shells, they stepped to one side, letting the next couple take their place.

In pairs, they advanced down the stairs, then spread out on the balcony overlooking the ballroom. As soon as Luke was clear, he darted into a room and used the bayonet to stake half a dozen vampires before it broke. Hastily, he slung it around his back and pulled his gladius.

The sound of steel on steel drew Luke's attention as Roxi parried a thrust from a vampire before beheading it.

He pulled her rudis from its scabbard and handed it to her. "Top up. You're going to need it."

Nodding, she took it and hunched over the downed vampire. He stood watch over Roxi while she spoke the incantation. When the gentle white light flared, he stepped back out into the hallway to rejoin the fight now that they'd cleared the nearest room. A last few shots popped off and then were silenced as Luke's wolves dropped their guns and shifted. An automatic flared briefly before it was halted as the user was ripped in two by a furious werewolf.

The wolves advanced down the wide balcony three wide, tearing apart any vampire or enemy werewolf. A few of the wolves, bored with waiting, leapt over the banister to the ballroom below. As Luke advanced to the front, he peered over the edge to make sure they were OK. They'd formed a half circle with the wall backing them. A beachhead.

When one of the wolves fell to the ground, taken down by several vampires, Luke darted in to clean the vamps off his friend. After he finally eliminated the last vamp, the wolf was covered in goo and dust and a healthy dose of their own blood. As they stood, they stumbled, unable to hold much weight on one of their legs.

"Go to the infirmary. Now!" Luke pointed and turned around to keep up with the advance.

One of the other wolves had stepped into the downed wolf's spot, taking its turn paying back the fanged vermin that had invaded their party. While he waited for his next opportunity to engage, he took another look to ensure the wolves who'd gone over the side were still good.

"Luke!" Roxi yelled.

Luke turned as several vamps jumped out of a room that hadn't been cleared. One of them opened fire, blasting Roxi back and onto her ass as she slid across the stone floor.

"No!" Luke screamed, the corners of his vision tinging red.

Unleashing all his speed, he slammed into the gun-wielding vamp before it could turn the barrel on him, smashing him into the wall. When he'd gone in, he'd lowered his sword and skewered the vampire. He yanked it out with a nasty twist and cut a backhand slice to the nearest fanger, taking its head. Taking the gut-stabbed vamp, he shoved it into the last vamp, crashing them both back through the door. He fell on them, ending their undead existence with two stabs through the heart.

He turned to run to Roxi, but saw her on her hands and knees, wheezing and crawling toward the headless vamp.

She pulled out her rudis, and gasped out, "I know…"

Below, he heard a piteous yelp followed by a second from a different werewolf. His body went rigid. If two had gone down, the rest were vulnerable as outnumbered as they were. He ran to the banister, placed his hand on it, and vaulted over the edge, landing in the shrinking shadow of the safe space the wolves had created. Springing up, he kicked a vampire in the face, knocking them off the downed wolf, and used a second to unsheathe his rudis.

With two swipes, he decapitated two vamps on the pair of downed wolves. They could handle the remaining vamps with the odds evened. Luke stepped up into their place and unleashed a storm of blades. Luke's only care was creating carnage. Arms, heads, legs—

all belonged to him as he collected them on the edge of his swords. As the crowd of vamps tried to make space, he squatted down and eliminated two fangers, then stood back up and closed on the nearest vampires.

They'd tried to shove too many vampires in the ballroom to get to Luke and his friends. It didn't help that their assault off the stairs and onto the balcony had packed them in tighter. Now, their attempt to overwhelm Luke and his friend had backfired. With no shortage of targets, Luke allowed his anger to boil over, the fear of his glance nearly as potent a weapon as his ancient swords.

With a quick glance to his left, he saw his friends working their way down the wide stairs, ripping apart anything in their way. The sheer ferocity of their counterattack broke the momentum of the vampires who'd been attempting to take the last floor of the house.

Luke had to keep the intensity up, keep the momentum on their side. They were still drastically outnumbered, and if the vampires regained control of their forces, they could press Luke and his friends against the walls and pick them apart one at a time. The occasional gun still went off, but even the vamps must have been running low on ammo after the amount expended on their initial probing attacks and then their huge assault. Occasionally, a shot was followed by a yelp of pain from one of his wolves.

As the pain of his wolves soaked his brain, he found new levels of aggression to apply to his enemies. It wasn't until a gun went off and slammed into his chest that he slowed, staggering backward, his lungs struggling to find air. A second shot rang out, hitting the other side of his chest and doubling his breathing problem. As everything went into slow motion and he tipped over backwards, a silver streak jumped over him, accompanied by the furious, high-pitched scream of a woman.

It seemed like forever before he got the first taste of air into his lungs, but the wellspring of its beneficence encouraged more air until the spots cleared from his vision enough for him to see Roxi take up his spot, raining death with her swords. Each strike of her blades she punctuated with a curse, driving her enemies before her with word and weapon.

Struggling to get up, he forced himself over onto his knees and pushed up, still fighting to take in air. His eyes went wide as he saw vamps break from the group and streak toward Roxi. He launched himself forward, propelling himself on all fours as if he were one of the wolves he led. As he collided with the vamp, tangling in its legs, he groaned at the impact on his delicate ribs. As claw and teeth slashed at him, he struggled to keep the vampire from his neck.

Seeing his predicament, Roxi moved to assist, dispatching the vamp with a quick spin that brought her sword down through the creature's neck. With the struggle suddenly gone, Luke heaved the body off and rolled back, grabbing his swords.

Weariness dragged his body back as he tried to reengage. When he heard more shouting and gunfire coming toward him, it nearly brought him to his knees. Taking a deep breath, he rotated his shoulders and stepped toward Roxi. If he was going to be dragged down by his enemies as a new wave flooded over them, he was going to do it next to her and die alongside a woman he loved.

He didn't have it in him to shout or make bellicose sounds at this late hour; he had no energy to spare. With each swing, his arms burned, but the pain brought with it separation. He could feel the pain of his fatigue but it became diffused, as if there was a second Luke to feel the pain, allowing the main Luke to swing his arms. There was a tether between the two Lukes; he couldn't quite escape the pain, but it allowed him to turn himself into a machine, hacking and stabbing, slicing and punching, kicking and blocking.

Screams of pain washed over him as his swords made contact with his victims. The occasional punctuating grunt of exertion from Roxi accompanied the screams until the general din washed over his ears as one indistinguishable pummeling to his damaged eardrums.

When bipedal werewolves poured into several of the entrances, he nearly gave up until he recognized Pablo's form, ripping the head off a vampire. Off to the other side, he saw Simone in her bipedal form, tearing through vampires and the remaining few enemy werewolves with a bulky blade and her claws. At her side, Delilah and her jian carved bloody swaths through the crowd. Behind Pablo, a naginata poked through the door. Somewhere at its end was Sam. Their friends had arrived.

"Roxi…" Luke gasped out. "They're here. Reinforcements."

As the new arrivals met in the middle, they ensured at least one avenue of escape was open to the vampires, letting them choose to flee instead of a vengeful last gasp against the wolves.

"Do you feel it?" Roxi gasped out.

As he tried to control his breath, he couldn't make sense of her words. "What?"

"That low level presence… It's gone."

He took several deep breaths, hoping it would steady him, but as he pushed out his thoughts, she was right. He didn't know if it had been caused by the reinforcements, but the sense of wrongness hanging over him and the manor since early in the vampires' assault had disappeared. Though it should have reassured him, its absence inspired a question: what next? What other darkness would replace it? Shaking his head, he pushed it out of his mind for the moment. He'd cross that bridge when he got there.

Luke pulled Roxi toward the wall and into a pocket of quiet. They kept their swords ready and their eyes sharp as they leaned against each other, gasping for air. After all this time and work, his condition still hadn't returned to his pre-capture levels. He couldn't imagine how unfathomably tired Roxi must be after wasting away to next to nothing as the compulsion destroyed her slowly. Even after being restored, getting a few weeks of good food and exercise, and topping up on a couple vampires, she was still a shell of her former glory, but she'd given everything she had.

The last of the vampires had been torn down or fled. His legs trembling, he coaxed Roxi toward the antique wooden bench against the wall.

"Let's sit down." Luke sat on one side, the bench groaning under him.

Roxi finally let her legs go and sagged onto the other side. With their armor on, they barely fit, but it was enough until the legs and joints of the bench groaned and snapped, spilling them into a heap. Roxi let out a raspy sound that drew Luke's attention, thinking she was hurt until he realized it was the laugh of a woman pushed beyond her current capacity.

Despite his own lungs struggling to catch up, he couldn't help but join Roxi in her laughter at the ridiculousness of the two of them breaking the antique bench and their current disposition. A few nearby werewolves chuffed their wolfy laughs. As good as laughing felt, Luke couldn't keep it going as his body struggled. He prayed nothing else went wrong.

He didn't have enough in him to handle it.

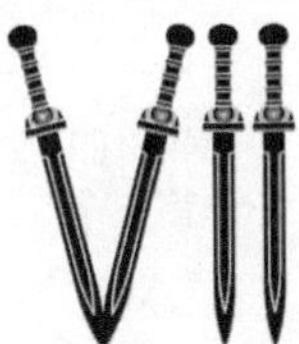

DELILAH, pushing her way through the crowd, shook her head at Luke and Roxi. "If you two kids are done playing around, we need to get this place evacuated fast. There are still a lot of vampires out there."

Off to the other side, a small commotion broke out as someone tried to push through the crowd toward Luke. A few growls broke out among his pack.

"What now?" Luke struggled to get up until Delilah offered a hand and hauled him up.

The crisp voice of Sam settled everyone down. "Let them through. They're allies."

Luke helped Roxi out of their pile of debris, then turned to see who the "allies" might be.

Sam shoved her way through the crowd, naked and carrying the huge naginata she liked to use in her bipedal wolf form. A tall blond woman and a muscular hairy man joined Sam, both also nude after making the change from their wolves.

Luke nodded at Heidi. "I believe an apology is in order, Heidi. I haven't been terribly polite to you as of late."

"We can discuss that later. I'd like to introduce you to Jean-Paul Aquitaine." Heidi gestured toward the man.

"Oh, we've already met a few times," Luke replied, a hint of mischief fighting through the weariness in his eyes.

Jean-Paul's brows furrowed in confusion. "I believe you must be mistaken. I've never met you before, and I'd remember meeting the Centurion Immortal."

Luke pulled the medallion out from under his armor, engaging it in the process. "How about now? Does this face look a bit more familiar?"

"Ah, Your Excellency, I did not realize you were one and the same." He looked at Heidi. "I was just told the Centurion Immortal needed my help against Mathis and the vampires he's been funneling money for."

Ah, ha, Luke thought. "Please, call me Luke. The title was useful for its purpose, but it's not who I am."

Jean-Paul squinted at him, tilting his head. "Are you really the Comte de Maubeuge?"

Luke nodded. "I didn't lie to you about how I came to the title, although all the names in between were pure fiction, but I do hold the title under the alias the Comtesse preferred."

They stopped when the sound of feet rushing distracted them. "Sam?" Someone said around heavy breathing. "We found explosives in the basement."

"Anyone know how to defuse a bomb?" Sam yelled, asking the room.

"Sam, let's just go. We've got to evacuate the building quickly." Luke drew in a deep breath. "People with keys, get your cars ready to go. Delilah, you organize the defense of the vehicles." He turned to the wolf who'd just warned them. "Where is it?"

"Under the kitchen, near the gas lines."

"Go, people! We're on a ticking clock," Luke yelled. "Let's get the wounded out of here. Twenty people are enough to evacuate the third floor. The rest, get outside and protect our escape route."

People exploded into motion. Sam pointed at people and stormed upstairs to evacuate the wounded.

"Luke, you should evacuate your art," Roxi said, taking his hand.

"They're just things, Roxi."

"They're wonderful pieces, and it would be a loss to the world if they burned." She stepped away from Luke and pointed at several werewolves who were milling about, still unsure what was needed of them. "Take out as much art as you can to the truck. Hurry."

They seemed to be happy to receive orders to carry out. They scurried about, grabbing paintings and statues, sprinting out toward the truck, then making more trips.

The crack of a rifle drew Luke's attention. It sounded like one of their Steyrs. Although the European vampires had preferred the weapon as well—that's who Luke had taken them from—so the shot could very well be from the vampires.

"Luke!" Someone pushed their way down the stairs and leaned over the balcony, scanning the crowd until he saw Luke. "Connor says they're trying to send in someone close to the building."

"Which side?" Luke asked.

"The kitchen, I think."

"Shit." Luke looked around, trying to get his weary brain working. "The bomb. It must be remote."

"There's a lot of stone in the foundations of this place. It could be cutting down on the range of whatever they're using for a detonator," Delilah said.

"Right." He looked up at Rebecca. "Tell Jung-sook to get up on that roof with Connor. Stop anyone from getting close to the house. Gather up a few of those grappling hooks and ropes. When we start blowing car horns, tell them to get off the roof and make for the caravan."

Roxi stood by Luke's side as they watched the activity, the occasional shot of the sniper rifles singing out. As the last of the wounded passed by, Luke stopped Sam.

"Everyone cleared out up there?" Luke asked.

Sam nodded. "Yeah. Except for the snipers on the roof. Third floor is empty."

They both stopped as the bodies of the dead, wrapped in blankets, followed the living wounded. The sound of doors slamming upstairs broke his eyes away from the dead as he looked up.

"Second floor is clear," someone called.

"Alright, let's go. Everyone to their evac vehicles," Luke yelled.

Sam sent word ahead as she joined Luke and Roxi to usher everyone out. A minute later, gunfire opened up outside, an occasional quieter responding shot answering as the vampires fired back. After fighting to survive inside the confines of the manor, the fresh air of the outside world felt like a delicious slap to the face. Luke inhaled deeply, wanting to let the clean air fill his lungs, but only coughed and groaned when his ribs strained, sending pain shooting through his chest. Two shots to his armor had probably bruised or broken some ribs—again. He should have drained a couple vamps while they waited to evacuate the wounded, but instead he'd stood there foggy-brained, watching as the wolves walked around the room, staking them all to ensure they didn't rise again to haunt the living. Hobbling along, he coughed and tried to keep from breathing too deeply.

"You going to be alright, dōšagīh?" Roxi asked.

He nodded, trying to calm his lungs and keep them from causing the muscles around his ribs from spasming. "I'll be OK."

Together, they headed to Luke's BMW while Sam took off toward the vehicle she'd arrived in. Charlie fired up the engine as soon as Luke and Roxi slid into the back.

"Charlie, lay on the horn a few times," Luke ordered.

In between the honks, Luke heard the Steyrs fire off a few last shots before going silent. A few more horns took up the call. A minute later, Luke saw two shadows shimmying down the side of the manor and sprint across to their cars as Charlie pulled into the line sweeping up the narrow driveway.

Luke's stomach felt like a pit of wriggling worms the closer they were to the break in the thick barrier of trees leading to the narrow country roads heading away from his manor.

With his mind focused forward, he nearly had a heart attack when the bombs went off in the basement of his manor house. Without Jung-sook and Connor on top to shoot anyone trying to get close with a detonator, the vamps had set off the C4. As the explosion ripped apart the gas pipes, flames spouted from the northwest corner of the house.

Twisting painfully around to look out the back windows as they sped away, stone, wood, and debris rained down, causing a few cars behind them to swerve to dodge the falling scraps of the Comte de Maubeuge's house. Thankfully, the road out was on the south side of the house. Had it been on the north side, it could have been far more dangerous and deadly to the rear of their caravan.

"I hope your insurance covers bombs and vampire damage," Ahmed said from the front passenger seat.

Luke nearly jumped out of his skin as intently focused as he was on the fire spreading through the newly renovated manor house. Normally, he'd be much more generally alert and less hyper-focused, but fatigue wore heavy on him, and they still had a ways to go before they reached the safety of the cottage.

"Yeah. I'm not sure how I'm going to write up that claim. I guess the Comte de Maubeuge really exploded onto the social scene with that party."

Everyone in the car groaned. Roxi reached over and patted his knee.

"Did…did you just make a bomb pun, Luke?" Charlie said.

"Sorry. That was terrible and I'm exhausted. I'll do better in the future." Luke shook his head in shame. "I wish we had something to drink. I'm parched back here."

"Well, if we get away safely, we can stop and get something at a petrol station," Ahmed said, looking down at himself. "I guess I'll go in, seeing as I'm the only one not dressed in steel or blood-soaked."

"There are advantages to being a werewolf. You keep your clothes clean if you don't wear them to fight." Roxi smiled through her weariness at Ahmed.

"Yeah, but now I have to fetch stuff," Ahmed replied, a smile on his face.

Luke winked at him. "It's what a good bodyguard does."

"Ha! I guess so." Ahmed turned back, facing forward.

Luke yawned, his body dragging him down as the adrenaline left his system. "I'm going to pass out here. Wake me if anything happens."

Slouching in his seat to adjust to a slightly more comfortable position—next to impossible in his armor—he jostled as the car bounced, hitting the slight bump that meant they were now on the road leading away from his burning manor. Roxi's warm hand sliding into his as she moved over to sit closer drew a faint smile to his face before he succumbed to the exhaustion.

WHEN THE BMW came to a stop, Luke woke, the first rays of sunlight conspiring with the sudden stop to drag him from the embrace of sleep.

"Where are we?" Luke asked.

"A gas station outside Mons," Charlie said, turning the engine off.

"Mons?" Luke asked, sitting up and looking around.

"Orders," Charlie replied. "Sam wanted us to split up and take circuitous routes. Once the sun's fully up, we can head back to base, as long as we're sure we're not being followed."

"The vamps should be tucking in by now." Roxi sat up and untied her armor's lacing. "Luke, be a dear and help me off with this. I need to use the restroom."

Luke helped her slide out of her armor then set it in the back, draping it on top of everything hastily tossed in the trunk of the BMW X5 M. Luke untied the thong holding his armor together, letting Roxi help him slide it off in the tight confines of the back seat. The cool air hit the sweat-damped shirt, causing a small shiver to go through Luke's body.

"There should be some change up in the console. Mind handing me some so we can use the restroom?" Luke asked.

"I'll get drinks. What does everyone want?" Ahmed asked.

Charlie volunteered to stay in the car and keep an eye on things while everyone else went into the gas station to use the restroom and get drinks and snacks. When they paid, the cashier looked Luke and Roxi up and down in their stained and torn clothes.

"It was a hell of a party," Roxi said, hoping to deflect the cashier's questions.

After they stepped out, they stood around the car, looking around.

"Luke, do you sense anything?" Ahmed asked. "Are we clear to go back to base?"

Luke twisted the top off the bottle of sparkling mineral water and took a swig, letting the exploding bubbles burn in his throat. Exhaling, he closed his eyes and cleared the sound and smells of the gas station from his mind. Nothing. Nothing tickled at even the farthest reaches of his vampy senses.

"I've got nothing." He turned to Roxi. "You got anything?"

"All clear, as far as I can tell." Roxi took a drink of her beverage.

"We all clear to go home?" Charlie asked.

"Yes. I can't wait to sink into a hot bath and soak the sweat and death off my skin, then crawl into clean sheets. So please, drive us home, Charlie." Luke reached out and grabbed Roxi's hand.

"Alright, if everyone's ready, let's mount up!" Charlie called, sliding back into the driver's seat.

Now that they wore no armor, Roxi rested her head on Luke's shoulder as they wound their way south to Dinant, then to Luke's house on the Meuse River. As the BMW smoothly ate up the kilometers, Luke found his head drifting again. The sound of Roxi's steady breathing further enticed him toward the gentle embrace of sleep. Having no reason to stay awake, he let his head drift to the right until it settled onto Roxi's hair as he drifted off.

"LUKE, ROXI? WE'RE HERE."

Luke forced his eyes open. The large house everyone affectionately called the cottage loomed in front of them. Roxi yawned and sat up straight, shimmying to the door, and stepped out. Several of the vehicles were parked around the open space between the cottage and the cliff, but not all.

While others moved about, unloading the BMW, Luke stood bleary eyed and foggy brained, exhausted from the intense battle to survive the vampire's assault on the Comte's manor. Roxi sidled up next to him and wrapped her arms around him.

"Luke. Where do you want me to stay now that I'm mostly healed?" She rested her forehead against his arm, not looking up into his eyes.

"What do you mean? Why would you... Oh." Luke wrapped an arm around her shoulder.

Now that she'd returned to some semblance of health and had a future ahead of her, she wanted to know where Luke saw her in his future. They'd been sleeping in the same bed for weeks, but maybe in her mind it was the comfort a dying person requested. The thought of asking her to sleep somewhere other than next to him hurt, and in a body filled with the aches of battle and wounds, that specific hurt eclipsed all others.

"The same place you've already been sleeping."

She smiled up at him, her eyes a mix of happy relief and sad uncertainty.

He moved, so he stood in front of her and held her at arm's length by her shoulders. "Roxiustana"—he spoke in the middle Persian they used for privacy—"now that I have you back, I don't want to let you go. There is plenty of future to talk about, but right now, I need you. Please stay with me."

She smiled, a note of triumph joining the rest of the emotions playing across her face and eyes. "I'm going to go draw a bath for us. Don't take too long." She brought his face down and kissed him before turning and heading into the cottage.

He watched her walk away, the gently sway of her hips entrancing him even though he knew she probably wasn't trying to do so as tired as they both were.

"Dude, what are you doing standing around out here when she's walking away like that?" Pablo said, stopping next to him.

"I should probably help unload and make sure everyone makes it back." Even to his own ear, his voice sounded strained and exhausted.

"Luke," Sam stopped next to them. "Go to Roxi. You two have been mooning over each other since we dragged you out of that hell hole." She sighed. "Even when I first met you, I don't think I've seen you so sad and lost than after when Roxi left. Put aside your responsibility and go be with her."

"But—"

"Luke, honey, there is no but." Sam took his hand and looked deep into his eyes. "You and I have had these conversations, and I'm going to be brutally honest with you because I love you. You're one of my best and truest friends." She paused, ensuring she had his attention. "I know you don't really think you deserve to be loved, not in a real tangible way. You're still awed by how much Maggie loves you. I see it on your face. And now, you have Roxi, and she loves you—painfully so. And you love her, and you love Maggie. You don't have to choose, Luke. Do you think Maggie's love for Zel diminished when she fell for you?"

Luke shook his head.

"You're right. Maggie loves and adores Zel. She also loves and adores you. Both things can be true. You can love Maggie and also love Roxi. Do you think love is a finite resource? I know that's what the world seems to want to tell people, but it's not true. You have the capacity to love them both in the way they deserve and in the way you deserve. You care so hard for everyone around you, but neglect yourself. Don't do that. Not with this. You'd die for that woman. You would have torn the world down for her. You were a little scary when we went to rescue her. Go be with her, truly. You can figure out how to sort out the details later, but you don't have to sacrifice one for the other. Luke, you have more than enough love for them both."

Luke pleaded with his eyes, looking at Sam, then Pablo. Delilah, who'd been standing nearby directing people, slid up and pulled Luke into a hug.

"Go to her and don't hold back, Luke. You deserve this. Now get going. You've made her wait too long. Or I'll kick your ass." Delilah pushed him back and kissed him on the cheek.

He chuckled, overwhelmed at his friends' words.

"Go, buddy. We'll take care of everything here. Go be with her and put yourself first for a change. The world will be here waiting for you after, but maybe it'll look a little more joyful when you come back to it." Pablo smiled at him, his eyes conveying his love and friendship.

Luke nodded and turned toward the house, taking the first step —then the second. As he walked into the house and through the entry way, people reached out to pat him on the back, offering words of friendship and wellbeing after they'd survived the brutal fight in Maubeuge.

Despite the burn of his thighs, he practically jogged up the stairs until he stood in front of the door to his suite. Before he could stop himself and walk in, he reached out and knocked on the door.

"Roxi? It's me." He cringed at the nervous quaver in his voice.

"Come in, Luke," Roxi's voice drifted through the door.

He opened the door tentatively and peeked in before stepping all the way in. The sound of water falling into the tub sent up a soothing noise, filling the suite with a spicy and floral scent carried on steam. Roxi stepped out of the bathroom wearing a simple white robe. Without a word, she pushed the door shut and stepped in front of Luke, unbuttoning his shirt, then helping him slide it off before she tossed it toward the closet area.

"Roxi—"

She placed her forefinger over his lips. "Shh."

She unbuckled his belt and pulled his pants down, then pushed him onto the edge of the bed so she could remove his boots and then his pants. The cool air of the suite drew shivers from his exhausted body as he sat naked, waiting for Roxi to finish. Standing, she offered her hand to him. He took it and let himself be led to the bathroom. Two glasses filled with dark beer sat on the ledge around the large tub in the middle of the floor. With her hand steadying him, he stepped into the tub and let the warm water lap at his calves and knees, then sank into it, releasing a sigh. The scent of the soap drifted up to relax him.

Reaching over, he grabbed the glass, the flick of cloth catching his attention. Roxi untied her robe and let it slide over her shoulders, then stepped into the tub, settling in on the opposite side from him. They quietly sipped their beers.

"Roxi, I love you. I just need to start with that. Know that I love you with every fiber of my being. I don't know what my future holds, but it doesn't matter to me if I can't hold you. I need you, Roxi. Now that we've found each other, I don't want to let you go. Don't leave again."

Roxi drew her legs in and slid in between Luke's, caressing his cheek before kissing him. "I'm sorry, Luke, I—"

"You don't need to apologize. It's been a hard few years for us both." He ran the back of his fingers over her cheek. "I want to be with you. I've drifted for years, going through the motions of life. It wasn't until I met Pablo and made a true friend, then I met everyone else, and then Maggie. I started feeling more in touch with the world, with myself. I've built the beginnings of a real life, but now that I've met you, I want you to be part of it—I need you to be part of it. Right now, I'm exhausted, but all I can think about is being with you and how miserable I'd be without you."

Roxi smiled, her eyes twinkling but tired. "I'm tired of drifting, Luke. In your eyes, I see a home, a place to belong. Your friends have been so kind to me—made me feel welcome. I want to be with you and fight by your side. I love you."

Luke pulled her in, kissing her deeply and passionately. When they pushed back from the kiss, they smiled at each other, drinking in each other's faces and the prospect of a future together. Roxi turned and pushed her back into Luke's chest. Reaching out to grab her beer, she took a drink. Luke curled an arm around her and over her chest, enjoying the steady rhythm of her heart as he finished his beer.

"I'm so sleepy and the water is getting cool," she said, resting her head on his shoulder.

"I could sleep for a week, if they let me. I happen to know where a warm bed is."

Standing, they toweled off and crawled under the covers, snuggling together. Roxi's body felt right against his. For the moment, the rest of the world could wait. They'd accomplished their mission for the moment, exacting vengeance and breaking up the werewolf power block the vampires had been trying to set up in Western

Europe. Roxi's body had been returned to her, and now she was on the path to recovering her strength and health.

He smiled, wanting to laugh with joy because he had Roxi and her desire to build a future with him, to join forces against their enemies and to join hearts to find joy in each other. He didn't know what tomorrow held, but today, he held Roxi.

CHAPTER
SIXTEEN

MOST PEOPLE SLEPT LATE the next day, recovering from the exertions and stress of battle. Luke slipped out of bed, leaving a sleeping Roxi, and headed downstairs to seek out coffee. After he made one for himself, he made a cappuccino for Roxi and took it upstairs to her.

When he opened the door, she greeted him with a broad smile. "Good morning, dōšagīh." She inhaled deeply. "I smell coffee. I hope that's for me."

He set the coffee on the nightstand and bent over for a good morning kiss. "There's food downstairs. People are moving about."

As if on cue, her stomach grumbled, and she chuckled. "Apparently my belly has demands. Let me get dressed."

Luke took his coffee and sat down in the chair, enjoying Roxi's nude body as she looked through the drawer set aside for her.

"Ugh, more borrowed clothes. They'll have to do. It's too cold to walk around naked." She pulled a pair of jeans and a T-shirt from the drawer and slid into them, then cinched a belt tightly around her waist to hold the baggie jeans in place.

When she finished, she took her cappuccino and practically shot it down in one go, finishing with a lusty sigh. "Damn that tasted good. I think I'll need another to go with breakfast."

Holding hands, they walked downstairs and out into the solarium where a couple of the pack had set up a breakfast station, making eggs and pancakes as well as bacon and sausage. With full plates, they joined Luke's leadership team at one of the bigger tables. It felt wonderful to sit with the people he cared about most, though he missed Gwen's presence.

Now that he and Roxi had talked about exploring a relationship, he needed to figure out how he wanted to navigate his relationship with Maggie, but he pushed that thought aside. He didn't want to bring confusing thoughts into this morning. He'd speak with Roxi. She knew he was in a polyamorous relationship with Maggie, even if he'd only been dating her. They'd figure out how to make things work, but for now, he just wanted to enjoy the good natured conversation with his friends while celebrating their victory and Roxi's return.

"How are you feeling, Roxi?" Sam asked.

"Still quite tired, but ecstatic to be alive and on the mend. It's such a beautiful day."

Sam raised an eyebrow and turned to Luke. "And you, Luke?"

"My ribs are pretty sore, but I'm feeling pretty damned amazing, all things considered," Luke replied.

Everyone turned to look at the glass walls and ceiling covered in heavy streams of rain coursing over and down the side. Sam smiled warmly, her eyes flicking between Luke and Roxi.

"It is, indeed." Sam picked up her coffee and held it over her face to cover her grin.

Delilah winked at Luke and reached out to grab Simone's hand.

"Where's Pablo and Pieter?" Luke asked.

Sam shrugged. "Not down yet that I've seen. Though they could have come and gone already."

"Well, we'll have to round them up for a little post battle confab." He sipped his coffee.

"Ah, speaking of the devils," Sam pointed toward the door leading into the solarium as Pablo and Pieter walked in together. "Good morning, sleepyheads."

They both sat and grabbed cups to pour coffee into. Pablo reached for a pastry while Pieter slouched into his chair.

"Give me a minute to finish my first cup, then we can talk," Pablo said.

Pieter nodded his agreement.

"Should we wait for Maggie?" Delilah asked. "I don't think I've seen her."

"She was up quite late dealing with the wounded. Fortunately, she had Émile's son to help." Sam refilled her coffee cup.

When Pieter's phone started buzzing, he sat up straight, setting his coffee cup down. "Let me go take this."

He walked away, then answered the phone. Since no one seemed too chatty, they waited until he returned. He strode back, looking more alert with a grin on his face.

"You look like the cat who caught the mouse," Sam said.

Pieter sat down and refilled his cup, blowing over the steamy surface. "There are still some rats to deal with, but we might have some more cats."

"Well, are you going to tell us the news, or just grin like a goofball?" Sam asked.

Luke smiled, squeezing Roxi's hand under the table.

Pieter fixed his gaze on Luke. "Apparently, after our little party broke up, Jean-Paul went to Cologne with Heidi. They are interested in meeting with the Centurion Immortal over here in order to discuss matters of importance."

Luke sat up. "That is indeed interesting. I'm amendable. When and where?"

"That's up to you. Jean-Paul is quite excited about meeting you when it's not a running battle. I've known him for a long time. I'm not sure I've ever heard him this giddy before."

"I'm not sure I'm interested in signing autographs." He leaned forward, resting his elbows on the table. "Let me run some thoughts by you, Pieter."

Pieter nodded, his brow furrowing.

"I've had a few interactions with Jean-Paul and got a good vibe from him. Is he trustworthy?"

"As long as I've known him, I've considered him a friend. You can trust him," Pieter replied.

"He did show up to help when he only thought he was helping a new acquaintance," Sam said. "That's got to count for something."

"I'm guessing both he and Heidi are fairly well known amongst the region's werewolves?"

"You could say that." Pieter chuckled. "What are you thinking?"

"If they're willing to wear blindfolds, bring them here. Tell them they can bring two escorts each, if it makes them feel more comfortable," Luke replied, sweeping his eyes around the table as his friends stared back.

"Are you sure you feel comfortable bringing them here?" Delilah paused and looked around the table, getting several nods of agreement. "Even after Jan?"

"They've both proven themselves—" Luke interrupted himself when Maggie walked in, rubbing her eyes and yawning.

"I hope there's some coffee for me. It's been a long night and short sleep," she said, taking the empty seat next to Luke.

Roxi grabbed a cup and slid it toward Luke, who snagged a carafe and filled the cup, placing it before Maggie.

"Mmm." She held it up to her nose, inhaling deeply. "Thank you."

Sam pushed the tray of pastries toward Maggie. "We were just talking about a conference with Heidi from the Rhein Pack and Jean-Paul of the Paris Pack before you walked in. Luke was going to invite them here."

"With suitable precautions. If they'll agree to it, they and their minimal escorts will be blind folded before they're brought here—"

"What if they're followed?" Delilah interrupted.

"We'll run interference and come in circuitously to ensure we're not followed. I'll leave the planning in your hands, Dee." He smiled and nodded to acknowledge his trust in her. "Plus, the Mithraeum will drive off any vampires or their toadies. And while Heidi and Jean-Paul are on the property, it will scramble their memory of the location, especially if we don't give them the passcode before bringing them here. I'm not saying we give them the keys to the place."

"Those sound reasonable." Maggie sounded unsure, either from being suddenly thrust into the conversation or from lack of sleep and caffeine. Maybe both.

Luke shifted in his chair to direct his attention to Maggie. "You lived in Paris for a while. Do you know the Paris packleader?"

"I don't know. I haven't kept up with the pack since left. I think they changed packleaders sometime after I departed for London though. What's their name?"

"Jean-Paul Aquitaine," Luke replied.

Shaking her head, she risked a sip of coffee before answering. "No. I'm not familiar with the name."

"So that takes us back to Pieter's opinion on Heidi and this Aquitaine and Luke's impression of them," Pablo said.

"What do you all think?" Luke asked.

"It's your house," Delilah said with a half shrug.

"Unless any of you have any objections, let's see if they'll go for it? It could all be a moot point if they're unwilling to agree to our terms." He waited until all his friends nodded. "Pieter, could you relay our terms, please?"

"On it." He stood up and walked away from the table.

"Do we need to bring Holly in on this?" Luke asked.

"No." Sam replied. "She knows what we're doing and trusts us. We have five council members here. That's enough to make these kinds of decisions."

Luke nodded. "Alright. So we have a plan for now." He sighed, clenching his jaw before releasing it. "While Pieter's making his calls, we should plan the memorial service for those who died yesterday."

He couldn't be sure if the rainy sky had grown darker, but his suggestion had drawn a shroud over the table as his friends looked at each other, the earlier cheer gone.

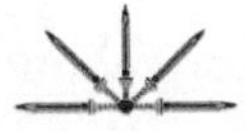

LUKE PACED NERVOUSLY around the sitting room. Though the fire burned, the few people who'd been sitting around the room opted to go elsewhere as Luke fidgeted and moved about. He tried sitting down at the piano, plucking out a few notes before pushing off the bench and returning to pacing.

Pulling his phone from his pocket, he checked the time. They should be back now with Jean-Paul and Heidi. Pablo and Pieter had signaled they were at the pickup point and were loading up, but he hadn't heard from them since. Although they weren't really that late, Luke still couldn't contain his anxiety.

When the door cracked open, he stopped, a small smile breaking out at the sight of Maggie. Her blond hair cascaded down around her shoulders. She wore a thick sweater in a Nordic pattern and curve hugging jeans.

"You're looking lovely today," Luke said.

"I look lovely most days."

Luke chuckled, a bit of the tension leaching out of his shoulders. "That you do."

"Mind if I come in?"

Luke gestured toward the love seat in front of the fire. "Not at all. Would you like to sit with me?"

"If you can stop pacing for a while."

"For you, I think I can manage it." He strode to the love seat and sat, making room for Maggie next to him.

"You're unusually nervous today." Maggie slid her hand onto his thigh.

"Yeah. I guess so." He paused. "We just really need these alliances to take some of the pressure off the pack and to stabilize the region. With so many packs falling to Le Mousquetaire, the whole west of Europe is in a precarious position."

"Especially as we try to sever the ties between the vampire-loyal packs and their overlords."

"Do you at least feel good about removing Mathis from the board?" Maggie asked.

"Yeah. That felt good. I should have put a camera in the office so

I could have recorded it as I disassembled him. Then I could play it whenever I needed a pick-me-up."

"I would have liked to see that. You're such an impressive man when you decide to be scary, though I prefer the sweet man that you are."

"Thank you." He held his hand in front of his eyes and rubbed his temples for a few seconds.

"Tired?"

Luke lowered the hand and wound his fingers through Maggie's. "Yeah. I was hoping to get a week or so of rest after everything that went down in Maubeuge. I also think I'm getting a bit of a tension headache."

"It's only been three days since everything. You should have pushed this meeting further out."

"I know, but this is too important, and I want to strike when the iron is hot. I'll be fine." Luke gave her a tired smile.

"You should take a couple ibuprofen before your meeting. You don't want to be grumpy when it's time to charm our potential allies. Your ribs could probably use a little pain relief as well."

"I guess I'd better. You are the doctor after all."

Someone knocked on the door of the sitting room, then poked their head in. "They're just coming down the ramp now."

"Thanks," Luke replied.

"I'll run up and grab a couple ibuprofen. Go greet our guests."

When they stood, he pulled Maggie in for a tight hug and a kiss. "I've missed your lips."

"Me too," Maggie replied. "Now shoo!" With a laugh on her lips, she pushed him gently toward the door.

He followed his orders and trooped down the hall, grabbing a coat and the beautiful over-sized scarf he'd purchased in Antwerp before stepping out into the biting cold. He waited at the top of the steps leading up to the entrance of his manor house. The three cars they'd sent to bring the two pack dignitaries and their escorts—plus a security team to make sure they didn't get up to any trouble— turned off the ramp and stopped in the parking area.

The security detail jumped out of their vehicles and opened the doors, helping their guests out of their vehicles.

"Can we take off these blasted masks before I vomit forth my breakfast on His Excellency's gravel?" Jean-Paul's robust voice carried easily across the short distance.

Luke nodded then descended the stairs as he made his way toward his guests. Heidi and the four attendants waited by the cars.

Jean-Paul twisted his torso, stretching after being crammed into the back of the car. "If I'd known you lived at the end of so many damned windy roads, I'd have told you to shove this mask up your ass. Respectfully of course, Your Excellency."

Luke laughed. "Just call me Luke, Jean-Paul. The expediency of the Comte's identity is not necessary at this point."

"Are you *not* a Comte?" Jean-Paul extended his hand in front of him.

Luke took it and received a hearty handshake. "I am, plus a few other titles that are meaningless in the scheme of things. Tell you what. I won't pretend to care about the proprieties if you don't."

"Deal." Jean-Paul patted Luke on the shoulder.

"So this is what your man called a cottage? I see you all like understatements."

"It's a fair bit smaller than my house in Maubeuge," Luke replied.

"Not anymore. I guess maybe if you had an ashtray large enough."

Luke shrugged. "Fortunes of war."

"You're being awfully blasé for a man who just lost a huge property. You must have the only home insurance that covers vampires."

"Like I said. The fortunes of war."

Sam stepped out of the cottage, stopping by Luke. "What he's not saying is that it's not his fortune."

Jean-Paul's eyebrows shot up.

"We'll fill it all in when we sit down," Luke said. "If you don't mind, can we switch to English? Not many of our friends speak French, Flemish, or German."

Maggie joined the small group, standing next to Luke. "Luke, I have your…" Her eyes narrowed as her jaw dropped. "Louis? Is that you?"

"Magda?" Jean-Paul asked.

Before Maggie could react, Jean-Paul moved forward and wrapped his arms around her in a fierce hug. Then he spun her around, her feet flying out in a circle.

"Louis! Put me down, you giant oaf!" Maggie said, laughing.

Jean-Paul set Maggie down, careful to stabilize her when she staggered.

"I take it you two are acquainted," Luke said.

Maggie, trying to catch her breath, returned to Luke's side, sliding her hand into his. "Yes. Louis was a very dear friend when I lived in Paris."

"I'm going by Jean-Paul now. I decided to go back to my old name." Jean-Paul smiled fondly at Maggie.

"Whatever happened to that person you ran off to London with?" Jean-Paul asked, his eyes drifting down to Luke's and Maggie's hands. "Oh, unless that's an indelicate question."

"We got married. They stayed in Portland."

"Zel has been gracious enough to keep an eye on my ward while I'm here," Luke added.

"But you two..." He pointed toward the hands, wagging his finger back and forth between them.

"We're polyamorous," Maggie said.

"Hmm, good for you. You got yourself a good woman there, Luke."

"Of that I'm sure. Shall we head inside?" Luke gestured toward the cottage.

"As long as I can get a beer after that ride."

Maggie let go of Luke's hand and slid her arm through Jean-Paul's arm. "I'll show you to the bar."

As they walked away, Luke smiled at Heidi and approached her. "Welcome to my home, Heidi."

"Thank you for hosting this meeting." She sounded a bit stiff and unsure.

He tried to fix a warm smile on his face. "Before we head in, I'd like to apologize for how I treated you. I was struggling with trust issues after...what happened."

"That's understandable. What Mathis put you through would test anyone's ability to trust."

"Thank you for coming to our rescue in Maubeuge." He extended his hand.

Heidi relaxed and shook it. "I'm glad you and Maggie are still together. You make a good couple."

"Thank you. Let's head inside." Luke led the way into the house and turned left into the bar.

Jean-Paul was already bellied up at the bar with a glass of Bavik Pils in his hand. When he saw Luke and Heidi walk in, he lifted the small glass toward them, then downed the rest, sliding the glass back to Maggie for a refill.

"What can we get you, Heidi?" Luke asked.

"You don't expect me to drink Belgian lager, do you?" Heidi winked, a smirk spreading across her lips.

Luke chuckled. "We have a lovely strong dark and a white ale. I didn't think to lay in any German beer."

"The wit will do nicely."

Maggie nodded and grabbed another glass and held it under the tap.

"Are you still bartending and waiting tables, Magda?" Jean-Paul asked.

Chuckling, Maggie handed Heidi the glass. "No. I'm a doctor now. I'm in charge of the North Portland Pack's medical team."

"She's also on the pack's council," Pieter said as he entered the bar.

"Pieter!" Jean-Paul pulled the Belgian man into a crushing hug.

"It's good to see you too, my old friend," Pieter wheezed.

Jean-Paul released Pieter from the hug, but held onto his shoulders, looking into his eyes. "I didn't get to say it at the time, but I'm sorry to hear about your father's passing. He was a great man and a good friend."

Pieter nodded, his jaw clenching. "Thank you."

Pablo wandered into the room with Sam and Jamaal. "Hey, barkeep. I'll take a pils."

"Barkeep?" Maggie replied, raising an eyebrow.

Pablo grinned broadly. "Please? Most beautiful keeper of the ales and lagers?"

Maggie rolled her eyes and filled a glass for him. Sam and Jamaal waved her off when she indicated the tap tower to ask if they wanted anything.

"Roxi joining us?" Sam asked.

"No. She still tires easily. She's opted for a nap." Luke looked around the room, counting heads. "Looks like we're all here. Do your people need any drinks?"

"Do you have a place they can warm up? I don't need them here for this," Jean-Paul asked.

Once Luke and Maggie collected the orders for the escorts, Heidi and Jean-Paul sent their people down the hall to the sitting room. Luke locked the door behind them then herded everyone toward the long table they'd assembled from the smaller tables.

"I'd like to thank everyone for being here and welcome you to my home. Since not everyone knows each other, I'll make introductions." Luke gestured toward Jean-Paul. "Jean-Paul Aquitaine is the packleader of Paris. Heidi Sauerwein is… What are you now?"

"I'm the provisional packleader of the Rhein. I mean it's a done deal, but it's still a delicate situation."

"Not alpha?" Pieter asked, raising an eyebrow.

Heidi rolled her eyes. "No. After Netzke, uh, disappeared." Her eyes flicked to Luke briefly before continuing. "I discontinued that title."

Luke was happy to hear that. Based on what Pablo and Sam had told him about the various packs, those that used Alpha and Beta terminology weren't always the best or most welcoming.

"Everyone here knows Pieter," Luke continued. "Now for my friends. All the Portland wolves are members of the pack's council, as am I."

"A human on the council?" Jean-Paul pushed his lips out and nodded appreciatively. "Very interesting."

"Pablo Sandoval is the pack's second and owner of one of the finest brewpubs in the city. Sam Wakamatsu is the wife of our packleader. Jamaal Burton is the pack's head of tech. Maggie Rabinowitz you already know, but she's in charge of the pack's medical team."

"Quite the distinguished team you've brought with you." Jean-Paul nodded. "And of course, you are the Centurio Immortalis. The immortal man and implacable enemy of the vampire."

Luke tried to fight the blush spreading over his cheeks. "Luke will suffice."

He wasn't sure he cared for the shift in dynamic. When he met Jean-Paul, the packleader of Paris had treated him as a friendly near equal. Now the man seemed to be enamored of Luke's history and reputation, forgetting they'd played cards together and evaded vampires in the Paris catacombs.

"Most of the time he's just a grumpy old guy with a cat and a kid," Pablo shrugged, winking at Luke so Jean-Paul couldn't see it.

"He's also a slightly above average poker player," Jean-Paul added.

"But he is a top tier vampire antagonizer," Sam said.

Jean-Paul chuckled. "And that is a woman directing the conversation onto the topic." He turned to Luke. "So what did you do to antagonize Robert Beaufort? Besides taking his money at the card table."

"Do you want the long version or the short version?" Luke asked.

"Start with the short version, then if I decide I want more beer, we can do the long version."

Luke made eye contact with Pieter. "Do you mind if I take this one?"

"Not at all, you know all the pieces better than I do."

"Alright." Luke looked around the table. "Stop me if I miss something. A vampire lord named Le Mousquetaire, through his surrogate in Wallonia, kidnapped Pieter's half sister and her mother. That's when Jan engaged me to rescue them which I achieved then returned home to Portland."

He took a quick drink. "Once I arrived home, the vampires started turning up the heat in Portland, eventually shipping in vampires through the ports in Antwerp and Rotterdam to Portland.

After we stopped that, Pieter was recalled home by his father. They were losing their advances in Wallonia to the vampires. They suspected a leak in the pack, so they called me in to help."

"When was all this?" Jean-Paul asked.

"It started about three and a half years ago. I returned to Belgium a little over a year later?"

"Damn. That was a busy year. Please, continue."

Luke nodded. "As soon as we hit the ground, the vampires kidnapped Pieter's father. We went into hiding to investigate and try to rescue him. We discovered they were holding him in Cambrai. We also found out that Le Mousquetaire was subverting werewolf packs and contributing to the ethnic and racial cleansing of those packs."

Luke paused for a breath and another sip. "We attempted a rescue, but the vampires had planned a multi-prong attack and took the rest of the south from the Flanders Pack. Unfortunately, we weren't able to rescue Pieter's father. Once we reconnected with Pieter, the vampires negotiated an exchange—Pieter's father for the full withdrawal of the pack from Wallonia, including Brussels."

Jean-Paul's eyebrows shot up. "That's not much…"

"Well, turns out that's not what the fangers actually wanted. We snuck in to provide a bit of cover and to get to the bottom of the vampire problem—"

Pieter stood up quickly, shoving his chair back, and walked toward the door. Luke waited until he'd unlocked it and left before he continued.

"Is he OK?" Jean-Paul asked.

"No. He's still dealing with the fallout of what happened next," Luke replied. He took in a breath and exhaled heavily. "Jan had his bodyguards subdued Pieter. Then Jan murdered his father. One bullet to the heart then one through the forehead."

"My god…" Jean-Paul covered his open mouth with his hand.

"Yeah. We barely managed to rescue Pieter and get out of the country ahead of a vampire/werewolf army. We snuck into Luxembourg with the vampires hot on our tail. Mathis gave us sanctuary while Netzke provided passports for the kids we rescued."

"Wait. What? What kids?" Jean-Paul sat up straight, looking

around the table, shock written on his face.

"The vamps had collected werewolf children from the packs they'd been subverting, including the Flanders Pack."

"So if Mathis helped you rescue those kids and provided sanctuary, why are you trying to destroy him?" Jean-Paul asked.

Luke grimaced then replaced it with a look of pure loathing. "He betrayed us—betrayed me. He sold me to the vampires. He shot me with a tranq dart and turned me over to my enemy. When I woke up, I was in a tiny cell."

Luke swallowed, a pit opening in his stomach. Taking in steadying breaths, he worked to calm his heart rate. Finally, he took a deep drink of his beer. "They'd built an arena in the mountains of Wyoming. They forced us to fight for their amusement. We were locked in that hellhole for a year and a half."

Jean-Paul's brow knitted. "You keep using the plural. Who is 'we'?"

"That would be me." Roxi pushed the door closed behind her.

Luke stood and hugged Roxi, kissing her on the cheek.

"I saw you fighting at the Comte's manor." Jean-Paul stood and bowed. "I'm Jean-Paul Aquitaine, packleader of the Paris Pack. At your service."

Roxi bowed, her long hair sweeping off her shoulders to fall in a curtain around her face before she stood. Reaching up with both hands, she pulled her hair back off her face and fixed a steely gaze on Jean-Paul. "I'm Roxiustana Surena, servant of Mithras, devotee to Selene, the terror of Tehran, the murderer of Mumbai, enemy of the vampire, and dōšagīh of the Centurio Immortalis."

"That's…that's a mouthful." Jean-Paul swallowed nervously. "Those are quite the titles."

"Some of them were given to me by my enemies. I like them." Roxi smiled sweetly, but her eyes held a threat of veiled violence. Her hand slid down, clasping Luke's.

"She can be quite intimidating when she wants to be," Sam said, smiling. "I'm glad I'm on her side."

Luke appreciated the veiled threat. Like Samantha, Roxi could be utterly ruthless when the occasion called for it. And though he trusted Jean-Paul, or was at least starting to, it felt good to have the consequences clearly out in the open.

Jean-Paul pealed his eyes away from Roxi and visibly relaxed. "So what are you going to do to Mathis when you catch him?"

"Oh, I already caught him. He's currently cooling his heels in my little prison. Along with that useless sack of shit, Netzke," Luke replied, looking toward Pieter. "Now all we have to do is finish Jan."

"Are you in, JP? Or do you not like fun?" Pablo asked.

Mouth hanging open, Jean-Paul looked around the table at a sea of serious faces, eventually stopping on Maggie. "These Americans are very plain-spoken, aren't they, Magda?"

Maggie nodded. "It has its charms. You know where they stand. At least this group." She gazed over the table, a warm smile on her face. "These are some of the finest people I've had the pleasure of knowing. You could do far worse than throwing in with Luke."

"What say you, Sauerwein?" Jean-Paul asked.

Heidi's face slipped from slightly amused to serious. "We can't sell our souls to the vampires, Jean-Paul. That way lies madness. We lost one of the great packleaders to patricide and several packs have teetered into the madness of white supremacy. That's a road Europe can't go down again. If they'll have me, I'll bring the Rhein Pack to their side."

Luke nodded respectfully to Heidi. "We're glad to have you on board."

Luke leaned toward Jean-Paul, resting an elbow on the table. "So what do you say, Jean-Paul? Do you want to bring justice to a patricide then help me hunt down the vampire that's sewn chaos and murder throughout the region?"

"But what does this have to do with Robert Beaufort?" Jean-Paul asked.

"Robert Beaufort is Le Mousquetaire's alter ego."

Jean-Paul whistled, his eyes going wide. "He's been a busy little vampire." He paused for a few moments, then shrugged. "Why not? I wasn't doing anything at the moment."

"Let's celebrate!" Pablo said. "I think I saw some Champagne behind the bar."

CHAPTER
SEVENTEEN

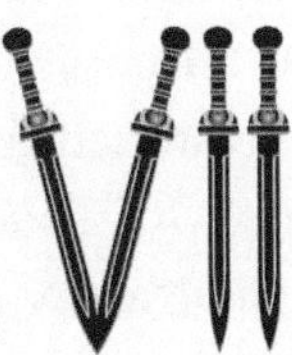

LUKE KEYED in the code leading into the section housing the prison cells. "Be careful, don't touch the walls."

"Are they electrified?" Jean-Paul asked.

"No. They'll only hurt werewolves. And I imagine vampires too, though I'd never bring one here."

"It doesn't look like silver."

"It's not. Are you sure you're ready to delve that deep into my world?" Luke stopped, raising an eyebrow.

"I'm curious."

"You know what they say about curiosity and the cat."

"I'm not a cat." Jean-Paul folded his arms across his chest.

"The power to contain my prisoners is divine in origin."

"You're not kidding are you?"

"No. What Roxi said was true. We are servants of the god Mithras and the moon goddess Selene is our protector," Luke replied.

"How can she affect werewolves?"

Luke rested a hand on Jean-Paul's shoulder. "She holds a unique place in the history of werewolves. She is their divine protector, their goddess from ancient times."

The blood drained from Jean-Paul's face. "Gods are real?"

"I don't know if all of them are, but I've met a few."

"Did she create werewolves?"

"No. That's a dark story for another time, but she did take them in, along with Artemis, when they fled their evil creators. She is kind and gracious."

Brutus shoved his head under Luke's unattended hand so he scratched the giant dog's ears.

Jean-Paul shook his head and turned around, taking a couple steps away from Luke before turning around. "You're dropping a lot of things on me."

Luke chuckled. "You came here to meet the Centurion Immortal. You're just getting the VIP meet and greet. If you'd like, I can introduce you to Selene."

Jean-Paul snorted.

"I'm serious. One minute and you'll never doubt her existence ever again."

"I'll think about it."

Luke nodded and descended the stairs to the prison level. Keying in the code, he opened the second to last door on the right. Mathis scrambled back toward the opposite wall but went too far, his back hitting the wall. He screamed and tumbled forward into a heap in the middle of the floor. After Jean-Paul stepped into the room, careful to avoid touching anything, Luke pulled the door shut.

"Good afternoon, Mathis," Luke said, holding his hands behind his back.

"P-p-p-please, sir..."

"Please what? Do you think you can bribe your way out of this? Do you think you have anything I want? I already own all your debt. I've reclaimed my sword and armor. Hell. I've even taken that little Picasso from your parlor."

Mathis cringed away from Luke, careful not to back into the wall. He kept his eyes fixed on the ground between them. "Please, Jean-Paul... We're friends... Our fathers knew each other."

Jean-Paul looked down at the sniveling coward before him and sneered, looking nauseous. "We were never friends. You only liked playing cards with me or borrowing money based on our history. I know the kind of things you said about me to people you thought you could trust."

"There's no one left who wants anything to do with you," Luke said nonchalantly.

"Gabriela will find me." Mathis sounded confident.

"When I had you kidnapped in Monaco—"

Mathis gasped and looked up before his eyes darted back to the floor.

"Oh yes." Luke grinned cruelly. "That was me. She couldn't find anyone who would loan her the money to ransom you. I was her last resort. Now I've taken her from you." He laughed mirthlessly. "You tried to sell your wife to me. She found that recording most heart-breaking. Though the photos with you and your various mistresses made her more angry than sad. She sold me your house and every-thing in it that wasn't hers. I might sell it." He shrugged. "I might burn it to the ground and roast marshmallows in its embers."

Luke squatted down, resting his forearms on his thighs. "You. Have. Nothing."

"Is there any reason to keep him alive?" Jean-Paul asked.

"That's entirely up to Mathis here. I mean, with time, Jamaal could crack all his passwords, but we have other things to attend to. So if he'd like to give me all his passwords, I might considering letting him live."

"What's to keep him from lying? He's a notorious cheat, sneak, and liar."

"Oh, he'll give them directly to Jamaal. And for everyone he gets wrong, I'll carve something off his body. Slowly."

Mathis cringed back further, looking shocked.

"Oh, you take me for a rube because I'm ancient? Because I'm not a power-hungry monster? I have no compassion or pity for you, Mathis. You sold me into slavery for things you regarded as trinkets. You sold me to garner favor with your masters. You should be grateful I'm only interested in destroying you."

Jean-Paul's lip quivered in disgust. "So his life is in his hands?"

"Jan… Jan will hunt you down," Mathis whined.

Luke snorted. "Do you think he's going to show up for you? He can barely stand you. The only reason he tolerated you is because you held the secret of his father's murder and your role in it. If you're removed from the map, he's not sending any rescue parties. He'll keep your money and celebrate your disappearance."

Mathis gasped.

"Oh, I know everything, you worthless worm. Besides, Jan has bigger things to worry about right now. Do you think he was going to escape my wrath? I wiped Netzke from the map, then you. Jan is mine for the taking. You have no one who gives a shit about you."

Jean-Paul inhaled through his teeth, making a hissing sound. "Sounds like your only hope is to appease Luke here."

Luke stood up and grabbed the door. "We'll give you time to think about it. But don't take too long. I've only so much patience for you."

"I could go for a beer, Luke," Jean-Paul said, following Luke.

"That I can arrange, my friend."

"Please," Mathis said, barely above a whisper.

Luke cupped his hand around his ear. "What? I didn't quite hear you."

"Please, Luke, I'll do anything you ask."

"Excuse me? I didn't say you could be so familiar with me." Luke's voice cracked like a whip.

"I'm sorry, sir. I'll do whatever you want."

"Good. I'll think about it and decide if it's worth letting you live." He slammed the door behind him. As he walked away, he thought he heard Mathis sobbing. A satisfied grin spread across his lips.

Without coordinating, Jean-Paul had played his role perfectly as if he and Luke had been doing bad cop worse cop for years. He also knew the display would serve as an example to the Paris packleader. Betray Luke at your own risk. Between Roxi's veiled threat and his more open threat by proxy, he almost felt bad for how he was starting the alliance with Jean-Paul, but he couldn't afford to take chances, not with so much at stake. He'd never been so close to striking at the heart of his enemy.

Once they emerged back into the weak sun and cold wind outside Luke's network of caves, Jean-Paul sighed heavily. "You and your Roxiustana kind of sapped my enthusiasm for meeting the Centurion Immortal."

Luke stopped and faced Jean-Paul. "I'm sorry, Jean-Paul. I've never been much for adulation, even when I led a legion. Don't think of me as the Centurion Immortal. Just think of me as the man you played cards with and shared drinks with. That's closer to the real me than any stories and legends. I'd rather have a friend than a fanboy. And if I can't have a friend, I'd take a reliable ally instead."

"I think I can manage friend. As long as you don't turn Roxiustana loose on me." He shivered. "She is terrifying."

Luke chuckled and held out his hand. "Friends?"

Jean-Paul shook his hand. "Friends."

Luke nodded and smiled. "Roxi is a sweetheart, but we've come through two thousand years of pain and loneliness to be together. I threatened to kill a god to save her. Neither of us will allow anything to come between us. Though we met because of my abduction, she doesn't want anyone to betray me again."

"You…you threatened to kill a god? And you didn't get smote with lightning?"

"No. Lightning is not Mithras's province. Though he took the threat seriously and relented."

"You threatened a god, and he was scared of you?" He shook his head, looking at the ground. "What have I got myself into?"

"You've started a friendship with someone with unique abilities. But you will find few more loyal friends than myself and the Portland Pack. I would kill or die for every one of the people here. They saved my life with their friendship. They gave me a reason to live."

"So you're dating both Magda and Roxi?" He chuckled. "That's a whole lot of woman between the two of them. If you've earned Magda's love and trust, that speaks volumes about the kind of man you are."

"Maggie's friendship with you told me more than my own interactions with you. I've known some exceptional women over the centuries. Maggie is special."

"I imagine with your reputation, you must have had women lining up for a chance to be with you."

"Adulation never interested me. It made me uncomfortable, even when I was a young man flush with power and responsibility. It took me over two centuries to fall in love for the first time."

"You're an unusual man, Luke."

He shrugged. "I am who I am. If you'll place your trust in me for a while longer, I'd like to share something special with you."

Jean-Paul stared at Luke for a moment, then nodded. "Why not? As the Brits say, in for a penny, I guess."

Luke turned and gestured over his shoulder for Jean-Paul to follow, leading him to the outbuilding marking the entrance to the cave and his Mithraeum. If this went well, he'd invite Heidi to visit his cave as well. He looked to the sky for the moon, but it was too early, though it didn't matter for what he needed.

My Mistress, will you meet me in the Mithraeum? I have someone I wish for you to meet. He leads a powerful pack of your children. He cast the thought into the ether.

He felt the goddess's approval as he keyed in the code for the second door.

"Damn, you've got a lot of secret doors and hidden caves. You're nothing if not intriguing. It's like you're a Roman Batman."

"It would be accurate to say I'm a Belgo-Gallic Batman. I was born about an hour's drive from here near the Hallerbos. I'm the last of my stock. They're all dead or interbred with the Germanic invaders that flooded in when the empire fell."

"Where were you when Gaul fell?"

"In the Sassanid Empire grieving for the loss of my wife Marpesia." He couldn't help the sadness that filled his voice, even after all this time he couldn't wall it off.

"I'm not familiar with the Sassanid Empire."

"Persia. They replaced the Parthians. Who replaced the Greeks who replaced the ancient Persians."

Jean-Paul laughed. "I've never heard of the Parthians either."

"You met one today. Roxi is Parthian. The last of her people. Her father was a powerful general."

"What have I gotten myself into..."

"I don't know. When you find out, let me know. I'm still trying to figure it out myself." Luke ducked into the tunnel, lowering his head to slide under the lower overhang. "Watch your head here."

He hadn't bothered with a flashlight. Selene's silver glow poured out of the cave, illuminating the way. Stopping before the entrance, he turned to halt Jean-Paul. "This is my Mithraeum. Though in truth, I spend far more time with Selene than I do with Mithras. She is waiting to meet you."

Jean-Paul swallowed and nodded, taking a step forward. Luke led the way in. Selene, standing tall and glowing gently, waited in the middle of the cave, her hands clasped in front of her.

"My Mistress." Luke placed his fist over his heart and bowed deeply. "This is my friend Jean-Paul Aquitaine, packleader of Paris."

Jean-Paul, seemly unsure what to do now that he was confronted by a goddess, bowed awkwardly.

"May I approach you?" Selene asked.

Jean-Paul nodded shakily.

The goddess towered over him but smiled gently as she brought her palm to his cheek. Jean-Paul froze, a look of awe lighting his face.

"He is a fine example of my lupine children, my brave soldier. He is worthy of your trust."

"Thank you, My Mistress. He has pledged his loyalty to our cause, at least as it pertains to this region of the world."

Selene narrowed her eyes and bent slightly, looking at Jean-Paul. *"He is nearly to the point where he'll follow you further."*

Luke's eyes widened as his eyebrows shot up. That was a shock. Jean-Paul always seemed glib. Jovial, yes, but not one to stand with in the trenches. Unsure what to say to her, he bent his neck in acknowledgment.

Removing her hand from Jean-Paul's cheek, she stepped back. "Know that you are welcome, Jean-Paul Aquitaine. You have my blessing, my child."

Jean-Paul stood, shaking. Gaining some control over himself, he bowed. "Thank you, My Mistress."

He continued to surprise Luke.

Selene took Luke's hand. "How fares Roxiustana?"

"Well. She's still regaining her strength and stamina, but she is on the mend," Luke replied.

"Excellent." She shifted to speaking into his mind. *There is still no word from Mithras on what happened to her old rudis or what the entity is, but we are searching. He is a wily and elusive one for sure.*

"We are close to moving against one of the important vampire lords. Also, I'm hopeful we can get some inside information on their network soon," Luke replied.

"That is indeed good news." She switched back to the spoken word. "It was a pleasure meeting you Jean-Paul Aquitaine. Trust in your heart and your new friends, and you should do well."

"Thank you," he replied.

"Lucius, convey my regards to Roxiustana, please."

Luke bowed. "I shall, My Mistress."

Selene's silvery glow intensified until Luke was forced to close his eyes. When the light dimmed back to the normal level the divinely powered braziers provided, Jean-Paul sat on one of the stone benches. Luke joined him, choosing a bench across from him. They sat quietly for a while.

"She's something else," Jean-Paul finally said, breaking the silence.

"She is. I've followed her since she took notice of me..." Luke paused to check his math. "Since she took notice of me almost exactly one thousand nine hundred and five years ago. Her affection has been one of my guiding lights, especially during my darkest years, and I've had too many of those."

"You're really almost two thousand years old?"

"This spring will be my nineteen hundred and thirty-sixth birthday."

"And Roxi is as old as you?"

Luke chuckled. "She's a few years younger, but not many." He shook his head, a smile spreading across his face. "We actually met for the first time that winter when Selene took notice of me, though at the time I was fleeing from her as she pursued me across the snowy mountains of Armenia."

Jean-Paul ran a hand through his hair. "What have I gotten myself into?" he asked again.

"You're a werewolf who has signed up to fight vampires. Is your world really that much bigger?"

"Yeah. I think it is. I'm sitting next to an immortal who serves a god, a real life divine being. I think that's a fair bit bigger than my world was before I walked into his cave." He stared at his hands.

"If it helps, just think of it as protecting your city and your pack. Robert Beaufort is moving on your territory and has supplanted the vampire lord you had a treaty with." Luke gestured around the temple. "The rest of this, just think of it as a brief tour through history."

Jean-Paul chuckled, then sighed. "Disassociation and delusion?"

"If that's what you need to do."

"So now what?"

"We walk back outside and plan the next phase of my campaign." Luke slapped his knees lightly, then stood up.

"And that phase is?"

"We bring down the father murderer in Antwerp."

CHAPTER EIGHTEEN

"LUKE, YOU GETTING ANY RECEPTION?" Pablo asked.

"No, we're on our own down here."

Pablo huffed. "My first trip to Antwerp, and I'm wading through the fucking sewers. I'm severely disappointed in you, buddy."

Pieter laughed. "Just be glad they converted the sewer system to pipes. This could be a lot worse."

Luke nodded. "Sorry, Pablo. Maybe if this goes well, we can get a beer later."

"Fuck!" Pablo slapped his neck. "These mosquitoes are huge."

"And mean." Luke scratched an earlier bite.

Pieter, running point, stopped and turned around. "We can always break into my brother's wine cellar, Pablo. It's full of some exceptional vintages."

"Now we're talking," Jean-Paul said. "You Belgians and Americans can keep your beer."

"Boys, we have other things to focus on right now," Roxi chimed in.

Sam chuckled. "Nice to have someone else here to help keep them on task."

Roxi smirked at Sam and gave her a wink.

"They're right," Luke said. "How far out are we, Pieter?"

"It shouldn't be too much further. A few more turns and we should be at the entrance."

Luke nervously tapped the pommel of his gladius with this thumb. "Are you sure Jan doesn't know about this door?"

"I'm pretty sure. But there are no guarantees in life. We should go silent from here."

Luke sighed, gripping the handle of his sword tightly. "Lead the way."

He checked his phone. They were running on time; he just hoped the other team was running on schedule. Grunting, he swatted another mosquito. He really owed the team an apology for this mission, but at the time it seemed like the safest option, parasites excepted.

Without the distraction of banter, he had more brain space available to worry about the other team. Ahmed, Delilah, Jung-Sook, and Simone were more than capable of leading their people, but it was their allies he worried about. Their training and abilities were unknown, with only their desire for regime change guiding things. And even that was only as strong as the weakest believer. It would only take one leak to blow this whole thing apart.

Roxi slid up next to him and squeezed his arm, giving him a reassuring look. Of course she knew where his mind was drifting. He smiled and nodded. His people were well-trained and highly experienced. They knew how to fight, but more importantly, they could improvise if things went sideways. He just had to hope they didn't get a sudden case of the overconfidence and try to force it if too many things went wrong. He firmly believed it was better to retreat and live to fight another day.

You don't win a war by dying for your country. You win by making the other poor dumb bastard die for his country. It was sage advice from General Patton and one of the guiding principles he'd learned early on in the legions. Do the job, stay in line, and kill the enemy. Going rogue meant death—both personally and for comrades.

By Luke's calculations, a left turn and a short stretch would bring them to their destination. Pieter slowed them down to keep the splashing of water down. Luke used the opportunity to give Roxi's hand a squeeze. Behind them, weapons readied and guns cocked. Reaching down, Luke made sure the tranq gun was ready to draw.

Once they made the turn, they slowed further. This section was darker, splitting off from one of the more main spurs. The added caution, though galling, was needed. Now was not the time for someone to turn an ankle or worse.

As soon as Pieter gave the signal to stop, Luke pulled down the ski mask, covering his face. The rest of the team followed suit. Pieter handed his gun to Pablo and rubbed his hands over the bricks of the sewer wall. Gliding forward slowly, Luke stopped near Pieter and watched.

Pieter signaled for more light and pointed to a spot so Luke took out the light from his belt and turned it on. Pieter huffed and moved on, pointing to another spot. They repeated the procedure a couple more times until Pieter thrust out his fist, giving a thumbs up. With both hands, he pushed on the brick he'd found. The sound of mortar grinding on brick simultaneously brought a feeling of victory and dread as he hoped no one was close enough on the other side of the wall to hear.

Luke put his back against the wall, his tranq gun out and ready. Pablo stood on the other side of Pieter similarly armed. As soon as the brick door opened enough, Pieter flashed in a light, moving it around to ensure no one waited on the other side. So far, Luke hadn't felt any vampires. A small opening, measuring about a meter by a meter, stared back at them about a foot above the water level.

When Pieter signaled the all clear, Luke, with the help of Pablo and Pieter, climbed into the opening. He stood in a narrow shaft that rose into deep lightlessness. Rusty iron rungs driven into the wall climbed into the dark. His flashlight beam disappeared as the shaft above him devoured it.

Holstering his tranq gun, he clipped the flashlight to his tactical straps and signaled he was proceeding. Carefully, he tested the rungs, making sure they'd be strong enough to hold his weight. They seemed solid. When he climbed onto the first one, he bounced a couple times. They held.

He licked his lips, the tip of his tongue rubbing over the knit of his ski mask, then started climbing. When he cleared about ten feet, he paused and looked down. Pablo was busy stripping down to his birthday suit, handing his clothes out to someone in the sewer tunnel. As soon as he wolfed into his bipedal form, he strapped on a tactical strap similar to Luke then fixed a tranq gun onto it as well as a machete. They'd found him one with a larger grip for his werewolf paw.

When Pablo grabbed the rungs, Luke resumed his climb, moving slowly. After he'd advanced maybe thirty feet, he waved his foot to signal a stop. Bracing himself, he unclipped his flashlight and shined it above him. He thought he could see something besides the shaft and rungs. It might be their destination.

He swallowed then took a deep breath. With every rung, he was careful to place each hand, each foot delicately to avoid making any noise. Werewolves had incredibly sensitive ears, even in human form. As he let the rung take his weight and lifted his hand to grasp the next one, the only warning he got was a slight groan of metal and then it snapped. He let out a startled yelp as his feet scrabbled to find purchase.

The momentum of the fall coupled with his one-handed grip twisted his body to the side. Flashlights from below skittered up and around him as he dangled precariously. When he found something to put his foot on, he desperately tried to get a grip on it, but it didn't feel solid like metal. Below him, Pablo grunted in pain—the hand Luke stepped on yanked out from under his foot, returning him to dangling. Iron rungs shoved into his side, pushing his armor segments into his ribs.

Forcing his mind to focus, he stilled his body and swung himself flat against the rungs and got a second hand onto the rung he hung from. Once he secured his grip, he carefully felt around with his feet until he found a rung. As he put weight on one foot first then both, he gripped tightly with his hands in case this one was likewise at the end of its life.

His heart thundered in his chest as he breathed heavily, secured for the moment. He wasn't sure how long he stayed there, but it couldn't have been more than a dozen or so seconds when the whispers from below refocused his attention. He'd halted the advance. Forcing his hand off the rung, he reached up and grabbed the next one, then lifted one foot and brought it up extra high.

His toe caught on something. Making sure his grips were secure he drew his foot back to free it, whatever it was tugged at his foot. Risking a look down, the broken rung, barely attached on one side, had tangled in his boot lace. No matter how he moved his foot, he couldn't untangle it.

Taking a deep breath, he moved the foot enough to rest on the portion of the run still attached to the wall and stamped hard with his foot. He heard the slight groan and crack of metal but it didn't give. He stomped again. A bit more. On the third time, it snapped off but stayed tangled in his lace.

Now that the initial adrenaline dump had lessened, he grew increasingly annoyed and frustrated with the situation. Heaving a heavy sigh, he resumed his ascension. Each time he lifted his left foot, the dangling chunk of iron bounced or scraped the nearest rung, creating a steady low-level clatter.

As he neared the top, he slowed then stopped when he reached a level where he could poke his head out of the shaft and see what was waiting. On the first look, he relied on the light spilling out of the shaft from all the flashlights below him, finding nothing but dust and cobwebs then impenetrable shadows. On the next look, he moved his flashlight's beam around. Same thing—cobwebs, dust, and distant shadows.

It looked like they were in between two old brick walls. Very old walls. They weren't the clean and perfectly squared modern bricks but the old ones dominating the architecture of the oldest parts of the city.

Ducking his head back into the shaft, he whispered, "All clear."

A few soft yips replied, acknowledging his assessment. He pulled himself out the rest of the way and took a moment to untangle the rung from his laces. He was halfway to tossing it aside when he stopped himself. Even something as simple as the ring of tossed metal could alert anyone inside to something in the walls far larger than rats. Shoving it in his pocket instead, he crawled out of the way, stirring up dust where he moved.

He reached up and adjusted his ski mask to make sure his nose was covered. An unwelcome sneezing bout would be a hell of a way to announce their presence. Before standing, he checked the head clearance. It looked like there was plenty of room. He led with the gladius, swiping the cobwebs out of his way as he went. He tried to wind the webs on his blade to clear as many as possible for the people following.

With his flashlight, he swept the beam over the ground, looking for any tripping hazards. He was concentrating on the floor so intently, he missed the low beam and whacked his forehead into it. Grunting, he pulled pack, his eyes watering. Fortunately, he wasn't moving quickly, but it still smarted.

He ducked under the beam and highlighted it with his flashlight for the people behind him. Pieter covered his mouth with a hand, his body shaking, probably in silent laughter. Luke held up his hand, leaving the middle finger up, then flashed the light beam over the hand before turning and continuing down the dark path. When he reached a junction, he waited for Pieter.

Silently, Pieter moved his beam over the corners at about chest height. When he was satisfied, he pointed for Luke to continue straight.

He nodded and moved past the junction, clearing cobwebs as he went. When he reached the end of the straightaway, he turned right, the only option other than reversing course, and proceeded, ducking under another low beam.

Sniffing carefully so he wouldn't inhale dust, he thought he caught the faint whiff of wood smoke. The further into the tunnel, the stronger the scent grew.

When Pieter grabbed his shoulder, Luke nearly jumped out of his skin, his heart rate spiking again. He scowled at Pieter's silent chuckle and shook his head. Pieter signaled he wanted past, so Luke squished himself against the wall and let his friend slide through.

Pieter gasped and hurriedly swiped a cobweb off his face. It was Luke's turn to quietly laugh at his friend. Taking a page out of Luke's book, he pulled a short sword from his hip, one he'd borrowed from Luke's enchanted stash, and swiped the way ahead of him clean. After another twenty steps, Pieter stopped and signaled for Luke to stop. He passed the signal down the line.

Pieter sheathed his sword, turned off and put away his flashlight, then squatted facing the wall to Luke's right. He carefully worked at something on the wall until he pulled a loose brick out. The scent of smoke increased as a few tendrils trickled through the brick. Swatting the tendrils out of his way, Pieter inched closer, peering through the gap he'd created. After a minute, he stood up and stepped out of the way, waving Luke forward.

He turned off his flashlight and squatted down where Pieter had just been. Luke, mindful of a potential burn, held his hands close to the bricks. They didn't seem to hot, so he quickly set a finger on one of the bricks. Warm, but not too hot. The fire must not be too big. Careful to avoid inhaling the smoke, he leaned forward and peered through the hole made by the missing brick. The the smoke and heat waves made the view look like a flashback scene from a 1960s movie.

A man sat on a couch on the opposite wall. As he scrolled through his phone, he'd occasionally reach out and grab a can of beer to pull a drink from. Luke shifted his position, trying to take in as much of the room as he could. As far as he could see, the man playing on his phone was the only one in the room.

Turning to Pieter, Luke held a hand with one finger pointed up. Pieter nodded in return. Luke set his gladius aside and pulled the tranquilizer gun from its holster, holding it up for Pieter to see. He shrugged and nodded.

Luke leaned away from the hole in the wall and took a deep breath then released it before dropping to his knees to form a more stable base. He poked the barrel through the hole then set it on the brick. Leaning forward he aimed down the sights and took aim. With a held breath, he squeezed the trigger.

The dart thwacked into the chest of the man sitting on the couch. In shock, he stared down at the dart sticking out of his chest. When he finally went to reach for the foreign object, his hands shook, distracting him from what he was doing as he stared at his trembling hands. A moment later, his hands dropped and his head slumped onto his chest. He loved the magic anti-werewolf darts Selene had blessed.

He holstered his tranq gun, grabbed his sword, and stood, moving out of the way. Pieter stepped into Luke's spot and reached up to grab a handle on a chain dangling from a rod. When Luke nodded his readiness, Pieter pulled the chain down. A faint snick of metal grinding and a final thunk told Luke it was time to go. He reached over and pushed against the brick wall. Nothing.

Putting a shoulder into it, he tried to budge it, but still nothing moved. Pieter, still holding the handle, slipped it onto a hook to keep it engaged and moved out of Luke's way. Taking a step back, he pressed his back against the opposite wall, reared back, and slammed against the wall with all the strength he could muster in the confined space.

The wall gave way, grinding open as it swiveled on a central axis. Luke's momentum carried him through the gap and dumped him in a heap on the floor. Rolling aside, he scrambled to his feet, sweeping the room with his eyes. A man, mouth open and eyes wide, stood in a doorway leading into the room.

"What the fuck?" the man hissed out in Flemish Dutch.

Luke grabbed the tranq gun from his holster like an Old West outlaw and squeezed the trigger. Nothing. He'd forgotten to reload it. Launching forward, he raised his sword. Behind him, he heard the sound of a fired tranq gun. Not wanting to chance it, he kept going, slamming into the man and crashing to the floor. What little struggle the man mustered, the dart sapped the rest of it.

Disentangling himself from the now unconscious man, Luke grabbed his legs by the ankles and dragged him into the room. Behind him Pieter, his lips clamped between his teeth, shook with laughter. Pablo chuffed quietly, his hand on Pieter's back as they laughed at Luke and his tackle.

Luke pulled out a couple zip tie handcuffs, yanked the men's arms behind their backs, and cinched them around the wrists of the two downed men. Then he cuffed their ankles as well.

When he finished, he took his tranq gun from Pieter who'd

picked it up. Removing a dart from the pouch on his belt, he reloaded it, ignoring Pieter and Pablo's mocking eyes. As soon as the last person emerged in the room, Pieter unhooked the chain and pushed the wall back into place, then showed everyone the release mechanism on this side of the wall. They tested it a few times to make sure it worked so several people could find it in case it was needed.

After Pieter's demonstration, Luke sidled up to Pablo who'd been keeping watch from the side of the door. Luke peered around the room, making sure everyone was ready.

"What's going on down there?" someone called from upstairs.

The creak of noisy wooden stairs froze Luke. Pablo slipped back out of the way as Luke pulled his tranq gun and waited. Soon, they'd get their shot at Jan.

CHAPTER
NINETEEN

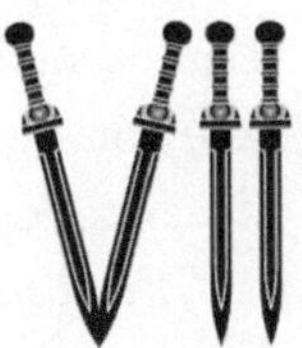

BETWEEN THE TRANQUILIZER GUNS, Pieter's knowledge of his brother's house, and the audaciousness of their sneaky home invasion, they'd taken out the first several layers of muscle milling about the lower levels of Jan's large old mansion. While the ease of the incursion would have normally been a good sign, they still hadn't found Jan.

While Pablo and Pieter swept ahead, Luke dropped back to check in with Sam who was supposed to check in with the other team once they had reception again.

"What's the word?" Luke whispered.

"Not much resistance yet. No sightings of Jan yet either."

"Damn it, where is he?"

Sam's phone vibrated, so she answered it. "They say there are people gathering outside the compound."

"Police?" His heart rate increased as his stomach twinged.

"Not that they can tell. No lights, no uniforms." Sam's brow furrowed in worry.

Luke thought about it for a moment. "Damn. You stay here and keep open the line. I'm going to see if we're almost done here."

Sam nodded and squeezed Luke's arm. As he worked his way quietly up the stairs to join the team clearing the floor above, he checked his tranq gun, not wanting a repeat of the earlier gaff. It was loaded.

Peeking around the corner, he saw several of his people waiting outside of rooms so he walked down the hall, nodding at his friends as he passed. He could hear Pieter mumbling from a door at the terminus of the hallway. If Jan wasn't on this floor, where his bedroom was supposed to be, they were quickly running out of places to look.

"Find anything?" Luke asked, leaning against the door jamb as Pieter and Pablo dug through drawers and closets.

Pieter straightened up and stretched his back. "No. This is his room. This is his stuff, but no Jan. Damn it. I wish we'd left someone conscious so I could interrogate them."

"Yeah. We were very thorough, but it seemed like the safest idea if we were going to do this without raising a ruckus," Luke replied.

Pablo took a pair of underwear from a drawer, hooked his thumb in the elastic band, drew it back, and shot it across the room at Luke. The undies fell short of Pablo's target.

Luke ignored the antics, keeping his attention on Pieter. "Are there any other secret rooms or doors or hidey-holes around here?"

"Not that I'm aware of. I only ever found the secret way into the sewers." Pieter sighed heavily, sounding exasperated. "He's so fucking slippery, the little slug. Any word from the other team?"

"Yeah, initially no real resistance, but there might be some people gathering near the property. No sign of Jan."

"Fucking bloody hell."

"Luke," Sam said, squeezing past him into the bedroom. "Delilah's getting concerned. They're getting people probing around the perimeter."

"Is there anything else we can do here, Pieter?" Luke asked.

"No. Not that I can think of. If our people are still trying to lock down the pack building, they won't have enough to stop a concerted effort to take it if they have to split forces. We need to reinforce them." Pieter hung his head, shaking it.

"Don't suppose you know a secret tunnel to get there, do ya?" Sam asked.

"Unfortunately, no."

Luke pulled out his phone. "I'll call in our evac team." He dialed the number. "We need evac. Rendezvous point three. We'll be there in five. Out."

"I'll get the crew gathered up so we can boogie." Sam exited the bedroom and started issuing orders as she passed by their teammates.

"Pablo, quit rifling through Jan's undies. We need to go. Time to take off your Wookie costume and put on some street clothes."

Pablo stuck his tongue out, then picked up Luke and moved him out of the way before jogging downstairs to find whoever had his clothes.

"He is a ridiculous man," Pieter said.

"That's one of the reasons I love him. He keeps me laughing when times are dark," Luke replied. "I'm lucky to have his friendship."

He waved Pieter ahead of him, then followed him downstairs to gather in the living room. Doing a quick head count, Luke came up two short.

"Where are… Never mind."

Two people came up from the room where they'd been stashing all the unconscious werewolves, completing their team.

"OK, everyone, let's move out to the extraction point. We're headed over to the pack house to reinforce the other team. Ski masks up. Keep it quiet and try to look natural."

Sam, waiting at the door, opened it, letting out people in groups of three or four so it wouldn't like a giant flood of people suddenly leaving the house. Luke and Pieter were the last to leave, pulling the door shut. The cold evening air felt good on his sweaty face.

With his hands in his pocket, Luke walked quietly, keeping his ears peeled for the sound of encroaching footfalls or the distant sound of a siren. Walking briskly, they covered the last couple of blocks and arrived just as a couple of vans pulled to a stop. One of them was painted to look like an ambulance, the other a large box van.

Luke climbed into the passenger seat of the ambulance and

buckled in. "Hey, Maggie. We need to get to the other team. They may be in trouble."

"Right. I'm on it." Once the doors into the cargo area were closed and people were settled, she pulled onto the street and took off.

"Luke," Sam said from the back. "Delilah reports they're spreading out toward the various entrances of the pack house."

Luke twisted his head to look into the back of the van. "Shit, I thought Pieter was with us."

"No, he's guiding the other van," Sam replied. "What's up?"

Luke held up his hand and dialed Pieter's number. "Pieter, we need a plan. We can't just go in and fight our way through on the streets."

"Yeah, that might not go down well with the locals," Pieter replied.

"Here's what I'm thinking. What's the safest, most dependable part of the building?"

"Top floor. There's only a narrow staircase leading up, but that's also the only escape route."

"Can we send everyone up there except for a couple pairs who can delay the incoming attackers as they fall back?"

"Yeah, I think we can manage that."

"Good. Tell them to tranq a couple wolves from the window before they fall back. Give your brother's forces something to think about. I want you to call Delilah and relay that plan to her. We'll be there in five minutes, but I want to go in slow so we don't attract any more attention than is necessary."

"Got it. I'll call back when I'm done." Pieter hung up.

"Dee, I'm hanging up," Sam said into her phone. "Pieter is going to call with the plan since he knows the building better."

A few minutes later, Pieter called with the confirmation.

"Almost there," Maggie said.

"We'll leave you a couple people to keep a look out." Luke opened his tranq gun, ensuring it was loaded, then moved the darts around to the easier to reach empty spots.

Maggie hit the brakes a bit too hard, throwing everyone forward. "Sorry, this is a bit nerve wracking."

Luke chuckled and squeezed her thigh gently. "No worries."

She leaned across the middle of the van and kissed him, then patted his cheek. "Do you think you should activate Selene's disguise?"

"No. I think not. They know I'm alive. I want them to know who's hunting them."

Maggie squeezed his hand briefly. "Good luck."

Luke nodded and joined the rest of the team gathering in a narrow and poorly lit alley. Roxi was the last out of the box van, giving him a smile once she saw him.

Luke winked at her, then held up a hand to gather everyone's attention. "OK, team. You know your assignments. Let's keep things quiet."

Pablo grinned, shoving his hands in his pocket. "Fly casual."

Luke snorted quietly and waved his team after him. Following Pablo's example, he shoved his hands into his pockets and walked casually. They didn't want to hurry too much. They needed Jan's people to take the bait. When they neared the turn that would take them to the Flanders Pack's headquarters, he split his group into smaller units to keep from looking like a mob descending on anyone left out to watch the outside of the building.

Strolling around the corner, he squinted, seeing three profiles lingering outside the entrance onto the pack house's estate. He drew his tranq gun, carefully keeping his body angled to minimize the chances the guards would see the movement. With a stop, he turned and quickly stashed the gun inside his coat, using his arm to keep it pinned against his side. Luke nodded to the two people with him and waited until they'd similarly stashed their tranq guns.

Luke slowed down even further as they approached the guards and pointed at a few cool looking buildings. "Hey, at least we get to see come cool buildings while we're lost. I'll ask these dudes if they can point us to the hotel," Luke said in English.

Luke picked one of the guards and approached him, giving his two teammates time to get in position. "Excuse me, sir. My friends and I are having trouble finding our hotel. Do you think you could help us?"

"Look it up on your cell phone, American, and keep moving," the guard replied.

"Sorry, but my phone is dead. It can't be far from here. You look like you know your way around."

The guard rolled his eyes and pushed off the post he was leaning against. "Fine. What's the name of the hotel?"

"I wrote the name down in my note pad. I can write your directions in it. Let me grab it." Luke slipped his hand inside his coat as if reaching for an inner pocket but wrapped his hand around the grip of the pistol and whipped it out, firing.

The dart punched into the guard's arm. He staggered back, getting wobbly, while he slurred a few Flemish curses. Luke lunged forward and swatted aside the hand trying to reach for the dart. Wrapping an arm around the guard's back, he guided the stumbling man inside the gate.

"Looks like you had too much to drink there, buddy," Luke said loudly but not loud enough to draw too much attention. "Just sit down here for a few minutes and see if that helps."

The other two guards were being similarly moved inside the wall where they could be hidden. Soon, Luke and his two partners were surrounded by the rest of their team as they filtered in and moved into the shadows. Luke took a moment to reload his gun while he counted heads. Delilah, if things had gone as planned, should have taken out the security system, but they needed to move before someone looked out a window and saw Luke and his team. He gave the order to advance.

The team piled up around the door. Luke gave the signal, and the door was pulled open, letting Luke push through, gun raised. Catching movement out of the corner of his eye, he tracked it with his barrel and fired. A glint of metal flashed toward him, so he ducked and rolled out of the way. The person following Luke in the door fired, taking the potential shooter down. Desperate to keep advancing, Luke scrambled for a dart to load. As soon as he had it, he pushed off the ground and swept through the floor, firing when needed, then ducking out of the way to reload.

Another movement from the shadows drew his eye. Tracking it

with his gun, he pulled up at the last moment when he recognized Pablo's black and red track suit. With all the teams now in the building, Luke gathered his squad and headed for the nearest stairway while the others gathered the downed Flanders packmembers and stashed them out of the way, binding their hands and ankles in the process.

Staying close to the rail, Luke crept up stair by stair. He could he hear shouting from upstairs that sounded Flemish, but he couldn't distinguish the shouted words. A handgun firing sent a spike of adrenaline through his veins. He hoped it wasn't aimed at one of his people and if it was, that it'd missed. Whoever was shooting, they needed to stop before things got too noisy and the police showed up. Maybe they'd get lucky and the size and brick construction would muffle the sounds enough for them to blend into the cityscape.

Someone popped out from the wall at the top of the stairs. Luke dropped as whoever it was darted back. He drew a bead on the place where they'd disappeared and waited. As soon as they poked their head out, Luke fired. The person screamed and pulled back out of sight. Grabbing another dart, Luke squished out of the way as the rest of his squad ran up the stairs and burst around the corner. The sound of tranq guns popping and bodies falling drew him back to his feet as he took the rest of the steps two at a time.

When Luke cleared the top step, he found three bodies on the ground, including the one he shot. He hadn't seen what he'd hit, but a dart poking of the man's cheek caused him to wince. He and Connor quickly zip tied them while their other two teammates watched over them. Splitting up, they held both sides of the staircase as the rest of the squads made their way upstairs after clearing the ground floor.

Using the tactics they'd practiced and used for years as a team from the freighter to all the house raids in Portland, they cleared the second floor with ease. As far as Luke could tell, whoever was up on the third floor was more concerned about taking out Delilah and her team holed up on the top floor.

If it had been him or one of his people, they'd have made sure the stairways were watched and guarded. But as long as Luke was fighting against the Flanders Pack, stupid enemies were better.

Luke checked his dart count and had a few of the people with extras spread them around to Luke's squad since they were about to head up to hold the stairway to the third floor. As soon as his team was ready, he stormed the stairwell, opting for a bull rush instead of a slow ascension. They needed to take the top of the stairway and hold it so their teams could make it up. If they snuck up, it might give the Flanders Pack a chance to mount a defense.

He picked his target as soon as one appeared, fired, then dashed forward, tackling a man as he raised a gun. Luke's squad followed, placing darts with precision, while Luke struggled with the Flanders werewolf, trying to keep his mouth covered without getting bit. Once someone had a hand to spare, they helped Luke immobilize the man, shooting him.

After they secured the stairway, Luke reloaded the tranq gun, then holstered it. The last team up the stairs dropped several duffel bags and opened them up, handing out shotguns loaded with the silver and wooden anti-vamp shot. While it wasn't as effective against werewolves, it still had a good shot of killing and if it didn't, it burned like hell.

Luke took his squad and headed toward the position where Pieter said the stairway to the top floor was nestled. Pieter took his squad around the other way. Every creaky floor board and every shout thickened the tension. It would only take one unlucky break to turn their plan upside down at this point.

When they burst around the last corner, Luke pumped a shell into his shotgun, the rest of his team following suit. The sound of a dozen shotguns being pumped froze the eight remaining members of the Flanders pack. Delilah and her team had done well, holding them off with their tranquilizer guns.

"We can take them. There's not that many. Let's rush them," one of the Flanders Pack members mumbled in Flemish.

Luke picked the nearest and fired, blasting his knee full of silver and wood. The werewolf dropped, screaming as wisps of smoke rose from the silver pellets. Pumping another round into the chamber, Luke took aim at the face of the one who'd wanted to rush them.

"I'll fill your face with silver if you so much as breathe in a way I don't like. Understand?" Luke asked in Flemish.

The man nodded, his eyes wide with fear.

"Someone take care of the screaming," Luke ordered.

Pieter pulled his tranq gun out and fired it, knocking the man out. After about fifteen seconds, he quieted, his writhing slowing, until he was unconscious. The wounds still smoked from the silver.

"I'm glad we understand each other," Luke said, keeping his shotgun raised. "Pieter."

Pieter stepped out of the crowd. As soon as the Flanders werewolves recognized him, the blood drained from their faces.

"Who here feels like singing?" He looked around, then pointed to one of his old packmates.

Once he made his selection, several tranq guns fired off, leaving only the one Pieter had selected.

"Karel. I'm only going to ask once. If you don't answer, try to equivocate, or lie, I'll let my trigger-happy friend over there put a round in something sensitive. Those silver ball bearings we use are big, and it'll burn right through your body. You'll never be able to heal out of that injury. You don't want to know where the second shot will go if you try to evade my question a second time. Do you understand me?"

Karel nodded enthusiastically. Luke took a step closer and aimed at Karel's knee. His eyes flicked back and forth from Pieter to the gun barrel and back again.

"I'm glad you're choosing to be smart about this. Where's my father-murdering brother right now? He wasn't in his house, and he's not here."

"He's in your father's old house. That's where he takes his whores."

Pieter reached out and casually backhanded him. "Don't call them whores, Karel. So my father's house?"

Karel nodded, his eyes wide and unblinking.

"I believe you're telling the truth." Pieter turned around, stepping away from Karel. "But if I find you've lied to me, I'll come back and pay you in kind. Now. If someone could take care of him, I don't need him anymore."

Sam stepped out of the crowd, a vicious grin on her face, and shot him in the crotch. Karel collapsed, grabbing at his groin. Several people winced. Pieter winced as well, then smirked and nodded his approval.

Delilah stepped out onto the stairs and descended. "Nice shot, Sam."

"How you doing, Delilah? Any injuries?" Luke asked.

Delilah shrugged. "Not really. They didn't come in heavily armed. Simone got winged, but it's healed already. She's more annoyed about the rip in her shirt."

"Good. Gather up your people. We're moving out." Luke patted Pieter on the back. "Great job with the plan."

Pieter nodded. "What now?"

"How far is it to your father's house?"

"About three blocks."

"Want to play it like we played this place? Sneak up on the sentinels and then clear the house?" Luke asked.

"It should work. Let me draw out the house plan."

SINCE IT HAD WORKED SO well the first time, Luke played the dumb tourist with his squad and took out the guards, hiding them behind a wall when they were done. They'd caught them completely off guard, easily clearing the first two floors.

Even without knowing Luke was alive and on the prowl, Jan's defenses should have been better. Perhaps they'd drummed out and murdered too many of their old packmates—hoisted on his own petard.

They were about to work up to the top floor—the one where the main bedroom was located—when someone burst out of a cabinet, shoved aside Ahmed, and ran toward the stairs leading up to the top floor.

"Jan! Invaders. Run. Save your life!"

Sam yanked out her tranq gun and shot the man in the back. Tripping, he thudded face first into the stairs, then tumbled down a couple steps before wedging into the wall. With a quick gesture, Luke sent two of his people to clear the stairs. As soon as the body was out of the way, Pieter dashed up the stairs, a shotgun in his hands. Jung-sook tossed Luke one. She brought her Steyr SSG69 to hand.

Luke sprinted up the stairs after his friend. Ahead, a woman's scream followed glass shattering. Bursting into the hallway, he followed Pieter into the room he'd designated as the main bedroom.

A white woman clutched blankets to her chest, her watery eyes wide with fear. Pieter stared out of a window, shards of broken glass dangling from the pane. Peering over Pieter's shoulder, Luke watched as a shadow grew smaller as it dashed away from the house. When the fleeing person, likely Jan, he guessed, passed near a lamp-post, it exposed his bare skin. Jan had jumped out of the window naked.

"Pieter, step away from the window. Jung-sook, see if you can get a shot." Luke backed into the corner as Jung-sook laid her sniper rifle across the bottom of the window and aimed at Jan. When the shot cracked out into the night, Luke smiled. He thought he heard a faint scream in the distance.

Leaning over Jung-sook's shoulder, he found the lump on the ground that was Jan van den Bergh. He turned around and waved Ahmed forward. "See where he is? Take a squad and go fetch him. Hurry."

Ahmed nodded and dashed out of the room, issuing orders as he gathered some people to go with him.

"Luke…" Jung-sook whispered.

He followed her finger to the lump on the ground. Jan moved slowly, pushing up to his hands and knees, then staggered up, stumbling surprisingly fast despite his erratic movement. He veered toward the nearest building.

"Hit him again," Luke said.

Jung-sook chambered another round and took aim, but it was

too late as Jan disappeared into a nook that put him out of reach. A couple moments later, a handful of people dashed toward where Jan had fallen.

"We should get going," Jung-sook said. "Before someone comes to see about our noisy handiwork."

"You're right." Luke turned to the woman trying to remain unnoticed in the bed. "I suggest you get dressed and get out of here. No one here is going to hurt you."

"Luke…" Jung-sook whispered, pointing to Pieter, who was still staring out the window.

Blood dripped from Pieter's hands. Gently, Luke grabbed them and flipped them over. He had several gashes in the palms of his hands. The woman, after she'd dressed, brought out a couple hand towels and handed them to Luke. He wrapped them around Pieter's hands and tied them as best as he could.

Jung-sook reemerged with a damp towel and cleaned the blood from the window and the floor where it had dripped. She must have put some soap on the towel, given the suds. Within a minute, she had the spots looking as clean as possible without doing heavy duty cleaning.

"Miss, you can follow us out. We can escort you home if you wish," Luke said in Flemish.

"It won't be necessary," she replied.

Luke nodded, his frustration growing. "Bring the towel with us."

"Right," Jung-sook replied, grabbing her rifle.

They quickly stowed the weapons in the bags, then in small groups, disappeared into the night to meet back up at their rendezvous points. Luke took one last look at the house that had once belonged to Pieter's father. Faint flashing lights caught his attention in the distance. He didn't know if they were headed to check out their handy work or some other nefarious activities, but it didn't matter. He jogged after his friends, then settled into a casual walk as they found a larger road, then found a bar that was open late and ducked inside to get off the street.

Pablo directed the silent and fuming Pieter into a table in the back corner, leaving Luke to grab beers. He was happy they hadn't taken any serious injuries, but the entire point had been to take out Jan. Luke felt for Pieter. To find his brother further defiling the memory of their father by using his former house as his love nest must be like pouring lemon juice into the open wound of his brother's patricide. At least they'd hurt Jan, sending him fleeing naked with a gunshot wound—though it would probably heal quickly once the bullet was removed. The slimy bastard had evaded his comeuppance yet again.

CHAPTER
TWENTY

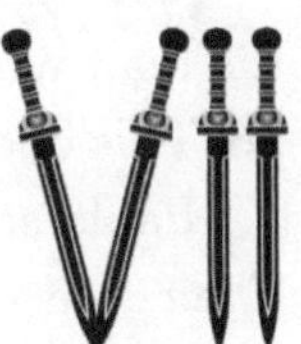

IN THE LIGHT OF DAY, the Flanders Pack house was a marvel of Antwerp architecture, hearkening back to the city's heyday at the height of the Flemish Renaissance. It had likely been a guild house back in the day, though Luke couldn't guess which.

This time when he approached the gates, he was welcomed with a smile. "Beats having to fight our way in."

Pieter chuckled. "Yeah. It does." Shaking his head, he sighed.

"You OK, buddy?" Pablo asked.

"It's weird being back without my father. The last time I was in this building, he was alive and we were trying to figure out who the leak was. Little did we know then it was the man sitting next to us—my father's son and my brother."

Pablo squeezed Pieter's shoulder. "At least we kicked him out and humiliated him in the process. I can't provide any hard evidence, but I'd like to think Jung-sook's shot hit him right in the ass."

"Maybe. Either way, we hurt him physically, but the damage to his ego will be far worse," Pieter said. "I know he'll be hurting after we've kicked his ass off my father's seat." He shook his head. "I can't believe he turned my father's bedroom into his place to meet with his mistresses."

"I don't mean to be cruel, but after what he did, did you expect him to have any sort of line in the sand he wouldn't cross?" Luke asked. "Though it seems very intentional, as if he were trying to desecrate your father's memory by using his bedroom like that. It's like your brother's still trying to prove something, mostly to himself."

"He's not my brother. I don't know who he is anymore other than the man who murdered my father." Pieter rubbed his temples. "Let's go. This conversation is depressing."

Pablo squeezed Pieter's shoulders and led him to the meeting hall. The centerpiece of the room was a long rectangular table surrounded by heavy but comfortable looking wooden chairs with cushioned red velvet seats. The largest chair stood watch at the head of the table. Someone had placed a portrait of Pieter's father—Pieter van den Bergh the elder, also known as Pieter Bruegel the Elder during his first life—on the arms of the chair to look out over the proceedings.

Luke nodded to his friends as they milled about in one corner out of the way of everyone else. Jean-Paul hadn't arrived yet. The only member of the Belgian delegation he recognized was Augustin Lusamba and the bodyguards who'd accompanied him to their meeting deep in the hills of Wallonia.

When Augustin saw Pieter, he nodded and smiled before letting his eyes drift to Luke. He responded with a cordial nod. Waving off his guards, Augustin slid through the crowd and pulled Pieter into a hug before turning to Luke. "You must be the Centurion Immortal. It's an honor to meet you."

Luke smiled slyly. "We've already met." Slipping his hand inside his shirt, he touched the medallion and transformed into the image of the man who'd escorted Pieter to the secret rendezvous.

Augustin inhaled and took a half step back. "My god..."

Luke released the image, returning to his normal visage. "Sorry for the shock, but anonymity was the order of the day. You can call me Luke. Alex was a convenient alias."

"Pleasure to meet you, Luke." Augustin stuck his hand out to shake.

Luke shook his hand, but before he could say anything. Augustin's eyes drifted toward the door and the sound of people entering the conference room. Turning to see who it might be, he smiled when the loud voice of Jean-Paul Aquitaine drifted through the door, followed shortly by the man himself.

Once he saw Luke and Pieter, he made a beeline toward them. "Pieter! So good to see you home again. Luke!"

"Jean-Paul," Luke replied.

"What are your goals, Luke?" Augustin asked. "To set up your own empire?"

Luke narrowed his eyes and focused on Augustin for a moment. "No. I have zero interest in that. I never have. If it were, I'd have marched my legion to Rome and set myself up as emperor, and we'd all be speaking Latin still."

Pieter snorted, covering his snicker with his hand.

Jean-Paul raised an eyebrow. "That's an interesting topic I'd like to dive into over a bottle or three of wine, but I don't blame my Belgian friend here for wondering. You're an intriguing man shrouded in mystery and ancient rumors."

"And were any of those rumors about my desire to rule over people? Have I ever set myself up as a ruler?" He leveled a serious gaze at both Jean-Paul and Augustin.

"Not that I've ever heard of, and I've chased down rumors about you for a long time," Jean-Paul replied.

"My only goal is to kill vampires and seek out a bit of peace and quiet in some corner of the world where I can be with my friends and be left alone."

Augustin nodded, a bit of the tension draining from his shoulders and face. "That's plainly spoken enough. I guess we should get going since everyone's here now."

Turning to face across the room, Augustin raised his arms. "If everyone can take a seat, we can get started."

Luke and his friends picked a series of seats on both sides of Pieter. Luke, by Pieter's request, sat next to him. Roxi slid into the seat next to Luke on the other side. Augustin sat on the opposite side. Looking around, Jean-Paul sauntered over to the foot of the table and sat down, the handful of people he brought taking the chairs on either side of him. There were still many spots left open at the giant table.

"Welcome friends," Augustin said by way of starting the meeting. "It's good to have such distinguished people here looking out for the interests of the Flanders Pack. First, a reminder we're recording this meeting so that people can't say we're hiding anything. I'd also like to speak to the security of this meeting. We have people posted on the roads leading into this building, plus around the property."

"I also have plenty of people nearby to call in if we need them," Jean-Paul added.

Augustin nodded politely. "Thank you. Thanks to Pieter and to Luke, we have a trained sniper keeping watch from the top floor, plus an elite team of specialists if the need should arise. With that out of the way—"

A commotion at the door interrupted Augustin. One of the people stationed at the door to the conference room strode across the room and leaned over to whisper into Augustin's ear. They whispered back and forth for a minute, then the guard stepped back.

"There is a delegation wishing to join us. They are…supporters of Jan."

Pieter stiffened next to Luke. "How supportive?"

"Were they his inner circle?" Luke asked.

"Not exactly his inner circle, but they represent a powerful voice in the pack," Augustin replied.

Luke leaned over and whispered into Pieter's ear. "Would you know if they're the kind of supporters who can be swayed?"

"Possibly. I remember the name and face of everyone who was there that night." Pieter's eyes flicked toward the door. He sat straight and addressed the room. "I'll accept their presence on one condition."

Augustin raised an eyebrow. "And that is?"

"If any of them were with Jan on the night of my father's murder, they're to be taken into custody and questioned." The muscles in Pieter's cheeks flexed as he stared across the table at Augustin.

"That seems reasonable, as long as it's a fair questioning."

Pieter nodded, so Augustin sent his guard to escort them in. As soon as they entered the room, Pieter stood, staring intently at them. The blood drained from their faces when they saw him.

"They may join us, but only if they agree to listen to the evidence and keep an open mind," Pieter said.

The small group nodded among themselves, then headed toward an empty bank of chairs that put them as far as possible from the other groups. Luke didn't hold out much hope for them, but if they wanted this to be a meeting that would start the Flanders Pack on a new path, they needed as many people to buy in and not think of this as a fait accompli.

Augustin cleared his throat. "Thank you for joining us. We want this meeting to be open to all who wish to listen and learn so that we can set a new course for this pack. I'd like to invite Pieter to recount the events leading up to Jan's assumption of pack leadership."

Pieter stood, cleared this throat, then took a drink from a nearby glass. When he could stall no more, he started in with the abduction of Amiata and her daughter Olivia-Adelisa, then he moved onto the attack of the vampires as they invaded the south with the aid of an internal leak.

When he got to the part about his father's murder, he had to stop for a moment and collect himself before going on. "Then Jan shot him in the heart and then in the head." He dashed tears from his cheeks.

One of Jan's supporters leapt up from his seat and yelled, "Lies! Jan said the vampires murdered him."

Luke stood up and starred daggers at the man until he cringed away and sat down. "The vampires are responsible, but only in the sense that they provided Jan with the support to execute this plan. Jan leaked the information to the vampires about the pack's positions in the south. He leaked his father's location so he could be kidnapped. Then he coordinated the pack's withdrawal from the south. He sealed that deal by murdering his father and turning over Brussels. Jan has manipulated you all to put himself in power."

"What proof do you have?" the man, regaining some bravery, challenged, though he kept his voice more modulated this time.

Luke smiled humorlessly at the man. "I'm glad you asked." He turned to Roxi. "Can you bring our first witness?"

"Of course, dōšagīh." Roxi disappeared from the room and reappeared a couple minutes later with Delilah, Pablo, and Sam escorting a man in heavy ankle and wrist cuffs.

They sat him in a chair and cuffed him to it.

Augustin rose and approached the prisoner. "State your name and position."

"Erik Merckx. I was Jan's bodyguard."

"Where you with Jan when our Packleader, Pieter van den Bergh, was killed?"

"Yes."

"Who did it?"

"Jan. Jan pulled the trigger," Erik replied.

"Did you witness it first hand?" Augustin asked.

"Yes. I held back his brother Pieter and kept him from interfering."

Augustin narrowed his eyes and leaned toward the witness. "This sounds cold-blooded. Was the murder of our packleader premediated?"

"Yes. I and everyone on the list I provided knew about it in advance. My job was to subdue his brother if he tried to interfere." Erik stared forward, avoiding eye contact with everyone.

The man who'd objected earlier stood again. "I'd like to ask some questions."

Augustin looked toward Pieter, who shrugged. "Go ahead, Dries."

"Were you tortured?" Dries asked.

"No. I've been treated well enough," Erik replied.

"Are you being paid for these lies?"

"They're not lies, and no." Erik seemed to stiffen as he looked toward Dries. "You won't get any more loyalty payments from Jan. The money is all gone. There's nothing left, so sit down and shut the fuck up, Dries." He looked away from Dries and stared angrily at the wall.

That seemed to shut Dries up for the moment as he sagged back into his chair. Those surrounding him seemed to pull away from him as if he suddenly stank.

Pieter stood up. "Why? Why did my brother want to do this?"

Erik sighed. "He was tired of waiting and he thought that if your father turned the pack over to anyone, it would be his golden boy son—and not Jan."

"I've never wanted to lead the pack. I would have let him have it."

"He didn't want your charity. He wanted you to bow to him."

Pieter sank into his chair and rested his head in his hands.

"Do you have any more questions, Augustin?" Luke asked.

When Augustin shook his head, Luke had the man returned to his cell. They brought Mathis back with them. Like Erik, he was in chains, though looking more disheveled and dirty after spending a lot of time in Luke's prison cell.

Augustin started his questioning of Mathis Heinen, and Mathis sang, spilling everything about his dirty web of lies, corruption, and murder. How he'd approached Jan on behalf of Le Mousquetaire. How he'd funneled money to Jan and helped set up the network of vampires to do Jan's secret bidding. How he'd suggested to Jan that he should be the packleader, and how to take power.

Dries seemed content to listen to the litany of crimes stacked at Jan's door now that he'd learned his loyalty payments weren't coming anymore. As the French and Belgian werewolves listened to Mathis's confession, they grew more and more disgusted as their faces went from neutral to holding a mix of sneers and nauseous expressions. The web Mathis created was truly epic in its scope, with the single focus being his own enrichment and aggrandizement.

Luke found it ironic that Mathis had gone to such lengths yet had squandered it all before his fall. He'd used the money and power to try to gather more power, but Luke had stepped in and sucked up his debt, throwing the whole delicate juggling act off.

When Mathis was done spilling his guts, the once robust man looked deflated. Luke's lips curved into a satisfied smile as he stared maliciously at the former Luxembourgian packleader. Luke had taken everything from the man and now all he had left to give was his life, though Luke wasn't sure how he wished to spend that yet.

Luke stood and walked over to Mathis, squatting in front of him so he could look into the man's eyes as he stared at the floor. "Does anyone have any more questions for this maggot?"

When Luke heard no more questions, he directed Roxi and his people to take him back to his cell.

One of the wolves loyal to Augustin raised a hand. "Will the Flanders Pack be allowed to try and punish him for his crimes?"

"No. His fate belongs to me, but rest assured, he will pay for his crimes." The intensity of Luke's voice and expression quieted any attempts to counter him. When he thought everyone was clear on Mathis's disposition, he called in Jamaal, who handed out thick binders to everyone at the table. "This is Jamaal. He is our tech expert and has been inside both Jan's and Mathis's computer systems."

Jamaal smiled and nodded. "Thanks, Luke. The binders before you contain a selection of both the financial transactions linking Mathis and Jan, as well as their email communications. In the pocket is a thumb drive with the complete forensic breakdown covering all the mischief they got up to—if you need to see the full details."

"How…how did you do this?" Augustin asked.

Jamaal grinned broadly. "I've been in the Flanders Pack's computers for two years, since we were invited to help investigate the leak. I found all kinds of things when I nosed around. Mathis, he was stupid enough to give us his Wi-Fi password. Then we put some pressure on him, and he was more than happy to provide the passwords we needed."

"It's a web of corruption that links packs throughout the region, small and large, including the Rhein, Flanders, Luxembourg, Bordeaux, Nord Pas de Calais, and more." Luke turned to Jean-Paul. "You'll even find some names from your pack. Given time, Le Mousquetaire and his surrogate Mathis would have tried to topple you as well to install their puppet."

Jean-Paul shifted uncomfortably, much of his usual confidence and bravado replaced by fear and shock.

Luke turned to address Augustin. "I don't know if you've had time to look, but Jamaal can work with you to protect your system and help you take it over. You'll also find that the Pack's coffers are empty, as are Jan's personal accounts."

Augustin started back in his seat as if Luke had struck him. "What…what happened to it? So much money comes through the ports…"

"To be blunt. I took it all." Luke looked to Jamaal. "And every penny that's coming in is flowing right back out to end up in safe accounts we set up."

"The pack is ruined." Augustin covered his open mouth with a hand as he stared in shock.

"No. Jan is ruined," Luke replied. "Pieter will be in charge of the money and will repatriate it to the Flanders Pack once Jan's toadies are ferreted out and dealt with—minus some expenses used to bring down Jan."

Augustin found his confidence again, turning to Pieter. "Is this foreigner installing you as our new packleader as a condition of returning the pack's funds?"

"No," Pieter said. He stood and looked to Luke and Pablo and the rest of the Portland wolves. "I'm not interested in leading this pack. It's time for new blood to take over. I'm content with my place in Portland. When this is over, I want to live a quiet life with my friends and help Amiata raise my half-sister. I might take up painting again. The memories here are too painful. But I will help you form a transitional council until the pack can decide its own future."

Luke's eyes opened wide in shock. He hadn't expected Pieter to fully commit to his life in exile from the Flanders Pack, but he was also glad he'd get to keep his friend nearby.

Augustin exchanged a respectful nod with Pieter and stood. "Jean-Paul, what's your role in all of this?"

"Pieter's father was my friend, and I want to see justice. Also, it appears I now have a much more personal stake in this venture. I can provide some extra muscle that will aid the transitional council. Though, once Flanders is stabilized, I'd ask for your alliance and aid in helping stabilize the smaller packs around France that have strayed from the light."

"What is going to happen to Luxembourg?" Augustin asked.

"Heidi Sauerwein of the Rhein Pack is currently working with the council there to stabilize things since Mathis is currently unavailable," Luke replied. "She is also currently leading the Rhein Pack since Netzke's disappearance.

"Did his disappearance have anything to do with Mathis and Le Mousquetaire?" Augustin leaned his butt against the table and crossed his arms.

"Not as deeply as some, but he was taking money to let the vampires move freely through his territory. His deeds are tied in with Mathis's crimes against me. His fate is not your concern."

"What crimes? Am I in danger of suddenly coming down with a case of the crimes if you decide you don't like me?"

"Only if you conspire with vampires to do harm to me or mine. Other than that, I don't care what you do. I've come and gone for centuries without bothering the werewolves of the world. But make no mistake, if you strike at me, I will strike back." He exhaled sharply and loosened his shoulders as he tried to soften his expression. "Augustin. This is the land of my birth. This is the first time in nearly two thousand years I've interfered in the local packs, and that is only because they directly attacked me and orchestrated my kidnapping on behalf of Le Mousquetaire and his masters."

He paused for a moment. "If you don't want to have anything to do with me, you'll never see or hear from me. I'll come and go as I always have—just another tourist traveling through."

Augustin relaxed some and uncrossed his arms. "That's fair enough. Pieter trusts you, and I've always trusted Pieter and his father. I'm sorry for accusing you of bad intentions."

"Apology accepted. I'm sorry for being terse with you."

Pablo laughed. "You're very good at being grumpy."

Luke grinned at his friend. "Hush, Pablo."

Augustin nodded at Luke. "Very well, Luke. I appreciate your candor. So where does that leave us?"

Luke shrugged. "That's entirely up to you and your transitional council. I think we've provided all the evidence you need to prove to the pack that Jan was not acting in its best interests and, in fact, was doing some pretty sinister stuff. You have plenty of his flunkies to interrogate to corroborate our evidence. Jamaal will turn over access to the pack's systems so you don't have to break through Jan's security."

Luke gestured toward the Paris Packleader. "Jean-Paul has graciously offered some folks to help you secure the transitional council. Me and my friends, we have a rendezvous in France with Le Mousquetaire, so we'll be otherwise occupied."

Pieter stood up. "You have your pack back, Augustin. You can return it to a place where all are welcome. The money we used to bring down Jan is a pittance, so the pack won't have to worry about financial ruin when we move the money back into the pack's accounts. My family's time leading the pack is done. Take the Flanders Pack into the future."

"What about those of us loyal to Jan?" Dries said.

Augustin's face hardened. "That depends on whether you renounce your loyalty and come clean, though some crimes are unforgivable. If anyone was involved in the murder of packmates, in the kidnapping of our children, then forgiveness will be hard to find."

"This sounds like an internal matter, Augustin," Luke said. "If you have no need for me or my friends, we will depart. Though, Mathis will be coming with us. We have mighty deeds that are yet undone."

"Thank you, Luke. I hope I speak on behalf of all in the Flanders Pack in extending our thanks and that you will someday renew your acquaintance with us so that we might build a friendship," Augustin replied.

"Fairly spoken. I look forward to that day. But in the meantime, on behalf of the North Portland Pack, I can make an offer of alliance for such a time as the Flanders Pack is ready."

Jean-Paul stepped up to Luke's side. "And you have Paris's friendship as well. Don't hesitate to call on me."

"Thank you, Jean-Paul. And thank you for the extra hands. They are much appreciated." Augustin shook Jean-Paul's hand, then Luke's.

Taking their cue, Luke's friends stood up and followed him from the conference room along with Jean-Paul and his people while Pablo grabbed a couple people to go fetch Mathis.

"We're headed back to my cottage to get ready for our move to France. You're welcome to join us, Jean-Paul," Luke said.

"I'd love to, but unfortunately, you've created a bunch of work for me, and I'd better return home to mobilize my people. We'll need to gather the disaffected wolves of France if we're to unite all the packs against Le Mousquetaire," Jean-Paul replied. "But when you arrive, please let me host a dinner for you and your friends."

Luke nodded and smiled. "It's a deal, my friend. I'll see you in Paris. Though we might make a small diversion to wine country first."

A wicked grin spread across Jean-Paul's face. "Bordeaux?"

Luke's grin matched Jean-Paul's. "Bordeaux."

CHAPTER
TWENTY-ONE

LUKE LOOKED out over the valley toward an elegant château surrounded by ornately landscaped gardens, a faint smile playing across his face. Roxi's scent alerted him to her presence just before she slipped her arm around his waist.

"It's a very lovely estate," Roxi said. "It seems a shame it's infested with vampires."

"Indeed," Luke replied, wrapping an arm around her shoulder. "I forgot how beautiful Bordeaux is."

"Luke," Pieter called. "I've got it set up if you want to inspect it."

"I'm sure it's fine. Your training is more recent than mine." He turned to Roxi. "Shall we, my love?"

Roxi nodded and took his hand, leading him to where everyone else was clustered.

"I've got the range set, and a blank to test the range so we can keep quiet until we're dialed in," Pieter said.

Luke nodded. "Everybody, step back please." When they'd stepped back to a safe range, Luke nodded at Pieter.

Pieter took the first round and dropped in the mortar blank, ducking after releasing it. A second later, the mortar round flew out of the tube with its characteristic explosive crack. Raising binoculars to his eyes, he watched the château. As the mortar round arced down, it bounced off the roof, falling behind a wall surrounding the château.

"Nice shot, dude," Pablo said. "Can I have dibs on the first live round?"

"Maybe we should let Owen go first," Sam said. "He's the one who procured the weapons and was gracious enough to meet us here with the mortar."

Owen, his arms folded across his chest, nodded at Sam. "I'm good, but thanks for thinking of me, Sam."

Luke patted Pablo on the shoulder. "Sorry, Pablo. Simone deserves the first round."

"That's true." Pablo squeezed Simone's shoulder.

"Pieter, set the round for impact detonation." Luke waved Simone forward. "Simone, the first live round is yours, if you'd like it. No pressure if you're not interested."

She looked back at Delilah who nodded back. Turning back to Luke, Simone's answering grin was vicious. She stepped forward and knelt next to Pieter as he gave her a quick lesson on what to do. She took the live round and dropped it into the tube, ducking as the mortar flew into the air.

With held breaths, they stared at the château in the valley below them. The answering explosion rocked them back as debris and black smoke spouted from the roof of Le Mousquetaire's château. Simone's face glowed with the wide smile the explosion had caused.

"I think Luke and Roxi deserve the next rounds," Sam said. "They also owe Le Mousquetaire for the arena."

"Roxi?" Luke gestured toward the mortar.

"Why thank you, dōšagīh." She walked up and took the round Pieter handed her and dropped it in, ducking as the mortar round flew out.

This time when the round exploded, flames burst out, catching a few spots. Luke took his turn, sending up another incendiary round. This one dropped through the previous hole, a ball of flame rising from inside the château and out of the destroyed roof. They had three rounds left, so Pieter adjusted the aim to undamaged portions of the château. Pieter took one, then Pablo finally got his chance. Delilah was offered the last one, but deferred to Simone, allowing her girlfriend to take the last shot at the vampire that had corrupted her pack and killed her parents.

After she dropped the last one in and watched it explode, tears shone on her face, the emotion of exacting vengeance from the vampire who'd tormented so many of them there overwhelming her. Delilah enfolded Simone in her arms, letting her cry.

"Do you think we got him?" Sam asked.

"Le Mousquetaire?" Luke shrugged. "Maybe. Probably not. But a house for a house seems fair."

"We better pack up and get out of here before someone shows up to check on our handy work," Pieter said as he and Owen took down the mortar and gathered the tubes the mortar shells had come in.

"Alright, do you have your selected route?" Once he saw the team nod, he smiled. "I'll see you all back in Paris for our dinner with Jean-Paul."

They scrambled down the hill and through the woods toward the tiny road they'd parked off of. Delilah and Simone joined Luke and Roxi in their rental car. As soon as belts were buckled, Luke took off. Everyone had their own escape route planned. They didn't want it to look suspicious for a group of cars to be traversing away from the site of so many explosions. Feeling cheeky, he hit play on La Batteria's "Vigilante" as they sped away.

JEAN-PAUL PULLED out all the stops for them, having his chef and sommelier prepare a gorgeous multi-course meal. Luke and Roxi joined Paris's packleader and his wife at the head table—along with Maggie and Sam—sharing wine and laughs. Jean-Paul insisted on watching the video Sam had recorded of them bombing Le Mousquetaire's chateau several times.

"I wish I could have been there, but alas, there's just too much going on with calling in all the unhoused werewolves of France. We've even set up an industrial lathe to make stakes." Jean-Paul shook his head and giggled under his breath, watching the flames spread over Le Mousquetaire's home yet another time.

They dined late into the night, doing heavy damage to Jean-Paul's wine and liquor stores. Gradually, people snuck out to go to bed or find other adventures for their night in Paris. Saying goodbye for the evening, Luke hugged Jean-Paul and kissed his wife on the cheek before taking Roxi back to their hotel room.

After the exuberance of the day, Luke and Roxi fell into each other's arms to continue their celebration in a more personal manner. When Luke finally fell asleep, it was covered in sweat and with a smile on his face as Roxi curled into him, already asleep.

LUKE CHECKED his phone to see what time it was. It was hard to tell under the steely gray clouds of winter that blanketed Paris. He was thankful it had been a few days since the last snow—the roads and sidewalks were well worn. It was hard to hide movements in fresh snow.

"Are you sure you remember the right mausoleum?" Ahmed asked.

Luke turned his head slowly toward Ahmed and blinked steadily, his mouth drawn into a thin line.

"Right. Sorry. Just nervous."

"Do you have a problem with caves and underground spaces?" Roxi asked.

"They're not my favorite, but I can manage them. It's just this place was something else, and being trapped down there with so many vampires last time… It kind of felt like I might not ever see the light again." Ahmed shivered.

"I'm sorry, Ahmed. If you need to, you can return to headquarters. Another guard on duty there wouldn't go amiss." Luke felt bad.

He hadn't checked in with the team after their trip into the Paris catacombs. They'd always bore up well no matter the circumstances, but perhaps the trip deep into the underground maze of the catacombs and mines of Paris was something a bit different from the usual fare of houses and street fights.

Ahmed stiffened his spine. "Thanks, Luke. But I have a job to do and a team to look out for. I can manage."

Luke nodded and patted Ahmed on the shoulder. "OK."

Roxi squeezed his shoulder and said something to him in Arabic. It was too quick for Luke to understand with his extremely rusty and limited knowledge of the language. Whatever it was, Ahmed grinned at the friendly gesture.

Luke waved the team in closer, as if he were a tourist guide gathering his wards. "I want to give everyone a fair warning. It's going to be dark and confined in there. We'll be doing deep under the city through winding tunnels. Each of you has a GPS with a programmed path on it. If you get lost, trust it to get you back to the path. The radios will have limited reliability with so much stone surrounding us. Rely on your teammates. Rely on your friends. We'll get through this by working the plan and taking care of each other, like we always do."

The nods and pats among friends as well as mumbled encouragement told him the pep talk had worked and been needed. This wasn't like any of the other missions they'd run, and it was his failure as a leader to not acknowledge it earlier. Roxi slid her hand into his as they resumed their walk toward the cemetery he'd visited on his last trip to Paris.

"And if you get desperate, go wolf and follow the scent trail," Sam added.

"Well spoken, dōšagīh," Roxi said to Luke in Middle Persian. "They needed a little something extra."

"Thanks. I should have noticed it earlier. Give me a heads up if I'm missing something going on around me. I've been working with them for quite a while and have gotten used to their calm professionalism. You're new to working with them and can provide a new perspective," Luke replied in the same language.

"What's that language?" Ahmed asked. "It's got some vague hints of Farsi."

"Do you speak Persian?" Roxi asked.

"Not really. I dated a Persian man for a while and he taught me some."

"It's middle Persian, though not my native dialect of Pahlavi or Parthian." Roxi laughed. "I'm still trying to teach Luke to speak a proper tongue."

"How did you learn middle Persian, Luke?" Sam asked.

"After Marpesia died, I moved to the Sassanid Empire for a while and learned it while I lived there, though enough people spoke Latin and Greek that I didn't learn the native language as well as I could have. I wasn't in my best frame of mind for a long time." He smiled sadly as Roxi squeezed his hand. "But it's the language Roxi and I first communicated to each other with in the arena. It has come in handy since we're the only two speakers left in the world."

"I mean, there could be some vampires that are that old and from that part of the world, though I've tried my best to ensure I'm the last native speaker." She bumped into Luke affectionately as they walked. "I thought I was losing my marbles when I heard a voice through the stone wall speaking a language from my youth."

Luke chuckled. "To be fair. I think we both were losing our marbles by that point. Finding you saved me."

"Finding each other saved us both, dōšagīh."

"What does that word mean? The one you keep calling Luke." Sam, with eyes narrowed, grinned knowingly.

"Beloved," Roxi replied.

A few people responded with an "ahh."

Sam patted Luke's arm. "I thought it had to be something like that. No one puts that kind of emotion into word and have it mean something pedestrian."

"I'm sure you have all kinds of Japanese pet names for Holly," Luke said.

"That is true."

Pablo nudged his way into the lead group. "Ha! Our boy Luke has come a long way since he was oblivious any time someone flirted with him. He's practically a real smoothie. I mean, he's no Casanova like me."

"No one is like you, Pablo," Sam said.

"That's probably a good thing. We'd never get anything done if you were all unbridled raw sexpots like me." Pablo hooked his thumbs in nonexistent suspenders and pulled them out.

That got a fair share of chuckles, laughs, and groans—a pretty average mix for a Pablo joke. No wonder Pablo made such an effective number two to Holly. He could defuse the tension in any situation and was a good balance for her serious demeanor. The lighthearted banter had gone a long way to helping the group relax as they navigated the streets of Paris.

Taking in a deep breath, he held it, letting it flex his lungs as he savored the scents of the city. A nearby cafe smelled of espresso and baked goods. Somewhere near, a restaurant sent the aroma of grilling meat out into the city. He'd much rather be in one those places with his friends than leading them into the city's catacombs where the dead outnumbered the living on the order of hundreds of thousands to one, and that was just the bones stored there. Luke had no idea how many vampires infested the tunnels.

Luke held up a hand to catch everyone's attention. "OK, team, let's keep it quiet from here on out. We're getting close to the cemetery. If you want to ask touristy type questions, go for it. It'll help us blend in and look like a tourist group, but other than that, lips sealed. The fangers may be asleep, but they have other servants, including those with ears as good as yours."

Maggie might have been able to perform as a better tour guide since she'd lived here much more recently, but she was currently with her medical team ready to respond to the needs of the pack. Though this time, she had the entire Paris Pack's medical team to assist her. She was enjoying her time, reacquainting herself with some of the friends she'd made during her years here.

When they approached the cemetery, Luke slowed down and pushed out with his senses but picked up no vampires. He doubted one would brave the surface or hiding in a mausoleum to serve as sentinel, but it was always better to be cautious. He waited until he received the signal from Sam that none of them scented anything in the area that might give them pause—including other werewolves.

He turned to address the team. "Alright team. You know the plan." A vicious grin spread across his face. "It's time to go fuck up a vampire's whole night."

TWENTY-TWO

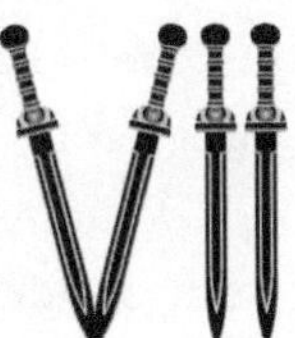

THE METAL DOOR of the mausoleum clanged lightly onto to the blanket wadded up on the ground to catch it as it fell. Waving the scent of acetylene out of his face, he checked to make sure no one was coming to see why someone was using a cutting torch to slice their way into a mausoleum.

Luke hated to do damage to the structure, but the crossbars the vampires had affixed to the other side made it a necessary evil. Once they judged it cool enough, a team of werewolves picked it up and moved it out of the way. Flashlight beams swept around the inside of the mausoleum, stopping on the empty sarcophagus. Sword in hand, Luke stepped in first to make sure there weren't any security features or booby traps. When he gave the all-clear, he stepped outside so the muscles could address the sarcophagus's lid. It opened easily, but it wasn't empty.

The stench of putrefying flesh rolled out of stone box, driving the werewolves out of the tight confines of the mausoleum as they gagged and coughed. Luke stared into the sarcophagus, anger rising in his gut. The bastards could have just sealed the sarcophagus, but instead, they murdered someone and stuffed their body in the box. He didn't know if it was meant to serve as a warning or just to be a brutal reminder of who lived through that door. Somewhere off to the side, someone vomited.

Pulling out his phone, he stepped into the mausoleum, doing his best to hold his breath. He took several photographs of the body, focusing on anything that might identify the poor person. It might just be some random Parisian, but he doubted it, not if this was directed by Le Mousquetaire.

"What are you doing, Luke?" Delilah asked, her scarf held in front of her nose and mouth.

"Playing a hunch. This probably isn't a victim of chance." He texted Jean-Paul and warned that gruesome pictures would be incoming. When he got the OK, he sent the images.

While he waited for Jean-Paul's response, Luke stepped outside to get some fresh air. A moment later, Jean-Paul sent his reply.

"He's going to send in a medical team. Apparently they have a coroner in the pack," Luke said.

"Are we supposed to wait?" Sam asked.

"No. We're going to need to move it. Hand me that blanket we used for the door. Also, I'm going to need a volunteer. Someone who isn't squeamish. And those gloves."

Sam gathered up the blanket and gloves, handing them to Luke.

Roxi followed him into the mausoleum, taking one of the pairs of gloves. "You sure know how to show a lady a good time."

"Not sure handling a cadaver is on the top ten list of Parisian dates, Roxi," Sam said from a safe distance away.

Luke and Roxi did their best to lift the remains from the sarcophagus and lay them on the blanket. Though even Luke had trouble handling the guts that tumbled out before they could get the body onto the ground. Gritting his teeth, he piled them onto the blanket while Roxi stepped out of the tight space to get a breath of fresh air. When only bloodstains were left in the stone box, he covered the remains with the sides of the blanket. With Roxi's help, they lifted it out and set it out of the way.

Everyone studiously avoided looking at the covered body.

"What's next?" Sam asked.

"I need the chainsaw," Luke replied.

Although it was a battery-powered chainsaw, it was still a long way from being silent, especially when he cut into the wood the vamps had used to block the entrance into the tunnels. Still unwilling to go completely without caution, he pushed the chain down in the middle and let the tool do its job. When he cut through without meeting resistance, he moved to the edge and started cutting. He almost didn't notice the scent of burning until he realized his chainsaw wasn't gas powered and spewing exhaust.

He smelled petrol and burning.

"Get down!"

Everyone scattered.

Luke dove out of the mausoleum and rolled out of the way as an explosion sent stone and smoke spraying out the door. Luke's ears whined as he coughed and blinked smoke from his lungs and eyes. Shaking his head, he rolled onto his butt and knocked the debris from his hair.

"Everyone..." He shook his head again and rubbed his ear. "Everyone OK? Any injuries?"

Once they reported in, it looked like a few scratches, cuts, and bruises were the worst of it. Using the corner of the mausoleum, he stood and peered inside. The sarcophagus was rubble and the inside of the walls were pitted with dents and chips, but the structure had held. If it hadn't, the injuries would have been far worse. All the explosive power had focused through and out the door. The crypts and statues directly across from it were a bit worse for wear.

Smoke still rolled out of the door, though progressively less. Someone took off their jacket, using it to waft the smoke out to clear the mausoleum.

"Anyone have a flashlight? I appear to have misplaced mine. Also, we need to post a couple people and keep an eye out for cops. We're pretty deep in the cemetery and the building contained most of the explosion, but someone's bound to come investigate." Luke took the offered flashlight and stepped into the mausoleum, being careful where he put his feet so he wouldn't roll an ankle on debris or fall through a weakened floor.

Where the entrance into the tunnels had been a clear door, now it was a ragged mess, but fortunately, the stone steps underneath looked relatively unharmed. The explosive charge either wasn't that well set or wasn't that big—maybe both. Either way, Luke and his team had been lucky.

"How are we looking, Luke?" Roxi asked, poking her head in.

"OK, I think. We'll need to be careful and watch out for booby traps along the way."

"It's going to slow us down to crawl." Roxi pursed her lips and shook her head.

"The cave coming down on top of us would slow us down a lot more," Luke replied.

Roxi folded her arms in front of her chest. "Yes, but that doesn't mean I have to like it."

"Let's head down. You and I can scope it out. Grab another flashlight."

Roxi disappeared and reappeared a moment later with two flashlights. "I'll check high, you check low?"

"Right." Luke took in a deep breath and exhaled noisily. "Here goes…"

The steps near the tunnel entrance were covered in chunks of stone of various sizes. He did his best to scoot them carefully out of the way without knocking them into the unknown, where they could trigger a trap they hadn't found yet.

Once he was under what had been the bottom of the sarcophagus, he ran his flashlight's beam along the bottom edge. Based on the burn marks and debris, he found where the explosion had been set. Then, he finished the circuit, stopping when the beam moved over a gray lump and bits of metal. Edging closer, he found a lump of C4 that hadn't exploded.

"Everyone, back up and get out of the blast zone. I found more explosives," Luke called out of the hole in the floor.

Returning his attention to the bomb, he examined it closely, finding the detonator. He inched his hand closer and carefully gripped it before slowly extracting it from C4. He sighed in relief, a bit of tension leaving his body. He double checked that there wasn't another, then pulled a knife from a sheath on his belt and pried the C4 away from the stone. With a quick look over, he didn't find any other detonators hidden in it, so he tossed it into the dark, then set the detonator on the ground. Grabbing one of the rocks the other bomb had made, he brought it down hard on the detonator, smashing it to open. Just to be on the safe side, he did another sweep with his flashlight, finding nothing.

He poked his head out of the hole and called, "All clear," before dropping back down into the hole to descend a few stairs.

Roxi and her flashlight joined him a moment later.

They'd taken thirty steps when a flashlight alerted them to someone's presence. "Psst, Luke. Roxi."

Luke turned around carefully. It was Pablo.

"What?"

"Sam says they hear some sirens in the distance. What do you want to do?" Pablo asked.

Luke made eye contact with Roxi. The look of steely resolve he got back from her matched his. Down seemed like the safest way to avoid detection by the authorities. Besides, tonight, their destiny was under Paris.

He looked up toward Pablo. "Pack up the tools and gather everyone up. We're going in."

"What about the body? The police will find it up here."

"Shit." Luke bit off more curses. "I guess we have to bring it with us. We'll stash it in a safe place where it can be retrieved later. Tell Sam to let Jean-Paul know to have his team back off for now. We don't want them blundering into the cops if they are indeed coming this way."

"Right," Pablo said. "Should we prop the door up so it looks closed? We'll have to leave a couple people on the outside to do it."

Roxi set her hand on Luke's shoulder, then turned to Pablo. "Just rope it around the top the of the door and pull it up from the inside. If the rope gets pinched, cut it and push it down to the gap to pull it through."

"What she said. Roxi and I will move ahead as quickly as we can to clear the way." Luke saluted Pablo casually.

"Have fun! Don't let us catch you making out in a dark side tunnel." He made kissy noises as he departed.

Roxi checked to make sure Pablo was gone. "Is he always like that?"

"You have no idea. He makes me laugh, though, and is a true and loyal friend."

"I guess I'll have to earn his approval."

Luke chuckled. "You already have his approval. You have everyone's approval, not that you need it."

She grinned, then reached out and grabbed him by the back of the neck and kissed him intensely. "Be careful. I don't want to stitch your body back together again."

Butterflies exploded into his stomach. He tried to speak but came up empty. Clearing his throat, he nodded and resumed their descent, though they picked up speed. They were nearly to the bottom before Luke called a stop.

He squatted down, flashing his light onto a taut wire stretched across a step a couple down from where he stood. He followed the line of wire to both sides of the stairwell, a faint reflection of something dark and metallic drew his attention. Checking the step below it, he moved down slowly, setting one foot on the step above the wire and one on the step below it.

"What do you have there?" Roxi asked.

"Can you put your beam right here?" Luke pointed with his flashlight's beam.

With Roxi's added light, Luke found the business end of the booby trap. He handed her his flashlight so both his hands were free. Working carefully, he extracted a fragmentation grenade from a hole in the wall, careful to keep the spoon depressed. After he secured it, he pushed the pin the rest of the way back into its hole to render the grenade safe. He took out the multi-tool on his belt and clipped the wire from the pin then tossed the wire out of the way. He exhaled heavily to expel some of the tension; Roxi, probably for the same reason, sighed as well.

"That was nice of them to leave us a grenade," Roxi said.

"Yeah. I'll be sure to give it back to them." He stashed it in his belt pouch for later retrieval.

"You're a very thoughtful man."

The approaching flashlights of the rest of their team told them it was time to get moving. They resumed their trek down the stairs, finding nothing. Once they reached the bottom, they continued down the tunnel that lead straight from the stairs.

Luke hated the slow progress the booby traps necessitated, but at least he and Roxi were moving quickly, their ability to work well together reasserting itself.

"Luke. Stop." Roxi moved her flashlight up to a nook in the rough stone ceiling, highlighting another frag grenade.

"I don't see the trip wire." He swept his flashlight further down the tunnel, stopping when he saw a glint about fifteen feet in front of him. "I think that's it. Am I clear to move forward?"

Roxi double checked the path ahead with her beam of light, then brought it back to the ceiling. "Go ahead."

Luke licked his lips and inched forward, trying to keep his heart rate down and his eyes focused on finding any hint of a trigger for the trap that might be closer than the suspected one. When he arrived at the wire he'd spied a moment ago, he stopped and ran his light along the length of the wire, finding its anchor. Then he followed it up into the darkness of the ceiling and found where the wire had been anchored with eye bolts.

"How does the pin look, Rox?"

"I'm seeing more of it exposed than I'd like to, that's for sure."

"Should we clip it and tie it off? Or do we try to lower it and secure it?" Luke asked, staring at the wire that ran along the floor.

"Either way, it's going to jiggle the grenade. It'll probably be smoother if you clip the wire, then lower it slowly."

"Right." He pulled out his multi tool and grabbed the wire, careful not to pull it. "Ready?"

"No, but it's not like we have a choice."

Taking a steadying breath, he gripped the wire tighter and slowly placed the wire cutter along the wire. "Clipping now."

The wire slipped from his hands and zipped forward. Lunging

forward, he grabbed it before it slipped through the first eyelet and out of his reach. He could feel the vibration of the grenade wobbling on the other end.

He panted heavily, his heart thundering in his chest. Roxi's heavy breaths joined his.

"Luke. The pin pulled a bit further. It's just barely hanging in," Roxi said, panic tinging the edge of her voice.

"OK. I'm going to lower it slowly." Reaching forward with this other hand, he gripped the wire after the eyelet and let go of the other end of the wire. He scooched closer to the wall and stood up, careful not to jostle the wire. "Here we go."

He slowly lowered the grenade, keeping his movement as smooth as silk until it dangled just above Roxi's head. She reached up and wrapped her fingers around the grenade and secured the spoon in place. He gave her more slack on the wire as she lowered it and shoved the pin back through the hole.

"I nearly had a heart attack." Roxi handed the grenade over to him.

"I still might." He wiped the sweat from his forehead. "That was more excitement than I was looking for from this portion of the evening."

Pablo, a grin on his face, stopped when he reached them. "What's the matter? You two taking a break? Too much work for you old fogies?"

"Hush, you," Roxi said, giving a fierce and friendly scowl.

"Disarming booby traps is nervous work, Pablo. You're welcome to take the lead if you'd like to, though. We'll catch up to you, or the pieces of you, eventually."

"Nah. I wouldn't want to deprive you two of all the fun you're having." Pablo leaned against the wall and waggled his eyebrows.

Luke shook his head and turned away from Pablo, pulling Roxi along with him. Without a word, they resumed their sweep. When they found the first junction in the tunnel, Luke pulled out the GPS map he'd made during the first time down here and checked it.

Once he had the direction, he waited for Pablo to catch up again and posted him there to direct everyone into the correct tunnel.

Hitching a thumb over his shoulder, Pablo asked, "Should we stash the body in this side tunnel?"

"No. If the cops discover the door and come down this way, it's the first turnoff. Not the best hiding spot," Luke replied.

Giving Roxi's hand a squeeze, they resumed their hunt for booby traps, except what they found wasn't an explosive, but a freshly constructed stone wall. Luke carefully tested the mortar, looking for weaknesses.

"What do we do? Do we try to find another way?" Roxi asked.

"No, that could be a bigger danger than this wall." He sighed through his clenched teeth, rendering it into a frustrated hiss.

Roxi wrapped an arm around his lower back and pulled him into her. "We'll get there. Then we'll get to repay them for all the annoyances they've caused us along the way."

He snorted. "I do like the way you look at the world."

"I may be sweet to you and your friends, but there's a reason the fangers call me the Terror of Tehran. I'm more than happy to remind them why."

A smile tugged up at the corners of his lips as he stared into Roxi's eyes, his gaze half-lidded. "You're an incredibly sexy woman, do you know that?"

"I do, but it's nice to hear it from your lips." She leaned forward and kissed him.

Someone coughed behind them. "Not sure this is the time and place…"

"Sorry, Sam. Luke was just telling me what a sweet, polite lady I am."

Sam snorted. "I heard what you were saying. You're terrible, Roxi."

Roxi grinned at Sam. "Aren't you glad I'm on your side?"

"Very much so." Sam turned to Luke and gestured with her head toward the wall. "Want me to bring up the sledges?"

"That might be the quickest way, though we'll have to be careful not to bring the whole thing down on our heads in the process."

The wall brought everyone together in one clump, so Luke moved them back while Pablo and Connor changed into their bipedal forms and took sledgehammers to the top of the wall. The added height and strength of their bipedal wolf forms worked nicely to knock the rocks back onto the other side of the wall, though the smashing of rocks was an unfortunate noisy side effect. By Luke's memory, he thought they were far enough back from the vampire's circus that it shouldn't be a problem, unless they had werewolf patrols. No plan was perfect, and sometimes they had to make adjustments.

In short order, they had a significant chunk of the wall torn down. After another couple of minutes, Luke called a halt. The space cleared would work well enough. Pablo, still in his wolf form, climbed through and started handing stones back through to Connor who set them out of the way. When Pablo was finished, he stuck his paw through and gave them a thumbs up then waved them through.

Roxi and Sam went through to work ahead, leaving Luke to guide the team through, including the body. He wished they'd had time to make a stretcher, but they'd be able to ditch it shortly. After a few more turns and side tunnels, Luke decided they'd taken the body far enough. He swept ahead, looking for booby traps, but found none. Once they dropped the body off, Luke and the two carrying it rejoined the rest of the team. He was glad to be rid of the poor cadaver, a feeling probably more than shared by the two who'd carried it all the way from the cemetery.

Luke moved through the pack until he reached Roxi and Sam at the front and called a halt. It was time to gear up for the next phase of the mission.

TWENTY-THREE

LUKE SLUMPED to the side and brought his leg up to dangle over the edge of the throne. Roxi, her sword laid bare across her lap, slouched in the smaller throne next to his, her feet propped up on the table in front of them. Six heavy oak tables flanked the central table they were using, three to each side. A series of blood bags were laid out on the wood surface. They'd placed a lantern on the table between them to provide some light while they waited for the vampires to show up. Even in deep dark tunnels like these, vampires still preferred to sleep during the day.

"It's past sunset, and I don't feel any vamps. Want me to take care of the bags?" Roxi asked, uncrossing her legs and recrossing them on the table.

"We can do it together."

Roxi chuckled and stood up. Slowly, she stabbed the point into the bag and then twisted the blade to open it up more before proceeding to the next one. Luke, following her example, opened the ones nearest him then returned to his seat. The coppery tang of blood permeated the air. If it was this strong to his only slightly enhanced supernatural sense of smell, it would be salivatingly enticing to the bloodsuckers.

It didn't take long. A few minutes after opening the bags, Luke felt the first twinges of approaching vampires, the feeling growing more oppressive as more drew near.

"You feel them?" Roxi whispered.

"Yeah. Hard not to."

Luke resumed his casual and disrespectful position in Robert Beaufort's throne. "Did I tell you about the little entertainment they threw when I was last a guest here?"

"Was it better than the entertainments we were part of in the arena?" Roxi asked.

Luke snorted, pushing back the hollow feeling conversations about the arena always brought to the surface. "Yeah. This time, I got to sit in the audience."

"Are you still struggling…from the arena?" Roxi asked, her voice tentative.

"Yeah. It's hard not to when so much of what we're doing right now forces those memories to reside just below the surface. I've never really had a chance to put these feelings into perspective. It's like I'm dragging them along with me all the time."

She nodded. "Yeah. The only thing keeping my panic at bay right now is the fact this cavern is so big and you're here next to me." She reached down and gripped the handle of her sword. "And I have my tools with me."

"We'll get through this together—" He held up his hand to halt the conversation.

"Yeah, I feel it too," she whispered.

The sensation of vampire was drawing tighter like a noose slowly shrinking, though the vampires weren't fully surrounding them. The strongest presence was coming from the back right portion of the massive cave and spread to both sides of that point to a weaker degree. The tunnel they'd come from as well as the one Jean-Paul was using still felt clear.

Wanting to add sauce to the display, Luke grabbed a bottle of wine he'd set by his chair and opened it, pouring it into two wine glasses. He handed one to Roxi and kept the other for himself.

"Here's to you, Roxi, and a successful venture."

"Together, we can do this, dōšagīh," Roxi said, clinking her glass against his.

After a sniff of the wine, he took a drink, savoring the rich, brambly flavors of the southern Rhone wine. Even for a charade, he couldn't bring himself to settle for a cheap bottle. "This is quite good."

"I know. Excellent choice."

"It doesn't feel right to toast to our evening plans and do it with an inferior wine."

Roxi laughed. "You're a ridiculous man."

"I am who I am."

A light flicked on toward the back of the cavern, highlighting the irregular entrance to the tunnel. Another light joined it to the right, quickly followed by another to the left. A moment later, silhouettes moved into view and out into the main cavern, though they filed around the edges instead of crossing the floor to investigate the lone lantern illuminating the two trespassers sitting on Robert's and Antoinette's thrones.

"They don't seem too curious," Roxi said.

"No. They're probably waiting for someone with some authority to come tell them what to do. Low level henchmen rarely want to make decisions that could result in their own punishment." He knew the vampires could hear them with their supernatural hearing. They weren't speaking quietly.

"Their ilk rarely displays any kind of bravery until they're in large numbers when they can bully others." Roxi winked at Luke and took another drink of the wine.

"They only have their soul removed when they're made into vampires, not their spine."

"What use is a spine without a soul to stiffen it?"

Luke laughed, adding more to it than he otherwise would have for effect, though Roxi's cutting comment had earned the laugh.

From the main tunnel, the fangers blocking it created space as a single silhouette emerged from the depths. A moment later, Robert Beaufort—Le Mousquetaire—strode from the tunnel, through the gap opened by the other vampires, and continued toward the center of the cavern.

"You're sitting in my chair," Le Mousquetaire said, stopping about twenty yards from the table.

"I believe my ass is currently planted in it, Robert."

"An annoyance I aim to rectify." He crossed his arms. "You were not invited here, Your Excellency. Pierre. Or whatever alias you're using. And you appear to be a bit outnumbered." He snapped his fingers and more fangers streamed out of the three tunnels the others had come from.

"What do numbers matter to such as we?" Luke asked, slowly drawing his gladius from its sheath. He angled the blade so it caught the light of the lantern and reflected it. "For two thousand years, we have cut through your kind like a thresher through wheat."

"I'd have killed you if your pack of dogs hadn't rescued you," Robert spat out.

"Yet here I am." Luke took a drink from his wine. "Really an excellent little bottle, Robert. Too bad I don't feel like sharing."

Le Mousquetaire let his hand drift to the hilt of his rapier while scowling at Luke and Roxi. "Well? What are you waiting for? Are you just going to sit there and talk us to death?"

"You always seemed to enjoy a nice chat before the main event," Luke replied.

"You destroyed my château. I'm not much in the mood for banter." Robert sneered.

"It makes us square then." Luke drew an invisible square in the air with his index finger. "Tell you what. I'll let you live another day if you tell me where I can find Constantius and Eusebius. If you want to earn my permanent ignorance about your existence, throw in what information you have on the entity that calls himself Zalmoxis."

Le Mousquetaire narrowed his eyes as he shifted on his feet. "What do you want with Constantius and his pet monk?"

"We have unfinished business that doesn't concern you. It's far older than your petty life."

Robert shrugged. "I couldn't say where they're at currently. I'm not exactly their social secretary."

"And Zalmoxis?"

"He is everywhere, and he is nowhere. Don't call his name unless you're prepared to deal with the consequences." He turned to address Roxi, pointing a finger at her. "You, though, you have consequences coming your way for what you did to my Antoinette. To me."

Roxi, her sword held point down with the tip of the blade poking into the wood surface of the table, spun it. "All I've heard is talk. Where's this great vampire lord I heard about? The one that subverted werewolf packs and orchestrated the kidnapping of the greatest vampire hunter to ever walk the earth? All I see is a wrung out dishrag flapping his gums." She held up her other hand and pantomimed a mouth opening and closing.

"Your doxy is going to get you killed. We're trying to negotiate here."

Luke laughed. "You told me you didn't have the information I wanted and are too afraid to give me the other piece. Sounds like negotiations are over."

Luke put his fingers between his lips and let loose a shrill whistle. A moment later, Luke's werewolves dashed out of the tunnel where they'd been hiding. Unlike the vampires who'd filed in and let their leader address the invader, the werewolves charged in, guns blazing.

As soon as the first shot barked its bright muzzle flash into the darkness, Luke and Roxi used their divinely enhanced strength to tip the massive wooden table on its side to act as a barricade and defensive position. It was sturdy oak and thick enough to probably block most small arms fire.

Luke grabbed the shotgun he'd taped to the underside of the table and took aim toward the vampires, pumping all six rounds into the crowd as they scrambled to find safety. As soon as he was empty, he ducked down and Roxi took his place, firing off her full magazine.

The sound of screaming vampires and gunshots echoed around the stone cavern creating a horrible pain-filled din of death. Each inhale bit with the stench of dead vampires and spent gunpowder.

As quick as he could, Luke shoved shells into the magazine of his Winchester M12 and popped up when Roxi ducked back down. This time, he took his time and aimed, dusting five of the six vampires he'd aimed at before returning to cover. In all the chaos, he'd lost track of Le Mousquetaire.

After he reloaded and popped up again, he swung his barrel around to engage. His eyes went wide as a dark streak charged him. With a yelp of surprise, he ducked as a silver streak slashed where his head had been a moment earlier. He tried to bring the shotgun around to his attacker but was too slow. A silver blade arced toward his head as he cringed away. The blade, moving nearly faster than he could see, knocked the gun aside and bit into the flesh of his forearm on its path toward his head.

The aggressive scream of a woman and the clang of steel on steel interrupted what should have been a sword cutting through his face. Forcing his eyes open, he tried to steady his body and get his brain back into the situation. Roxi had intercepted the blade with her own but was having trouble gaining her feet. Le Mousquetaire had the advantage.

Luke dropped his shotgun and snatched up his gladius. Springing to his feet, he blocked Le Mousquetaire's next attack. The adrenaline of his near brush with mortality drove his speed, and his hatred for all vampiredom bolstered his strength. Le Mousquetaire's smug face soon shifted to one of supreme concentration as Luke drove him back, allowing Roxi time to gain her feet. Between the two of them, he'd have no hope of surviving the engagement.

As Roxi dove into the fight, Le Mousquetaire found a new level of speed, blocking every stab or slash Luke and Roxi directed at him. Though there were two of them, he had the advantage of blade length and used every inch of it to distance himself from them.

When Le Mousquetaire cleared the row of tables, he made a wild stab toward Roxi's face, forcing Luke off balance to block it. The vampire rolled to the side just under the edge of the table and popped out, leaving several feet of oak between him and the vampire hunters. With a wily grin, he turned around and dashed through the heaps of wounded vampires, sprinting toward the central tunnel he'd originally come through.

"Damn it! He's getting away." Luke made to run after him, but Roxi reached out and stopped him.

"Dōšagīh, our guns."

Luke nodded, then scooped his M12 off the ground and vaulted over their turned-over table.

"Cease fire!" Sam yelled. "Melee, advance."

Luke cast a quick glance toward their lines, his brow furrowing, and frowned. He didn't see Jean-Paul or any of those who'd gone with him. But what he had was a bunch of combat-tested werewolves shifting to their bipedal forms. Sam, sticking to her human form, dashed forward with her naginata leading the way.

Sheathing his sword as he ran, he fired off his six shots then slung it over his back. Roxi followed his example and unloaded her shotgun on the vamps before drawing her Parthian sword. There were too many vampires between him and the fleeing Le Mousquetaire. He and Roxi would serve their friends better by staying to help.

Luke was surprised at how many vampires were still moving about, and with the gunfire now ceased, they were peering out from their hiding spots and readying to receive the incoming attackers. Only the shotguns had anti-vamp ordinance; the rest of the team had been using lead, copper, and steel ammo because they'd been out of range. A vampire could absorb an obscene amount of damage as long as it wasn't their head or heart. Now, they'd have to rely on claws and hand to hand combat or risk shooting their packmates with silver.

Luke reached over his left shoulder and yanked the rudis from its scabbard. The nearest vampire stared at him wide eyed as he brought the gladius through its neck, sending its head tumbling. Roxi, a split second later, pierced its heart with her blade, sending the dead vamp splatting to the floor in a pile of sludge.

With her Selene-enchanted naginata, Sam surgically carved a wide swath of death—slicing into hearts or bisecting necks when a heart wasn't available. If she couldn't get the head, she'd remove arms and legs. Off to the side, their wolfy allies were tearing into the vampires rushing to meet them. Pablo had kept the sledgehammer he'd used earlier on the wall and seemed to take particular delight in pulping fanger heads.

The sheer brutality of their assault sent the vampires in the back into a panic as they screamed and fled down the tunnels they'd emerged from in the first place. The vampires currently engaged fought with a fiendish frenzy trying to get away from the onslaught. The odds were quickly tipping in favor of Luke and his allies as vampires either escaped or were put down.

Luke, his arms growing tired from the intensity of engaging so many targets, panted as sweat poured down his forehead, collecting in his eyebrows only to oversaturate and drip into his eyes. As the last ambulatory vampire disappeared into the tunnels leading away from the giant cavern, Luke dragged his sleeve across his forehead, trying to keep more sweat from dripping in his eyes.

"That was hot work," he gasped out between breaths.

"Uh huh," Roxi replied, bending over, her hands on her knees.

Once he got his breath calmed a bit, he sheathed his blades and helped Roxi back to the tables so she'd at least have something to lean against. Though she was on the mend, it would take a long time for her conditioning to recover after knocking at death's door thanks to Mithras's brutal compulsion.

"How are you doing, Rox?" he asked, still short winded himself. "We should drain a couple vamps."

"I'll be alright…once I catch…my breath… Then I'll top up."

"Hey, Luke," Sam said, her naginata propped on her shoulder. "I've got the gang staking anything that hasn't turned to dust or sludge yet. You two OK?"

"Yeah. I think so. Just a bit winded," Luke said.

Sam's eyes flicked to Roxi briefly.

"I'll be fine, Sam."

Sam looked sheepishly away.

"I'm winded, not blind."

"And very sharp."

Luke chuckled.

Sam turned and yelled over her shoulder, "Bring a couple vampire corpses over here for Luke and Roxi."

Pablo strode over, naked and in his human form. "I love this sledgehammer. Do you think I could charge money and splatter vampires on stage? I'll be the Gallagher of werewolves."

Sam rolled her eyes. "I'm not paying for that, at least not for front row. Maybe balcony, though."

Roxi chuckled weakly, shaking her head.

A couple werewolves emerged from the crowd dragging bodies toward them.

"Hey, Sam. We staked them all. Now what?" Connor called from across the cavern.

"Luke…" Roxi said, a note of concern tinging her voice.

"Shit!" Luke yelled. His eyes flew wide as vampires poured from their tunnels, the glint of cold steel in their hands. "Get to cover!"

A shot cracked out from the far corner. Sam dropped in front of him. Luke, his body going into high alert, grabbed Roxi and yanked her across the table and onto the ground behind it. They landed in a heap, knocking the air from his lungs. Even as he gasped for air, he forced himself up. Gripping the edge of the table, he put his legs and back into it, and flipped the table on to its side. Splinters flew at him as he ducked behind its thick protection. Reaching out, he dragged Roxi behind the table and covered her, placing his back against the wood of the table and adding his body to her protection as bullets thudding into wood.

He forced his eyes closed but couldn't escape the screams of his friends as the vampires poured bullets into the cavern. Le Mousquetaire had rallied his forces.

CHAPTER
TWENTY-FOUR

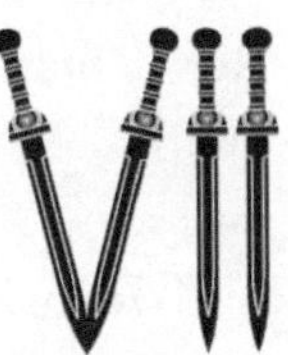

AS BULLETS THUDDED into the wood hiding him, Roxi curled into a tight ball as he wrapped his body around her. Wood splinters showered down on them as Luke felt spikes of pain bite into his neck, scalp, and the back of his legs. Either they had higher powered weaponry or were firing enough shots to dissolve the wood under their assault.

Shot after shot rang out in a nonstop deluge of hot metal and explosive concussions. He had no idea how long they huddled there. It could have been a minute or an hour, but the gunfire never seemed to stop. Instead, it only seemed to get louder. Under him, Roxi's body shuddered and quaked, an occasional scream punctuating her crying.

Luke's ears roared. After a while, he could no longer tell what was happening around him. All he knew was he had to keep his body between the vampires and Roxi. He grunted as something slammed into his back below his shoulder blade.

Clenching his jaw, his ears popped, providing a slight relief to the pressure of sound around him. He thought he could hear shots coming from both sides of the cavern. They'd been surrounded. They would be no escape today.

"Luke!"

The sound barely registered in his brain.

"Luke!"

Someone shook his leg. When he didn't respond, they tried again.

"Fuck you, you toothy bastards!" someone shouted, then fired an automatic weapon.

Luke twisted his around and freed his face from the thatch of Roxi's hair. Blinking his eyes clear, he saw the shadow of someone on one knee shouting and shooting over the table from just a few feet away.

"Jean-Paul?" Luke's voice felt harsh and raw in his throat.

Jean-Paul ducked down, laughing, and shoved another magazine into his gun before popping back up to return fire at the vampires. Luke blinked hard to flush the acrid smoke of gunpowder from his eyes. It wasn't a hallucination. Jean-Paul and his team had finally arrived.

Keeping his head low, Luke sat up, wincing as needles of pain twisted in his legs. The table behind him was nearly shredded, with gaps missing in places. The table Jean-Paul had flipped over was still in decent shape. Luke leaned over and squeezed Roxi's shoulder, moving the hair covering her ear.

"Roxi, we need to move. This spot isn't safe anymore."

She bobbed her head and tried to rise to her hands and knees but slipped back to the ground, her limbs trembling. Luke helped her up and together they crawled behind Jean-Paul to crouch in the shadow of that table. Carefully, Luke unslung his shotgun and propped it against the oak protecting him.

"Roxi? Do you think you can reload for me?"

Nodding, she fished her gun around and handed it to Luke. He took it and rolled up, taking aim toward the end of the cavern where the vampires had been. Finding targets, he fired off the full magazine, then set it down, picking up his shotgun to empty it. Roxi had the other reloaded in time to replace it.

Periodically, a pluck of pain from the back of his legs would momentarily distract him. Round after round he poured toward the end of the cavern. The expelled smoke of so many shots drifted about the cave like an acrid, foggy miasma. The constant flash of muzzle flair happened so quickly and frequently from nearly all parts of the firefight as to almost be a strobe light.

Setting his gun down and picking up the other, he chuckled, a touch of hysteria in it. "Worst dance club ever," he mumbled.

"What?" Jean-Paul ducked down and reloaded.

Luke shook his head and fired off his gun. He was getting punch drunk and a bit giddy. Roxi kept reloading, and he kept emptying the shotgun, aiming toward any movement along the back wall where the vamps were trying to secure a beachhead to push out further. If Jean-Paul hadn't made his timely arrival, Luke and his friends would likely be hamburger by now.

They had to be low on ammo. He'd dropped his belt for Roxi to use several rounds ago. He was having trouble finding moving targets through the haze of smoke. Finally, Jean-Paul bellowed a cease fire order out into the cavern. The thick fog and stench of gunpowder reminded him of his times in the trenches of Flanders and France during WWI.

As his mind drifted along with the shifting eddies of the smoke, he waited for the usual waves of a panic attack to surge over him. When they remained in the background, merely the ripples of a puddle, he furrowed his brow in confusion and wonder. It would probably come later once he was out of the immediate danger of combat.

He tried to pop his ears. The whine of his tinnitus and the silence of the cease fire were nearly as loud as the recent barrage of gun fire. Roxi, thanks to the rhythm and purpose of reloading Luke's shotguns, knelt next to Luke, poking her head over the edge of the table.

"Do you see any vampires, Jean-Paul?" Luke asked.

"I don't know," he whispered. "It's hard to see anything in this mess."

"Do you feel anything, dōšagīh?" Roxi asked, squeezing his arm.

"It's hard to tell. There are probably live vampires smeared all over the floor and walls." He squinted and looked for any signs of movement. "You?"

"I'm having the same issue. My mind is in sensory overload and I can't distinguish anything at this point." She reached over and plucked something from his hair.

"Ow." He cringed. "What was that?"

"You're covered in slivers from the table. I've been pulling them out in between reloads. Didn't you feel it?"

"No. I was a bit occupied," he whispered.

"Luke. My people are going to sweep from the back of the room to our position. We'll help you sort through the carnage."

"Shit! Sam." He popped up and looked where she'd gone down. He didn't see her anywhere, or Pablo. "Sam! Pablo!"

He fumbled for his radio but when he brought it up, it was nothing but shards of plastic held together by a few wires. Roxi handed him hers.

"Come in, this is Luke. Can I get a status check on Sam and Pablo?"

"This is Delilah. She's back here with Pablo. He carried her out. They're pretty shot up—"

"Use your CB handles..." Sam's voice sounded thin and weak from the background.

"As you can hear, Spartacus, *Bandit* is alive and conscious."

Relief washed over Luke, his body trembling from the release. If he'd been standing, he'd have probably collapsed. Roxi, probably sensing his distress, slipped an arm around his waist.

"Roxi and I are OK."

"Horse girl," Sam called in the background.

Luke chuckled—even shot, Sam's good humor shone through. Even if it was a coping mechanism at the moment.

"You stay there and organize our people. We'll coordinate with Jean-Paul up here," Luke replied.

"No, Sam...sorry, *Bandit*, I'm not going to...no..." Delilah sighed in exasperation. "Fine. Tell *Frenchy Le Beefcake* to take care of you two and keep you alive."

Jean-Paul narrowed his eyes and raised an eyebrow. "Frenchy Le Beefcake?"

"Sam likes giving people radio handles, ostensibly to protect our anonymity, but mostly because it amuses her." Using the table, Luke pushed himself to a standing position then helped Roxi up.

When Jean-Paul's people made it to them, Luke and Roxi followed Jean-Paul around the tables. His people sorted through the mess of bodies strewn about the cavern floor, staking any vampires they came across. When they found a wounded werewolf, they hustled them back to a safe place where they'd set up their de facto field hospital. The dead were set aside so they wouldn't be resting in the growing pool of vampire sludge.

Luke stared at the growing pile. So many. Too many. Roxi slid her hand into his and squeezed tightly. A hollow pit opened in his stomach as numbness seeped into his veins and spread around his body. The bloody face of Agatha, who he'd rescued from Cassius over two years ago. James, who'd been shot and evacuated from the freighter before that. Jepson from the Coast Pack, who'd helped rescue them on Mt. Hood.

"Dōšagīh, don't get lost. We have work to do," Roxi said quietly, wiping a tear from his cheek with her thumb.

He nodded, weakly at first but more firmly as he went. "Right. Right." He turned away from the pile of his dead packmates and pulled his rudis from its scabbard. "We should grab a couple vamps for ourselves, Roxi."

"Alright." She pulled hers and they went looking for bodies with enough heart left that they could use them to refresh their bodies and heal their wounds—the physical ones, at least.

He let Roxi take the first as he protected her. When they found another, Luke took it. The slash in his arm sealed, and the aches and pains and muscle weariness lessened. They only found one more each. Jean-Paul's werewolves were extremely thorough in their staking duties.

"Has anyone seen the body of Robert Beaufort?" Jean-Paul called out.

Nobody replied with an affirmative.

"Do you think we got him?" Roxi asked.

"I don't know. I want confirmation," Luke replied.

As if to answer, a handful of bodies tumbled away as someone crawled out from under them and out of the cavern and down the central tunnel the vampires had emerged from earlier. Either he'd been trapped under the bodies in the counter attack or he'd created a shield of vampire flesh to hide under until it was safe enough to flee.

"That's him!" someone shouted.

Without thinking, Luke took off after Le Mousquetaire.

"Luke!" Roxi yelled.

Behind him, he heard the pounding of foot on stone and the harsh breathing of someone chasing him. As he neared a corner, he glanced over his shoulder. It was Roxi. He slowed for a moment and moved to the side, letting her catch up before returning to a speed they could both keep up.

Despite draining two vampires, cuts and the slivers Roxi hadn't removed twinged and burned as he forced his muscles to contract and release in his dash after Le Mousquetaire.

Ahead, he could barely see the vampire lord of Paris running hard and making wide turns through the rough stone of the illuminated caverns. They weren't gaining on him, but neither was he increasing his lead. It was too late now, but Luke hoped they didn't run into any other vampires. Every side cave became one more opportunity to get lost or ambushed.

When they made yet another turn, Luke caught a pale smudge behind them. Sparing a moment for a glance, he saw the giant form of Brutus loping after them, along with a wolf he didn't recognize. He was glad the dog had made it through safely. It was for the best that they'd sent him with Delilah's group when he refused to stay behind.

"We have company," Luke gasped out between breaths.

"Danger?" Roxi asked.

"No. Allies."

After a few more turns, their luck ended when a vampire leapt out at them. Seeing a flash of metal, Luke made a rolling dive to avoid whatever it was and kicked out with a leg. The shattering of bone and a pained scream told him he'd made contact. Roxi slid to a halt and staked it through the heart, then tore off after Le Mousquetaire. Now it was Luke's turn to catch up to her.

"Luke… Do you feel that?"

"Shit. Yeah." A surge of vampires moved toward them from ahead and to the left.

"Do we keep ahead of it or address it?" She swiped sweat from her forehead.

He took a moment to think about it then cursed. "No. We should address it. If they're fresh, we can't try to outrun them."

He slowed down, waiting for Brutus and the wolf to catch up then focused his concentration on the incoming vampires. They were close. He spared a last glance for Le Mousquetaire as he disappeared down a side tunnel heading to the right.

"It's up ahead." Luke slowed to a walk, his lungs heaving.

The tunnel made a slight bend to the left. About half way around the bend, they found a tunnel entrance taking off to the left. Luke held up a hand to halt his little party.

"Wait here with Roxi, Brutus." He looked at the werewolf and spoke in French. "I'm assuming Jean-Paul sent you?"

The wolf's tongue lolled out, and it nodded.

"Good. Listen to Roxi while I'm gone."

The wolf nodded again.

"Be careful," Roxi whispered.

"Hey. It's me." Luke gave her lopsided grin.

Rolling her eyes, she shook her head. "You ran into vampire caverns without backup."

That was true. Not the most careful of moves. He shrugged and jogged into the cavern. Soon, the light spilling in from the main tunnel disappeared. Running his hand along the side of the wall, Luke felt the ground with his boots. The fangers were getting closer.

He blinked. A stray beam from a flashlight moved across the tunnel. A few more joined it. There must be a side tunnel or a sharp turn ahead that they were approaching. A few voices drifted his way. Stopping, he brought his hand down and felt something hard and round in his pocket. A feral grin spread across his face.

He switched his gladius to his left hand and pulled out one of the frag grenades they'd liberated earlier. Now seemed a good time to return it to its owners.

While keeping the spoon firmly bolstered against his palm, he hooked the pin with his left index finger and pulled it. He couldn't tell how high the ceiling was here because he didn't want to lob it and have it ricochet off the ceiling and fall short. Taking a couple side steps away from the wall and toward the left side of the tunnel, he got into position. Then, thinking better of it, flipped his gladius around and sheathed it on his left hip.

Waiting, he tried to make a rough guestimate of how far the tunnel was from his spot. The light beams grew strong as did the sound of the vamps' voices. As soon as he saw the first vampire turn the corner, he coiled his body. They still hadn't noticed him. More vampires streamed around the corner.

Luke cocked back his arm and took a couple side steps forward and hurled the grenade side-armed. The spoon pinged away as the grenade left his hand. After a second, the dark swallowed the grenade. Overcoming the urge to watch, he turned and sprinted back the way he'd come. He slid to a halt and dove behind the wall, pulling Roxi with him. Brutus and the wolf lunged after them just in time.

The grenade detonated sending screams, dust, and pebbles rolling out the entrance to the tunnel. Luke was glad he hadn't stopped to watch. The confined space of the tunnel had contained and pushed the explosion both ways. He'd likely have blown out his eardrums or worse if he'd stayed to gloat.

Roxi grinned and tipped her lips up. "Beautiful music."

He kissed her quickly but firmly. "We should see if we can find Le Mousquetaire's trail.

Brutus gave a low woof and snuffled around the floor then jogged down the tunnel and stopped, looking back to see if anyone was a following him.

"We know what tunnel he went down. We can run hard to make up some time, then we have Brutus's snoot if we need to pick a turn." Roxi jogged after Brutus.

"Sounds like a good plan to me." Luke put one foot in front of the other and caught up Roxi and Brutus, the werewolf following on his tail.

CHAPTER
TWENTY-FIVE

LUKE BREATHED DEEPLY as the crisp cold air of the outside world filled his nostrils and lungs. They'd had hints of the end of the tunnel for a few hundred yards now. Soon, they'd emerge somewhere in Paris. Brutus's ability to follow their quarry allowed them to slow down instead of rushing blindly after the vampire lord of Paris. No matter the twists and turns, the giant dog kept the trail.

Roxi glanced back at the werewolf trailing behind them. "Is he going to cause any trouble out in the city?"

"I don't know. Brutus is pretty big, and Armenian Gramprs kind of have a touch of wolf in the appearance, so hopefully he'll blend in with Brutus." Luke shrugged. "If we can find some clothes, he can convert back to human, otherwise, he'll have to pretend to be a dog."

The wolf's tongue lolled out into a wolfy grin.

"It'll have to work."

As pitch black darkness of the cave—only broken by their flash-lights—lessened, revealing the faint irregularities of the stone tunnel, Luke grew eager to be under the night sky. Even if he couldn't see the stars and moon, he knew they were there, unblocked by the earth's crust.

Next to him, Roxi breathed deeply, picking up her pace. They were both ready to be quit of Paris's tunnels. Reaching out, he stopped Roxi then focused on his vampire senses. Nothing.

"Do you feel anything, Rox?" Luke asked.

"No. All clear."

"We should still take caution. He could have some werewolves or thralls hidden ahead."

She squeezed his hand. "Age has brought you wisdom."

Luke frowned, his brow furrowing. "You're nearly as old as me."

"But I'm still younger." She smiled smugly.

"You can't hang around Pablo anymore. You're picking up his bad jokes." Luke shook his head but smiled.

Roxi patted his cheek and returned to her march out of the tunnel. Even in the middle of a brutal and long night, she could bring a sense of joy to his life. He followed along, catching up to her.

When they finally saw the outside world, they spread out wordlessly, one on each wall. Brutus slipped behind Roxi while the werewolf fell in line with Luke. Raising his nose in the air, Brutus snuffled the currents moving into the cave then slid around Roxi. The werewolf joined Brutus, and together they slunk along the edges of the cave as they worked their way out.

Luke caught Roxi's attention and gestured that they should follow. Careful to set their feet noiselessly, they crept out of the tunnel. A couple minutes later, they emerged into the pre-twilight night. Off in the east, the horizon shifted into a slightly lighter deep blue.

Depending on Le Mousquetaire's destination, he might be caught out in the morning light. Luke would love to witness the torturous death of the vampire who'd manipulated the last three years of his life from his first unwitting encounter with Le Mousquetaire's apprentice The Mistress to the murder of his friend followed by his kidnapping. Though, he doubted he'd be so lucky.

The vampire no doubt knew plenty of places to hide. Or he could simply glamour someone and force his way into their house.

It felt good to be under the open sky once again, the tension leaching out of his muscles. He inhaled deeply, letting the fresh air fill his lungs.

"It feels tremendous to be out of those caves," Roxi said, then gave a full body shiver. "It felt like being trapped in our cells again. I used to have nightmares of escaping and just wandering around forever in perpetual darkness. I nearly couldn't enter that first tunnel. It was like my skin was crawling every moment we were down there."

"Yeah. It wasn't pleasant." Luke squinted and looked around. "I suppose we should go find the pooches."

Up ahead, Brutus barked, the low sound quiet but pitched toward Luke and Roxi. They worked their way through the trees until they found Brutus and the werewolf. They lay on their stomachs, facing each other like two sphinxes. As soon as Roxi and Luke approached them, they popped back up and headed off, their noses to the ground.

As they descended from the hilly park, they weaved their way through trees. A couple times, Luke was tempted to use his gladius to hack through a bush.

"Everyone halt." Luke lifted his sword. "We should probably stow these away."

"Yeah, not sure the late night early morning crowd is ready for a couple of sword-toting vampire hunters."

Luke shucked his coat and unclipped the scabbard from his hip. Sheathing his gladius in it, he handed it to Roxi, who clipped it onto his tactical straps for a right hand over the shoulder draw. He helped Roxi take off her coat and move her sword to her shoulder, then slide her coat back on.

"We should maybe rub some dirt over these patches of vampire sludge," Luke said, pointing to a couple large patches on his pants.

"Right." She bent over and grabbed a handful of mud and smeared it over the shiny, dark reddish patches.

Luke followed her example.

"Do I have any more spots I can't see?" Roxi turned and faced away from him.

"You've got a couple. Want me to get them?" Luke asked.

"Sure."

Luke grabbed some more mud and smeared over a couple spots on her upper legs and on her butt.

"My coat and armor tails kind of cover that area. You just wanted to touch my butt." She grinned and winked at him.

"Better to be thorough… Mind checking me out?"

"Sure, handsome." She patted down a couple spots then gave him a sharp swat on the butt. "Looking good there."

"Thanks," Luke replied, chuckling.

If it was possible for a dog to look impatient without bouncing round, Brutus huffed and returned to the trail as soon as he judged his people were ready. Whoever or whatever the dog was, he was an interesting being.

Soon, they transitioned from the dirt and grass of the park onto the stone of sidewalk. With the added illumination of street lamps, Luke spotted an occasional dab of something dark and shiny along the trail Brutus and the wolf were following. Usually, if a vampire was this ambulatory, they'd have healed enough not to be leaking. They must have put some silver in a larger vein that wasn't sealing up.

The thought of Le Mousquetaire in constant pain brought a smile to his face. After all the suffering he'd caused Luke and his friends, the vampire deserved it and more.

Luke cinched his coat tighter and flipped the hood over his head. The one advantage of being deep underground was a constant mild temperature and no wind. He thought he heard the chattering of Roxi's teeth.

"Are you cold, Rox?"

"Yeah. This coat isn't exactly the thickest. It just happened to be the only one of the offered garments long enough to cover my armor." She wrapped her arms around herself and rubbed her arms.

"I'd let you have my coat, but then it'd be sword and armor out to the public. Not sure being a spectacle while we're trailing a vamp is the best idea."

"I know, dōšagīh." She sighed. "My body still hasn't recovered all the way, and it's having trouble regulating."

"I'm amazed you're doing as well as you are. If you need to, we can call a cab and you can go rest." He slid his arm through hers.

"I know. I can manage. I'm not done in yet, but I'll let you know if that changes. I'll probably need to sleep for a couple days after, but I'm good for now."

"OK." He smiled softly at her, then stepped away to give her space to move more easily. "At least we'll get to experience a Paris sunrise together."

Roxi chuckled. "I'd rather be sound asleep after a night of drinking fine wine, then making love until all the wee hours of the night, but a Paris sunrise with you will do well enough."

"I like your plan better than this one. Maybe we can make that happen if this goes well."

"I look forward to it."

She sounded tired. They still had more mission before they could call an end to the day. He just hoped Le Mousquetaire hadn't jumped into a car and drove off. Brutus appeared to be a good smell hound, but Luke doubted even an animal worthy of being imprisoned in the vampires' super max security section of their arena could track a vampire after he removed his body from the street.

Luke hoped the rest of the team was doing OK after the brutal counter-assault the vampires had launched. "I'm going to check in with Maggie and get an update if she's got one. When we get to the next street corner, let's stop so I can give her a location."

At the next corner, Roxi leaned up against a lamp post and crossed her arms to keep a bit of warmth in.

Hey, Maggie. Roxi and I are in pursuit of Le Mousquetaire. I'll attach the map location. Any updates on the rest of the team? he texted.

He wanted to wait for a reply, but they had their own task to attend to. "OK. Let's get moving."

Roxi nodded then bent over and scratched behind Brutus's ears. The wolf slid up and rubbed over her leg like a cat, so she gave him a scratch behind the ears as well, sending his wolfy tail wagging. Luke chuckled and pointed down the street. Wagging his tail, Brutus resumed his task.

They worked their way through the quiet, mostly residential

neighborhood. It looked affluent, though no neighborhood in Paris was entirely single purpose. When they passed by bakeries, the scent of fresh baked goods tantalized his senses. It had been a long time since dinner, and he'd burned a lot of energy in the brutal fight and the mad dash to chase Le Mousquetaire.

"I would literally kill someone for a fresh baked croissant right now," Roxi said.

"Right? All these bakeries are killing me right now. If my stomach growls much louder, I'm afraid Brutus might decide it's trying to start a fight."

Roxi chuckled. "I'm sure you're safe. Brutus seems to like you."

Hearing his name, Brutus lifted his head and woofed lazily, his tail swishing slowly back and forth, then returned his nose to the sidewalk to continue following the trail.

His feet ached. It'd been a while since he'd bought his last pair of boots, and he was probably due. Tonight's intense work had done them in, though they still had more time together. He couldn't help feeling sympathetic for Roxi. Like all her garments at the moment, her shoes were borrowed and no doubt well broken in by whoever had been gracious enough to give them to her. He vowed to himself to take her shopping so she could rebuild her own wardrobe. He wondered what happened to all her possessions in London.

She'd been based there despite making trips around the Middle East, South Asia, and Central Asia to fight vampires. But she hadn't been back to London in well over two years. Unless she had rent payments set to autopay, no doubt her landlord had cleared out her stuff when the rent payment dried up. Though, she might own her own place. If she'd paid for it, all her stuff might be there waiting for her, just a bit musty and dusty after being left unattended for so long.

He knew so little about her immediate history. They'd shared their deep histories, and Luke had given pieces of his current life. But she'd told him so little about what her life was like before she'd been abducted. Maybe her recent history was similar to his—soul crushingly lonely.

"Luke. Pay attention. You almost ran into that lamp post."

He blushed. "Sorry. I got lost in my head."

"You can tell me about it later. Brutus is getting tenser. I think we're nearing our destination."

That sobered him from his wandering mind. "Right." He felt embarrassed for wool gathering on a mission, so he tucked away his desire to know more about Roxi. Tonight's mission would bring him closer to a time where he could live a life. Any life he wanted. He wanted Roxi. And Maggie. Shaking his head, he snapped himself from his distractions and looked around him.

They'd wandered into an old neighborhood, a moneyed neighborhood. Neither of them looked like they belonged. They were dirty and wearing ill-fitting clothes. They looked sweaty and disheveled. They looked like the kind of people rich people would call the police on to harass them out of the neighborhood. Somewhere near, a bakery or cafe was springing to life. The aromas of baked goods and coffee drifted on the morning breeze.

Then they stopped.

Brutus sat down and stared at a house. It didn't look any different from the other residences in the neighborhood, but the trail ended here.

"What do you sense?" Luke asked.

"It's faint." She looked to the east.

The glowing orb of the sun was nearly all the way over the horizon. It was almost the point in the day when all but the most powerful of vampires had to respond to their nature and seek the oblivion of their kind and rest for the day. That also meant it would be nearly impossible for them to feel their presence. But even the absence of information was in and of itself information.

"Now what?" Roxi asked. "Do you want to go in?"

In the light of day and after the encroaching exhaustion of all they'd gone through, his better reason stepped to the fore. "It's just the four of us, and we have no idea what's waiting inside. It could be packed with werewolves like sardines in a can." He looked at Roxi and gave her a tired smile. "We're good, but I don't think we're that good."

Roxi nodded and reached down to scratch the ears of the werewolf. "Can you sense any werewolves in there?"

If it was possible for an animal to shrug, that was the sense he got from the werewolf.

"I don't think we should risk it. We're here. We know where he's at. Let's take a step back and make sure we do this right." He pulled her in and wrapped his arms around her.

"Good. I'd have gone in with you, but this is a smarter choice." She squeezed him.

Luke chuckled. "I occasionally make the right choice." He squatted in front of the werewolf. "Can you run back to the pack and alert them to the situation?"

The werewolf nodded, his tongue lolling out.

"Alright. Be safe."

The wolf took off, loping away from them. He hoped whoever they were wouldn't run into trouble, but he had to trust to their knowledge of their own city. Who knew? They might have clothes stashed around for such occasions.

"Do you have any cash on you?" Luke asked.

Roxi crossed her arms, pursed her lips, and blinked slowly at him. "I own virtually nothing. Everything except the steel on my back is borrowed."

"Sorry." He fished his wallet from his pocket. "Can you get us a couple of coffees and something to eat? I think I can smell a cafe nearby."

"That I can do." She stuck out her arm, palm up.

He gave her a couple of twenty euro notes, then shoved his wallet back in his pocket.

"Anything particular you want?" Roxi asked.

"Several shots of espresso and a pastry, something with cherries, if they have it."

Roxi stepped into him and laid her hand on his cheek, bringing his face down to her lips for a kiss. Resting her forehead against his, she stroked his short beard for a moment, then stepped back. "I'll be back shortly, dōšagīh."

With the hint of a smile on his face, he watched Roxi walk away to find them something to revive their spirits. As if she knew he was watching, she added a bit of extra pop to her hips as she strode away.

Chuckling to himself, he smiled broadly as she walked away, disappearing around a corner.

He didn't know how he'd come to be so fortunate to fall in love again after all this time, let alone twice with two impressive women like Roxi and Maggie. He turned back to the house where Le Mousquetaire was most likely hiding and sighed heavily.

If they managed to catch the villain and end him, it was still only one more step closer to the top of the mountain—a mountain peak that didn't even have a proper name. Whatever waited for him inside, he'd get through it and finish the fanger that had been his most recent tormentor. It didn't matter what was waiting inside. In the last millennium, he'd never felt such an intense desire to survive and thrive. For the first time in ages, the dangerous light of hope kindled a desire to not only survive but prosper. He'd slaughter everyone and everything inside that building if it meant another day with Roxi and Maggie in his life. If it meant a chance of seeing Gwen grow up and find her own joys.

His spine stiffened with the steel of resolve. He finally had a life worth living, and he wouldn't let anything get in his way of living it.

Brutus, sensing the agitation of the human who'd adopted him, rose from his spot on the concrete and slipped his head under Luke's hand. The scruffy fur of the dog grounded Luke as he patted the animal, occasionally scratching behind his ears and around his neck.

"This is it, Brutus. I know I've been at this for nearly two thousand years, but the last three have felt particularly long and hard despite all the good things. We'll get to the end of this. One way or the other," Luke said quietly, the words more for himself than the dog.

Brutus's tail thumped on the ground then settled after a few seconds when he spread out, laying his head across his front legs. With a giant yawn, he closed his eyes and started a nap. Luke tried not to look too suspicious just standing on the street, but he felt awkward anyway. So far, only a few people had stirred from the surrounding houses to go about their days.

He yawned as his stomach growled, unsure of which urge was the stronger at the moment—sleepiness or hunger. To keep his mind occupied, he pulled his phone to see if anyone had reached out yet. Still nothing from anyone. He hoped everything was going OK and his people and Jean-Paul's hadn't been attacked again. Between both groups, they'd be able to hold the cavern until they could evacuate the wounded and the dead. He pulled up a social media app and tried to distract himself from focusing on those they'd lost. As tired as he was, he'd spiral downward into a pit of self-recriminations, and he had too much to do to finish this mission.

Brutus's ears perked up and pointed toward the direction Roxi had disappeared earlier. She returned, but she brought friends with her in the form of a small box and a couple of coffees in to-go cups. He raised his hand and smiled.

"I don't know if you've ever looked so beautiful." He took the coffee she'd handed him and sniffed the rich roasty notes.

"I guess I should always carry coffee and baked goods." She winked at him then sighed. "I hope this coffee does the trick because I'm really dragging here."

"Me too." Luke braved a scalding and took a careful drink of his coffee. The time it had taken her to return had rendered it the perfect temperature. "Oh, this is good. Thank you."

"Have you heard anything back?" Roxi asked.

Luke shook his head, then took another drink to delay responding. "I'm getting worried. We should have heard something from someone by now."

"It's still early. Those tunnels run deep, and I doubt the vampires installed Wi-Fi. As long as it took us to get out, it'll take them longer if they have to wait for the medical teams before evacuating." Roxi set the box down then squeezed Luke's arm.

"I know you're right, but I'm still worried."

"So how many people do you think Le Mousquetaire could have stationed in this house?" Roxi asked.

He appreciated her abrupt change of topic in an effort to keep him distracted from his own thoughts. "I don't know. It's pretty big, and who knows how much illicit underground infrastructure they might have installed. That's kind of why I don't want to go busting in there."

"We should maybe move to the other side of the street then, in case someone comes out to investigate. I saw a bench that's reasonably covered but should allow us to watch this house easily enough."

"Lead the way." Luke scooped up the box and patted Brutus's back. "Up ya go, boy. Time to move."

The big dog lumbered up and followed Roxi. Luke trailed behind. Roxi was right. The bench was in a good spot. He hadn't seen it from his spot in front of the house because a bush blocked it from this angle. Even if the view was blocked from the bench, all it would take was a couple steps to check in on it. When they arrived at the bench, Luke took a seat.

"Hmm, the view's blocked. Oh well, it'll work well enough."

Roxi handed him her coffee. "Mind holding this?"

He took it. With her hands empty, she pulled the belt off the coat and reached into the bush and used the belt to tie a branch to another one, creating a gap they could now see through. With their vision sorted out, Luke opened the box and found four pastries and what looked like a baked dog treat in the shape of a bone.

Roxi snagged it and called Brutus over, handing it to him. He took it gently, his tail wagging, then laid down to crunch it up. Luke started with one of the chocolate croissants she'd picked up. They sat quietly eating while Brutus snuffled up the last crumbs of his dog biscuit. When Luke finished, he checked his phone again to see if anyone had returned his messages. Seeing one from Delilah, he opened it.

Bruh, Where did you go? Are you alive?

Roxi, Brutus, a werewolf, and I chased Le Mousquetaire. We're waiting outside a house that he disappeared into, he replied. The message immediately showed as being read.

Why haven't you gone in and finished this?

We don't know how many are inside. It could be full of werewolves or thralls.

At least you have the sense not to break in by yourselves. Delilah texted back.

What's the situation there?

Seven dead, five of ours. Several wounded, mostly healed over bullets, though some will require serious surgery. Maggie and the other doctors are taking care of that. What about you?

We were waiting to hear from anyone. We sent the wolf to get someone from his pack. We're hidden nearby. He sent her the map location. *Can you relay the details to Jean-Paul? I'd like to have a team diverted to assist us. We also could use some clean clothes. We're pretty messy after the fight.*

OK. I'll get on it. I'll keep you updated. Delilah sent a gif admonishing them to stay out of trouble.

"What's the news?" Roxi asked.

"Delilah says seven dead, five from our pack, and a lot of injuries, some serious." Luke rubbed his temples.

"I'm sorry, dōšagīh." She slipped her hand under his and squeezed it gently. "I know it's small consolation, but it could have been a lot worse."

He sighed and nodded. "At least we heard from them."

"Now what?" Roxi asked.

"We wait and watch."

CHAPTER
TWENTY-SIX

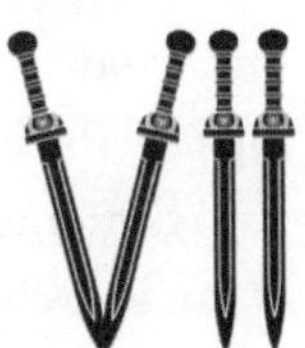

LUKE YAWNED, his jaw popping. After rubbing his eyes, he brought the binoculars back up. Other than a few shadows behind curtains, no one had exited Le Mousquetaire's house or entered it. When Jean-Paul had been notified of the situation, he turned over the evacuation of the cavern to his second, formed a mixed team of Paris and Portland wolves, and hustled over.

"Was this house on your radar?" Luke asked.

Jean-Paul lowered his binoculars. "No. We'd seen him kicking about the mansion of the Paris vampire lord—I guess I should say former lord—but this area hasn't been of interest to the vampires."

"Robert is good at popping up where he's not expected."

Nearby, Roxi snored quietly on a bench seat that ran down the side of the box van they were spying from. Brutus took up the rest of the seat, his head draped across Roxi's lap. The addition of the van from the Paris pack made for a much more comfortable situation. Sitting out on the bench in the cold winter air had grown steadily uncomfortable as his body settled after the fight and pursuit of Le Mousquetaire.

"When do you want to go in?" Jean-Paul asked.

"I think a couple hours before sunset. I want to clear the house while the fangers are down for the day. Then I'm going to free the world of Le Mousquetaire and his violent scheming."

Jean-Paul set his binoculars down and pushed back in his chair. "I can't say that I'll be disappointed to be rid of Robert. Since he's risen to prominence in the ranks of the vampires, he's done nothing but create chaos. We had a good stalemate with the previous vampire lord of Paris."

"Stalemates and treaties only give fangers the time to come at you from a stronger position. You can't trust vampires, not with their desire to exploit and dominate," Luke replied, his anger simmering under the surface. He was too tired to let it out now, needing its energy for later.

Jean-Paul nodded sheepishly. "Yes. It didn't turn out so well. While the treaty kept the peace in Paris, he used that time to bolster his power around France, then took over the local nest."

"Like fascists, there can be no peace with vampires. Their very philosophy is inherently violent. When you can use magic to force a human to do your bidding, to become your food source, you rob them of their consent. When they strip a human of their soul, they condemn that human to an immortal existence of brutality." He sighed and rubbed his temples, a headache from too much caffeine was blooming behind his eyes.

"You should catch a couple hours of sleep while you can. We could be busy this evening."

Luke nodded and curled up along the side door next to Roxi's legs. Despite the constant stream of thoughts running through his head, he fell into a deep sleep.

SOMEONE SHOOK HIM AWAKE. Not sure where he was or with who, he reached for his gladius but found nothing but the cloth of his hood. He blinked furiously, trying to get his vision to clear.

Jean-Paul held both of his hands up and leaned away from Luke.

"Sorry to startle you, Luke. You wanted me to wake you up when it was time to get ready."

Luke nodded, a yawn forcing his jaws apart. "Do you have some water?"

Jean-Paul handed him a bottle. The cold water felt amazing sliding down his parched and sore throat. Breathing so much gun smoke in the cavern had done a number on it.

"If you need a restroom, there's one nearby," Jean-Paul said.

Luke took the instructions and returned to the van fifteen minutes later, relieved but still tired, though the nap had taken off the worst part of the exhaustion.

"Where's Roxi?" Luke asked.

"I think she and Jung-sook went to the cafe. They took that beast of a dog with them. They should be back soon." Jean-Paul looked at his wrist and the large, high-end watch.

"Brutus is quite sweet."

"I saw what he did to those vampires he brought down last night." Jean-Paul shivered.

"It's no different from a werewolf using one of their forms to take down an enemy. Gramprs are a guard breed. They're very protective of their people." Luke tried to stretch from side to side to work out the kinks in his back but gave up. The tension had no interest in relinquishing its grip on his muscles.

"Grampr? Is that what he is?"

Luke nodded. "It's an Armenian breed."

"Hmm, never heard of it before," Jean-Paul replied.

"Is everyone briefed on the plan?" Luke asked.

"Yes. Your people will lead, mine will follow and assist. We haven't had any luck getting the blueprints for the building. It's too old."

"No worries, we'll just be methodical. It's far from our first house raid."

"It'll be interesting to watch pros work. If we're going to clean out our city of its fanged denizens, we'll want to ensure we do it properly." Jean-Paul perked up and looked toward the rear doors.

A moment later, they opened and Roxi climbed in, pulling the doors shut behind her. "Good afternoon, dōšagīh. I have a sandwich for you."

"Thank you. Is our team all accounted for?" Luke asked, taking the box Roxi handed him.

"Jung-sook is getting them ready now." Roxi slid onto the bench seat next to Luke.

"My people are ready. We just have to gather and move in." Jean-Paul crouched low to avoid hitting his head on the low ceiling of the van. "I'm going to go over the last details with them while you finish your sandwich."

The sandwich hit the spot. Setting the box aside, he helped Roxi with her weaponry and armor then let her assist him. Lastly, they slipped their coats on and stepped into the brisk late afternoon air.

The teams were gathered in small groups, chatting idly to get to know each other. Once Luke and Roxi emerged, they all quieted down and stared at them. Luke felt awkward with all the eyes on him, so he did his best to ignore it as he joined Jean-Paul, Delilah, Jung-sook, and Simone.

Luke stretched his neck, trying to work out the kinks. "Hey, Delilah. Do you have an update on the rest of our people? How are Pablo and Sam?"

"Pablo and Sam will be fine. Maggie is busy working on the wounded. She sends her love," Delilah replied. "Are you ready?"

Luke nodded. "As I'll ever be. Is your lock picker ready, Jean-Paul?"

"He is, since it's me."

Luke raised an eyebrow.

Jean-Paul shrugged. "I've led an interesting life."

"I bet you have. Remind your people—guns are last resort, and if they find humans, they're to be considered non-combatants unless they give no other choice." He checked his phone for the time then looked to the west to see how close the sun was to the horizon. "The vampires should still be down pretty hard, so we can go cautiously."

"Anything else?" Jean-Paul asked.

"Nope. If you don't have anything to add, everyone to their

teams." Luke reached up and checked his weapons to make sure they weren't tangled in his hood.

Roxi slid her arm through his, resting her other hand on his forearm. "Shall we go pay a little visit to our friends?"

Luke grinned viciously. "That sounds delightful."

They stepped to the edge of the sidewalk and waited for the light traffic to clear before striding across the quiet street. Jean-Paul followed in their wake. Once they hit the other sidewalk, they let Jean-Paul take the lead as one of the Paris werewolves they hadn't met joined them.

Trying not to look suspicious, they simply walked up the short sidewalk to the stoop. Luke reached out and pretended to push the doorbell. While they stood around looking like they were waiting for the doorbell to be answered, they surrounded Jean-Paul and blocked him from view while he squatted down and started working on the lock.

Luke reached out and held his finger over the doorbell another time to buy more time. A series of clicks were accompanied by a triumphal sound from Jean-Paul as he stood up and grabbed the door handle. Checking in with the team, he turned the knob and stepped through the door. Luke followed him and pulled his swords as soon as he cleared the door and stepped into the dim recesses of the entryway. Roxi stood next to him, her sword held at the ready.

Jean-Paul pulled a stake from his coat and stepped out of the way of the door, turning it over to the fourth member of their party whose task was to let the other teams in. So far, nothing stirred in the house.

Brutus, who was supposed to be waiting in the van, shouldered his way through the door and came to heel on Luke's left side, his ears flicking about as he snuffled the air. A low growl rumbled in his throat. Reaching down, Luke rubbed his knuckles on the back of the dog's neck, careful to keep the blade of the rudis from getting too near the animal's thick fur.

"I smell it too, Brutus," Luke whispered.

Jean-Paul sniffed the air. "What?"

"Death," Roxi said.

Luke eased forward, his body coiled and ready to strike if called upon. Brutus swung wide, leaving room for Luke as they moved through the sitting room. The room was filled with beautiful antique chairs, settees, coffee tables, and shelves. When he found the staircase, he crept along one side while Roxi took the other. Brutus and Jean-Paul followed in their wake. When they reached the first landing, they waited and listened for activity, but when he didn't hear any, he nodded toward the next flight of stairs and ascended.

When he reached the landing of the third floor, he peeked down to make sure Delilah, Simone, and their team were in place. Once he got a nod from Delilah, he waved his team after him as they snuck toward the first door. Roxi reached down and took the knob, then turned it quietly before pushing it in gently.

A profound stench nearly bowled them over. Luke pulled back and turned his face away until his body calmed. Jean-Paul ran back to the landing, gagging and dry heaving. Even Brutus seemed repulsed by the smell. When Luke got the nerve to look inside, he wasn't surprised at what he found.

Three bodies were splayed out on the bed, looking thin and drained like empty husks. Their stomachs and chests had been ripped open, probably for no other reason than for the feeder to vent its rage. Luke checked the wardrobe and found it empty save for a few pieces of ratty clothing. Slipping out into the hall, Roxi pulled the door shut, turning the volume down on the stench but not eliminating it now that it had escaped.

Luke and Roxi checked the other five rooms on the floor, finding similar results. Since Jean-Paul was struggling, they sent him to watch the landing while they proceeded. Each dead and abused body stoked the intensity of Luke's anger. He had to force his jaw to unclench so he didn't grind his teeth. Flicking his eyes over to Roxi periodically, he saw a similar expression on her face. She'd no doubt seen this sight too many times herself. When he was done with this, he'd need to stand in a scalding shower to wash the filth off.

After they cleared the last room, they rejoined Jean-Paul, the werewolf looking sad and troubled. He'd probably never seen the full extent of what a vampire could do to its victims. Luke squeezed his shoulder, then headed downstairs, stopping on the middle floor. Delilah and Simone had finished with the last room and were bringing their team down the hall.

"Anything?" Luke asked.

Delilah shook her head, looking angry. "Just dead bodies."

"They smelled fresh too," Simone said.

"OK. Let's go check in to see if they've cleared the ground floor." Luke descended the stairs quickly.

Jung-sook, standing near the bottom of the steps, waved as Luke stepped off the last stair.

"Anything here?" Luke asked.

"Clear so far. Just empty rooms," she replied.

Luke nodded. They needed to get creative. He sheathed his rudis, then reached down and rubbed Brutus's neck.

"When you get the last all-clear, gather the team leaders," Luke said.

While Jung-sook attended to her teams, Luke went and found a bathroom and relieved himself. After he washed his hands, he splashed some water on his face to try to revive himself, but he'd been going too hard for too long the last couple days. Hell, the last couple months.

When he stepped out, Roxi stopped, wrapping her arms around his waist as she rested her head on his shoulder. He pulled her in tighter and rested his cheek against her hair.

"Uh, Luke, sorry to interrupt, but I've got the team leads gathered." Jung-sook turned around and returned to her duty.

Roxi let go of Luke and took his hand, leading toward where the team leaders were gathered.

Luke cleared his throat. "It's secret door time. Check anything that looks like it might be a trigger. Books, vases, anything. Paintings. Look for hidden panels that could contain a switch. Be methodical, but work quickly. If you find something that looks suspicious, let me know."

"You heard the man," Jung-sook said, scattering the team leaders to their various locations.

Luke squatted down in front of Brutus and scratched around his neck with both hands. "Hey, buddy. Do you think you can pick up that trail we followed earlier?"

Brutus huffed, bathing Luke's face in doggy breath augmented with flecks of slobber.

"Thanks." Luke stood up and wiped his face off.

Roxi, hand covering her mouth, tried to keep the quiet snickers from escaping but mostly failed. Brutus turned around and snuffled the floor, working his way back and forth until he picked up a trail he wanted to follow. Luke followed the dog as he snuffled his way into a large study or library.

Moving back and forth around the room, he seemed to be having trouble. He stopped at a carved bust, then moved to a bookshelf, then over to a couch, and back to the same bookshelf again. With a huff, he flopped down in the middle of the floor, laying on his stomach with his head between his paws.

"If he's followed Le Mousquetaire's trail again, it might be this room since the trail goes all over the place," Luke said, looking around the edges of the bookshelf. "I think I feel some air moving from here."

He placed his hand over the spot, then moved his face closer and sniffed. He thought he detected a faint mustiness reminiscent of dirt and stone and air that belonged underground. Starting with the wall around the shelf, he looked for any kind of latch or hinge, then moved onto looking for any hidden switches.

Jean-Paul looked around the couch since it was one of the spots Brutus searched. Roxi searched for the opening mechanism around the bust.

"Luke, I think I found something," Roxi said.

He turned to the sound of stone lightly grinding on stone as she twisted the head off the bust. When she set the head aside, there was a button under it.

Luke poked his head out of the study. "Jung-sook, gather every-one. I think we found it."

"Do you want me to push it?" Roxi asked, her finger hovering above it.

"Not yet. Not until we have everyone gathered."

Roxi slumped slightly, her face falling. She looked sad about not getting to push the button, but waited nearby so no one else could take the honor. Slowly, the rest of their teams filed in or waited in the hall as the room got crowded.

Luke leaned against the fireplace mantle, his arms crossed. "Jung-sook, I want two people on each door into the house. And another pair to wait in this room. They can open the door for us or catch anyone trying to flee."

"Right." Jung-sook pointed to pairs and sent them to their posts.

"I want shotguns out and aimed at the door." Luke stepped away from the shelf and pulled his gladius from its scabbard. Once everyone was ready, he nodded to Roxi, who smashed her finger down on the button.

Something heavy clicked from behind the bookshelf, then it opened. Flashlights shined into the dark maw in front of them. When nothing came out of the opening, Luke waved the shotguns down and pulled his own flashlight. It flickered on, then faded to a dim beam before flicking off.

"Crap. Batteries are dead." He put it back into its belt pouch.

Someone handed him theirs before he had to ask. He shined the light around the entrance to a narrow hallway that ended in a steep staircase. Feeling along the walls, he found a panel that folded in to reveal another button. He reached out and pulled the bookcase closed, locking himself behind the bookcase. The bookcase swung back open when he pushed the button.

Luke pointed to the panel, pushing it open for everyone to see. "Here's the other button, so be sure to memorize the spot if we have to come out hot."

Roxi joined him as he headed down the short hallway. He took the stairs slowly, not wanting to take a tumble down the steep rise which wouldn't pass US building codes. After about twenty steps, he arrived at a small landing that switched back to another set of steps heading down. He waited until those following him were bunched up then headed down into the darkness.

On the next landing, they found a hallway leading away from the stairs. Luke left a team of four to watch the stairs. When they cracked open the doors, they found empty cells. In one, they found another dead body, though it appeared to only be drained of blood. Behind the door that capped the end of the hall, they found someone they didn't expect.

"Hello, Jan," Luke said. He brought his sword up and laid it across his shoulder. "You seem to be an unwelcome guest of your master."

"Luke? I thought you were dead." Jan stood up from his cot and crossed the couple of paces to the thick bars, grabbing them. "Have you come to taunt me before you kill me?"

"It's the least you deserve."

"I'm surprised my tenderhearted brother isn't here with you. Are you going to murder me before you let Pieter get a shot at me?" Jan sneered at Luke and turned around.

"I could just leave you here. Then after I clean out the rest of this place, I'll just lock it up and throw away the keys. Maybe I'll leave you plenty of water so it takes longer for you to just waste away and die." Luke shrugged. "It won't comfort your father's soul, but it'll amuse me to think of your end."

Jan whipped around, fear in his eyes. Luke was almost impressed when Jan forced his face into the disdainful nonchalance he usually wore.

"It's been a lot of fun orchestrating your downfall after you betrayed me and my friends and your father and brother." Luke leaned up against the wall. "I took out Netzke, then I ripped Mathis's empire of cards down. Now here we are. I stripped you of your power and your pack, and now you're not even worth anything to the master you sold your soul to."

Jan narrowed his eyes and pushed his head forward. "How…"

Luke laughed and slipped his hand under his hoodie, activating the medallion, calling forth the visage of Pierre Luc-Thibaut Archambeau, Comte de Maubeuge.

Jan gasped and pointed a shaky finger at Luke. "You…"

Pushing off the wall, Luke sketched an elegant bow. "At your service." He touched the medallion and deactivated it. "Did you think you could become my enemy and live to tell the tale?" Luke waited for an answer, then continued when Jan kept quiet. "Many have tried, but all have failed. But thanks to you, and Mathis and Netzke, word of your fate will warn a new generation *not to fuck with me.*" Luke yelled the last five words, a bit of spit flying out with his anger.

Luke turned and signaled for everyone to move out. Luke nearly reached the stairs when Jan finally broke.

"Luke! Please. Don't leave me here to die that way. At least give me a clean death. Luke! LUKE! Lu…ke…"

When Luke started down the stairs, he heard Jan break down and start sobbing. The team remained silent as they worked their way down the stairs.

It wasn't until they reached the landing before another switchback that Jean-Paul broke the silence. "Annabelle, please put a note in my calendar to never ever fuck over the Centurio Immortalis."

"You got it, boss," she replied.

Luke chuckled quietly and shook his head. He'd come to know Jean-Paul well enough to know the Parisian was making a joke to lighten the mood while meaning every word he'd said.

Once they found the next floor, everyone cleared a path and let Luke move to the front. In teams of two, they swept down the hall, peeking into the doors they found. They looked to be the sleeping quarters for lesser ranked vampires—small, with multiple empty beds in each room. The thought of all those vampires dead brought a mirthless smile to Luke's face as he turned around and headed to the stairs.

On the next floor, they found a few rooms with occupants who they quickly staked. Luke checked his phone. They were about an hour from sunset, yet still had more work to do. He hoped the exertion and wounding would force Le Mousquetaire to sleep late. Otherwise, this could turn into a mess if they were trapped deep in the bowels of Le Mousquetaire's mansion with vampires waking up angry and hungry.

Luke heaved a sigh of relief when they reached the bottom of the stairs with no more heading down. There were only a few doors on this level—large,` heavy oak numbers that would have been at home in a castle. Luke had bashed his way through more than a few doors in the last few years, but these thick monstrosities were beyond his supernaturally enhanced strength, and maybe more than a werewolf or three could take down. When they tried the first door, it was locked.

Jean-Paul reached into his pocket and pulled out his lock picking set. "These old skeleton locks should be easy enough."

Luke set his hand on Jean-Paul's shoulder. "Hold on. Can you get the big door at the end of the hall first? I think that's the one I want."

"Right." Jean-Paul strode to the end of the hall and quickly picked the lock.

"Guns ready, Roxi and I will go in first. If he's still asleep, I want you to open the rest of the rooms and clean them out."

"You're the boss," Jean-Paul replied.

Luke pulled his rudis out and handed it to Delilah. "Can you stake one for me? I'll drain it on the way out."

Delilah raised an eyebrow in question, but nodded and kept quiet.

He nodded as he took the handle of the door and pushed in, shoving the door wide open. Two shotgun barrels were raised and pointed into the room, but nothing stirred.

As Luke surveyed the room, he snorted. "This asshole actually sleeps in a coffin?"

Jean-Paul snickered as he turned to attend to the other doors.

Roxi stepped into the room and began rifling through the armoire. "Damn. No cowled black cape lined with red silk. I figured he'd go full Dracula if he was going to sleep in a coffin," she said as she closed the armoire's doors.

Luke was more focused on the Monet on the wall. That was coming with him. When he turned around, his eyes went wide; a Bruegel painting was staring back at him. He'd give that to Pieter.

Roxi slipped up behind him and leaned her chin on his shoulder. "What you doing?"

"Planning an art heist."

"That's an interesting painting."

"It's a Bruegel. Most likely either Pieter or his father. He'll be able to tell us."

Roxi slipped her arms under his and squeezed him, contracting the bands of his armor. "How do you want to do this, dōšagīh?"

"Would you like to stake him?" Luke asked, caressing her arms as he stared at the painting.

"I couldn't deprive you of this, not after all he's done to you and your friends."

"If you'll play along, I have an idea." He twisted his head around and kissed her cheek.

"Of course."

He filled her in on his plan and made sure she was on board with it. "OK. Let's get the lid off his sleeping coffin."

Roxi stepped back and walked to the foot of the elaborately carved coffin. On the count of three, they lifted the lid and set it aside, tipped against the wall. Le Mousquetaire lay perfectly still, his arms crossed over his lower ribs. When Jean-Paul stepped into the room, Luke held a finger to his lips to keep his friend quiet. Jean-Paul nodded and raised his shoulders in question. Luke pointed to the wall at the foot of the coffin. Roxi set her sword aside and pulled her rudis from its scabbard. She waited nearby.

Luke, standing at the head of the coffin, stared at the face of the vampire that had made his life hell for the last three years. The rest of the team must have finished cleaning out the other rooms; they gathered and filled the space around the door, standing back but still there to enjoy the show.

It had to be near wake up time for the fanger. He checked his phone. It was officially sunset. The sun would release its hold on the vampire soon. He couldn't keep still as he waited, opting to pace back and forth at the head of the coffin. Each pass, he'd check only to find a still perfectly motionless vampire. So he continued his silent pacing.

When he turned for the latest pass, he stopped when Roxi went into motion, raising her rudis to her side. Le Mousquetaire stirred.

Luke stepped up to the head of the coffin and crossed his arms, resting them on the ledge of the coffin. He laid his head on his crossed wrists and waited. Roxi stood over the coffin, her rudis held in the reverse grip with both hands and poised to strike just over the vampire's heart.

Le Mousquetaire sniffed the air, then his eyes shot open and filled with terror.

Luke grinned broadly. "Good morning, sunshine."

The fanger started to move, but it was too late. Roxi plunged her rudis into Le Mousquetaire's heart. He ceased moving.

"Beautifully done, Roxiustana."

"Thank you, dōšagīh." She leaned across the coffin toward Luke.

He obliged her by leaning in for a kiss.

"Goodbye, Robert Beaufort," Jean-Paul mumbled quietly.

"They're very weird," someone said in thickly French-accented English.

"You have no idea," Delilah replied.

Parting, Luke stared into the sparkling brown eyes of the woman he loved. Straightening to his full height, he pointed to the paintings. "I'm keeping these two, if someone would take them down and carry them out."

Jean-Paul pointed to a couple of his people who jumped to, quickly pulling the paintings off the wall and taking them from the room. "We found several in the other rooms that'll make nice additions to our pack house."

"Only seems fair." Luke reached into the coffin and rifled through Le Mousquetaire's pockets, finding a heavy key chain filled with a variety of keys, including some skeleton keys. He tossed them to Jean-Paul. "Congratulations, you're the proud owner of a vampire den."

Jean-Paul chuckled and stuffed them into a coat pocket.

"Anything else we need?" Roxi asked.

He felt around the coffin but didn't find anything of interest. "There's nothing here."

Roxi's eyes flicked down to her rudis then to the observers then to Luke. Nodding, he smiled gently at her then turned to face the crowd.

"OK, everyone out." He walked around the coffin, blocking the view and pointed down the hall with both hands.

Jean-Paul helped usher everyone out then followed, leaving Luke and Roxi alone. Roxi laid her forehead on the end of the pommel and recited the incantation to activate the rudis. Light moved down the handle from her forehead down the blade and silver filigree into the vampire's chest then back out, making a return trip to disappear back into Roxi's forehead. Standing up, she sighed, looking refreshed. With a twist, she yanked the rudis from Le Mousquetaire's, leaving a dusty pile in the coffin.

"Shall we?" Roxi held her arm out.

Luke took her arm and walked from Le Mousquetaire's bedroom and grave. When they passed the room with the vamp Delilah had staked with his rudis, he stepped in and drained it.

With the added energy from the drained vamp, the stairs didn't seem so onerous, especially after ending the powerful vampire lord.

"Hey, Luke. I found a couple laptops. I snagged them for Jamaal," Delilah said.

"Nice job," Luke replied.

When they arrived at the prison cell level, Jean-Paul stopped and stepped out of the line. "Should we really leave him here?" He hitched his thumb over his shoulder toward the end of the hall.

Jan lay in a heap on the floor, clinging to the prison bars. Luke fought back the wave of pity. The man deserved to die horribly, but Luke wasn't the only one he'd committed crimes against. He sighed and shook his head.

"Delilah, I need the tranq gun."

Delilah stopped and pulled the backpack from off and fished out the tranq gun. "I'm not sure it'll be safe to carry him up those stairs, even with werewolf strength."

"Annabelle, go get some appropriate bindings for our war criminal," Jean-Paul called.

Luke took the gun and marched to the end hall, pointing it at Jan. Jean-Paul grabbed Le Mousquetaire's keys and readied them at the lock.

"You're coming with us, Jan. You can stand trial for the crimes you've committed. If you cooperate, you can walk out of here. If you try anything, I'll shoot you with this. It won't be pleasant for you if I have to do that. Understand?"

Jan lifted his head, hope kindling in his eyes.

"Don't try me."

Jan nodded eagerly.

Jean-Paul unlocked the door, and Jan walked out, keeping his hands raised to chest height. Luke poked the gun's barrel into his back and marched him out and up the stairs. When they reached the house, Annabelle called from the other room that she had the manacles.

Jan, body tensed, spun lightning quick and knocked the gun from Luke's hands and darted out of reach as people lunged for him. He dashed out of the study, bowling over several unprepared people. Luke chased after him just in time to see Jan smash through the front window and take off across the street to disappear into the park.

"Fuck!" Luke yelled, restraining himself from finding something heavy to kick.

"Do we go after him?" Jean-Paul asked.

Luke, rubbing his temples, sighed. "That's up to you. My people are done for and don't know the city."

"As are we after last night and this. I'll put a bounty on his head," Jean-Paul replied.

Luke sucked at his cheeks and popped his lips as he unclenched his jaw. "I'll match it." He sighed. "Pieter's not going to be happy his brother escaped yet again. I'll call him on the way back. Let's get out of here before someone calls the authorities."

Pausing to stow the weapons, people left in small groups, carrying out the various weaponry and paintings they'd pilfered. Luke found a love seat in the sitting room and dropped into it, fuming. Roxi sat next to him and took his hand in hers. They sat quietly together.

The feel of Roxi's warm hand helped assuage his anger, as did the song she quietly hummed under her breath. A few minutes later,

Jean-Paul stepped into the room and leaned up against the wall across from them.

"You've managed to take out all your enemies. What's next for the Centurio Immortalis?" Jean-Paul asked.

Luke looked over at Roxi, a hint of a smile teasing at his lips, then to Jean-Paul. "Unfortunately, not quite all of them. But Jan aside…" He paused for a moment, then exhaled sharply. "I'll need to talk to my team first, but I think after my people heal, it's time to go home. I have a kid I miss, and a cat that needs some scritches."

Jean-Paul chuckled. "Good, that gives me time to plan a farewell party for you and our new Portland friends." He pulled his vibrating phone from his pocket. "Our ride is here."

Luke stood and offered Roxi a hand. They followed Jean-Paul out to a fancy SUV. He held the doors for them, then climbed into the front passenger seat.

"Take my friends to their hotel. I think they could use some rest," Jean-Paul said.

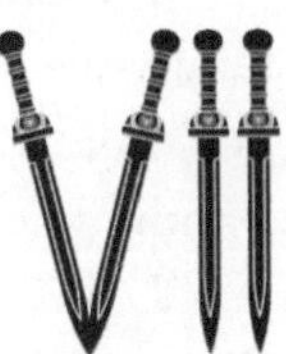

CHAPTER
TWENTY-SEVEN

LUKE AND HIS LEADERSHIP TEAM—AHMED, Delilah, Jamaal, Jung-sook, Maggie, Owen, Pablo, Pieter, Roxi, Sam, and Simone—arrived at the appointed time at the Paris pack house. Jean-Paul met them at the door, graciously ushering them in and to the large conference room. The jovial Parisian had snacks and beverages prepared, including plenty of bottles of wine.

Jean-Paul, at the head of the table as the host, stood and raised his arms to draw the room to silence. "Welcome, my friends! Please take a moment to grab some hors d'oeuvres. I've selected a nice variety of French wines to help facilitate our convivial conversation. Help yourselves."

After they'd assembled their food and drinks, they returned to their seats, testing their treats with sips and nibbles.

Jean-Paul returned to the head of the table. "Luke tells me this is a tradition when an important mission has been completed." He sat, raising an eyebrow, and turned his attention to Luke. "That implies that you have completed a task?"

Luke looked around at his people then nodded at Jean-Paul. "We have. We removed Netzke, dismantled Mathis's schemes, toppled Jan, and eliminated the vampire lord that brought them all together to create chaos throughout Western Europe. I think that's enough for one trip."

Jean-Paul raised an eyebrow and smirked through his beard. "That's a fair tally of regime change. So what's next?"

"It's time to go home. We've been away for too long. We have family we miss and lives to return to."

"That's it? Just hop on the next plane and go?" Jean-Paul asked, leaning back in his chair with his glass of wine.

"Luke," Jamaal interrupted. "I just got a message from Holly, she's ready."

"Let's bring her in."

Jamaal hooked up the laptop to a large screen with a camera sitting on it. A moment later, an image of Holly appeared on the screen.

"Hello, Holly," Luke said. "You know everyone here, except for our generous host and new friend, Jean-Paul Aquitaine. He's the packleader of Paris and played a key role in helping with our plans."

"It's a pleasure to meet you, Mr. Aquitaine," Holly said.

Jean-Paul stood up and bowed. "Enchantée. And please, call me Jean-Paul."

"I'd appreciate it if you'd call me Holly."

"Of course. And let me start by passing on my condolences for your fallen packmates. Depending on their families' wishes, it would be an honor to inter them in our pack cemetery. They will be given a place of honor for all they've done to help preserve our pack and return peace to the region."

"That is most gracious of you, Jean-Paul. I'll allow Sam to manage that. All of our packmembers completed instructions for such an occasion. She'll be able to handle the disposition of their remains. I wish to extend my thanks for ensuring more of my pack-mates won't be joining them. You and your packmates will always be welcome in Portland as our friends and guests." She shifted her head to address Luke. "Well done, Luke. Sam gave me a summary. You've done well to lead our people with so few casualties."

Luke nodded. "I wish it could have been less, but all things considered..."

"And I see you got Roxi back." Holly smiled and looked toward the Parthian woman. "Will you be returning to Portland?"

Roxi smiled nervously and gave a small wave. "That is my intention, as long as I'm still welcome."

"Of course you are. You've fought and bled for our packmates. You've kept my wife and friends alive to come home to me. If you wish to make Portland your home, the pack welcomes you."

Pieter cleared his throat and sat up, leaning over the table. "Holly. I would like to make my official request to make Portland my permanent home. I've spoken with Amiata, and we've both decided that our future isn't in Belgium. We'd love to continue being surrounded by our new friends."

Holly smiled warmly. "I'm glad to hear it. Amiata and I have become quite close as we've worked together to integrate the former Flanders people into the pack. I'm glad my friend will be staying. You'll both be a welcome addition to the pack, and I'm sure Gwen will be happy to know her best friend isn't leaving."

Pieter relaxed and sank back into his chair. "Thank you, Holly."

Luke quirked an eyebrow up. He knew that Gwen and Olivia were friends, but he was glad they'd found each other. Olivia needed a friend after being taken from her home, especially after the murder of her father. He was glad Gwen had someone she could claim as a best friend. He hoped to get some more time with his ward; he'd missed too much of her life.

"You should have some wine for the meeting, Holly," Jean-Paul said, raising his glass, and smiled broadly.

"It's a bit early here." She lifted a coffee mug into the camera frame. "I'll have to settle for coffee. So, Luke, what all do you have left to do and when can we expect y'all to come home?"

"I'd like to start sending the peripheral people home at the earliest point when it's convenient. Once everyone is in Paris, we'll send them home via commercial flights. I'll keep the core group to take care of logistics on our new acquired toys and everything else we brought with us."

Jean-Paul interrupted. "Also, you can't leave until after the treaty meeting. Everyone involved has requested you be a signatory to it."

"That's a great honor, Luke," Holly said. "It'll bring prestige to our pack. Who all will attend?"

"Paris, Flanders, and the Rhein are the big three, but several smaller packs will be there."

"What about Luxembourg?" Holly asked. "Since a lot of this started with them…"

"The pack is no more, at least independently speaking. The remaining temporary council that replaced Mathis has requested to join the Rhein Pack," Jean-Paul replied.

Pieter and rested his elbows on the table, leaning forward. "That's good. Heidi will keep them in line but make sure there's no resentment."

"Any word on the rogue packs?" Delilah asked as she reached over to take Simone's hand.

Jean-Paul, on his way to the wine, stopped and turned to the camera. "Word is being spread that if they take the ringleaders into custody and hold them, that we will provide support and conduct the investigation and hold the trials afterwards. If some packs decide to hold out and fight, the alliance will hold them to account. With the vampires interfering in pack politics, sewing dissent and hatred, it's time the larger packs played a broader role in the neighborhood and make sure everyone is united against the common foe."

"Also, if packmembers know they can find sanctuary with the bigger packs, maybe things won't go like they did in mine," Simone said.

Jean-Paul's face, normally jovial, saddened. "Yes. It is to our eternal shame that we didn't protect those who needed it. We were too focused on ourselves and didn't pay attention to what was happening only a few hours away. We let down your family and many others. I aim to see that it never happens again."

Simone nodded, her jaw set. "Good."

"Is there any word on Pieter's brother?" Holly asked.

Pieter scowled. "No. Jan has found some hole to hide in. He's as slippery as an eel, and twice as slimy."

Jean-Paul snorted and smirked. "We've placed a sizable bounty on his head. Our Belgian and Dutch allies of the Flanders Pack are most interested in asking him a few pointed questions about his dealings. At this point, his head is more valuable to others than it is to himself."

"We'll be sure to keep an eye out for him here, if he decides to come after Amiata and Olivia," Holly said. "What word on the vampires?"

"They're scattering like roaches when you turn the lights on. Without Le Mousquetaire, the few remaining elites are fighting for the scraps. After your friends here swept through town, there seem to be a whole lot fewer vampires left." Jean-Paul raised his glass and tipped it toward Luke. "Luke and his friends have agreed to provide more training on how to handle vampires so we can be more efficient about it. We have a team producing stakes and other anti-vampire equipment. The pack is very eager to clean up the city."

"Plus, all the treasures you're taking from the vampires makes for a good incentive," Sam said, raising her glass to Jean-Paul.

"We're just doing our patriotic duty to repatriate French treasures," Jean-Paul replied piously.

Luke chuckled. "You are a true son of France, my friend. Anything else we can tell you, Holly?"

"I think that's all I had for the moment. It'll be a rolling conversation as you disembark from Europe, so I'm sure we'll be in contact constantly." Holly held up her coffee up and smiled. "We'll see you all soon. Stay safe."

As they waved or said good bye, Holly's screen blinked out. Jamaal grabbed his laptop and put it back into his backpack.

"Have you had any luck cracking the computers we took from Le Mousquetaire's mansion?" Luke asked Jamaal.

"Not yet. I'm working with Jean-Paul's tech people, but so far the vamps have us stymied. We're making some bulk copies of the drives so we can spread the work out," Jamaal replied.

"Will we be able to work on it when we get home, without tying up one of our French speakers?" Luke looked at his teammates.

"If we have to, that's a priority, so we can move someone to help," Sam said.

Maggie raised her hand to break into the conversation. "There's no need. Herschel is fluent. He escaped from France before the Nazis took over."

"That's convenient," Luke said. "Unless anyone has anything else, I think we can call it for today and everyone can get back to their tasks."

When no one spoke up, he thanked them for attending, sending them on their way.

He spun his chair to face Roxi. "We have the afternoon and evening free, any thoughts on what you'd like to do?"

Roxi's brow furrowed. "I hope this is alright, but I think I'd like to take some quiet time to myself and wander around and maybe get an early night's sleep." She leaned forward, quickly adding, "It's just that I'm not used to being around so many people all the time."

Luke chuckled and grasped her hand, squeezing it. "I totally understand. I took me a long time to get used to being around people again. After we get home, I think I'm going to hide for a while and only see my favorite people. All this forced interaction, especially having to spend time with people I loathe while pretending to like them. It's draining."

"Yes, it's a lot, especially since I didn't get the small lead up you did with Delilah and Pablo."

"Yeah. I got a bit of a warm-up on peopling. Anytime you need quiet time, don't hesitate to talk to me. I want you to be happy," Luke replied.

"Thank you. I appreciate that. Why don't you ask your pretty doctor to show you around Paris? I'm sure she would love some Luke time." Roxi smiled reassuringly.

"I think that would be a good idea, if that's OK with you?"

"Of course. I don't want to interfere with your relationship with Maggie. I just want to be a part of your life, not monopolize it."

Luke picked up her hand and kissed the back of it. "Thank you."

"Why don't you give me a kiss and go catch up to Maggie before she heads back to the hospital."

Leaning over, Luke slid his finger under her chin and drew her closer for a deep kiss that ended too quickly. "Enjoy your day."

"You too, dōšagīh."

Luke squeezed her hand one last time, then briskly walked out of the conference room. He found Maggie standing in front of the pack house with Sam.

"Hey, Luke," Sam waved as he approached.

Maggie smiled warmly. "Big plans for your afternoon?"

"That depends on you. If you're available, would you like to show me around Paris?" Luke asked.

"I could be available. Do you mind if we stop by the hospital first? I just need to check on a couple things, then I can clear my schedule for the day."

"I'll catch you two later," Sam said. "I think I'm going to go find a coffee. Delilah and Simone invited me to go to a couple dance clubs tonight."

"House beats and flashing lights?" Luke shivered. "Not my scene."

Sam laughed. "Didn't you go to a dance club in Portland and dance?"

"That was for work, and it was more hip-hop. Also, all the dance moves I know are older than either Delilah or Simone, and I don't feel like being laughed at in multiple languages for my dusty moves."

"Besides, I have other plans for him." Maggie slipped an arm through his.

"You two have fun." She hugged Maggie and kissed her on the cheek, then gave Luke the same treatment. "I'll talk to you tomorrow."

"The hospital isn't too far away, and it's not too cold. Would you like to walk?" Maggie asked.

"Sounds lovely."

"It's nice to spend some time with you. You've been so busy with everything and with Roxi finally on the mend… Are you sure Roxi is OK with this?" She held her hand up, gesturing between them.

"It was her idea. We're working out the details, but she doesn't want to interfere in the relationship you and I have."

"That's good. I just wanted to check in. It's important to keep open lines of communication." Maggie smiled sweetly.

"I appreciate your concern for Roxi. She's still getting used to being around people after living a solitary life and wanted to have some alone time. So I'm all yours," Luke replied.

"Then I think we'll head back to the hotel and pick up a change of clothes." Maggie stopped and pulled Luke in close. Running her hand over his cheek, she leaned in for a kiss that stretched and intensified until they were both left breathing heavily when they finally parted. A mischievous smile spread across her face. "Bring your change of clothes to my room. I think we can find something to do to keep ourselves busy this afternoon. Afterward, we can clean up and head out. I feel like experiencing some fine dining and wine."

Luke opened his mouth to speak, but the butterflies in his stomach robbed him of his words. Instead, he kissed her until his words returned. "That sounds perfect."

EPILOGUE

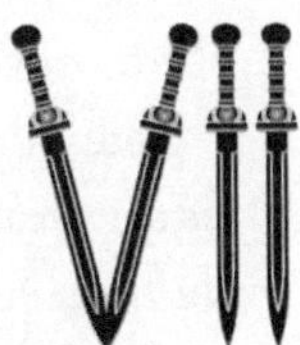

LUKE STOOD ON THE TARMAC, overseeing the loading of their gear into the private jets they'd chartered to fly them back to Portland. As he watched every corner and every shadow for any signs of something amiss, his breathing grew shallow.

Roxi slid her hand over his shoulder and ran her fingers over the back of his neck, massaging the muscles at the base of his skull. "Dōšagīh, Jean-Paul asked if there was anything else you needed from him at the moment." Her voice was a low, even though Jean-Paul probably heard it easily with his werewolf ears.

Luke coughed lightly to buy himself a few seconds. "I'm sorry. I got distracted. No. I don't think there's anything else. Looks like we're almost loaded and ready to go."

"Luke, it's been a real pleasure meeting you. I want you to know you're always welcome in Paris." Jean-Paul smiled broadly.

"The feeling is mutual." Luke reached out to shake Jean-Paul's hand.

Instead, the big man pulled Luke into a hug, air kissing his cheeks. "Safe journey, my friend." He released Luke and kissed Roxi's cheeks. "Roxi. It was wonderful meeting you. Try to keep this guy out trouble."

Roxi laughed. "If I spend my time doing that, who'll keep me out of trouble?"

Sam poked her head out of the lead jet. "You ready to go, Luke?"

Luke startled at the sudden call from Sam. "I think so. We'll be there in a moment."

Sam nodded and withdrew into the jet.

"Jean-Paul. Thanks for everything. If you ever find yourself in Oregon, you'll be my guest, and I'll show you around." Luke fixed a smile onto his face he hoped read as genuine enough.

"I'm due some vacation time. I might have to take you up on that offer. Now, go! Your departure time is quickly approaching." Jean-Paul shooed them toward their plane.

Luke nodded and turned around, taking Roxi's hand. Together, they strode toward the jet, Luke guiding Roxi up the stairs first then following her. Once he sat down next to Roxi and buckled in, he waited for the door to close, then for the plane to taxi toward the runway. Breathing shallowly, his brow furrowed and every muscle in his body wound tight.

As soon as the plane lifted off the ground and the G-forces increased, pushing him back into his seat, he exhaled explosively.

"Are you alright, dōšagīh?" Roxi asked.

He inhaled deeply, holding it then exhaled and repeated it a few times, expanding his chest and trying to get his muscles to relax. "I was afraid we wouldn't make it off the ground. I guess I didn't realize how much trauma I was carrying with me from my abduction. The situation was nearly identical."

"Except Jean-Paul is an honorable man and your ally," Roxi said.

"Yeah. I tried to keep that in mind, but my reptilian brain was trying to take over there. Thanks for stepping in. I think you staved off a full panic attack."

She squeezed his hand and kissed his cheek. "I'm glad it helped. You know, I had a nice time in Paris, but I can't wait to stop living out of a bag and have a place to call home for a while."

"Only for a while?" Luke asked, raising an eyebrow.

"Who knows what our future holds, and where we'll be called off to fight? It'll just be nice to wake up in the same place." Roxi leaned into him, resting her head on his shoulder.

Luke liked the sound of "we." She was right, though. For a while, they might settle in and create a home together, but it'd only be a brief respite until their next campaign in the long war against the vampires. For the first time in ages, maybe ever, Luke thought there might be an end in sight. They had met and survived an entity that claimed to be the master of the vampires. If they could find it or draw it out, they could try to kill it, and by killing it, maybe end vampiredom entirely.

Then he would be free. Free to love Roxi and Maggie and his friends, and to finish raising Gwen, though he'd done precious little of that since she moved in with him. He planned to correct that, though, and do everything he could to ensure she had the best upbringing she could ask for.

Roxi reached up and ran her hand down his cheek and jaw. "What's got you so pensive, dōšagīh?"

"Just thinking about the future," he replied.

"What about?"

"Just that I might have one."

"Oh, Luke. Of course, you will. Everyone here wants to end this so we can build the world we want without monsters hunting us, at least supernatural ones. I want to have a future, and I want it to be with you." Roxi snuggled into him.

As Roxi's words sank in, Luke realized that not only might he make it to a future in which there wouldn't be vampires, but he had a spark of longing for that future and the good things he could build into his life. The things he wanted weren't just for others' safety and prosperity, but his own. He wanted a future, and he knew who he wanted to share it with.

"I want that too, Roxi," he replied.

She straightened up and turned Luke's head for a kiss. "I love you, Lucius Silvanius Ferrata."

Luke smiled, hope burning in his eyes. "I love you too, Roxiustana Surena."

Luke Irontree will return in Ancient Sword Falling.
Available Now!
Keep Reading for a short preview.

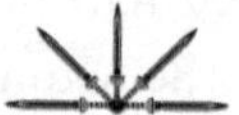

LUKE IRONTREE WILL RETURN IN

ANCIENT SWORD FALLING

LUKE IRONTREE WILL RETURN IN

ANCIENT SWORD FALLING: BOOK EIGHT

CHAPTER ONE

Luke's heart raced as the private jet took off from the small Parisian airport. The last time he'd attempted to board a private jet offered by a European packleader, he'd been tranquilized and kidnapped as he watched his friends fly away, helpless to aid him.

Gripping the armrests, he thought he might rip them from the seat. Roxi did her best to soothe him as his foot tapped nervously on the airplane's floor. He appreciated Roxi's efforts. Though the only thing that worked was gravity pushing him back in his seat as the plane's wheels left the ground. The jet climbing, he took his first deep breath. And once the relief settled in, he felt hollowed out.

He did his best to push the tension away once they leveled out and were safely away from the airport, though he never could break entirely free from it. Next to him, Roxi slept, alternating between resting against the inner wall of the private jet and snuggling up on his shoulder. When she leaned on him, he turned his head and kissed the top of hers, her wild hair tickling his nose. She hadn't had a professional haircut in a long time, according to her, but even when freshly styled, it still liked to fly away. The other bonus of her proximity was her scent. It tantalized and calmed him all at once.

He'd spent months bringing down the three packleaders who'd betrayed him, exacting bloody vengeance and utterly destroying them. But saving Roxi and reversing Mithras's compulsion ultimately was the most important to him.

If the choice had been Roxi or vengeance, he'd have forsaken his own revenge for her life. Fortunately, he didn't have to do either. Mathis had been taken down then cast out to try to survive; no doubt there were multiple bounties on his head from all those he'd betrayed in his hunt for power and wealth. Without his money and connections, he was useless to his vampire overlords. In fact, he was a loose end for them to tie up. Permanently.

Heinrich Netzke, Cologne's former alpha, had been turned over to his pack for trial and justice. Luke didn't bother asking what that meant in the scheme of things. It wasn't his business. Heidi, the new packleader, could manage her own affairs.

His only regret was that he hadn't been able to bring justice to Jan, the man who'd murdered his own father to gain control of the wealthy Flanders Pack, their control of Belgium and the south of the Netherlands, and the mighty ports in Antwerp and Rotterdam. Luke had helped orchestrate his fall, removing his wealth and leadership of the Pack, but he'd slipped through their fingers and escaped the justice everyone wanted to bring to the patricidal fuckhead.

Luke felt for Pieter, who'd have to wait a bit longer before he could avenge his murdered father. Sometimes Pieter was hard to read. Mostly, he looked weary. Luke would have to get some private time with his Belgian friend for a heart-to-heart when they were both settled after their travels.

With a stop in New York City to refuel, they still had a long day before they landed back home in Portland. Luke couldn't wait to see his girlfriend Maggie—she'd been one of the first to depart after their conference in Paris—and his adopted child Gwen and bestow some well-earned scritches on his cat Alfred.

His life before becoming involved with the North Portland Pack had been a lonely and tedious life with only his cat Alfred to keep him company. At first, he'd feared involving Pablo and Delilah in vampire hunting, but if he'd not given in, he'd probably have been dead multiple times over by now. He'd been reluctant at first, but they'd become so much more than allies of convenience.

He turned in his seat and smiled at Pablo and Delilah. Pablo grinned and winked at him. Delilah nodded, the corners of her lips quirking up. They were family. And knowing them had helped him grow his family further.

He would never have met Maggie. And even though the circumstances of their meeting were dark, he'd never have met Roxi. She'd have died alone in that prison under the arena or in one of their arenas fighting to entertain the soulless bloodsucking monsters.

So many lives intersecting with his would have been irrevocably altered had he not taken the chance and made two new friends. Now, he loved and was loved. He had a girlfriend and, though they hadn't discussed official terms, another budding relationship. He had friends, and he had a young teen he needed to guide to adulthood. He also had a weird dog whose presence locked in one of the high security cells of the arena was still a mystery.

When they hit a patch of rough air, Roxi startled awake, her eyes wide. Her unfocused gaze flicked about as she clung tightly to Luke's hand. When her breathing calmed, she looked a bit sheepish.

"Sorry. I didn't know where I was. I sometimes wake up and think I'm still in that cell under the arena," she mumbled just loud enough for him to hear it.

"That's OK, Roxi. I still struggle with the memory of the arena, too. I haven't had enough time to really unpack it with my therapist, not with the full half year we've had since getting out. It's a lot." Resting his hand on her cheek, he turned her head and kissed her.

"I'm glad I can wake up next to you, even if it's on this rinky-dink plane. It feels more secure to be near you. For so long, you were the only bright light. Now I have more to look forward to than seeing your face through a hole in the stone."

Luke chuckled. "Yeah. It's a bit of an adjustment not being in that cell, but the last few weeks with you have been wonderful. It's weird to say, but I wouldn't trade it for anything."

"Yeah. It's the one good thing I can say about the arena—it brought me you." Roxi kissed his cheek.

"It might be more than just one positive. In all the years I've been doing this, I've never had a target to aim for. I've killed powerful elite vampires by the legion, but I've never had a true target to aim my gladius at. We've brought down some powerful associates of the vampires and spoked the wheel of their plans in Western Europe. We've got a whole bunch of financial intelligence we'll need to sort through, but I think we have a real chance of doing something meaningful and potentially permanently disabling to the vampires." Luke could feel his excitement building at the thought of maybe being able to end it all.

Roxi looked scared and hopeful all at once. "Do…do you really think that's possible? To, you know, end it? For real?"

"I hope so, and for once, that hope might actually have some evidence to back and bolster it." He squeezed Roxi's hand.

"I truly hope you're right, Luke. There is nothing more I long for, well, other than being in your arms, but ending vampires would be a close second."

Luke chuckled at the sweet grin on her face. "Roxi, I love you."

She patted Luke on the cheek. "I know. Now let me out. I need to visit the loo."

He moved out and let her into the narrow walkway, then sat back down. He didn't want to let himself fantasize about a world without vampires, so he forced his brain to lean into the other fantasies he had—home and friends and loved ones. He was still amazed at how domestic his desires had become. Spending time with Gwen talking music or teaching her to fight. Goofing with his friends down at the pub as they shared beers. Kissing a beautiful woman he adored. Sleeping late and being woken by an insistent cat. These had become the goalposts for a good life for him, the things he truly wanted.

Sam squeezed his shoulder, interrupting his wool gathering. "Scoot."

He slid over into Roxi's seat, letting Sam take his spot. "What can I do for you, Sam?"

"Nothing specific. Just wanted to check in with you to see how you're doing. You seemed pretty tense this morning."

"Yeah. I was having some real trouble keeping calm until we got off the ground. I almost had a panic attack. About the only thing that staved it off was Roxi's presence. I was terrified something bad would happen."

Sam squeezed his forearm. "I bet. That was terrible last time. I don't know if anyone told you about the flight back after they saw what happened, but it was a very unhappy crowd of people. A lot of anger and tears. I honestly had some concerns as well, even with an official alliance with Jean-Paul."

Luke nodded. "I'll have to apologize to him if I seemed weird and unappreciative. I'm sure he'll understand."

"Yeah. He seems like a genuinely good man. I'm glad to have met him. He'll make a good ally."

"Plus, he has connections we don't and can get us in contact with other key packs in Europe. Hopefully he can bring them into the cause, or if nothing else, at least assure their neutrality. We can't afford to be fighting big, rich packs and vampires. He's working on a side project for me."

"Oh?" Sam asked, raising an eyebrow.

Luke grinned mischievously. "Just a little surprise in case we need some bigger firepower. The vampires seem to be upping the ante on us."

"You're not wrong there." Sam shook her head before smiling. "We can talk politics later. How are you and Roxi doing?"

Luke nodded and grinned. "We're doing well, I think. We're talking about a future together."

Sam chuckled. "Do you remember the first time we flew to Europe together? When we flew to Belgium?"

"Yeah…" Luke squinted his eyes at Sam, unsure where she was going with the conversation.

"Remember when I asked if you were going to look for someone to date besides Maggie, since you had the option as a person in a poly relationship?" Sam grinned mischievously, her eyes twinkling with mirth.

"Yeah. I do remember that now that you mention it."

"Well, it seems you are ready for a second relationship."

Luke chuckled. "I guess so."

"How do you feel about it?"

"Good but confused. A little anxious." Luke laughed at himself. "I've used 'confused' to describe myself so many times since meeting you all and having Gwen move in, then dating Maggie. Seems like the perpetual state of being with my personal life."

Sam smiled brightly. "It's good, though, right?"

"Yeah. It is. I'm having positive thoughts about the future, and all my fantasies are terribly domestic and simple."

"Luke Irontree, I think you're becoming a real boy!"

"Ha! I'm still a puppet. Haven't managed to cut those divine strings yet. But I can handle feeling more real, more attached to a life of meaning beyond the end of my sword."

"It's a powerful incentive to have meaningful things to fight for, to protect. I know you've been working your whole life to protect humanity, but billions of people are abstract. Maggie and Roxi and Gwen, those are all very tangible and real entities."

"And you, Delilah, and Pablo, and the rest of the crew. But you're right. I feel more integrated into humanity instead of just being an outside observer. I would have never thought it was possible to get to this place, not as old and outside of humanity as I've been, but here I am."

Sam nodded. "Here you are. I'm so proud of you, Luke. I don't mean this to sound condescending, but you've come such a long way since that first time we met. You were such a sad, lonely person. As much as you tried to pretend to be 'normal,' you couldn't hide the pain in your eyes."

Luke sighed and shook his head. "Sometimes I feel like a stray puppy Pablo brought home."

Sam chuckled, patting Luke's knee. "Yeah, he kind of adopted you, but I'm glad he did. You're a wonderful friend and a good man. My life is better for having met you."

"I feel the same about you, too." He leaned over and kissed Sam's forehead.

"So, got any big—"

Sam's question was interrupted by one of the pilots activating the intercom. "Sorry to disturb you, folks. But we're getting some troubling news coming in. We don't have much information yet, but it looks like a plane just crashed near JFK in New York. We're being diverted to an airfield in Maine. I'll let you know more when we can."

"Oh, my." Sam held her hands in front of her mouth.

Luke couldn't find the words and only nodded.

"Um, I see Roxi coming. I'll let her have her seat back." Sam stood up, looking unsteady and unnaturally pale after hearing the tragic news.

Roxi sat down and wrapped her arms around Luke. Feeling the

tremble in her body, he pulled her in tightly with one arm while he stroked her hair with his other hand.

"Did…did they say a plane crashed? It was hard to hear in the water closet."

"Yeah. Outside New York near JFK International. Are you OK?"

"I…I don't like flying, even at the best of times."

Luke squeezed her, kissing her forehead. "That's OK. It's understandable."

Holding her in his arms, he hummed the melody to the Gaulish lullaby she liked him to sing to her when she felt down. The simple sound seemed to calm her as she clung to him. He didn't know how long they were supposed to be in the air or how much time had passed since taking off, but landing couldn't come soon enough.

Behind him, the level of noise picked up as people discussed the snippet of news the pilot had given them. Luke wanted to tell them to be quiet as their speculation, loud enough for Roxi with her supernatural ears to hear, caused her to tremble more. He thought he heard her sniffle. It was confirmed when she rubbed her cheeks with her sleeve. A tear fell onto his arm, running down and falling onto his pants.

"Luke, please don't stop humming. If you could sing, it would be better, so I'd have something to concentrate on besides…"

"Sure." Luke kissed the top of her head and started at the beginning of the song, this time with the words.

By now, Roxi had heard it so many times, she knew the melody as well as Luke. It didn't take her long, not as a trained singer. It had been a skill she'd developed as part of her role as an assassin and spy for her father, the Parthian king's general, and for the Parthian Empire. It had also provided a valuable skill to allow her to move through society when women weren't granted much in the way of freedoms. Access to places where people drank allowed her to hunt where vampires preyed.

To focus her mind and distract it from her fear of flying, a fear exacerbated by the news of a plane crash, she played with the simple melody as she hummed along, adding more complex rhythms and tones. While she embellished the song, she made sure her voice enhanced the lyrics Luke sang to her instead of overwhelming them. As he worked his way through the melody, the conversation behind them quieted as people clued in to the music being performed for an audience of two. Yet, Luke didn't mind them eavesdropping on their private moment. It had caused them to quiet their speculation, which would help Roxi's anxiety some, he hoped.

He wished she'd told him she was afraid of flying—not that he could have done much about it. The announcement of the tragedy had clearly upset her coping mechanisms, letting the fear push past her point of tolerance.

The next time the pilot broke in over the intercom, his voice carried a tremble. "Folks, um, we've just gotten word of another commercial jetliner going down. This one in the air over the Atlantic. We still don't know much. We'll be increasing our airspeed to get you on the ground as soon as possible without burning too much fuel. Uh, please buckle up, we're about to head into some rough air. I'll give you an update as soon as we know more."

The second announcement stunned the cabin into silence. The only sounds Luke heard were seatbelts being buckled and someone maneuvering Brutus into his harness.

Roxi shook in Luke's arms, her breath shallow and ragged. One commercial flight going down was exceedingly rare. Two within minutes of each other was virtually unheard of. Whatever it was, he hoped it wasn't something interfering with plane electronics or some other environmental disaster that was affecting planes. He wished he knew which way the second plane had been going—west like them, or east.

It didn't matter; there was little he could do about it. He just hoped they'd get on the ground before anything else happened. Once they were safe from gravity's retribution, they could plan the next stage of their trip home. He sighed, wondering why nothing he was involved in ever seemed to go off without a hitch. Pushing that thought out of his head, he resumed his humming, starting with one of his favorite Parthian melodies.

**Luke Irontree will return in Ancient Sword Falling.
Available Now!**

NEWSLETTER

The Centurion Immortal is a Luke Irontree prequel novella and is exclusive to the Dispatches from C. Thomas Lafollette news-letter. Please sign up for your free copy and you'll also receive a twice-monthly news-letter with news, book updates, recipes, drinks tips, and other fun stuff. Your email will never be given out, rented, or sold.

CThomasLafollette.com/newsletter/

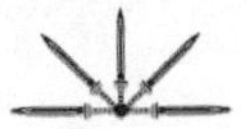

ACKNOWLEDGMENTS

I'd like to thank all the people who made this book possible.

Suzanne, your editorial eye has made this book and series infinitely better. Your belief in my vision for these characters has made this a kick ass team effort.

Ravven, your covers are amazing and really capture the essence of Luke and his world.

Amy, you're my alpha reader and my proofreader. These books wouldn't be possible without you.

C.D. Tavenor, you stepped up when I needed to change my copy editor and did a fantastic job.

Doochie, you've been my earliest reader and a great hype man as well as a wonderful friend.

To my critique group, thank you for all your hard work. Your eyes and efforts have made my writing better.

ABOUT THE AUTHOR

C. Thomas Lafollette is a writer of Urban Fantasy and Historical Fantasy and is the author of the forthcoming Luke Irontree novels. He earned a degree in Ancient History with a specialization in Classics at The College of Idaho. He's read poetry on stage with Yevgeny Yevtushenko and dined with the Belgian Prime Minister. C. Thomas has lived in Portland, Oregon for over Twenty years. He lives with his wife, fellow author Amy Cissell, his stepdaughter, and his three jerkface cats. He and Amy also run their own freelance editing business - Cissell Ink

facebook.com/CThomasLafollette

tiktok.com/@cthomaslafollette

instagram.com/CThomasLafollette

bookbub.com/authors/c-thomas-lafollette

amazon.com/C-Thomas-Lafollette/e/B09JMTR7W7

goodreads.com/cthomaslafollette

ALSO BY C. THOMAS LAFOLLETTE

Luke Irontree & The Last Vampire War

Book 0 - The Centurion Immortal

Book 1 - Dark Fangs Rising - March 22, 2022

Book 2 - Dark Fangs Raging - April 19, 2022

Book 3 - Dark Fangs Descending - May 17, 2022

Book 4 - Blood Empire Reborn - August 23, 2022

Book 5 - Blood Empire Avenged - September 20, 2022

Book 6 - Blood Empire Infiltrated - October 18, 2022

Book 7 - Blood Empire Burning - November 15, 2022

Book 8 - Ancient Sword Falling - March 21, 2023

Book 9 - Ancient Sword Unyielding - August 22, 2023

Book 10 - Ancient Sword Shattering*

The Luke Irontree Historical Adventures

Rise of the Centurio Immortalis - April 5, 2022

Fall of the Centurio Immortalis - May 31, 2022

The Moonlight Centurion*

The Highway Centurion*

Red City Reaper - A Dark Urban Fantasy Adventure

Book 1 - A Shot For Death* - Winter 2024

Book 2 - Death Orders a Double* - Winter 2024

Book 3 - Death on the Rocks* - Sprint 2024

*Forthcoming

Titles and release dates may be subject to change.